THE LOST BOOK 6

THE ROCK OF BATTLE

PETER NEALEN

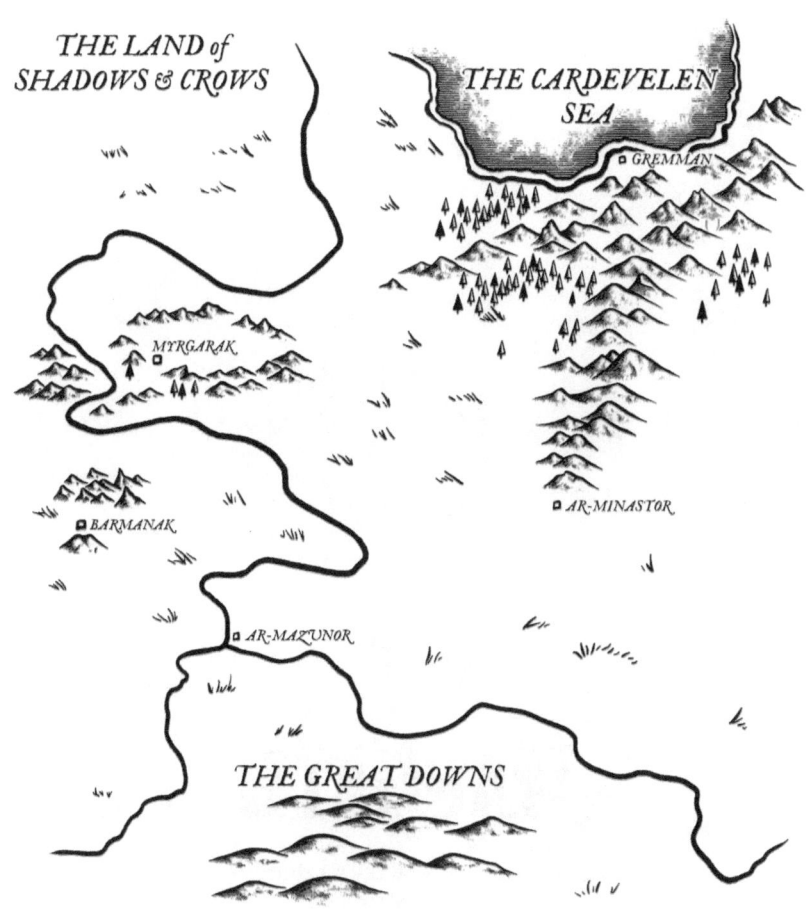

THE LAND of
SHADOWS & CROWS

THE CARDEVELEN
SEA

◻ GREMMAN

MYRGARAK
◻

◻ BARMANAK

◻ AR-MINASTOR

◻ AR-MAZUNOR

THE GREAT DOWNS

COR LEGEAR
and the NORTHERN
MARCHES of EMPIRE

WARGATE

An imprint of Galaxy's Edge Press
PO BOX 534
Puyallup, Washington 98371
Copyright © 2021 by Galaxy's Edge, LLC
All rights reserved.

ISBN: 979-8-88922-000-8

www.forgottenruin.com
www.wargatebooks.com

CHAPTER 1

THE wind whispered through the grass, and a hawk cried overhead. Other than that, there was no sound. The slope in front of us was still except for the faint waving of the stalks of grass gone golden as fall came on. There was a chill in that wind, but my cloak kept it off, while also concealing me in the grass almost as well as a ghillie suit. I wouldn't have thought it would, being a sort of grayish green at first glance, but it worked.

It was of Tuacha make, and therefore almost as wondrous as the people who had woven it.

I stayed utterly motionless, watching that slope. The creek at the bottom of a shallow arroyo about two hundred yards ahead was invisible from my vantage point, but I knew it was there, and I knew that the enemy's scouts were heading for that crossing point. It was the best ford for miles.

I cocked an eye toward the sky, where that hawk was circling. I was reasonably sure it was a real hawk. We'd encountered all sorts of weird flying things in this strange world, but over time we'd all developed a certain instinct for them. This wasn't some sorcerous construct or summoning spying on the battlefield. It was just a bird, hunting for its next meal.

That didn't mean its presence and activity were meaningless. I'd learned that some time prior. And a moment later, as it began to stoop on its prey, then veered suddenly aside, I got the indicator I'd been looking for.

We'd been riding the grasslands to the south and east of Cor Chatha for the last couple of days, and we'd spotted this bunch from a considerable distance, some hours before. Hopefully we'd picked them up from far enough away that they weren't aware of our presence, but even if they were, we'd gone to ground in a well-concealed spot with a good view of their probable approach, and if *we* hadn't seen them for a while, that meant they hadn't seen us, either.

Without turning my head, I reached down and gave the signal string underneath me a tug. It was an old method of intra-team communications in an ambush site, one that didn't get taught very often anymore, but one that I remembered from reading about Recon in Vietnam. A simple tug code meant you could communicate without saying a word or moving very much.

I got two tugs from Rodeffer, where he lay in a fold of the ground off to my left. Long and lanky, he'd gotten leaner over the almost two years we'd been here. We all had, but of all of us, Rodeffer had carried the least extra weight.

Two more tugs came from Farrar to my right, followed by fainter tugs from Santos, out on the flank. Everyone was dialed in and ready.

We weren't alone out there; Gurke's team was another rise over, invisible in the grass from our vantage point. We'd only recently started running team ops—there was too little support when all we had was the remnant of one

Force Recon platoon, a team of Tuacha, and a team of Menninkai with mortars—but we were getting used to it. It meant we had to be ready to act without *any* support, if we were to avoid detection, but there were certain advantages.

So long as we didn't get cocky or careless.

After what we'd seen since coming through the mists to this haunted place, not to mention the men we'd lost, that was somewhat unlikely.

Dust rose above the grass. As flat as that plain looked, I knew from our expedition to the north, toward Myrgarak and finally Gremman, that it was anything but. Those waves of gently undulating grasses disguised a rolling, often rocky landscape cut by arroyos and valleys that simply disappeared until you were right on top of them. It was no great surprise that we could see the enemy's dust before we could see the riders themselves.

Of course, we'd scouted this crossing thoroughly before we'd ever set in on it. I hadn't done a FORDREP— Ford Report—since BRC, but the knowledge had come in handy, if only for the purposes of target selection. So, I knew exactly what I was looking at, since I had a range card, drawn on one of the precious few sheets of Rite-in-the-Rain paper I had left, right in front of me.

That was how I knew that the lead rider was exactly two hundred fifty yards away when he crested the rise just on the other side of the stream. My finger was already taking up the slack on the trigger as the rest of the Imperial scouts came over that little finger of grassy ground.

The *crack* of the shot, muted though it was by my M110's suppressor, echoed across the nearly silent grassland. The lead rider jerked and went over his horse's hindquarters just as the rest of the team opened fire.

Six more riders went down hard before the survivors reined in and, quick as a flash, wheeled their horses and vanished into the low ground beyond. I cursed silently. I'd been hoping to get them all, but they'd reacted too fast. A couple more shots rang out from off to the north, where Gurke was set up, but from the looks of the dust still rising above the low ground, at least one rider had gotten away.

I moved back from my vantage point. "Rally up. We need to relocate."

* * *

As much as I wanted to go down and check the bodies, I knew that it was only a matter of time before the Peruni's react force showed up. This was the second scouting party we'd seen in the last couple of days. They were probing, and they were sure to have backup not far away. After all, Bailey and I had gotten eyes on the main body, as massive as it was, four days before, and they were now only about twenty miles from where we had set our ambush.

I was trying not to think about that part. Trying not to imagine the numbers we'd seen. I'd seen what the Galel had to garrison Cor Chatha, as formidable a fortress as it was. Even adding in the army King Uven had been able to raise in the aftermath of the fight at Cor Legear, it didn't amount to a third of what the Empire of Ar-Annator was about to throw at us.

And that was just thinking in terms of spears, swords, and horses. It wasn't even taking sorcery and monsters into account.

We knew the Peruni had both at their disposal. We'd been fighting them for the last several months.

Or, perhaps, the sorcerers and monsters ultimately had the Empire of Ar-Annator at their disposal.

That was a problem for another day. Right then, we were quickly shifting positions to a short bluff that overlooked the stream directly. A few short, scrubby trees provided some extra concealment as we hunkered down behind the rocks.

Not a moment too soon, either. By the time I was all the way down in the prone, getting behind my rifle and scanning the far bank, the first riders hove into view.

Since we were slightly closer and at a different angle, I got a bit better look at them this time. We'd gotten used to fighting the Avurs, wild steppe horsemen employed by the Peruni of Ar-Annator as auxiliary cavalry and scouts. They were a short, thickset people, for the most part, usually armored in lamellar breastplates and helmets, when they wore armor at all. We'd seen a few other tribes riding for the Empire, but most of their outriders had been Avurs.

These guys weren't Avurs, though. They were a scruffy, poorly equipped lot, mostly wearing homespun and carrying spears, axes, and battered oval Galel shields. From their faded and patched greens, oranges, reds, yellows, and blues, not to mention the preponderance of red, brown, and blond hair and beards, I gathered these were disaffected Galel, rebels who had gotten out of the kingdom ahead of the battles that had wracked it before a Dullahan, one of the ancient headless servants of the Summoner, had penetrated Cor Legear itself.

They approached the site where their predecessors had fallen with caution, circling the bodies. The horses—those that had survived the sudden burst of gunfire—had all run off, so all they had to look at were the corpses in the tall grass.

The leader, a tall, red-haired man with his hair and beard almost as shaggy and flyaway as our Tuacha teammate Bearrac's, lifted his eyes and scanned the seemingly empty country around them. I watched him through my scope, the variable dialed up to ten power, and saw that as feral as this man was, he was scanning his surroundings keenly. Nothing was going to get past this guy.

We were a little bit closer, but there were quite a few more in this group than there had been in the initial scouting party. I counted almost fifty. These guys were definitely the react force.

We *could* have dealt with quite a few of them with Santos's Mk 48, but I didn't trust that we'd get all of them. Fortunately, we had a bit more firepower on call.

I keyed my radio, my voice pitched as low as I could get it. My words shouldn't travel more than a yard or two. "Four, this is One. Request immediate fire mission on Target Reference Point Two."

"Four copies. Target Point Two." Orava's voice was still slightly accented, and the call for fire sounded a little different in *Tenga Tuacha* than English, but the important part of the message got across.

We'd set up target reference points around the ford for the Menninkai team's mortars. The stocky northmen had taken to mortars as soon as they'd found out such weapons existed, and they had proved to be superb mortarmen. They probably would have happily adopted mountain howitzers if we'd had the capacity to haul them along. Anything that went boom seemed to tickle the Menninkai fancy.

The target reference points allowed for quick engagement without needing to send a full call for fire nine-line brief. The Menninkai mortarmen already had the firing angles preset for those reference points, and they could hang and drop rounds within seconds of getting the call.

Which is exactly what they did.

"Shot, over." Orava's voice was flat and emotionless over the radio. The Menninkai tended to be pretty stoic as a culture, and it lent itself well to radio discipline.

"Shot, out." I kept my own voice even lower, even as the first *pop* of a round launching sounded from somewhere behind us. Redbeard out there had heard it, and his head came up quickly, looking for the source of the strange sound.

"Splash, over."

I could already hear the faint whisper of the falling mortar rounds. "Splash, out."

The warband weren't quite right on top of Target Reference Point Two. The dead scouts lay about fifty yards away, to the north and east, and these guys were slightly to the east of them. So, the initial sheaf didn't overlap their formation entirely.

It was still close enough that easily a dozen of them disappeared in the fountains of dirt, frag, and smoke as the first four rounds fell with a crackling roll of thunder.

"Left four, fire for effect." Technically speaking, they were already firing for effect. Adjust fire was usually called one round at a time. Using the target reference points and calling for an immediate fire mission had skipped a step or two. If I could walk them a little more on target, though, I would.

Orava read back my transmission dutifully, and seconds later, the next barrage was incoming. The riders were already scattering as the smoke began to clear, and Santos opened fire a moment later, ripping into several of the riders who were trying to flee to the south. Men tumbled to the ground limply, showering blood, and horses crashed to the dirt, screaming and thrashing in agony. A heartbeat later, mortar rounds hammered into several more of them, smashing them to the earth in a welter of smoke, flying metal, torn meat, shattered bone, and blood.

I knocked another one, a stoop-shouldered, sallow character in a faded, stained blue tunic that looked like it had been bled on more than once, out of his saddle with a well-placed shot that punched through his upper torso. Then the survivors were gone, riding down into the low ground about four hundred yards beyond the arroyo.

I called in fire on Target Reference Point Four, then. Orava could get a few more before they were out of range.

In the meantime, while I'd barely finished the call for fire, we were already pulling off the top of the bluff and heading for our third and final position on the crossing. There were only so many defensible firing positions, and we had to expect that any survivors were going to report where they'd taken fire from.

Even if they didn't, we had to assume that someone had noticed something. Back in the World, we might not have, instead holding our position and hoping to get a few more kills. Letting the ISIS dudes in Syria come get some worked sometimes, when they actually came back after getting shot to doll rags. They were usually no match for us in a standup fight. Here, though, we'd learned really fast not to take anything for granted, especially when it came to tactics.

The last position was to be on the sides of a small gully that ran into the stream during the runoff. We had only a few dozen yards to go to get to it, but someone on the other side *had* noticed something.

The wyvern came out of the sun.

CHAPTER 2

IT was tiny compared to the dragon of Gremman, which is why I call it a wyvern. It had a wide, spade-like head that seemed to be mostly mouth, a gaping maw lined with two rows of teeth, its eyes tiny points of hunger and malice set well forward. Its scales, colored a sort of blend of sandy tan and green, were smooth and shiny, and its wings stretched a good thirty feet to either side, dwarfing its serpentine body and two taloned legs. It stooped on us like a hawk with a rattling hiss, those talons outstretched to seize Rodeffer as its wings blotted out the sun.

Rodeffer pivoted and snapped his rifle to his shoulder, getting a fast pair of shots off before he had to dive into the dirt to avoid those grasping talons. He might have hit with both; I know he put at least one bullet into the monster. I saw the scale crack and a spurt of black blood, and the wyvern jerked and veered off abruptly, its talons snatching at air about two feet above Rodeffer's head. It flapped into the air again with a boiling water hiss, the spines along its back flexing.

After the dragon of Gremman, I wasn't eager to come to grips with that thing with only our rifles and Santos's Mk 48. The M107 .50 cal had hurt the dragon, but even that monster of a rifle hadn't been enough to kill it. Our 7.62 NATO weapons were more formidable than the M4s and M27s we'd come through the mists with, but they weren't dragon slayers.

I was sure the Sword of Iudicael could do a number on it, but that meant coming to grips with it. I'd stabbed the dragon of Gremman with the Sword, but that had been *after* Galan had given his life to pin it to the ground. This thing was still fully mobile, and those talons were as long as my forearm. Even if my Tuacha-forged mail held, they could easily crush bones before I could even get the Sword in to hurt it.

So, from where I stood, our best bet at that point was to break contact and get to cover.

Unfortunately, we were on the open plains. There wasn't a lot of cover to be had.

Gurke wasn't sitting on his hands, though. Even as I grabbed Rodeffer, levering him to his feet and shoving him toward the gully, a burst of machinegun fire tracked out of the weeds to our north toward the circling wyvern. At least a couple rounds had to have hit, as it dipped and screamed, flapping away from the bullets' sting.

We took full advantage, running flat out toward the hollow where we'd left our horses. It was a good distance; we hadn't wanted the animals to inadvertently give our position away. Fortunately, we were all in probably the best shape of our lives, despite the fact that we were all pretty worn down from months of riding, running, and fighting.

It's a good thing that some habits are hard to break. Rodeffer ran to a hummock in the ground about twenty yards ahead, then dropped to a knee, turning back to cover our six as Farrar and I ran past him.

He immediately opened fire, prompting me to keep going for another three paces past him before throwing myself prone and looking for the wyvern.

The wyvern wasn't our only concern. While Redbeard was dead, one of his lieutenants had rallied the survivors, and now they were coming after us, having regained some of their confidence with the wyvern overhead.

Rodeffer shot one of the spear-wielding riders out of the saddle, just before I laid my sights on the lieutenant. Or maybe he wasn't a lieutenant, but Redbeard's handler. The man was dressed similarly to the others, but he was taller, thinner of feature, slightly paler, and dark-haired. He looked more like a Peruni than a Galel.

I shot him through the upper chest. He jerked with the bullet's impact, but stayed in the saddle, even as bloody froth started to leak from his mouth, spurring his mount on, his spear held forward. He was determined to get after us, even as he was dying from a lung shot.

I might have shot him again, but there were other targets, and just then the wyvern came back around and dove at us again.

Santos hammered it with a long burst from the Mk 48, blasting fragments of its scales off and ripping a few holes in the leathery membrane of one wing. It veered off again, and then we were running once more, covered by another long burst of fire from Gurke's team, this time from another hillock behind their original position.

I hated the thought of breaking contact while Gurke of all people was standing his ground. It was petty, and I'd regret the thought once I had any time to reflect on it. But there it was.

The gully got narrower as we moved up, and we had to move farther to find cover. Mostly that amounted to cracks in the sides where the wyvern would have a hard time getting to us. It swooped on us a couple more times, and it almost took Farrar's head off, fended off by a mag dump that I could barely afford. I dropped the empty and kept going, even as it became evident that we couldn't afford to run much farther.

Not that we were too smoked, but we were simply running out of cover. In another dozen yards, we were going to be out of the gully and into the open, with nowhere to go to ground for far too long. Long enough that the wyvern was going to have one of us for lunch if we kept running.

"Consolidate!" Technically speaking, that wasn't the right term. Consolidation happens after contact has been broken or the objective has been overrun. It's for when you don't have any fight left.

The team got the message, though. Santos immediately threw himself down in a fold in the ground that looked almost too small for his massive frame, leaned into the Mk 48's bipods, and started laying the hate. Half a dozen more riders went down in as many seconds, and the remainder scattered.

With a hissing screech, the wyvern stooped on us again. I realized that we'd gone a little too far. We had no space, and the gully was too shallow at that point to keep the monster off us. Its leathery wings spread, it dove toward us, its maw open and its talons poised to snatch one of us up.

I shot it in the mouth, and it snapped its head back, the movement throwing it off and forcing it to one side.

It flapped its wings with another shriek and veered off, moving with surprising speed for a creature that big.

Of course, it wasn't an entirely natural creature, even though it was acting a lot more like an attack dog than the consciously and intelligently evil monster that the dragon had been. That wasn't a comforting thought, though, since I'd seen what a wounded animal could be like. This thing wasn't going to just give up and go away because we'd stung it.

It arrowed higher and off to the north, but immediately started to circle around again. At that moment, I got even more bad news.

"Conor?" Farrar hadn't lost track of the rest of the fight. He pointed over his rifle. "Two o'clock, that hilltop about three miles out."

Tearing my eyes away from the circling wyvern, I spotted the dust cloud almost immediately. Through my scope, I could just make out the riders, and the sun glinting off lamellar helmets.

The Avurs had arrived. Bad news. The Galel rebels so far had been poorly equipped, little more than flushers pushed ahead of the Imperial army, but the Avurs were born warriors and serious business. They'd have archers, which so far, the scouts hadn't. Worse, they could well have a shaman with them. With the sort of numbers I could see out there, that was almost certain.

We were already outnumbered. Being outgunned by that much was a disaster waiting to happen. I keyed my radio. "Prairie Fire."

That was an old, old radio call, going back to the SOG teams in Cambodia and Laos. We'd adapted it to our uses, and after a curt acknowledgement, Orava and Bailey responded.

Orava's team was actually split, with Orava, Lintu, Miero, and Ohto about a mile behind us with the mortars, and Huuhka, Kärsä, Noito, and Pöllö much closer to act as a react force. Bailey's team was positioned close to Orava's Bravo Element, for the same purpose. We'd known that this was going to get hairy.

As soon as I'd called "Prairie Fire," Orava and Ohto were already cranking the mortars into position for Final Protective Fires on our initial ambush position. That was still danger close, though we'd fallen back a decent distance since the wyvern had attacked.

The mortar rounds were already whispering down out of the sky when Huuhka and Applegate opened fire on the wyvern.

We'd gotten shots on that thing, but it's a little more difficult to get accurate fire on a monster that's attacking you while you're trying to bound back and stay away from it than when you're set in a solid position, which both machinegunners were. Stuttering streams of tracers converged on the winged serpent as it dove at us again, and this time, they put the hurt on it.

Bullets smashed into its overlapping scales, though they didn't do that much on their own. The rounds that got past the scales probably didn't penetrate very far. The wyvern still writhed and hissed, banking away from the stinging impacts.

Then one or both gunners found their target.

A burst ripped through one wing, tearing the membrane to tatters near the shoulder joint. The wyvern seemed to actually stagger a little in midair, and then the next couple of bursts continued to tear up the wing. Several rounds smashed into the bone and the joint that supported the batlike wing, and then it folded up and the wyvern tumbled from the sky.

The mortars landed a split second later, and I lost sight of the wyvern as a line of explosions just ahead of us kicked up a wall of dirt, frag, and smoke. The shock-waves rolled over us a moment after, and then we were up and moving. Trying to run any sooner, that close to the mortar impacts, would just have gotten one of us fragged.

Rodeffer didn't try to bound this time. We were far enough from the Avurs and the Galel rebels that we didn't need to worry about catching an arrow in the back, and the wyvern appeared to be down. We needed to make tracks, fast.

The horses were nervous, but they were warhorses, one and all, and several had been our mounts and companions across the plains to the east, there and back. Any panic had been worked out of them a long time ago. We quickly swung into the saddle, and I keyed the radio. "One is clear. Heading for Rally Point Seven."

Gurke echoed me a moment later. "Three is clear."

"Roger." Bailey sounded like they were already moving. The gunfire had died down, as they no longer had targets close enough to spend bullets on. "We're moving. See you at the rally point."

I spurred Allon toward the distant hill that was Cor Chatha, falling in behind Rodeffer, who was making tracks, not at a gallop, but enough of a trot that we could put some serious territory behind us before nightfall.

There was reason for haste, and not just to break contact from the Avurs and their rebel Galel allies.

We'd gotten eyes on the main body of the Imperial army, and we needed to get that reporting back to Gunny and Lord Tarvedum, posthaste.

Time was not on our side.

CHAPTER 3

WE joined up with a maniple of Galel cavalry about a mile from the walls. We weren't the only ones out there, scouting the enemy and harassing his scouts and flankers. The Galel, we'd learned, were not the sort to passively wait inside their fortifications as long as they had some maneuvering room left.

Furthermore, these weren't levies or auxiliaries we joined on the ride toward the gates. These were knights, heavily armed and armored, on the fastest, toughest warhorses the Galel could breed.

I didn't know any of these men; those Galel warriors I'd gotten to know were still a day or two out, with King Uven. These were the lords who had answered the call to garrison Cor Chatha, men whose lands and families were under direct threat from that vast army out on the plains.

A short, wiry man wearing an uncharacteristic brown cloak over his mail and a white horsehair plume atop his peaked helmet pulled his mount up next to me. I nodded to Lord Uurad. We'd met briefly before we'd ridden out on this reconnaissance, and he'd seemed to be a quiet, serious sort of man.

Now, while he seemed calm enough, I got the distinct impression that he was rattled. He wasn't pale, or shaking, or even talking overmuch. But he kept glancing over his shoulder, then back at me, and while he would then tighten his lips and watch straight ahead, squaring his shoulders, I could tell he wanted to talk. He just wasn't sure how to say what he wanted to say without revealing how scared he was.

I'd been there. It's not limited to new guys, either. From his scars, I gathered that Uurad had been in plenty of fights. Fights were not the same thing as the battle that was coming, though. The Galel hadn't fought a war like this in generations.

Neither had Americans. We were as green to this sort of combat as Uurad was.

Unfortunately, I found myself in the same boat with Uurad. I barely knew the man, unlike Galan, whom I'd formed a friendship on the passage from the Isle of Riamog aboard the *Radala Farragah*. I didn't know how he'd react if I tried to draw him out, and right then, I wasn't exactly feeling chatty, myself.

So, we rode toward Cor Chatha in uncomfortable silence, the quiet of men riding toward a battle they weren't sure could be won.

The hill—small mountain would probably be a better description—that was Cor Chatha rose ahead of us, still some distance away and yet dominating the western horizon.

Cor Chatha. The Rock of Battle. The largest and most formidable fortress of the Kingdom of Cor Legear, it had been built on and into a lone massif that rose nearly a thousand feet above the grasslands that spread out along the kingdom's southern frontier. The peak of the mountain rose another four hundred feet above the citadel, yet the rock was so sheer that it would take helicopters to get anyone up there.

Below that jagged peak, the citadel stood as an angular block of stone, overtopped by an equally angular, eight-sided tower, slightly offset to the south. From the top of that tower, you could see almost a hundred miles across the plains.

Its height was not the only defensive measure built into Cor Chatha. Six concentric walls, studded with square, stone towers, ultimately enclosed half the mountainside. In many ways, it reminded me of Vahava Paykhah, only larger.

Vahava Paykhah, however, had been a royal seat and a city in and of itself. Cor Chatha was different. It was a fortress, first and foremost, built and maintained to guard the border.

From that high tower, a man with good eyes could see any movement on that plain for miles. Even if an enemy tried to flank around to the coast, there were outposts equipped with beacons that could be seen for nearly as far that would pass the word as fast as fires could be lit. From that high promontory, the lord of Cor Chatha could hold down hundreds of miles of open grassland and farmland against an invader.

And since the rest of the border was guarded by the sort of mountains that surrounded Cor Hefedd, this was the most likely route for an invasion from the Empire of Ar-Annator. True to that assessment, we rode ahead of the biggest ground force I'd ever seen.

The men of Cor Chatha were on high alert, and another maniple of riders came out to meet us within the next half mile. We were too few to present much of a

threat—unless we had a shaman or a wizard with us—
but when you're facing a threat like the Empire, you
don't take chances, and the Galel were most decidedly
not taking chances.

They reined in a spear's throw away, the lead knight
holding up a hand. Beside me, Uurad doffed his helmet
and raised his own hand in reply. "I am Lord Uurad, son
of Mordeleg. I return with tidings."

The tall, ramrod-straight man wearing a gray cloak
and light blue tunic lifted his own helmet and grinned.
"It must have been a long ride, Lord Uurad, that you do
not recognize me."

Uurad seemed to slump in the saddle and smiled rue-
fully. "Fiachu. Forgive me. As you said, it has been a
long ride." He sobered. "We must make haste to Lord
Tarvedum."

The grin vanished from Lord Fiachu's face. "Follow
me."

I glanced over at Santos, whose face was as blank
and grim as Uurad's. He met my eyes and shrugged. The
Galel's challenge and pass was a bit less formal and a
bit more personal than we were used to, but these were
a people for whom fighting was their whole life, not just
a career for a set number of years. Most of these knights
really did know each other as friends, brothers, rivals,
and bitter enemies, and recognizing each other was probably better than a formalized challenge and pass.

Still, there were a lot of warriors holed up within Cor
Chatha's many-layered walls. They couldn't know everyone. It was fortuitous that Fiachu had been sent out,
and that he happened to have been one of Uurad's long-
time companions.

We rode past several more patrols on the way up to the gates. They were, if anything, bigger and more formidable than the gates of Cor Legear. Unlike that citadel, there was a drawbridge here, crossing a chasm that had been chipped out of the finger of the mountain that led up to the base of the walls. Beyond that drawbridge, which was currently down, allowing access to the fortress, not one but two massive timber-and-iron portcullises hung above the gateway, passing through the fifteen-foot-thick walls.

Of course there were murder holes lining the ceiling above the gateway. I didn't bother to look up as we went past; for one thing, riding under several thousand pounds of timber and iron held up only by a rope and a winch was not a comfortable feeling.

I've faced monsters and demons from the Outer Dark, but some of the basic human fears, like getting crushed to death, never really go away.

Some people think that to do what we do, as Recon Marines, means not being afraid. Truth is, if we weren't afraid, we wouldn't be human, or sane. You don't want a guy with no fear in combat. He tends to do stupid stuff that gets himself—or worse, his teammates—killed. Fear is natural. It tells you when you're in danger and that you need to be careful.

No, we just don't let the fear rule us. Someone once said—I've seen it attributed to John Wayne—that courage is being scared stiff and saddling up anyway. I never have liked heights. I jumped out of the airplane anyway.

The ride up to the citadel took the better part of an hour. Cor Chatha was *big*. Bigger even than Vahava Paykhah, though with a slightly smaller population. The knights and men-at-arms who accepted a tour there generally didn't bring their families. Those stayed in their home steadings, most of which were fortified, this close to the border.

In fact, while the houses and the palisades were mostly timber or stone, some of the villages we'd passed through on the way to Cor Chatha had reminded me of Syria. Or Afghanistan. Small, sturdy houses surrounded by thick outer walls.

The citadel was even bigger in person than it looked from a distance. It wasn't the prettiest bit of architecture, either. Big, blocky, and with only narrow arrow slots for windows, it had been built purely for defense. Aesthetics had taken a back seat to military engineering.

I had to look up at the doors. They were almost as large as the gate behind and below us and built of solid timbers. They were also at the top of a narrow staircase, much like many other fortifications we'd seen. There were certain commonalities to all defenses, especially when most fighting was done with swords, axes, and spears. An attacker would have to approach the doors from the side, and in single file, with their right hands closest to the wall.

Like the gates below, the doors stood open, for now. They'd remain that way far longer than the lower gates. It would take days of fighting and thousands—tens of thousands—of casualties before an enemy ever got to the final wall and the citadel itself. Still, a platoon of guards, wearing the gray and green of Lord Tarvedum's house, their spears glinting in the sunlight pouring down from behind us and the flickering light of the lamps deeper inside the entryway, stood between us and the interior of the citadel.

Lord Fiachu went through a somewhat more formal challenge and pass with these men. They were Tarvedum's nephews and cousins, most of them. They would know most of the garrison, but their ultimate loyalty was to the patriarch of their house, the lord commander of the fortress. They were going to be a bit more hard-nosed than a patrol leader out in the field.

That might not be the way I'd do it, but it was the way it was done in Cor Chatha.

They let us in, and Fiachu led the way up, past the great hall, past the garrison quarters and the defensive works, into the tower itself. We climbed up and up, legs burning and lungs feeling every mile we'd ridden, run, and fought for the last several months.

Finally, we reached the very top of the tower, high above the rest of the fortress and the plain below. The bare rock of the mountain peak loomed above us to the west, but everything else was laid out like a carpet at our feet. The sun was about to go down behind the peak behind us, and the shadows were lengthening on the timber roof as we stepped out and faced Tarvedum.

The castellan and lord commander of Cor Chatha was easily twice King Uven's age, but he looked even older. Short and stumpy, almost the size and build of a Menninkai, his snow-white hair flowed to his shoulders over a gray cloak. Of all the Galel, Tarvedum was the least colorful I'd ever met. Even his eyes were a sort of pale gray. Most of his countrymen wore brilliant colors as much as possible. Tarvedum liked his muted gray and green, and they seemed to suit him. He was the lord of a border fortress, and often fought enemies who could hide in the tall grass like ghosts.

He was currently leaning on a table set up against the eastern battlements, poring over a map studded with little flags. Several appeared to mark Galel forces, but a big block of those flags, bearing a hastily sketched version of the Empire's sunburst standard, was already gathering at the edge of the map.

Unfortunately, from what I'd seen, that block of red was a lot closer than Lord Tarvedum thought.

Uurad bowed. Our numbers had dwindled a bit on the way up; only the team leaders and the Galel cavalry leaders were needed up here. Gunny Taylor had joined us as well, his head still shaved as bald as he'd kept it back in the World, watching everything with that intense, unblinking stare of his that many men found unnerving.

I would, too, if I hadn't known the man so well. Bailey and I might be brothers from another mother, having gone through BRC together and finally become team leaders in the same platoon, but Gunny had become like a father to all of us.

In some ways, that had made Zimmerman's betrayal all that much worse. Captain Sorenson had been Captain Sorenson. Zimmerman, for all his contrariety, had been one of us. And yet, he'd turned entirely to the Outer Dark, to the point of firing on us while he tried to break Vaelor out of his mystic prison.

The castellan wasn't alone up there but had three of his senior knights standing off to one side, while Mathghaman and Bearrac stood to the other.

Mathghaman. The King's Champion of the Tuacha da Riamog was taller than all the rest of us, more kingly in bearing than King Uven, with auburn hair and beard, and steely gray eyes that missed nothing. We'd met him in the north, along with his wife, Nuala, and his companions. Since then, Mathghaman and his warrior companions had continued to accompany us, out of a combination of debts owed at first, followed by true brotherhood as time went on.

The Tuacha da Riamog are a strange and perilous people, stronger, faster, wiser, and much longer lived that most normal men. We were truly privileged to call such men our friends.

Mathghaman and the other Tuacha had stayed behind at Cor Chatha as we'd ridden out to scout the enemy's vanguard. Not because they were afraid of the enemy— that would never have crossed their minds—but, after the sorcerous insurgency we'd fought in Cor Legear itself, we knew that some heavy preternatural firepower was coming our way, and the Tuacha were the best equipped to fight that mystical battle. They'd been helping the garrison prepare for that front, as best they could.

Tarvedum straightened slowly and turned to face us, bowing in response not only to Uurad's homage, but also directly to Bailey and me. As the Sword Bearers, we'd come to be held in some reverence by the Galel, which was something neither of us were either used to or particularly comfortable with.

Neither one of us knew exactly why we'd been chosen to carry the Two Swords, weapons that were not of this earth. Legend had it that they had been brought down from on high by two messengers of Tigharn, centuries before, and bestowed on the kings of Silabor and

Commagan, before the latter had become a vast, corrupt empire that had collapsed into madness.

We knew the legends were true. We'd met those messengers, Iudicael and Categyrn.

And yet, the question remained. We were, if anything, even more aware of our personal flaws now that we were carrying these mystical weapons against the forces of the Outer Dark. Why we'd been chosen was something that bothered me, often late into the night. It certainly wasn't because there were no better candidates.

"My lords." Tarvedum's voice was deep and gravelly, with an undertone of weariness that never went away. "What news?"

"We intercepted a couple forward patrols of scouts at the crossing over the river." I didn't need to specify that it was the River Coul, since that was the only one out that way for miles. "They appeared to be disaffected Galel, judging by their clothing and weapons, though none of them were well armored or well-armed. They were backed up by a full company of Avurs…and a wyvern."

Tarvedum's shoulders slumped a little at that. "If they have such monsters with their forward scouts…"

I almost said that it got worse but decided to let the information speak for itself. This was reporting, not opinion time, and so professionalism was important. "We did get eyes on the main body, about six days ago. They're still about four days out, judging by the pace they were keeping. I would estimate their strength at between four and five hundred thousand, with about a hundred thousand of those being cavalry."

Now came the really unpleasant part. "We saw several more wyverns flying overhead, but that's not all." I took a deep breath. This was not unexpected, but it still wouldn't be pleasant to hear. "The twenty-nine remaining of the Thirty are with them, as well."

The low murmur didn't quite turn to cursing, but it was close. Tarvedum's face almost turned gray, and he turned away from us for a moment, looking east over the battlements as the horizon darkened.

The Thirty were the Dullahans, ancient sorcerers who had, according to legend, been the first of the Summoner's disciples, when he'd come to this world and seduced the ancients into sacrificing themselves to bring the Outsiders, the ancient demons of the Outer Dark, into the world. They were undead, their heads separated from their shoulders and carried around by various ways, though one—I suspected the worst of them—had his suspended in a column of green fire above the stump of his neck.

"They can be killed." I felt the need to point that out. "There are only twenty-nine left." It sounded weak and lame when I put it like that, but I'd fought one of them in Cor Legear. I'd very nearly lost, but with Iudicael's help, I'd stabbed its severed head with the Sword of Iudicael, putting its lights out forever.

"So few?" Tarvedum was trying to keep his voice light but failing. He had heard the full story of the fight in Cor Legear, at least as much as either Bailey or I could articulate. Most of the rest of the men in that chamber hadn't seen everything. They'd seen the flash of light that had dispelled the unnatural darkness brought on by the Dullahan and the shadow demon, but that was it. None could remember seeing the shining figures of the two beings of light that had backed us up against those terrible foes. "Forgive me, Lord Conor, but while I respect your own prowess and the power granted by the Two Swords, you faced one of them, and it seemed to fall to its own hubris. To face all the rest…"

I nodded. "I know. Even with the Swords, we can't fight all of them at once. I probably know that better than you think." To my right, Bailey nodded solemnly. We'd had to learn the truth the hard way—that simply being a Bearer didn't make us invincible. We'd only won when we'd called upon powers higher than ourselves.

It had been humbling, but it had been important. Humility was something that my mentors had emphasized back when I'd been a roper and then a new Recon Marine. It was a lesson that some of my peers hadn't picked up on, but humility is truth. Without it, you are doomed to fail.

Pride goeth before the fall.

"My point is that they *can* be killed. They're not invincible. It won't be easy, and Tigharn will have to be on our side in a big way, but we *do* have a chance."

Tarvedum nodded. "I appreciate your candor, Lord Conor. And you are right." He didn't look too cheered, though. "I pray that we can hold at least long enough for Tigharn to grant us a miracle.

"I fear it is the only way we will prevail."

CHAPTER 4

WE were prepping to go out again the next morning when things went south in a hurry.

The first warning was the thunderstorm that seemed to come in out of nowhere. One moment, the skies were clear. The next, they were being rapidly overtaken by boiling black clouds that blotted out the sun in minutes, lightning flickering through and underneath them.

The storm brought wyverns with it.

I heard the horn calls and bells of alarm first. Moving quickly to the window in the high chamber of the citadel that we'd been given as a sort of team room, I saw the winged, serpentine shapes swooping down on the outer wall.

"Machinegunners up!" Under different circumstances, that might have been Gunny's call, but he was currently passed out after pulling an all-nighter, and there wasn't time to wake him up and get him spun up. None of us had been long on sleep lately, and Gunny, being Gunny, was probably getting the least of all of us. He started awake as I bellowed across the team room, but Applegate and Santos already had their Mk 48s in hand and chest rigs full of linked 7.62x51 slung over their shoulders, heading for the door. Huuhka and Chambers were already grabbing for their own.

Since I'd opened the ball and Gunny was still getting fully conscious, I grabbed my own weapons and headed for the door myself. I'd have to take responsibility for deployment and make sure that we got fire on those wyverns fast.

I really wished, just for a moment, that we had some Stingers. None of us had ever trained on them, but if Afghan mujahideen could figure them out, then Recon Marines sure could. Granted, I had no idea if the Man Portable Air Defense Systems could even lock onto wyverns. They were heat-seeking missiles designed to track aircraft engines, which functioned at far, far higher temperatures than any biological organism, and even if the wyverns were more preternatural than natural, they probably still didn't put out enough heat for Stinger's seeker head. Even assuming we had any of the MANPADS, which we didn't.

"Watch your fires." I knew I really didn't need to say it, but we had just gone from zero to sixty in a handful of seconds, so it wouldn't hurt to throw out a reminder. "We're going to have to deploy up here, so you're going to be at range. Make sure you only engage when they're high enough above the battlements that you don't accidentally hit any friendlies."

"Means we might not be able to save any of 'em if they're under attack." Santos's objection was somewhat understandable. The outer wall was barely five hundred yards away, as the crow flies, and Santos had gotten good enough with that machinegun that, while he couldn't necessarily hit a fly off a horse's back with it, he could be pretty sure of his marksmanship at five hundred yards, especially with the *Coira Ansec*'s version of the TA648 machinegun ACOG.

"If we were taking single shots, I'd agree with you." I kept talking as we jogged up the steps toward the roof of the citadel proper. "But you and I both know that single shots of 7.62 ain't gonna do much against these things."

I could hear the grimace in his voice without looking over my shoulder at him as we climbed. "You've got a point."

We burst out onto the roof and the lower battlements, the tower looming over us. Lightning flickered overhead, splitting the sky with a deafening *crack*. That storm had moved in far too fast to be natural. I could feel the work of our enemies down there. This was Killaros and Cor Legear all over again, only worse.

In fact, as I peered through the dimness, thankful for the moment that the rain hadn't started yet, even though that made the lightning even more dangerous, I could see the dark line of the Peruni army in the distance. They were still a long way off, but they were pushing hard.

That meant the Dullahans were getting closer, along with the Avur shamans, Peruni wizards, and whatever other practitioners of the dark arts they had along.

I grabbed Santos and pointed him to the center position on the roof, then reconsidered and shifted him about a dozen paces left, putting Huuhka an equal distance to the right of the center and pointing Applegate and Chambers to the left. By the time they were in position, Santos and Huuhka were already going to work.

All of our weapons were suppressed, and the suppressors lasted a lot longer than anything I'd seen back in the World, so they opened fire with a hissing chatter instead of the rattling thunder that would have been the case without the cans. Red tracers reached out across the slope and down toward where the wyverns wheeled and stooped on the defenders, about five hundred yards out and another two hundred feet below us.

The first bursts missed as they got the range, one going high, the next passing right under the grayish wyvern's talons. Both men adjusted quickly and, while the wyverns were quick, they weren't as fast as bullets. The monster that had just tucked its wings and begun its dive at the gatehouse on the first wall seemed to stagger in the air as the 7.62 rounds, all 175-grain LR like our rifle rounds, hammered into it. Those rounds would have been prohibitively expensive to use as machinegun ammo back in the World. That was precision rifle ammunition. However, with the *Coira Ansec*, the mystic cauldron that King Caedmon held that could produce anything you asked of it—*if* you asked properly—providing us with our supplies and munitions, it was child's play.

The wounded wyvern banked away, dropping below the top of the wall, but we were still high enough that the two men could get at least one more burst into it. Then it was racing away, almost skimming the ground, its distant shrieks of pain and rage audible even up where we perched, and they shifted targets.

A reddish monster had flapped higher into the sky, looking for the source of the dashed streams of flying metal that had wounded its fellow. I didn't expect that there was much pack feeling among these things. No one who we'd talked to since that first encounter on the plains the day before had spoken of them as natural beasts; they were things of the Outer Dark, just like actual dragons.

Which meant they were bundles of pride and hatred, wrapped in bone, sinew, and scale. That didn't mean they wouldn't try to avenge each other, but not because they actually felt any sort of affinity between monsters.

It surged higher with each stroke of its massive wings, and unwittingly made itself a perfect target.

Santos's burst was so precise that he had to have had some supernatural help to get it on. Full props to my Assistant Team Leader's marksmanship, but at that distance, against a moving target, it takes even more of an artist than he was to shatter a wing joint with a single six- to eight-round burst. But he did it.

The wing folded in on itself and the wyvern screamed, an even louder and more hateful sound than any we'd heard from these creatures yet. It went into a flat spin, twisting and writhing around itself as it fell, and he caught it with one more burst, just to add insult to injury, shortly before it crashed to the ground between the first and second walls.

Galel warriors with spears were closing in on it fast as it thrashed around and roared its hatred and agony, the screams echoing off the mountain behind us. We left them to it.

Huuhka had gotten another one, though not as neatly as Santos. His burst ripped through the leathery membrane of one wing, though he missed the bone, so it could still get some lift out of it. Not a lot, though, and it limped off toward the enemy lines with another earsplitting screech. Huuhka gave it one more burst for good measure, though I was pretty sure that he just chipped a few scales at that distance and that angle.

More machinegun fire chattered off to our flanks as Chambers and Applegate plied their trade against the flanking monsters. One of the wyverns circled higher and higher, rising above even the tower overhead, then suddenly folded its wings and dove right at us.

It probably should have kept its mouth shut. Chambers put a burst right through that gaping maw and the creature jerked and went limp, turning into a ballistic projectile that slammed into the wall of the citadel with an impact that made the entire structure shake. Pulverized bits of masonry fell toward the ground below along with the body of the beast. It crashed to the ground with a heavy *boom* that sounded like a tree falling.

A new sound arose, echoing across the plain and off the mountain behind us. It was almost a horn call, but far louder. The trumpeting roar was so loud that it might have been put through an LRAD, one of those big sonic crowd-control devices. Almost as if a switch had been flipped, the remaining wyverns broke off the attack, banked to the east, and quickly winged away, though not without one last spiteful, hissing shriek.

Gunny had appeared at my elbow, moving as stealthily as he was wont to do, doubtless a little annoyed that I'd gotten the jump on him and directed this little fight without him. On the other hand, it *was* Gunny, so he was probably simultaneously irritated and satisfied, like a proud father whose son had just stepped up and done what needed doing.

"Good work, but we don't get to bask in the glory." Given Gunny's nature, his sarcasm shone through his deadpan voice. He jerked a thumb skyward. "Lookouts up there on the tower say that Avur horsemen and Peruni cataphracts are moving around the south flank, probably to cut the road that's the only good way King Uven can get here. We've been invited to come along, with all the explosive surprises we can bring."

I glanced to the south, but the light was failing fast as the black clouds spread across the sky. The wind was picking up, too. "Well, I think we can oblige them. Good thing Oncu brought as much as he did." The giant Tuacha had sailed from the Isle with a wagonload of ammunition, explosives, mortars, and pistols, long before any word could have reached them that we needed resupply. That wagon hadn't been small, either, and our pack animals hadn't enjoyed the movements since, but now we were probably going to end up using all of it.

"Yep." Gunny turned and started back toward the steps leading below. Santos glanced over his shoulder at him, then at me. Gunny usually wasn't quite that terse.

I shrugged. There wasn't much to say. We'd been in some pretty hairy situations before, but never quite facing half a million men, and twenty-nine of the thirty worst sorcerers in the world.

We headed toward the stairs, our gear, and our horses.

CHAPTER 5

THE ground to the west of the mount of Cor Chatha was rougher by far than the plains to the east. While the mount was pretty steep on the border side, where the fortress itself had been built, it fell away more gradually to the west, though that didn't make it easy to climb. In fact, if anything, the tumbled, broken hills that fanned out from that forbidding peak were steeper and more treacherous than any other mountain in the kingdom.

Fortunately, that would slow any attempt the enemy made at an end run or an encirclement. Unfortunately, it also slowed us down.

There was a road, high up on the mountain, that led back toward the west and the rest of the kingdom. By design, it wasn't wide or easy to traverse. It also wasn't easy to access, which made it next to impossible for an invader to try to set an ambush anywhere above the foothills, a good ten miles behind the fortress. That lent us *some* speed, but there's still only so fast you really want to ride when you're moving along a yard-wide track in the mountains, often with a sheer drop of easily a hundred feet to one side.

So, we picked our way down the road, hoping that King Uven's men had some good mountain packhorses, and that the distance the enemy had to cover cross-country to get around the mountain would make up for our lack of speed. Especially since the packhorses were carrying a *lot* of boom.

* * *

It was midafternoon by the time we reached a hill that had a good view of the road and the best approaches to it. The land flattened out quite a bit from there, though it was still slightly more rolling and obviously hilly than the plains to the east. A few of the farms that supported Cor Chatha were visible from our vantage point though, even given the arduousness of the trek up to the fortress, they were still set well back from the foothills.

There was no sign of the enemy yet, which was just as well. We'd have time to set in.

I scanned the clouds overhead as I dismounted. They were as dark as ever, turning late afternoon to early evening twilight, but I could still see just well enough that I was fairly certain there were no winged horrors watching us from above. We were, hopefully, still unobserved.

Uurad's maniple of cavalry sat their horses on the military crest of the hill, invisible to any enemy coming from the south. Uurad himself dismounted as we did, and immediately started getting the archers they'd brought deployed among the rocks at the top of the hill.

I pulled a kitbag down off my packhorse, shouldered it, and headed down below, following Gunny, who was half a step ahead of me.

He might have taken pride in his boys stepping up, but now that he was here on the ground, he wasn't going to let one of us get ahead of him again.

We didn't quite run down the slope, but we didn't walk sedately, either. We didn't have eyes on the Avurs yet, but we'd fought those stocky, tricky bastards enough to know that they could suddenly pop up right on top of you, arrows nocked and ready to rock.

With the Mk 48 gunners holding security, the rest of us got down to work. Charges were pulled out, primed, and hastily concealed along the base of the hill. We had some claymores, but without knowing exactly where the enemy was going to come, we didn't want to waste them.

After all, we couldn't be sure we wouldn't be falling back to the fortress under fire.

We got about a quarter of the explosives we'd brought set in before a chattering burst of machinegun fire announced that we were out of time.

I glanced up just in time to see an Avur horseman, his bow bent, bearing down on me from just over the hill to the east. They'd come up that narrow draw we'd passed and forced their horses up the steep slope toward the road, and now were plunging down the finger and across the hill where we were set up and putting in the explosives. Three of them tumbled from their saddles as Applegate walked his burst across them, but this guy was already ahead of them and coming for me, that arrow poised to slam right into my chest.

I threw myself to one side, hitting the ground hard as the arrow whistled past my ear. Grabbing for my rifle, I realized I didn't have the angle or the time to get it into action as he bore down on me, reaching for another arrow, and palmed my .45.

I hadn't been carrying it that much but, since that Dullahan at Cor Legear had snapped my family Bowie knife, I had a bit more room on my belt, and I felt light without that big pigsticker. That decision saved my life, as I shot the Avur out of the saddle with a fast, one-handed shot.

Frankly, I'm fairly sure that Iudicael probably steadied my hand for that one. I've never shot that well, one-handed and unsupported, from such an awkward position, before or since.

The bullet might not have killed him outright if I'd shot him center mass. That lamellar armor the Avurs wear is *tough*. Not tough enough to stop a .45 round, but enough to somewhat deflect and slow it. But I hit him slightly high, and the bullet glanced off one of the scales on his collar and caromed up under his chin. His head jerked, blood flooding down his neck, and he tumbled from the saddle, hitting the dirt only about twenty feet away as his horse kept going, thundering past me.

"Fall back!" Gunny was on a knee, his M110 in his shoulder, and he knocked another Avur off his horse a moment later. "Move!"

He was right. We were not in a defensible position right then, setting in charges that we hoped the bad guys would ride over as they tried to get to the road. I heaved myself up, shot at another Avur with my sidearm, and then I was running up the hill, leaving the kitbag behind. Sometimes you need to make sure you grab everything. Sometimes you've just got to fight the fight that's in front of you.

I got about ten paces before I had to pivot and throw myself to one side, the arrow meant for me thudding into the ground only about a yard away, and that because I'd flung myself about a yard to the other side. Rolling onto my back, I fired between my knees. I missed the horse-man, but I blew his horse's brains out and it tumbled, throwing him over its head as it crashed to the ground. My follow-up shot smashed through metal scales, bone, and lung, and then I was up and moving again.

The machinegunners were working in pairs, Applegate and Huuhka on one side, Santos and Chambers on the other, keeping up a constant, chattering roar of fire. One would let off the trigger just as the other took up the fire, maintaining a continuous, deadly rain of met-al on the attacking Avurs. They were going down fast, but even with talking guns using only six- to eight-round bursts, we were burning through ammo even faster.

Finally, just as I reached the top of the hill, the Avurs broke and fell back, quickly steering their horses into low ground where the machinegunners couldn't hit them.

It might have seemed strange that they understood cover and concealment against firearms, but these peo-ple were familiar with bows and arrows as well as slings and either stones or lead bullets. They knew projectile weapons, even when the projectile is moving so fast that it's invisible.

People are also a lot more likely to adapt to new stuff they've never seen before than some of the more con-ceited folks back in the World might like to think.

The machinegun fire died away. Oncu had brought a lot of ordnance, but it was still limited, and we had enough experience of being at the end of a *long*—or non-existent—supply line that we weren't just going to waste ammunition when we didn't have to. No targets, no fire.

I got Rodeffer and Farrar set in on either side of Santos, while I stayed up on a knee, watching the slopes below and around us carefully. I didn't think for a second that we'd seen the last of the Avurs, and the reporting we'd gotten from the lookouts suggested that there were quite a few Peruni cataphracts riding behind the lighter, faster Avur horsemen. They were doing their utmost to cut this road and encircle Cor Chatha, and that meant a full-court press. They wouldn't leave it entirely to the Avurs.

That also meant we potentially had more of a threat than just horse archers, slingers, and heavy cavalry to worry about. If the Peruni really wanted this route cut off, then it was entirely likely that they'd send wizards with the cataphracts.

I had come to really, *really* hate spellslingers. Not just because of the immediate physical threat they posed, but also because of the arrogance and palpable evil of them. These were men who had sold their souls for power, and were actively engaging with the darkest of entities, usually sacrificing human life and blood to do it.

"Gurke, make sure the six is covered." Gunny was standing at the crest, next to Uurad and Mathghaman. The Avurs knew we were there, and we had them out-ranged anyway, so there wasn't a whole lot of point in trying to stay flat. If those more lightly armed, pale-haired tribesmen we'd fought on the frontier up by Cor Hefedd were there, then it might be different, but they'd appeared to be footsloggers and, while most people in this place could cover a lot more ground, a lot faster, on foot than most back in the World, they still wouldn't have kept up with cavalry that were intent on getting to the objective with all possible speed.

Uurad's own men looked a little antsy where they stood or sat their horses around the hilltop. A few of the archers had gotten shots off on the enemy, but we'd done the bulk of the fighting, and that had to chafe on Galel honor. This *was* their territory, after all. We were supposed to be supporting them, rather than taking all the glory for ourselves. I didn't necessarily see it that way, but we were getting used to the somewhat different mindset of these people.

I moved up to join Gunny and Mathghaman. The King's Champion had apparently decided that they'd done all they could to prepare for the mystic battle to come, and so he'd retaken his place with the platoon.

Mathghaman, for his part, wasn't watching the enemy, or the ground where the enemy had disappeared. He was watching down the road. I followed his gaze wordlessly, but if he could see anything out there, I couldn't. King Uven was due at any time, but there was no telling—especially without radio comms—what sort of delays and obstacles he had faced, getting an army of at least ten thousand moving toward the fortress. We'd just fought a nasty little civil war, after all, and there were bound to be some of his lords who were still feeling a little froggy.

Unfortunately, even as I scanned our surroundings, I realized that we were only delaying the inevitable. We could head off this attempt to cut the road, but against half a million men and monsters, we'd eventually be forced back inside the walls. Cor Chatha had extensive stores of food and at least two springs for water, as well as massive cisterns carved into the rock of the mountain, but we'd never be able to hold this road indefinitely.

We just had to hold it until Uven could get there. And put as much hurt on the bad guys as we could in the meantime.

I'd been there before. None of us had ever thought that we'd make any kind of lasting impact in Syria. That illusion had died in Iraq and Afghanistan. We'd gone to kill as many bad guys as we could, knowing that we were only slowing things down.

That thought had barely ended when the next attack came.

CHAPTER 6

A volley of arrows whistled into the sky, plunging down onto the hilltop from out of the dim, darkened sky. The Avur archers had to have gone to full draw, aiming as high as they could without shooting straight up, and loosed. We still didn't have eyes on them, even as we scrambled for cover. There wasn't a lot of overhead cover on that hilltop, but we'd brought full-sized shields with us, borrowed from the vast stores of arms within the fortress. They weren't part of our ordinary kit. I'd taken to carrying a buckler, a small shield about nine inches across, attached to the scabbard of the Sword of Iudicael but, while it was good for parrying hand weapons and protecting my own fist, it wasn't great for protection against arrows. The oval Galel shield, however, was another matter. That had been Uurad's idea, and as three of the black, red-fletched shafts hammered into the hide-covered wood in front of my face, I was glad he'd thought of it.

Orava's boys had left the mortars back within the walls, for reasons of speed more than anything else, but right then I was wishing we'd had them along. There was a lot of dead space on our flank, where the Avur archers were hunkered down and launching their projectiles at us. We couldn't hit them with rifle or machinegun fire, but we could have dropped mortar rounds on them for hours, if we'd had the weapons along.

We didn't, though, so I grabbed Rodeffer and Farrar. "I'm heading up there." I pointed to a promontory that loomed above the road, about half a mile back the way we'd come. "We might have a shot at some of the archers from the top of that ridge."

"I'll come with you." While the Tuacha had originally been essentially their own team, as time had gone on and the original platoon had been whittled down by attrition, they'd started to spread out to the other four teams. Bearrac had sort of permanently attached himself to my Team One, occasionally joined by Mathghaman. Big, hairy, and aggressive, Bearrac was the bull of the bunch, often more eager to get into a fight than any of the rest. He was also as good with that finely engraved, somewhat musket-looking rifle of his as any of us were, even though he'd never touched one until almost two years before.

I just nodded. There was no way I was turning down Bearrac's help.

Another volley of arrows plunged down, intercepted by shields or slamming into the grassy dirt, for the most part, though I heard a cry as one of the Galel took a shaft through the foot. The Avurs didn't seem to have enough archers to darken the sky with their arrows, but they had enough and, try as we might, it was impossible to fit an entire man all the way under one of those shields. Again, they were better than my buckler, but they were far from perfect.

It was sheer luck that none of them had hit any of the horses we'd left in a hollow below the hilltop yet.

We got up to move as the shower of arrows stopped but, even as we turned toward the road and the promontory that I'd picked for an overwatch position, the cataphracts came around the finger to the south.

Their horses draped in iron scales, they looked almost like metal centaurs, their armor so like to their mounts' that it was hard to tell from a distance where one ended and the other started. That armor of overlapping, rounded plates was tough for a bullet to get through at range, never mind arrows, sling stones, or spears. And with the sheer weight they could bring to bear in a charge, all of it behind those massive, two-handed spears they carried, a full company of them could hit with the local equivalent of tank shock.

And those horses were powerhouses that could easily storm up the hillside toward us, which they proceeded to do, even as yet another volley of arrows forced us under our shields.

Even men in a medieval sort of society knew the value of covering fire.

By the time the arrows stopped falling, the lead elements of that charge were less than a hundred yards away and coming on fast. This wasn't like the hill where we'd last fought the Peruni, just over the ridge from Cor Hefedd, where we'd held in a nest of massive boulders that had acted as excellent defensive works and kept the cataphracts off us. This hill was a lot more open and, while we could still dominate the terrain by fire, provided we weren't pinned down by arrows, there were a lot fewer obstacles to a cavalry charge than I might have wished.

Fewer, but not none. We hadn't gotten all the charges set in, but we'd gotten enough.

"Heads down!" Gunny's bellow sounded over the thunder of hooves, and we buried ourselves in the dirt as far as we could. This was going to be danger close.

Gunny hit the clacker and the base of the hill erupted in fire, smoke, and flying dirt and rock with an earth-shaking *boom*. Men and horses went flying, when they weren't simply torn to pieces. The cataphracts' charge faltered as debris rained down out of the sky and, while we hadn't gotten all of the vanguard, they were smart enough that they didn't try to press the attack immediately, but wheeled aside, the wedge splitting and racing back down the hill, angling to either side of the smoking craters where the charges had been placed.

I suspected that most of the explosives we'd left down there had detonated sympathetically when the emplaced charges had gone off. We hadn't exactly had time to secure them, and I knew that some of those kitbags had been left awfully close to the bombs we'd already primed and buried.

Shoving my borrowed shield aside, I got behind my rifle and looked for a target, but those cataphracts had moved *fast*, faster than I'd expected riders that heavy to move. A horn call sounded, and I knew another volley of arrows was coming.

The Avurs couldn't have an infinite supply of arrows, any more than we could have an infinite supply of bullets, but there were enough of them that they could probably keep us pinned down just long enough for the cataphracts to ride over the hill, provided they figured out that we'd only had that one belt of explosives set in.

There was no way they could really know that, unless they had a wizard sniffing things out. We couldn't sit up there and rest on our laurels, though.

The storm of arrows was a little thinner that time, mainly because Uurad's Galel archers had figured out the range and were replying in kind. Their five-foot war bows were considerably different from the Avurs' compound recurves, but they still packed a punch. I'd seen those men launch a heavy arrow three hundred yards with some pretty decent accuracy, and now they were dropping those yard-long shafts over the finger at where the Avurs were holed up.

Of course, the Avurs weren't going to be staying in one place. That wasn't their style. Mathghaman knew it just as well as I did, and he had probably already figured it out as soon as the first arrows had whispered through the air.

He was up and moving, hauling me to my feet even as I started to rise. "We must move quickly."

We scrambled down the hill toward the road, momentarily out of the line of the enemy archers' beaten zone. Then we were pushing hard for the promontory I'd picked, though the ground was steep and uneven, and it was more of a clamber than a sprint. We should get up there before the next attack managed to materialize, but just barely.

I could hear the Peruni horns, deep, braying instruments that sounded disturbingly like the Fohorimans' signals in the north. They were already reorganizing quickly. They had to know that we were fighting to hold this road for a reason, and they wanted to cut it before King Uven could arrive.

A steep-sided gully, lined with bushes and short, stunted trees, ran up the side of the hill, and Rodeffer plunged into it, slinging his rifle to his back so that he could clamber over the rocks and through the brush with both hands. Speed was security at that point, and it was absolutely vital to getting up there while we could still make a difference. I tried to follow with my own rifle still in my hand, muzzle pointed at the sky, for a few yards before finally giving up and cinching it down across my back. The long rifle would catch on the bushes from time to time, but less than trying to maneuver it while climbing with only one free hand.

I could hear the horn calls and the renewed gunfire behind us as we scrambled up the gully. The next attack was already forming. If they were going to reduce the fortress relatively quickly, then the Peruni *had* to cut off any relief force, and that meant going through us. They couldn't afford to dawdle down there, and they weren't.

Rodeffer pushed hard, and I could hear him panting as he clambered over rocks and skipped the easiest route to try to cut a few seconds, at least, off the climb. Turning to the right, he started to climb up the steep side of the gully.

As he did so, I felt a pressure, a tension, in the air. The hair went up on my arms and the back of my neck. I knew that feeling. I recognized the sudden sulfurous, metallic stink on the air, too.

The Peruni had a wizard with them, all right.

I halted and looked around carefully, scanning for whatever the sorcerer might have just summoned. It wasn't a monster I had to worry about, though.

The clouds above the hill darkened still more, and then a purple-tinged lightning bolt slammed down into the hilltop.

The concussion was brutal. The thunderclap's shockwave hit as hard as if a satchel charge had just been set off. There was a definite hiccup in the outgoing fire for a second, but then it redoubled in ferocity. Our boys were *pissed*, which told me all I needed to know.

We'd lost some people in that lightning strike.

Rodeffer had stopped, too, looking back at me over his shoulder, his eyes slightly wide. I understood. That clifftop we were climbing toward was the highest point for a few dozen yards, and no one in their right mind wants to be the highest thing standing when there's lightning hitting nearby. There was nothing for it, though. "Keep going," I hissed. We *had* to get up there and get some fire on the Avurs. And, if the power up above was looking out for us, on that sorcerer, too.

Always kill the wizard first, if you can.

Rodeffer resumed his climb, though he stayed low as he got up on top of the craggy hill. I was right there behind him, and I confess that I did the same, moving up toward the cliff bent almost double, bringing my rifle around in front of me. Just because we really needed to get into that firing position didn't mean we needed to take stupid chances.

Sometimes stupid chances are the only way to get the mission done and save lives. Sometimes they only get you and everyone else killed. The trick's knowing the difference.

We threw ourselves flat at the edge of the bluffs and got on sights, searching for targets. I grimaced as I took in what I could see.

While we did have a shot on several of the Avur archers, they were already mounting up and getting ready to relocate as the Galel bowmen renewed their own flights of arrows, and we only had eyes on a handful of them, hardly the full band, even taking into consideration the casualties we'd inflicted on them during that first attack.

Still, it was better than nothing, so I shifted my hips to get myself well behind the rifle, flipped the selector to "Fire," and started to squeeze as I let out my breath.

You don't usually get a whole lot of time to practice the fundamentals of marksmanship in combat, which is why they have to be hard-wired into you before you go into battle. Fortunately, by that point they were as natural as breathing, so I hardly thought about it as I squeezed off my first shot, taking an armored Avur horse archer through the armpit from about four hundred yards. He crashed to the ground and out of sight as his horse freaked, and then we were just dumping rounds into the shapes of horsemen and horses as fast as we could shoot, reset, and find a new target.

I was pretty sure Bearrac was taking headshots, even at that distance and without any optics on his rifle. He was a Tuacha. They're like that.

There wasn't a whole lot of fellowship to be found among the Avurs. Those who could bolted, charging down the draw and out of sight, leaving the wounded and dead behind. I got one more high in the back and he arched in the saddle just before he and his horse vanished beneath the crest of the finger.

Then I shifted, looking for the Peruni, hoping I could spot that wizard. They don't always dress in robes and pointy hats, particularly not on the battlefield.

Just in time, I picked up the twin pincers of the Peruni charge. They had apparently decided to avoid the craters where we'd set the charges that had blown their vanguard to smithereens, and now were coming at the hilltop from two different directions, both steering clear of the craters and splitting our defensive fires in what was very nearly an L-shape. Even as the cataphracts rumbled up the hill, though, the Avurs rode around behind them, making for the road farther to the west while they loosed flights of arrows at the hill.

One Peruni horseman, dressed in especially fine armor, reined his horse in, spreading his arms wide as he chanted, his voice booming unnaturally over the thunder of hooves and the crackle of suppressed small arms fire.

Shadows seemed to move strangely under the sky as the clouds darkened again. The wind picked up, blowing dust and debris into the defenders' faces, Marines and Galel alike. And that thunderstorm tension started to build again.

Before he could call down another lightning bolt, this time probably targeted right on one of our machine-gunners, I put my reticle on his chest, adjusting the best I could figure for the wind and the distance, and squeezed the trigger.

His spell contributed to his death, because it made the shot that much easier. Though the wind blowing into our faces was hot and noxious, carrying more dust and grit with it than was probably natural, it was also what we'd call "zero value." Meaning I didn't have to adjust my windage to left or right to put a bullet right through his collarbone.

The round smashed through metal scales, leather backing, and bone, to plunge deep into his upper chest. It didn't kill him outright, but he jerked and swayed in the saddle, nearly falling before he grabbed hold of the saddle bows to steady himself.

My follow-up shot finished him off and he dropped as his horse panicked and ran off.

For a split second, as I watched through my scope, I wondered at a horse that would stand still through all that weirdness and sorcery, yet panic at a gunshot that killed its rider. Maybe he'd been forcing it to stay still through sheer force of will.

The wizard's death seemed to release the tension in the air, but it didn't stop the charge. Even as the wind died, the cataphracts came on, driving their horses hard to close the distance before our guys could start shooting again.

Wishing that I'd brought my M107, I shifted my aim to the lead cataphracts. The end of the windstorm had let our guys get some of their equilibrium back, and arrows were starting to fly into the advancing formations, even as the rest of the Galel formed shield walls bristling with spears and our guys opened fire. Santos cut two of the heavily armored cavalrymen nearly in half with a long burst, raking his fire across their front, just before Rodeffer and I took nearly simultaneous shots on another of them. Struck by no fewer than ten rounds, the man just went limp and fell out of the saddle, leaking blood from beneath those scales that remained intact, just before he was run over by the horse behind him.

They kept coming for a few moments, and very near-ly reached the front. Those lead cataphracts were *angry*, and they wanted blood. They were all nobles and very proud men, and they were getting torn up by foreigners without getting close enough to come to grips. Some of them probably would have gotten into the perimeter in the next few minutes.

But then a high, clear, brassy trumpet call echoed off the mountainside above us, and King Uven's knights smashed into the Peruni flank with a thunder of hoof-beats, clash of weapons, and shouts of warriors.

We ceased fire as friendlies and hostiles became hopelessly intermixed, but only a few moments later, even as lances shattered and men closed in with drawn swords, axes, and maces, that braying, evil-sounding horn call sounded again, and those cataphracts that could reined in, came about in relatively good order, and fell back to the east and south.

Several of them held their ground and fought, either to buy their fellows time, or, more likely, out of an un-willingness to retreat, even before the long column of King Uven's army, snaking its way down the road from Cor Legear.

For the Galel's part, they didn't mob the cataphracts who held their ground, but several of Uven's finest closed in to engage them in single combat. I understood, though I probably would have just shot them. Time was of the essence, and the longer that army was spread out on the road, the longer the enemy would have to launch a renewed attack higher up.

Still, it didn't take long. For all the weight of a cata-phract charge, their armor made them somewhat heavy and clumsy compared to the Galel knights, and they were unhorsed and killed relatively quickly. There was no quarter asked for or given. These men had known they were going to die, and they put up a hell of a fight, but the Galel were just faster and meaner about it.

The last one held his opponent off with that long, two-handed spear for a while, but the opposing knight, wearing a cloak of red and gold and a red crest on his gold-chased helmet, managed to get around behind him and hamstring the horse, his spear dipping beneath the long coat of scales that covered the animal's flanks. The horse screamed and collapsed, thrashing in agony, but the rider, despite the weight of his armor, leapt free.

While they were still a good distance away, I knew the knight was King Uven, just by his colors. It somewhat surprised me that Vepogenus had allowed him to go into battle, so soon after the wound he'd taken at the hands of a revenant summoned by an unholy alliance of Galel rebels and imperial provocateurs, but there he was, swinging down off his horse and hefting an axe with a big, half-circle blade as he waded in.

They came together, clashed, and then circled. The rest of Uven's knights had surrounded them, but it wasn't as if the cataphract was looking for a way out.

When the end came, it came quickly. The cataphract lunged, swinging his own short axe for Uven's head, and the king swayed aside, got his shield between his body and the enemy's weapon, then stepped inside and brought his own axe crashing down on the junction of the Peruni's neck and shoulder.

Even though I'm pretty sure the scaled aventail that covered a good bit of the man's shoulders kept the axe from cutting into him, the sheer force of the blow was clearly enough to shatter bone. He slumped and staggered away, his arm hanging useless, as King Uven stalked him.

Another, somewhat halfhearted swing of the Peruni axe was batted away almost contemptuously. Then King Uven feinted, quickly reversed the axe as soon as the cataphract tried to block it, and hit his enemy in the head so hard that I could hear the ring of steel on iron even from where I watched.

The cataphract fell to the ground and didn't move.

Uven turned and swung back into the saddle without a backward glance. I nudged Rodeffer with my boot. "Time to go."

CHAPTER 7

KING Uven stood in the hall, still in full armor and cloak, except for his helmet, held under the crook of his arm. His hair was plastered to his scalp with sweat. It had been a hard ride up that narrow, twisting road to the rear gate of Cor Chatha, and while the Peruni had retreated initially, as the column had threaded its way up to the fortress, they had returned. The Avurs had ranged up and down the column, harassing the Galel with sudden flurries of arrows before fleeing out of bowshot. Apparently, several of Uven's younger lords had wanted to go hunting them, but had been restrained by the older, more experienced knights. That was exactly what the enemy wanted. They *wanted* the Galel forces thinned out and scattered, where they could be isolated and defeated in detail, leaving fewer to man the defenses of the fortress.

"I had hoped to ride here with ten thousand." Even though he had recovered considerably over the last few weeks, Uven still looked drawn, his cheeks hollower than they had been, his eyes sunken. He'd been put through the wringer since we'd first met him, and now that he was in the middle of a fortress about to be under siege, things weren't likely to get much better. He sighed wearily. "Yet after what happened at Cor Legear..." His shoulders almost slumped. "We arrived with just over half that, and then we took some losses on the way up here."

He turned to us. Our relationship with the king was kind of an odd one. We were Americans, most of us, and with an American attitude that didn't much care for kings. Yet he clearly felt a certain brotherhood with us, one that I, at least, couldn't help but reciprocate. He was a younger man, full of piss and vinegar, and was a warrior through and through. Furthermore, Bailey and I had, arguably, saved his life and that of his queen in Cor Legear, when we'd fought off a shadow demon and killed a Dullahan. That neither of us had done it unaided didn't matter much to Uven. We'd still done it, and the awe in which most of the Galel held the Sword Bearers was added to a much more intense and personal gratitude when it came to the king.

The fact that he was just an all-around good dude helped, too.

"Once again, I owe you a great deal, my lords. We may well have been delayed at the pass long enough that the full might of the imperial army could have swept us aside, had you not been there ahead of us."

I shrugged. "We could use the manpower."

He laughed faintly, though there wasn't a lot of humor in it. When we'd first met him, Uven had been full of fire and energy. Now he seemed much older. Tired. Beaten down.

Turning back to the arrow slit windows, he took a deep breath, clearly fighting to maintain his equilibrium. It was getting dark out there, far earlier than it should, if only because of the ever-thickening, lightning-riddled clouds overhead. But it was still getting on toward evening, and now the countless campfires of the army of the Empire of Ar-Annator flickered in the dimness out there, spread out across the plains like the stars we wouldn't see that night.

"You say the Thirty are here?" He was staring hard out at the plain. I stepped forward, holding out my binoculars. I'd grabbed them out of my ruck on the way up, suspecting that Uven was going to want to get eyes on the situation as best he could himself.

He took them, examining them carefully. I showed him how to use them, and he put them to his eyes, though he needed to fiddle with the focus a little before he could see clearly. He grunted in some appreciation. He knew some of what we were capable of, but this was probably his first time looking through optics.

The binos were Swarovskis, some of the best glass we had, aside from the spotting scopes we were still hauling around. We could probably get even better ones from the *Coira Ansec* if we asked, but these were good enough that I'd made sure we held on to them even after reaching the Isle of Riamog.

Once he got used to the optics, he started to carefully and methodically scan the field of campfires out there. He was good; I'd had to train brand new boot Recon Marines how to scan properly, but King Uven picked it up like it was the most natural thing in the world. A lot of those new to observation will bounce from one point of interest to another, missing a lot along the way. The right way to do it is to slowly scan in strips, each one overlapping the previous one, and that appeared to be what he was doing.

He lowered the binoculars after a moment. "I think I saw one of them." He suppressed a shudder. He'd seen some weird and scary stuff as king, but some things never get better with time. Things that used to be men, toting around their own severed heads like footballs, are among those sorts of things. The whips made of human vertebrae didn't help, either. He squinted into the darkness. "They are some distance away, at least."

"They know we're here." Gunny was blunt. "We already shot down a couple of their wyverns. After Conor here sent one of their heads flying with a .50 cal round in Gremman, maybe they're being extra cautious."

"That would perhaps have hurt their pride, but little else." Mathghaman was every bit as blunt. "They are men who are, for all intents and purposes, long dead. They no longer live entirely on this plane." He shook his leonine head. "There are few weapons that might truly harm them."

"The Two Swords will." I folded my arms over my chest rig. "I know that for a fact." We would have burned the dead Dullahan outside Cor Legear, except for the fact that it had quickly decayed and turned to dust after I'd stabbed it between the eyes with the Sword of Iudicael. "*If* we can get close enough to them." I glanced out the nearest window, a short distance from where King Uven still stood. Even as I did so, I heard a hissing sort of croak, and I spotted a wyvern circling over the Imperial army. "That may have as much to do with their standoff as our firearms. Maybe more."

Mathghaman nodded somberly. "Indeed. They felt the final death of their fellow in Cor Legear, as soon as it happened. They will be warier, now."

I glanced over at Bailey, who was watching the myriad pinpoints of flame out there with an expression of frustration that I was sure mirrored my own. We weren't, either of us, cut out for sitting there waiting to get hit. We'd both had to do it from time to time. There had been more than one fight in Syria where we'd been able to watch the enemy gathering for over an hour before the first shot was fired. It still went against the grain.

But what could we do? Short of opening the front gates and running out in a frontal assault—and none of us thought *that* was a good idea—we were kind of stuck. The siege was beginning, and this wasn't Vahava Paykhah.

We weren't the only ones thinking that, though. Tarvedum was stroking his mustache as he studied us. He'd seen the army coming and probably had most of its numbers and dispositions memorized already. "What if there were a way to get you closer, my lords?"

Every eye in the place turned to him. "How, short of flying?" King Uven's words might have sounded sarcastic, but there was a note of curiosity in his voice, nevertheless. He had to know Tarvedum well enough to expect that he wouldn't venture a purely hypothetical, not right then and there. Hell, I *didn't* know him nearly that well, but I'd been around him enough over the last week that I didn't expect he'd talk just to hear his own voice. If he'd ventured the possibility, then he had something in mind.

"Lord Vurguist, the man who built this fortress, thought of many possible needs. How he managed it, I do not know, but there are secret passages that run underneath the mountain, opening up far to the south, north, and west. They could be used to evacuate the last of the

defenders, should the fortress's fall be imminent, or..."
He raised an eyebrow.

"As covert sally ports." Gunny finished the sentence with a glint in his eye, a look that I was sure we all shared. It appealed to the Sneaky Pete side of every Recon Marine's soul. To get around behind the enemy when he thinks he has you cornered, and show up where he least suspects, just to shove a blade in his kidneys.

"Where are these passages?"

* * *

Of course, we couldn't just go right into the tunnels immediately. There was a lot of preparation and planning that had to happen first. Mostly planning; all of our gear and weapons were already ready to go. I'd been pretty big on the "horse, gear, self" priorities since I'd first been an assistant team leader, what felt like several lifetimes ago, and it had only become more urgently vital since we'd come here. We never let our area turn into a gear bomb. Everything was always packed back up, weapons loaded, mags jammed, water full, and chow topped off, at least as much as possible. There wasn't a whole lot of prep to do on that front. Figuring out our plan of attack, though...that took some observation and thought.

Before we started, though, Tarvedum took us to show us the entrances.

Naturally, they were within the citadel itself, at the highest and deepest part of the defenses. I'd half expected to go clear down underground, but in fact the entrance to the catacombs was in the storerooms behind the kitchens, about halfway to the ground.

Tarvedum himself led us through the stacks of kegs and bales, the massive stores of supplies that were intended to keep the defenders fed for months. Most of the foodstuffs were dried and salted, in order to keep without spoiling for as long as possible. The storeroom was cool, partially cut back into the rock of the mountain, and it probably stayed that way most of the year.

He kept going, holding the oil lamp high, as we moved deeper and deeper into the stacks of supplies. It was getting dark enough that I turned on my weapon light just so we could see better. If not for that and the lamp that Tarvedum carried, we'd be in complete pitch darkness.

Coming to the back wall, he stopped. "It is here."

At first, it was almost impossible to see anything aside from stacks of timbers, very old timbers, set against the wall. They were probably there in the event that repairs needed to be made to the defenses. Shoring up the gates, things like that. There were similar stacks of lumber all over the fortress, staged near the gates for just that purpose. These were way back in the citadel, though, and they looked like they'd been there for a *long* time.

Tarvedum put the lamp carefully out of the way, and then started to move the timbers. We quickly stepped in to help and, after a few minutes, we were faced with a yawning opening in the rock. It was low, and we'd have to bend almost double to get through it but, when I shined my light inside, I saw that the passage got considerably taller the deeper it went into the mountain.

"It is many miles through the dark." Tarvedum had taken up the lamp again. "And while we stand on Galel ground, my lords, I must caution you. No man has traveled these tunnels in many years. We are not in the kingdom's heart any longer, either. This is the frontier, and many darker things have crept in closer as the years have gone by."

He looked troubled, even in the dim and flickering light. "Step carefully, and may Tigharn watch over you as you venture through the bones of the earth. I must hope for your success, but I fear for you, going down there." He seemed to hesitate for a moment. "There are stories that the fortress has a guardian. None know who or what it is, but some have said they have seen a faintly glowing figure walking the battlements. Perhaps he will protect you in the tunnels below."

There wasn't much to say after that. Bailey and I sort of had our own guardians, but I, at least, had come to the conclusion that such protection was somewhat conditional.

We'd seen some of what lurked out there, beyond the frontier. We'd seen some of the monstrosities that prowled through the "bones of the earth," as Tarvedum had put it. None of us were especially eager to face them again, but necessity is what it is.

This was a combat situation. There's no such thing as no risk.

We nodded, thanked him for showing us the way, and headed back upstairs to finish planning our end run.

CHAPTER 8

WE were relatively lightly equipped as we gathered in the storeroom again. I say *relatively* because we were still carrying as much ammunition as we could, along with chow and water for several days. No long-range radios or even explosives, though. We had a long way to go, and we needed to be able to move quickly.

I briefly remembered the sheer amount of stuff we'd been required to carry in Syria. Not for the first time, I was kind of glad we had come through the mists to a place where we could operate the way we figured we needed to.

The four team leaders were about to get down to a serious match of Rock, Paper, Scissors to determine our marching order. That was a matter of no small concern, since whoever was on point was going to get into contact first and, even after all this time, nobody wanted to let it be thought that he was reluctant to get stuck in. Gunny, however, had had it with our shenanigans, and probably figured we didn't have time.

"Knock it off, you friggin' teenagers. Team order. Let's go." He was already ducking through the opening.

I tried not to look smug as Rodeffer and I followed him, Bearrac and Mathghaman falling in with our team, just behind me. Granted, any smugness I might have felt dissipated almost as soon as I passed into the cool darkness of the tunnel itself. Things change once you leave the wire, even if it's somewhat metaphorical. It wasn't that I was scared of what we might meet down there, though I was. It was more that all the issues of pride and status fell away, and professionalism took their place.

It was a necessity to get over the fear, too. We were going to be a long way from support, even if Olgudach, who had taken over the lordship of Edernon shortly after the battle for Cor Legear, and was now gathering the greater army in the king's name, showed up in the next few days. Furthermore, we would be going up against some of the nastiest things we'd encountered since coming through the mists, with the possible exception of Vaelor, all by ourselves.

That's sobering. Faced with a mission like that, you either get icy professional or you panic. Panic wasn't an option.

So, I put my game face on, and we got moving.

Ordinarily, we spread out on patrol, getting about five yards between Marines. Down here, though, it was so dark that we didn't want to lose each other. In those claustrophobic passages we might turn a corner and find ourselves completely alone against whatever blind, pale thing was scratching away at the rocks under Cor Chatha at any moment. So, we stayed close.

Gurke had suggested moving in on NVGs, using the IR illuminators on our PEQ-16s to see by, but Gunny had kiboshed it, though not before some careful thought. It was true that most humans can't see into the infrared, but there were plenty of beings in this world that could, especially underground. The Tuacha didn't even need

NVGs in the pitch black. Meanwhile, we'd be limiting our own visibility because, even with the binocular vision you get with PVS-15s, it's still a pretty narrow field of view.

So, we moved with our weapon lights on. I was plenty thankful that the batteries the *Coira Ansec* gave us lasted a long, *long* time. We'd need them.

By Tarvedum's estimate, we had probably five miles to go through the tunnels before we reached the other side, about three quarters of a mile from the road where we'd fought the Avurs and the Peruni cataphracts. That was only an estimate, though. While he knew they were there, he'd never traveled the passages himself. There could very well be twists and turns that added a considerable distance to the trek we had to make through the dark.

It didn't take long for us to get beyond the faint glow coming from the storeroom, where Tarvedum and King Uven had seen us off by torchlight. Then we were alone in the dark, our way lit only by the actinic glow of our rifle lights.

The tunnels were rough for the first few hundred yards, clearly chipped out of the rock with chisel and pick, and held up by ancient, fire-blackened beams. After a short while, though, the tunnel opened up on a vast cavern.

I had no idea what geological processes had thrust the mount of Cor Chatha up from the plain, but it probably wasn't a volcano, since I had never heard of limestone caverns forming within a volcanic mountain. That was undoubtedly what these caves were, too, as we shone our lights around, the cones of white illumination glittering off stalactites, stalagmites, and flowing curtains of stone.

If I'd been thinking more in terms of aesthetics, I might have been struck by the primal beauty of that hidden place. As it was, I was thinking mostly about the amount of cover and concealment it might provide for any subterranean nasties that could have crawled into the cracks in the hills over the years.

Rodeffer paused at the top of the slick, gleaming slope and panned his light around, looking for the best way through. There weren't exactly any road signs, especially if no one had been through here in years. Finally, he fished his compass out of his chest rig and checked the direction, before half-climbing, half-skidding down the damp rock toward the southwest.

I followed as carefully and sedately as I could, my rifle pointed up at the ceiling and my finger very consciously well away from the trigger. A negligent discharge in there might result in a nasty ricochet, or worse, a cave-in. There was no way I wanted to be responsible for either.

It took well over an hour to navigate across that chamber, even though the whole place was probably only about a hundred fifty yards wide. The rock formations made movement in a straight line impossible, and several times we found, after a few false starts and doubling back, that we just had to climb over some of them and crawl between others. It was rough, exhausting work, but we were moving, even when we had to drop our day packs and drag them through a narrow crack after us.

Finally, though, Rodeffer found a sign that we were on the right track.

He was pointing his light at the rock wall as I dropped heavily from the ledge just above the tunnel ahead, where the chamber narrowed down into a passageway about six feet across. "What have you got?" My voice sounded achingly loud, even more than the rustle and thump of my landing had. Every sound seemed horribly amplified in those tunnels, and I had to fight not to flinch every time anything scraped or knocked against the rocks.

He nodded toward the circle of brilliant light cast against the wall, and I squinted at it. It was achingly bright this close, but after a moment I could make out what he'd seen.

The rune had been carved into the stone a long, long time ago. It was partly covered over by limestone deposits as water dripped down the walls, but it was still legible. It wasn't a Tuacha rune, but I could recognize the Galel signs, even though I couldn't really read them.

"Looks like we're on the right track, then."

"I hope so." Rodeffer was quite obviously not terribly comfortable with spelunking, and I couldn't blame him. I was acutely conscious of the millions upon millions of tons of rock above our heads, not to mention the fact that we didn't have a lot of good memories about roaming around underground since we'd come through the mists. Such expeditions had been fraught with frantic battles against horrific monsters out of nightmares. Even our escape through the caves beneath Taramas's citadel had been nearly ended by a cave serpent, some time after we'd gotten past the Fohorimans' servants.

"Only a few more miles." In truth, I didn't know that, but the definition of the word "few" is, fortunately, pretty flexible. It could be two or it could be six. We didn't know. We were going where we needed to, though, and that was what mattered.

He nodded, though the motion was jerky and nervous. I couldn't blame him. I wanted out of that hole, too, no matter how pretty the formations were.

The tunnel narrowed somewhat, and after about another quarter mile—just judging by pace count—we were walking hunched over to keep from scraping our helmets on the ceiling. It wasn't comfortable, but it was still better than crawling. I just hoped that things opened up again soon, because walking in a half-crouch gets painful and tiring awfully quickly.

Unfortunately, it didn't, and after a while we were crawling, dragging our packs and rifles along with us, cracking glow sticks for illumination since the weapon lights weren't going to work very well if we were going to be careful about not flagging each other with our muzzles.

It got harder to gauge distance while crawling, so I wasn't sure how far we'd gone that way before Rodeffer stopped dead, hissing back over his shoulder for quiet. I froze and held a fist behind me. Bearrac wasn't really making any noise as it was, and slowly, the rustle and scrape of men in combat gear crawling across the rock dwindled behind us.

While I wanted to know what had made Rodeffer stop, I also knew that asking him at that point would be counterproductive. He'd let me know when he had an idea.

We waited in the dark for a while, listening to the faint drip of water somewhere, and then I thought I heard it.

Something, somewhere in the tunnel, was tapping.

It wasn't water. There was a distinctly metallic sound to it, a ringing like someone or something was knocking a hammer against rock. There was someone or something ahead of us in the tunnels.

After a few moments, Rodeffer looked back at me, seemed to get frustrated, looked forward again, then started crawling once more. He got a few yards ahead and then found a slightly larger chamber where we couldn't stand up, but I could move up next to him.

"I can't tell how far away that is, but I'm pretty sure it's in front of us." He looked even more nervous in the green glow of the chemlights.

I peered into the darkness ahead, but of course there were no lights, no glow to tell us what we might be getting into. Only blackness and the little bit of rock we could see in the dim illumination of the chemlights. "Well, I guess that means that Tarvedum wasn't just telling ghost stories when he worried about something crawling around down here." I thought about it for a moment, but only for a moment. We really didn't have a lot of options. I sure didn't want to try to go back to the fortress and tell Vepogenus, Tarvedum, and the king that we'd turned around and ditched the mission because we heard some scary noises in the dark.

"Nothing for it." I glanced back at him. "You brought your .45?"

He grimaced a little and pulled it out of the pouch on his chest rig he'd started to use as a holster. "Yeah. Seemed to make sense, doing this tunnel rat shit. Still…"

"I know. But we've got one way out of here, and that's through." I didn't want to think too much about how we were going to get back inside.

We probably weren't. Once we were outside the encirclement, we were probably going to have to conduct constant hit-and-run attacks on the enemy until we could link up with Olgudach's relief force. Presuming it came. There was some history between Olgudach's house of Edernon and Uven's family.

I knew how bitter the men of Edernon still were that the kingship had passed to Uven's house over a century before. Still, I'd ridden and fought alongside Olgudach, and I knew that he was a man of his word. He'd already swallowed his pride to fight for the king he had, rather than help the Peruni and their dark masters.

That was a thought for another time. Too much woolgathering in a situation like that can get people killed. We had to get moving.

Rodeffer, as much as he clearly wouldn't have minded going back, grimaced and resumed his crawl through the narrow tunnel, his 1911 held in front of him in one hand. I waited until he had passed me, then I followed suit.

Fortunately, the passage widened after a few more yards, and we were finally able to stand up again. Rodeffer quickly holstered his pistol and got his rifle back up and ready, switching on his weapon light, which was absolutely blinding for a moment after what felt like several hours with only a vague green glow to see by.

As I squinted and blinked against the glare, I saw movement.

Rodeffer saw it, too, snapping his rifle up just as I moved up behind a multi-tiered stalactite that connected floor to ceiling. A pair of huge, lamplike eyes blazed in the illumination, much like a cat's, and a vicious screech echoed off the rock walls around us.

Suddenly, the walls of the cave were alive with movement, and I shot the first scuttling shape that threw itself at me. I could barely make out arms, legs, a too-large head, and jagged, sharp teeth before my bullets smashed through the thing's body and it went limp, crashing to the floor within a foot of my boot.

Rodeffer was pumping rounds into everything that moved, and I caught a glimpse of a bulbous head on a scrawny body, the eyes nearly the size of baseballs, with a lamprey mouth full of snaggle teeth. Then I was busy. I shot another one as it scrambled up a stalactite to try to throw itself at me from above, and it curled up like a dead beetle and fell.

Then things got strange.

I'd seen Iudicael manifest during the fight in Cor Legear, appearing as a figure of light and dispelling the sorcerous darkness that the Dullahan had wrapped us in. I'd seen him appear out of the corner of my eye, even put a hand on my shoulder from where I couldn't see all of him. So, I was getting pretty familiar with him, if such can be said about an angelic being who is a messenger of Tigharn Himself.

The glowing figure that swept down from the tunnel behind us was not Iudicael. I was reasonably sure it wasn't Categyrn, either. This figure was dimmer, more of a faint glow than a brilliant blaze, in the shape of a knight with sword held high, rushing down upon the pale, lamp-eyed little troglodytes. I could almost hear a shouted battle cry, though it sounded distant and muffled.

With the frantic scratching of claws on rock and shrill screams of what sounded like abject terror, the troglodytes suddenly turned tail and ran. They scuttled over rock formations and up stalactites like beetles, vanishing down the passageway ahead, both on the ground and clinging to the ceiling. In seconds, the only ones visible were the dead on the cavern floor.

That faint, glowing figure kept chasing after them, disappearing down the tunnel ahead of us.

Rodeffer was breathing hard, his rifle still leveled. "What the hell was that?"

"The monsters?" I lowered my own weapon and stepped up to join him. "Or the apparition that chased them away?"

"Yes." He finally lowered his M110. "Both."

"Well, I'd say the monsters look an awful lot like the Duergar in the north." Farrar flipped one over with his boot. "As for the apparition?" He spat into the darkness. "Offhand, I'd say we just met the 'guardian' that Tarvedum was talking about."

"Sounds about right." I hefted my own rifle and looked around. "Anybody catch a tooth or a claw?"

No one had. The engagement had been too short. Rodeffer and I had been the only ones to even get a shot off.

"Well, our thanks to the guardian of Cor Chatha." Gunny had clambered to the top of the pile of rocks behind to look down at us. "Let's get moving. We've still got a mission."

CHAPTER 9

I'D completely lost track of my pace count and the time, despite my best efforts. The dark seemed to stretch on endlessly, and the tunnels and caverns twisted and turned through the mountain. We were leaving marks to make sure we hadn't gotten turned around, but all the same, Tarvedum's estimate of five to six miles was proving to be a woeful underestimate.

There appeared to be more than one system of caverns under the mountain, connected by carefully excavated tunnels. A lot of thought and exploration had gone into these passages. I could only imagine how difficult it must have been with only oil lamps and candles.

After another short mine tunnel, we came out into a massive crack in the mountainside, and I looked up and saw the sky for the first time in what felt like weeks. It was still covered in clouds, and they were thick enough that it could have been noon or midnight, it was impossible to tell which, but it was definitely sky, ever so slightly lighter than the stygian blackness we'd been trudging through for hours. A flicker of lightning silhouetted the rock for a moment, and I started to breathe a little easier. We were still pretty deep, but we had to be getting close to the end.

Plus, it was nice to not have a mountain looming directly over my head, even if only for a little while.

We kept going for a short while before I moved up, stepping it out to catch up with Rodeffer and grabbing his shoulder. He stopped, and I steered him behind a boulder that looked like it had fallen from the sheer slope above, smashing several more graceful formations on the way down. I turned off my weapon light, and without anyone saying anything, the rest of the platoon followed suit over the next few seconds. If we were getting close to the exit, no one wanted to be the one who alerted the enemy to our presence.

I'd had to take my NVGs off my helmet and stash them in my dump pouch during some of the tighter areas behind us in the caverns, but now I pulled them back out, clipped them in, and dropped them in front of my eyes. The green was bright, but not as bright as the white light we'd been using up to then.

The crack in the ceiling overhead seemed to stop a few dozen yards ahead, but that might just have been another turn in the tunnel. In fact, I was pretty sure that it was. That wasn't why I'd stopped Rodeffer, though.

We'd been conducting security halts from time to time on the way, though more often since we'd made contact with the troglodytes. The gunfire, suppressed or not, echoing through the caverns hadn't drawn any more attention, or else Cor Chatha's mysterious guardian had driven it away. But we were being cautious anyway.

Now, though it was a little early, I wanted to halt again, because I thought I'd heard something.

We crouched in the dark, Rodeffer mounting his own NVGs again, and scanned the narrow slot in the rock ahead of us, straining our ears to hear. I'd been a Recon Marine long enough that I had some not-insignificant hearing loss, so I wondered if I was actually hearing anything or just listening to the tinnitus in my left ear getting creative. As time went on, though, I was able to catalog my breathing, Rodeffer's faint rustle as he leaned against the boulder, and the various other unavoidable noises that the rest of us—with the exception of the Tuacha—made as we knelt in the dark.

And those sounds that had made me stop weren't coming from us.

I could definitely hear movement, though it was hard to tell what was moving. A patter of footsteps, the occasional *clack* of a weapon or a tool against rock. A faint mutter that didn't sound like the *Tenga Galel*, akin as it was to the *Tenga Tuacha*, though it was so faint that I wondered in the next second if I'd really heard it.

Then I heard the scuttling and turned my eyes upward.

A dozen of the little troglodytes were scurrying along the ceiling, pouring out of the crack about fifty yards ahead. And a new glow, visible only in my NVGs, was starting to grow behind them.

This wasn't good. Somehow, I didn't think that the troglodytes had caused that flickering, wavering glow. It looked more like torchlight.

We weren't alone in that tunnel. Bad news.

I looked over my shoulder, where most of the rest had their own NVGs down again, and started to direct Santos and Farrar to move up into ambush positions. We were too close to turn back, and even if we did, if that was the enemy up there, then we couldn't let them get any deeper.

I was already starting to feel the dark fingers of despair clawing at the back of my brain. We were so close. If we couldn't kill all of these intruders, though, we were left with the only option being to collapse the tunnel and retreat back into the fortress.

That didn't sit well. I hoped we could kill all of them.

The troglodytes were cautious. These might have been the same creatures that the guardian had chased off, so they were understandably nervous about coming back in after that. They moved like frightened animals, the scuttling horde ebbing and flowing strangely. I was reminded of swarms of gnats, or some of the creatures we'd seen in the cursed lands we'd traveled through on the hunt for the vampire Unsterbanak.

The torchlight got stronger, and then the first warriors appeared.

They weren't Peruni or Avurs. They were as barrel-chested as most of the Avurs we'd seen, but considerably taller, and their armor was closer to that of the corsairs of the north, with banded cuirasses and flat-topped helmets. They carried small, hexagonal shields, and every other man seemed to have a torch. Those who didn't had their weapons out, short, broad, single-edged swords and hooked axes. They were clearly ready for a close-range fight. I didn't see any spears, javelins, or bows, which was a plus. We could hit them from a distance.

I already had my rifle laid over the top of the boulder, canted to bring my offset red dot to bear—it was far too short a range to need the scope itself, and it never works all that well to use magnified optics with NVGs—my finger taking up the slack on the trigger. Then I saw the dark figure looming behind them.

For a moment, I thought it was a Dullahan. It took a second to realize that the man was wearing a hood, rather than no head. It was a Peruni wizard.

I immediately changed my target priorities and shifted my dot to the wizard.

The hooded man spoke, his voice ringing through the cave, and the warriors stopped dead where they were, falling back and crouching behind their shields. Fat lot of good that was going to do them, but it put us at a new advantage.

Almost. One of those big bruisers was right between me and the wizard. I wondered if that was deliberate.

Nothing for it. I shot the big man through the skull from barely seventy yards, recovering from the recoil fast and shifting toward the sorcerer.

He bellowed something, and I could have sworn I caught a glimpse of a flash of light from his eyes behind that cowl. The gleam was green in my PVS-15s but somehow I knew that it would be red if I saw it with my naked eyes.

I fired, but he had already moved, even as the men in front of him began to convulse, vomiting a thick, black mist that quickly obscured that entire half of the cavern.

Every one of us started dumping rounds into that growing darkness at that. We'd seen what came next.

More awful words echoed hollowly from the blackness. That wizard was up to something, and it was going to be bad. I had sudden nightmare visions of the shadow demon we'd fought in Killaros and Cor Legear lunging out of the mist and tearing into the lot of us. We had the

Two Swords, and we even had Conall back, who was one of the quietest of the Tuacha, but also one of the most mystically attuned, but that thing could still do a lot of damage.

That was assuming that he wasn't just summoning whatever it was that had turned Clarence Nelson-Hyde to mist, up in the mountains above Taramas's citadel.

Slithering tendrils of blackness spread along the walls, the ceiling, and the floor, searching us out. At first, it just looked like shadow, somehow without that oily, burning tar look that the Outer Dark's minions often had. But then I saw that it was crushing and burning the rock underneath it.

"Get back!" Gunny's roar echoed through the cavern, though it was drowned out a moment later by the long, ripping burst Santos poured into that mass of darkness. None of the bullets seemed to have any effect, though.

I was up and moving, pulling Rodeffer with me, even as one of those tendrils crawled up the boulder we'd been using for cover, moving entirely too fast. Smoke hissed out from under it, but that wasn't the worst part. I could *feel* the sentient evil there. There was something alive in that creeping darkness, something terribly aware and *hungry*.

Rodeffer shot at it, which probably wasn't the best idea, since the bullet ricocheted nastily, whining upward to smack into the ceiling not far from one of the scuttling troglodytes. Not that it bothered the vicious little creature much, since it was currently being consumed by one of those crawling tentacles of shadow, smoke pouring off it as it shrieked and shriveled.

The entire cavern had turned into pandemonium, unholy screams still echoing from the heart of the shadow as the warriors that had formed the wizard's escort were still being consumed alive. Santos was still pouring fire into it, trying to hit the wizard, but he wasn't having much luck, and Gunny was pulling him back by the strap of his chest rig. He fell back step by step, keeping his weapon up and leaning into it as he stitched rounds back and forth across the opening.

I dashed back to the next boulder, barely avoiding getting my head taken off as Franks took a shot at another tendril slithering across the ceiling above us. When I pivoted and threw myself down on a knee behind the rock, I realized that Rodeffer wasn't with me.

He was up and moving, but he wasn't falling back. He was charging toward that mass of impenetrable darkness, already prepping the frag in his hand.

"Rod!" I couldn't find a target, so I just shot into the shadow past his shoulder, hoping I could hit the wizard, either by luck or guidance from above. Then I surged to my feet and ran after him.

I knew what he was doing. I was just a few yards too far away and a few seconds too slow to stop him. If I even should have.

Rodeffer wasn't the type to make speeches. There were no heroic last words. Not even a glance behind him as he dove into the middle of that opaque shade and disappeared.

He must have had more than just the one frag. Either that, or he was preternaturally gifted on where to place it.

The explosion rocked the entire cavern. Dust and smoke billowed through the crack, momentarily occluding even the dim view of the sky above. A few bits of frag whickered overhead, and several of the troglodytes fell limply from the ceiling to crash onto the rocks like broken dolls.

A moment later, something broke with an immense *crack*, and an enormous slab of rock calved away from the wall high above the turn where we'd first engaged the warriors. It slammed down with a *boom* that rocked the entire cave.

"Fall back! Move!" Gunny was holding his position but grabbing every man in reach and shoving him back toward the citadel. "Get your asses moving before we all get buried!"

The cave in was getting worse, but I confess that I hesitated, still looking back toward where Gene Rodeffer had disappeared, feeling icy fingers constricting my chest. It had been bad enough, losing Stanley and Smith. Rod, though, had thrown himself into that, knowing he was going to die, and I hadn't been able to do anything about it.

Hadn't been able to stop him and put myself forward in his place.

I had the Sword of Iudicael in my hand, though what I was going to do with it, I didn't know. I didn't even remember drawing it. The shadow was still there, still alive, still reaching for us, though it seemed to be getting weaker and thinner, and I slashed at it as it writhed up off a rock and stabbed for my face. It withered at the touch of the blessed blade, and vanished into smoke with a thin, distant scream of hatred and pain.

Then Gunny had me by the drag handle on the back of my chest rig. "Damn it, Conor, you are *not* going to make Rod's sacrifice a vain one!" He hauled me around as if I were a kid and shoved me, hard, toward the opening behind us. "*Move!*"

Half blinded by the tears, as well as the dust and the dark, I scrambled back toward the citadel as the cave in got worse, sealing the passage behind us with a thunderous roar and a cloud of dust.

CHAPTER 10

IT seemed to take even longer to find our way back. Part of that was probably because we were going uphill. Part of it might have been because Gurke's team was now on point, and Franks wasn't quite the pointman that Rodeffer had been. It's an old saying that *if you're not navigating, you're lost*, but not everyone, even in Recon, has always taken that to heart.

Part of it was probably because I couldn't quite accept that Rodeffer was dead, coupled with the near despair that the failure of our mission had wrapped around all of us.

It felt like days before we finally reached the storeroom, deconflicting carefully with the nearly thirty armed guards that Tarvedum had posted there, just in case. We dragged our way out into the storeroom, exhausted and covered in dust, as one of the guards ran for Tarvedum.

We were already on our way up to the great hall when King Uven, Vepogenus, and Tarvedum hustled down to meet us. The looks on their faces mirrored my own. They were a blend of concern, disappointment, and deep-seated fear.

Gunny shook his head as King Uven stepped forward. "They found the exit before we could get out. We ran right into them." He slumped wearily onto a bale of supplies. "Don't worry, they're not going to follow us. The tunnel's collapsed."

He didn't say outright what had happened, but I saw King Uven scanning our numbers. He didn't miss much. He noticed Rodeffer's absence, and he could put two and two together.

I'd been more than a little worried about what we might have been dragging behind us as we'd retreated, as the cave-in might have blocked the passage from an infiltrator, but those creeping tentacles of darkness had kept coming after us, burning and crumbling the rock as they came. Once we'd gone a certain distance, though, I thought I heard something like a distant horn call, and when I'd looked back with my light, the tentacles were vanished as if they'd never been there. Just a waking nightmare. The guardian still held sway in the heart of the mountain.

"What do we do now?" Gurke was obviously feeling a bit of the despair that I was desperately trying to fight off. I had gotten a bit of my equilibrium back as we'd climbed, though the weight of Rodeffer's death was still right there, threatening to choke me if I gave it an inch. "We're cut off. Our best chance was to go out there and hunt. Now we're stuck."

Gunny shot him a warning glance, and Diarmodh put a hand on his shoulder, almost as much to restrain him as to support him. He subsided, but it had been said.

I saw a bit of what might have been resentment flash through Vepogenus's eyes, though he shuttered it fast. We'd done a lot for the Galel already, and he had to understand that, but the sense that we were stuck *here with them* was unavoidable. As if we'd be better off ranging through the enemy's rear area while the Galel sat in here and took the brunt of the Peruni's assault.

No one thought that they were going to just sit out there for a prolonged siege. The timing wasn't right. Fall was coming on fast, and the chill was already setting into the air. The defenders inside the fortress had shelter, but those myriads out there on the plain below didn't. The Peruni couldn't afford a long siege. They had to re-duce Cor Chatha with a quickness, especially since King Uven was there.

That he had taken up residence in the fortress wasn't a secret, either. He'd flown his banner from the tower above for all the enemy to see as soon as he'd arrived. Wounded as he was, he wasn't hiding, and he was going to make damn good and sure that the bad guys under-stood that.

It was a very King Uven sort of thing to do. How wise it was I didn't know. I've always been more of the mindset that the less the enemy knows before you hit him, the better. But, while they were too well-versed in warfare to go Active Stupid, the Galel knights had some slightly different priorities than we did.

Their sense of honor couldn't be faulted. Particularly the king's. On some level, his actions made great stra-tegic sense. Cor Chatha was *the* defensive lynchpin of the southeastern frontier. It was also the single strongest fortress in the entire Kingdom of Cor Legear. If there was one place where the unstoppable force was likely to meet the immovable object, it was here. By proclaiming his presence, King Uven was challenging the emperor to come at him in the one place where he held most of the advantages. It made sense.

"We're going to do whatever we can." Gunny's voice was bleak but with the usual iron in it that brooked no argument. "We're here, and we're going to fight like hell until they're all dead or we are. That's just the way of it. It's been that way since we came through the mists, and not a damned thing has changed." He glared around at all of us, unblinking in that unnerving way Gunny had. "This is the fight we've got, gents. At least we're among friends this time, instead of Dragon Mask and his Dovos."

There was a murmured agreement, of varying degrees of intensity. The Menninkai actually looked the most nervous of all of us. They were adventurers, one and all, joining up just because they figured they could find the best fight along with us, but they still had homes and families, even if they were far away. We were homeless, clanless wanderers, despite the fact that we'd been welcomed by the Tuacha da Riamog. On some level, I think most of us would have been happy at some point to find a nice Galel girl—the Tuacha were too different, too ethereal in some ways, for us—and settle down somewhere. Yet the same warrior calling that had made us Recon Marines in the first place still tugged at every one of us. There was a hell of a fight out there, and no man living doesn't want to go down like a warrior, weapon in hand, surrounded by the bodies of his enemies. He might deny it but, on some level, some visceral, primal part of him longs for that kind of end. The kind that songs will be sung about for generations after.

Gunny had more than one purpose to his words, too. On the one hand, he was right, and we needed a bit of a shake, to get back on task. Like it or not, we were committed. The only way out was through, once again, even if it meant through that half a million men and abominations out there.

He had to get us on task to take our minds off the failure of our little raiding party, too. We'd been through a lot, but that could have more than one effect. On the one hand, we were tougher than we ever had been, but there was a bit of a brittleness there, too. Every man has his breaking point, and sometimes you just don't know where it lies. He had to get our minds off what had happened down there in the dark, and right then, the best way to do that was to get us looking at the next fight.

"What's the situation up here?" He turned to Vepogenus, implicitly turning the command over to him, and defusing some of that knee-jerk resentment that the older man might have felt.

"They sit just outside of bowshot from the first wall, while their monsters harass us on the battlements." Vepogenus was forced to turn and follow as Gunny started moving toward the hall. Once again, getting things moving, not letting anyone start woolgathering to the point of paralysis. Gunny was the man. He'd been around, and he knew his business. "We have struck a few of the wyverns with arrows, but they do little. Sling stones are better, but hard to hit with."

"I think we can help with that." Gunny glanced over his shoulder. "Everyone, get your gear and weapons squared away, top of mags, and grab some chow and water. We head down to the wall in thirty."

* * *

The wall really was a nightmare.

While the siege of Vahava Paykhah had been rough, the Menninkai had pretty well owned the battlements and, as long as each wall had held, they'd been able to rove along the crenellations, raining rocks, sling stones, and arrows down on their enemies. The situation was different here.

We could sense it before we even reached the base of the wall. The figures of the defenders weren't visible against the dim, clouded sky. From a certain angle, the wall appeared completely deserted. I knew that it wasn't, but it was eerie, nevertheless.

The steps up to the top were inside the defensive towers, and we hustled up to find the Galel defenders either inside, staying away from the arrow slits, or, if they were out on the catwalk atop the fifteen-foot-thick wall, they stayed low, dashing from crenellation to crenellation.

"What's going on?" Bailey frowned as he watched. "Don't tell me they've got guns."

It did, indeed, look like these guys were trying their best to avoid machinegun or sniper fire. The true explanation, though, was worse.

"We cannot remain in the open long, or the wyverns will stoop on us." The young knight in charge of that particular tower was black-haired and hatchet-faced, the narrowness of his features offset by a massive, sweeping mustache. "We have managed to scratch them slightly, but only slightly. They took three of my men and devoured them in the air before we started to take cover." He looked faintly haunted, his eyes fixed on the sky through the arrow slit, though I noticed that he never quite stood directly in front of it.

"The battlements aren't going to provide much overhead cover." Gurke nodded toward where a man-at-arms, in a short mail shirt and a simple iron cap, ran toward us, bent double as he sprinted from cover to cover. "So why aren't your guys just running straight for the towers?"

If anything, the knight seemed to get paler. "Any man exposed for long makes himself a target for their sorcerers. One was seized by something he could not see and *stretched*, until his neck broke. Another suddenly burst into flame." He shuddered. "The curses they send are bad enough. They have summonings out there, as well. They seem to be limited in how long they can remain on this plane, so they must be sent as soon as they see a man to send them at."

I shared a look with Bailey. We'd been there before. I remembered all too well the inky black horrors that had tried to tear apart the towers on the second wall of Vahava Paykhah. The Sword of Iudicael had banished them, setting them aflame but, once again, there were only two of the blessed blades there on the wall, and a lot of wall to cover.

"Well." I swung my ruck to the floor and started to unship the M107 where I'd had it broken down and lashed crossways to the top of the pack. "Let's see if we can't discourage some curse throwing, at least, shall we?" Sliding the upper and lower receiver together and locking them in place with the pins, I hefted the heavy rifle and rocked in a magazine of ten six-hundred-seventy-one-grain Raufoss rounds, racking the bolt with a heavy *clack*.

Fortunately, the towers were essentially living quarters for the men on guard, so they weren't as barren as those at Vahava Paykhah had been. There were furnishings, which meant I was able to set up more of a classic urban hide site, setting a bench and a table near the back of the tower with views out three of the arrow slits. They were extremely limited views, but I could still see and shoot. I'd just have to shift position constantly to use all of my field of fire.

Settling in behind the rifle, I got a good cheek weld and eye relief and started to scan.

It wasn't going to be easy. There were a lot of targets out there, and the sorcerers weren't going to necessarily stand out that much. However, from the young knight's description of the situation, it sounded like they needed to have line of sight to make their curses work. Which meant they couldn't hide all the time.

Before I could get a shot at a sorcerer, however, a wyvern dove on the battlements just outside, with that rattling, steam boiler hiss, snatching at one of the men-at-arms. Fortunately, the monster missed, and winged away with another hiss, sounding angrier this time, flapping those massive wings as it passed right in front of my field of fire.

I couldn't pass up a target like that. If it had been a full-sized dragon, I might have hesitated, since a .50 would have just pissed it off, but this was a smaller and softer target.

My lead on the first shot was a little overdone, and the bullet went past its nose with a supersonic *crack* that actually made the beast flinch. It was more aggressive than it was smart, though, and it reacted by suddenly banking hard, coming back around toward the tower, clearly intent on tearing whatever had had the temerity to attack it to pieces.

In the process, it gave me an almost perfect shot.

I blew a gaping hole through its serpentine neck, just behind its head. Scales shattered and black blood sprayed from the wound as the monster thrashed and twisted in midair.

For a brief moment, I was afraid I'd miscalculated, that this thing was much more otherworldly and therefore a lot more formidable than the oversized flying snake that it appeared to be. After all, most of the monsters we'd encountered were creatures somehow twisted or animated by spirits from somewhere beyond the veil.

It was already tumbling out of control, though, its throes apparently only a vestigial nervous reaction to having its spine severed. It crashed to the ground halfway across the no-man's-land between the wall and the front ranks of the imperial army.

I barely saw that, as I forced myself to get back on scope and look for the next target. That had been a warning, and I knew that the enemy was going to be looking for a way to neutralize me as soon as possible. It was what I'd do, if one of my biggest, nastiest monsters had just been shot out of the sky, and with one shot at that.

Sure enough, a moment later a flurry of dark little forms swarmed up from behind the ranks of Peruni and their auxiliaries, darting toward the tower where we were set up.

Something told me that I didn't want those things to reach the tower. They were far too small, too fast, and too numerous to try to engage them with the .50. So, while it was a struggle, I ignored the swarm and looked for where they'd come from.

Unfortunately, I suspected that the sorcerer hadn't needed line of sight to summon those things, whatever they were, and even if he had, he'd probably ducked for cover as soon as he'd loosed them. I still scanned the rear ranks carefully, dialing up the scope's magnification to be able to see details better. The darkness was getting deeper, but fortunately, there was something about the *Coira Ansec*–produced scope that meant I didn't need a MUNS to see in the dark.

It was like having a Tuacha's eyes. It was weird and cool all at the same time.

"Got you." To my surprise, the sorcerer wasn't hiding. Dressed much the same as the necromancer I'd shot in Killaros, except with less red and more black, gold, and midnight blue, he was standing on top of a platform that looked like it had been built from a wagon, his arms outstretched, his head bent. I couldn't see any lines going from his fingertips to the dark things zipping toward my face, but somehow I could sense they were there.

I didn't have a laser rangefinder to tell me exactly how far that platform was from the wall, but just from the tick marks in the reticle, I could tell that he was over a mile away.

That's a long shot, though I'd hit well past that with a .50. The thing is that the Barret M107 isn't *exactly* a precision rifle. It's a long-range rifle, certainly, and the *Coira Ansec*'s version of it was a lot more precise than the originals I'd shot back in the World, but the bullet still has some deviation due to atmospherics, barrel whip, and a few other factors. That's just physics. And the greater the distance, the more deviation there is.

Still, it wasn't like I was going to accidentally hit anyone we *didn't* intend to kill out there, even if I missed the sorcerer. We might still have to deal with the flying things, which I didn't want to do, but still. I let out a breath, my finger tightening on the trigger as my lungs emptied and the reticle stilled.

The concussion of a .50 is something that you never quite get used to. Everyone in the tower was already down on the floor or directly behind me after those first two shots, because the blast from that muzzle brake to either side is *brutal*, even when you're not down on the ground where it's kicking up every bit of grit and gravel it can. I was already partially numbed from that initial pair of shots, but I'd tightened up a little bit to try to get as stable as possible for this one. The shock of the shot, not to mention the bolt flying back inside the receiver next to my cheekbone, still felt a little like getting punched in the jaw.

But then, shooting a .50 always feels like that. Eventually, you just ride the pain and get back on target.

Somebody was looking out for me. I recovered from the recoil just in time to see the bullet tear into the sorcerer's upper left chest, smashing his collarbone and almost decapitating him as it tore his neck to shreds.

The flying attackers exploded into smoke, and I got back to searching for the next wizard, as Gunny, Bailey, and Gurke started to get the rest of the platoon spread out along the wall with every bit of long-range firepower we could muster.

It was going to be a long night. Or day, or whatever it was.

CHAPTER 11

NIGHT *was* coming on. I hadn't thought it possible, but it got steadily darker, to the point that I couldn't even see much through the fancy scope.

I'd still taken a few more shots, but whether or not they were effective was hard to tell. At least, as far as killing sorcerers went. I'd even taken a shot at one of the Thirty, even though I knew it wasn't going to do much. I didn't even manage to knock its head off, like I had in Gremman. For all I could tell, I hadn't hit it at all. It was more a matter of letting that thing know that I knew it was out there and I was gunning for it.

Now, though, I couldn't see well enough to engage anything, so I came off the scope, only then realizing just how desperately tired I was. Everything ached, including my eyes. Being on glass is taxing, which is why we tended to try to rotate guys out every thirty minutes to an hour. I'd probably been behind that gun a lot longer than that, though I couldn't tell for how long.

The rest of the platoon was spread out along the wall by then, and it was just my team in the tower. What was left of it.

Not for the first time, and far from the last, Rodeffer's absence was a gaping, open wound. I clenched my teeth and swallowed past the lump in my throat as I found myself looking around for him, since all I could see was Santos, Farrar, Bearrac, and Mathghaman.

Santos had already put Farrar down on rest plan. True to his stubborn nature, Santos himself was still up, and he would stay up as long as I did, unless I directly ordered him to go down.

The truth was, though, I didn't want to try to sleep. I knew that I desperately needed to. I wasn't sure when I'd last really slept, or how long I'd been awake. Fatigue has cumulative effects, and I knew that if I *didn't* get some rest, I was going to start making mistakes, mistakes that *were* going to get good men killed.

And yet I dreaded closing my eyes, knowing that as soon as I did, I was going to see Rodeffer plunging into that vast shadow, grenade in hand. In fact, I was sure that my subconscious was going to make it a lot worse than that and furnish all sorts of imagined details of his death.

Even if it didn't...

Rodeffer wasn't the first friend and brother I'd lost. Sooner or later you either bury everyone close to you, or they bury you. My first team leader had died in a car crash just after he got out. My second took his own life. I'd known men who'd been killed in combat in Syria, and we'd lost more than half the platoon in the first few months we had spent in this world.

The ghosts always come back. The closer you were to the dead, the more likely you're going to see them in your sleep. Not always badly. Sometimes it's just a chat with a man long dead, who you don't remember is dead until you wake up.

Those were somehow worse than reliving their deaths, in my experience. I wasn't looking forward to that.

Mathghaman's massive hand closed on my shoulder. "Rest now, Conor. The enemy will come all too soon."

I nodded wearily. He was right. And if we all went to sleep, Mathghaman wouldn't. He'd probably do whatever it was the Tuacha did, sitting against the wall in some state halfway between waking and dream. It was one of the main ways they were kind of spooky. That alone tended to emphasize just how different they were from normal men.

"Vince, you too." I wasn't going to lie down before Santos, and though it looked for a moment like he was going to argue, I glared at him until he nodded, pulled his poncho liner out of his ruck, and rolled up in it on the floor.

Then, with Mathghaman holding watch, tireless, seemingly imperturbable, I lay down and tried to get some sleep.

* * *

Sometimes, bone-deep exhaustion is a blessing in disguise. I passed out almost as soon as I put my head down, and I might have been dead for all the dreaming I did. It hardly felt like any time had passed at all when Mathghaman shook me awake.

"On your guard, Conor. Fell deeds awake."

Surprisingly, I was immediately alert. I'd come out of ops comas like that groggy and disoriented, but I think Iudicael was even then standing by me, alongside his

Sword, which hadn't been more than arm's length away from me for a long time.

I rolled out of my poncho liner, stuffing it back into my ruck with one hand as I snatched up my M110 with the other. I hardly thought about it. Being ready to break out and move had become such a hard-wired habit that it was second nature by then.

Even as I shut the pack, I could tell what Mathghaman meant. I could feel it.

It's hard to describe, but a feeling of dread had settled across the battlements, heavy and palpable. I felt it in a distant sort of way, but I think that was largely because Mathghaman and Bearrac were there. That, and I had the Sword of Iudicael on my hip.

Others weren't feeling it in such a distant sort of way, though. As I glanced out the door onto the battlements themselves, I saw several of the Galel defenders crouched below the parapet. No, not crouched. One was squatting down, his head in his hands. Another was curled up in the fetal position, shaking.

I looked at Mathghaman. I was about to ask a question I already knew the answer to, but the words died in my throat. He was busy.

The King's Champion had stepped to the arrow slit, his sword in both hands, his rifle slung to his back, and begun to chant. His voice, deep and resonant already, boomed out across the wall, joined a moment later by Bearrac's sonorous voice. Bearrac was the sort you expected to bull bellow everything, but when he chanted, he was as melodious as all the rest.

One by one, across the wall, the other Tuacha took up the chant. They sang in that ancient, inscrutable tongue they have always reserved for prayer and invocation. I would eventually learn it, but right then it was almost as opaque to me as ever it had been.

The effect was immediate, though. As that sound of rare majesty soared above the battlements, the fear and terror seemed to ebb, and I saw a few of the Galel defenders lift their heads and stop shaking.

Just in time, too. Horns blared, drums thumped and, as I moved up to join Mathghaman at the arrow slit, even though I was looking for the sorcerers I'd need to kill to end the spell of fear altogether, I saw the more immediate threat.

Ranks advanced behind wood-and-hide barricades, while the much bigger construct in the center, the size of at least two wagons put together end to end, had to be a battering ram. It rolled forward on crude wheels, overlapped by a hide-covered roof that also shielded anyone pushing it from arrows and slingstones coming from above.

It would have to get across the gap in the finger before the raised drawbridge, but there were dozens of wagons ahead of it, laden with tree trunks and rocks. They were going to try to fill the trench in, and if they moved fast enough, they just might pull it off.

I doubted the hide protection on the wagons and the ram would stop Raufoss rounds, but at the same time, I only had so many of them.

"Four, this is Five." Gunny's voice crackled across the radio net. We'd decided to leave the radios on, despite the risk that the enemy, especially those enemies that weren't exactly physical, could access them. We'd run into that problem at Killaros, as the voice of some thing of the Outer Dark had started to whisper through our net. "Let's get some eggs in that basket."

It said something about how much we'd come to understand each other, Marines and Menninkai, that that transmission didn't require translation. I suspect Orava had already been aimed in, anyway.

Farrar had already grabbed our thumper. He'd snatched it up from me a while ago, pointing out that I wasn't using it that much, and I usually carried the .50, anyway. Now he was at an arrow slit, the leaf sight on the M79—Santos had requested our thumper from the *Coira Ansec*, and he was a traditionalist—already flipped up, his finger tightening on the trigger.

With a series of faint *thunk*s, a barrage of 40mm grenades sailed out from the wall toward the wagons and the trundling ram.

The ogives detonated with a rippling series of explosions, kicking up billowing clouds of smoke, dirt, frag, and bits of hide, wood, bone, metal, and anything else that got torn apart by the concussions and the flensing shrapnel. Two hit the ram itself, while the other two sort of bracketed it, one falling just short, smashing the wheel of a wagon and throwing bits of rock and frag at the advancing barricades with enough force to punch right through the boiled hides, the second going long and sowing carnage among the troops advancing behind the ram.

Huuhka and Chambers opened fire with their Mk 48s, bursts of 7.62 fire hammering through wood and hide to smash into the troops behind the barricades. Those shields might have kept arrows and most slingstones off them, but against medium machinegun bullets, they didn't do much besides slow the rounds down, so they only went through one man instead of two.

Still, they came on, even as the wyverns came out of the clouds again, swooping down to attack our positions. *How many of those things do they have?* I grabbed the M107 and dashed out onto the battlements, risking the exposure to get a better shot.

As soon as I started to draw a bead on the gray wyvern that was even then spreading its wings to dip on the next tower over, where Applegate was laying the hate from the roof, Santos caught it with a long burst, hammering into its side. Several of the rounds just kind of spalled off the scales, but at least a few found a soft spot under the shoulder and shattered the joint. The wing folded like a cheap suit and the wyvern fell, though not without a scream of rage.

I came off sights and scanned for a new target. That was when I saw that the ram was not the only advance. In fact, the longer I looked at the situation, the more convinced I became that the ram itself was more of a feint.

A wedge formation was pushing ahead of the main line off to the north, moving at a trot beneath a formation of interlinked shields that reminded me of nothing so much as an ancient Roman testudo. The longer I looked at it, the more it looked like they were carrying something.

I squinted, forcing my tired brain to work, even as I put the .50 down and started to trot down the wall toward the point that wedge was making for. There was no gate there, so it couldn't be another ram. There wasn't enough of a structure for a ram, anyway, at least not one that could hope to punch through the timber of the gates, never mind the massive stone wall itself.

It clicked as the formation, shrugging off the sporadic arrows and stones that were being hurled down at it, reached the base of the wall. The mass of shields parted, and the ladders were quickly swung up toward the battlements. The steep and rocky ground below the first line of defense had dipped low enough that they could pretty much run right up to the base of the wall. It was the best spot for such an assault.

I broke into a run. They *wanted* all eyes, especially those behind rifles, machineguns, and grenade launchers, on the wagons full of fill and that ram. This was the real attack. While everyone was focused on the flashy threat, with the wyverns attacking near the gate to draw even more attention, this bunch was going to try to get enough men up on the wall that they could force their way to the gatehouse, drop the drawbridge, and raise the portcullises.

The Galel on the wall were trying to fend off the ladders, but just then another wyvern descended on them, whatever malevolent will that controlled the monsters having apparently decided that the diversion had played its part, and now they needed direct support. Before I could get close enough or take a shot, the creature grabbed one of the men-at-arms, lifted him high into the air, and let him go as it climbed, setting him on a screaming arc to smash onto the rocks to the north of the wall.

I shot at it then, though my 7.62 rifle barely scratched it. I'd need to get in there with the Sword or draw one of our machinegunners to support me. I momentarily regretted leaving the M107 behind.

It felt the sting, though, and came back around, its beady eyes, glittering with malice, fixed on me. It opened that wide maw, lined with jagged teeth, and dove at me, its talons spread.

It probably should have kept its mouth shut.

If I'd been confident enough in my marksmanship to be sure that I could take out its brain with one shot between those gaping jaws, I might have preserved the ammo. As it was, I dumped half my mag into it.

One round shattered a fang, two more skipped off the scales, one punched through a nostril, and then three or four went right through the roof of its mouth, bypassing its armored scales and smashing through cartilage and bone, right into its brain, or whatever it used for one.

The monster was suddenly a ballistic object, plunging toward the wall. It wiped out an entire ladder as it hit, making the enormous stone structure shudder with the impact, and then it turned over and fell, flattening close to a platoon of Peruni swordsmen.

Despite that devastation, however, and the two other ladders that the Galel had managed to push away from the wall with spears, there were still a good half dozen ladders now set solidly against the battlements, and the Peruni were climbing, even as the Avurs rained arrows on the top of the wall at a high angle, and another flight of those little, inky flying things swarmed around like giant flies, tearing into men as they did so.

Some of the Galel were still throwing rocks down at the climbing enemy, but even as I closed in, the first of the scale-armored Peruni swordsmen gained the top of the wall.

CHAPTER 12

THE first one over was a big bruiser who led with his shield, a short, broad-bladed sword licking out from over and around the rim at anyone near him. He had to have been picked to be the Number One man just for that sheer brute force approach alone, in order to clear a patch on the battlements for the follow-on forces.

I was still several dozen yards short, but I saw an opportunity. While the wall curved back toward the sheer cliff that formed the shoulder of the mountain, it didn't curve quite radically enough to provide those guys on the ladders with cover from me.

It wasn't an easy shot, even so. I had to really expose myself, leaning out between two of the crenellations, forcing Farrar—who had followed me even though I hadn't said a word to him about it—to grab my chest rig to make sure I didn't go over the side.

An arrow shattered off the stone within a few inches of my head. I was *really* exposed out there, and at least one of those archers had figured out what I was doing.

I had a better shot than they did, though, especially since another long burst of machinegun fire from one of the towers behind me answered that arrow a moment later, giving me a bit of a breather.

Non-standard shooting positions are non-standard because they tend to be unstable and difficult to engage accurately from. Some have gotten more refined over time, but there's nothing you can really refine about hanging out into space, hoping that you don't overbalance and fall, canting your rifle unnaturally just so you can bring the sights to bear on the men climbing the ladders toward your friends.

I struggled for a moment to steady the weapon, then accepted that I wasn't going to be making precise shots, and it was only about thirty yards, anyway.

My first shot missed, but only because Farrar shifted and I swayed slightly as I fired. Dragging the weapon back on target, I dumped the rest of the mag as fast as I could shoot, raking the line of bodies climbing toward the top of the wall with ten more rounds, punching through armor, flesh, and bone alike. I might not have been able to hurt the wyvern much with 7.62 until it showed me a soft spot, but even armored men—at least without anti-rifle plates, which the Peruni definitely did not have—didn't stand a chance against 7.62 NATO at thirty yards.

I'd almost just raked the entire length of the ladder, but at the last moment I kept my shots high. It worked out, too, as I dumped three of the higher climbers. Two out of the three fell almost straight down, wiping out easily a dozen of their fellows, all high enough up that there was no way they'd survive the fall. Some of the others might make it, but most of them were going to be a in a world of hurt.

Then Farrar hauled me back up so I could reload. He had his rifle slung in front of him and his pistol in his fist, his other hand wrapped around one of my shoulder straps.

I dropped the mag, hastily stuffing it back into my dump pouch—magazine retention is absolutely vital when you have the only mags for a thousand miles—and took stock. I'd put a hitch in the assault, but there were still easily two dozen men on top of the wall, falling into a hasty formation with interlocked shields, holding a chunk of real estate about twenty yards across. They were engaged with the Galel men-at-arms who were trying to retake that part of the wall and shove the ladders off on our side, while several of them appeared to be massacring the handful of defenders to the other side.

They had a foothold. This was bad. Worse, Farrar and I were cut off by our allies. We couldn't shoot at the Peruni without shooting through the Galel.

For their part, the Galel were doing a good job of holding their ground, though the wyvern attacks elsewhere on the wall were causing some trouble. Even as Farrar and I hesitated, looking for targets and a window to engage them, another swarm of black, flying horrors struck the defenders. They looked almost like bats with beaks, though it was hard to tell with the speed they were moving and the fact that they were so dark that they were essentially visible only as silhouettes. I tried to shoot one, but after trying and failing to track it for a moment, I shifted outward, looking for the wizard that had conjured these things.

He was being a little sloppy, especially given the fact that they had just seen me shoot a chunk of their assault force off the side of the wall. Cloaked in dark blue, not unlike the one I'd shot off the wagon with a .50, he sat astride a horse near the front of the line, his arms raised and his head bent, looking almost like a concertgoer who was getting *really* into the tunes.

It wasn't a long shot. Maybe a hundred fifty yards. From where I stood, though, I had to remember to aim a little low. High angle shooting can get complicated.

I didn't bother with the math, just put my crosshairs on his belt and fired.

Unlike some of the fantasy I'd read, played, or watched back in the World, there was no reason sorcerers couldn't wear armor. This guy had a solid breastplate beneath his robes, and the bullet *rang* as it slammed into it. I don't know what that armor was made of, or rather, what he'd done to get some Outer Dark monstrosity to strengthen it, but it stopped the one-hundred-seventy-five-grain bullet, which was still doing over twenty-five-hundred feet per second. It was a Level III-A plate, at least, which was unheard of here.

If I hadn't just shot at a wyvern, and wasn't trying to kill the dude controlling a buzzing swarm of horrors that was currently slicing a man to pieces only a few yards away, I might have blinked at that. Instead, I just shifted aim and put the next round about a foot higher.

His sorcery might have unnaturally strengthened the breastplate, but he wasn't wearing a helmet, and he hadn't managed to do the same thing to his skull. His head jerked and sprayed red. He stayed in the saddle for a long moment, blood dripping from the ruin of his head, and then he slid limply off the horse and crumpled to the ground.

The flying horrors let out a higher, angrier buzz. I thought that it hadn't worked at first, as they continued to whirl around the man they'd targeted, slicing deeply into his flesh, hitting him hard enough to keep him upright even as he bled out, screaming. Maybe I'd shot the wrong wizard. But then they suddenly dove in a cyclonic whirl downward, right into the rock of the wall itself, and disappeared.

The enemy stutter-stepped a little at that. I can only imagine it was like calling for air support and then watching the gunship get shot down before it really managed to drop any ordnance on your opposition. And the Galel took full advantage of it.

With a roar, the men-at-arms, having regrouped as the horrors disappeared, pushed into the Peruni line. These guys knew they were probably dead, but they were going to take as many of the enemy with them as they could. I saw one get hacked down, just before he thrust his sword through the throat of the man who'd killed him. Another found himself off-balance, started to fall, and grabbed a Peruni swordsman as he went, dragging him off the wall and to both their deaths.

Farrar and I had pushed up as close as we could get, though there were still too many friendlies between us and the enemy warriors on the wall for us to contribute much there. Instead, we both leaned over the battlements and started shooting the reinforcements that had started to climb up again.

In that brief breather, as the Galel front shoved the Peruni foothold back, one of the men-at-arms, wielding a big, two-handed axe, used the gap in men on the ladder to shove it away. He didn't have the leverage to throw it backward onto the enemy, so he hooked it with the axe and pulled it to one side, close enough that I could reach out and grab it.

I did, pulling hard. The ladder scraped against the stone, but the man in the orange tunic had pushed it far enough off kilter that I didn't need to move it all that far before it hit the tipping point, skidding and skipping down the face of the wall to crash to the ground at the bottom, crushing at least one more man, and shattering every bone in the one who'd been too high up to leap free by the time it started its fall.

Then the Dullahans apparently decided that enough was enough.

At least, I assumed that it was the Dullahans wielding the kind of power that made the very earth heave and crack, starting somewhere out there behind the enemy lines, throwing more than a few of the Peruni and their auxiliaries on their faces, swallowing some in the crack that opened in the ground as *something* arrowed under the trampled grass of the plain toward the wall.

Farrar and I were almost right at the edge of the devastation that followed. As whatever it was reached the wall, it heaved upward, pushing the wall itself a good ten feet skyward, making rock crack and crumble, the stones falling away in a cascade that crushed Peruni infantry on one side and Galel reinforcements on the other. Farrar and I were thrown to our knees as the wall bucked underneath us. Fortunately, we were just far enough away from that upheaval that we weren't thrown off the wall altogether.

Then the ground dropped away under that bulge in the wall, and the ancient defensive work fell with it.

That first fall of stones was almost a minor scatter of gravel compared to that collapse. The outer and inner faces of the wall fell like an avalanche, spilling outward and inward, the fill rolling down the fan of debris on either side. An enormous cloud of dust roiled up into the darkened sky and, for a moment, we couldn't see much of anything.

I didn't need to see that well to know what was going to happen next, though.

I grabbed Farrar, pulling him to his feet, and looked around us. The earthquake had knocked defender and attacker alike to their knees on the top of the wall, and at least one more of the ladders had fallen. The Galel were still picking themselves up, but as the first ones on our feet, I saw that Farrar and I had clear fields of fire.

We opened up, rifles canted to use our red dots, dragging muzzles from dim figure to dim figure, taking just enough time to identify the enemy warriors in lamellar plates and flat-topped kettle helms before squeezing the trigger. Our shots blended together into a single, crackling roar, and fortunately our Galel allies had the good sense to stay down as soon as the bullets started to *crack* over their heads.

There weren't that many left, and we ceased fire after a few seconds. The Galel had already gone through most of them like a buzzsaw before the wall had been hit.

The enemy hadn't been standing still while we'd been cleaning up their first assault, though. With the wall breached—and if ever we'd needed proof that the battering ram was a feint, we sure had it now—what looked like an entire division was surging toward the gap, right into the dust cloud that was being rapidly swept away by the wind.

There were too many of them for our rifles to accomplish much, and we were cut off from half the platoon. Bailey, Applegate, Synar, and Fennean were coming out of the nearest tower, firing down into the mob of warriors charging the breach. They were putting guys down, but even Applegate's machinegun fire was a drop in the bucket against the sheer numbers bearing down on that gap in the defenses.

Nearly a hundred were through the breach before the dust had settled. They weren't just rushing through pell-mell, going hey-diddle-diddle, right up the middle, all in a big mob the way Hollywood always portrayed this kind of warfare back in the World. Even with the speed with which they'd exploited the opening, they were still in formation—as much as was possible on the uneven footing of the mass of scree and debris left over from the collapse of the wall—with their shields up and their weapons ready.

I could see what was about to happen. They weren't slowing down and trying to secure the breach first, the way that the first assault on the top of the wall had held a foothold. They were flooding through as fast as they could get squares of men with swords and spears through, spreading out across the killing ground and keeping close to the inside of the wall.

They were going to cut off the defenders before they could get to the second wall. Before *we* could get to the second wall.

"Get down off the wall!" I roared. "Get back to the second wall, now!"

One of the Galel, clearly a knight from the quality of his arms and armor, his red and green tunic covered in dust, opened his mouth to protest, but then he looked down at the mass of men and spears below and saw what I saw. Worse, just then, the ground rocked once more, and more dust boiled into the air off at the other end of the wall, the roar of the collapse reaching us a second later. This wasn't the only breach.

"You heard the man!" The knight started grabbing the nearest men-at-arms and shoving them toward the tower and the steps. "Fall back while we still can!"

I hoped that he would keep the men in good order. A rout right then could be disastrous.

For a moment, I considered just going with them. We were a handful of men, and our fire wasn't doing much. We were dumping bad guys with every shot or burst, but there were a *lot* of them down there, and they were already getting closer.

But we'd do better to cover for the Galel as they fell back to the second wall. The Peruni were moving fast, trying to cut us off, but the need to stay in formation was slowing them down. They were going to get between our guys and the gate in another few moments, though.

Bailey read my mind. "Roy, let's help cut those guys a hole."

Applegate was already on the timber guardrail at the inside of the wall, bracing his Mk 48's bipods against the rail and leaning into the gun as he held down the trigger and played the stream of tracers across the Peruni's front. Farrar hauled out the M79 and immediately lobbed a grenade into the middle of the nearest square almost without aiming. The 40mm detonated with a *thud* and a burst of black smoke, and the shockwave rippled through the Peruni infantry as men dropped, falling on and against each other, many dead, dying, or badly hurt.

I was looking for an officer. We fought in a way that required little central direction, but formations like that needed one mind in control. Kill the officer, and the formation might not break up, but its movement becomes more uncoordinated.

Farrar had apparently beaten me to it, though. What was left of the square slowed, stretched, and started to break apart. The men in front didn't want to go forward, but they didn't want to fall back onto ground zero, either. The men in the rear *really* didn't want to go through the remnant of that black cloud, especially since it meant clambering over the bodies of easily a dozen of their fellows. And there was no officer to direct them.

Only discipline and the immediacy of battle kept them from immediately dissolving into a panicked mob. We went to work on that a moment later, as Applegate poured on another long burst, and the rest of us just shot whoever popped up in our sights wearing the colors of Ar-Annator.

The Peruni's arms and armor were a lot more uniform than the Galel's, which made targeting a little easier. They still weren't as uniform as an army back in the World, but everyone was similar enough that they were pretty easily identifiable.

As bullets tore through scale and lamellar armor, punched through mail and padded linen, and men fell, spouting blood from torn flesh and shattered bone, the front line wavered, then broke.

Voices and horns blared behind them, but for those few moments, as the vanguard square panicked and routed, turning into a frightened mob, scrambling to get away from the thunder and the meaty impacts of bullets, Farrar lobbed another 40mm ogive into their midst and they got in the following force's way, tangling that entire wing and holding back their encirclement.

"Time to go." I grabbed Farrar's shoulder and made sure he was moving toward the tower ahead of me. Bailey didn't say anything, but he didn't need to. It was as if we all saw the desperately thin opening for what it was and knew beyond the shadow of a doubt that if we didn't move, we weren't going to get off that wall alive.

Surrender to an army that took orders from the Dullahans was not an option.

The Galel defenders were nearly to the gates, but while they'd gotten past the wing of Peruni troops trying to cut them off, the imperial center was driving hard to reach the gates ahead of them. They were definitely going to get there before we could.

Fortunately, that was a contingency that had been discussed in planning, days before.

Without bothering with bounding, we sprinted down the steps and out onto what was now no-man's-land between the walls. Peruni officers with tall, black feather crests on their helmets roared and bellowed, trying to break up the chaos on that wing and get their troops moving to cut off any remaining survivors before we reached the inner wall. They were still a good seventy yards away, though, and we were moving, running up the hill at as close as we could get to a dead sprint on that slope.

The ropes were already dropping from the battlements of the second wall. This was going be rough, but the archers up there were already lobbing as many arrows as they could at our enemies, trying to cover for us. We weren't the first Recon Marines to reach the wall, either. I could hear more gunfire and 40mm *thumps* coming from up there.

I hoped that Santos had made it. I didn't want to lose him, especially not so close to Rodeffer's death. He probably had a better chance than we did, running with Mathghaman and Bearrac, but I still worried, even as I slung my rifle to my back and grabbed the knotted rope, climbing even as the man on the other end started to pull it up.

A few arrows shattered against the stone near me, but the withering hail of arrows and stones from the battlements above was keeping the enemy archers' heads down. I sped up the slightly sloped face of the wall as fast as I could haul myself and the man at the top could pull my considerable weight.

Finally, I reached the crenellations, slightly behind Farrar and a little ahead of Applegate. I reached up with a gloved hand, grabbed the battlements, and hauled myself over. The burly, red-haired and red-faced Galel who'd been pulling on the rope reached down to grab my arm and help me over.

I thanked him and looked below. We'd done better than I'd feared, but not everyone had made it back. Down below, about halfway across the open ground between the walls, about a hundred Galel warriors hunched behind their shields, drawn up in a tight ring, facing a forest of Peruni spears.

I got on my sights, looking for any target that might disrupt the enemy, give those guys a chance at escape. It was Mathghaman who stopped me, his hand coming down on my rifle's forearm. "Save the ammunition, Conor." His voice was bleak, almost haunted. As noble and composed as Mathghaman usually was, he had seen some shit, and while it had to pain him as much as it did me—more, probably—he knew that there was no saving those men. We couldn't put enough of a dent, fast enough, into that enemy force to give them a break.

We could only watch as they fought to the last man, under a black sky split by purple-tinged lightning.

CHAPTER 13

TO my considerable relief, everyone had made it back to the second wall. Everyone that was left of 1st Platoon, anyway. Too many of our Galel allies had fallen on the wall or the killing ground beyond it, but we still held the second.

For how long was the question that no one wanted to ask, but everyone was thinking. The first wall had fallen all too quickly. It should have held for days. Weeks, even. But that was against mortal men with rams, catapults, and ladders. Even mines, though the fortress was built on rock which made tunnelling beneath the walls extremely difficult.

Against creatures of the Outer Dark, it had lasted mere hours.

A pall of despair had settled over the fortress. What chance did we have against that? We had no wizards. We didn't even have any of the sort of living saints like Brother Saukko in Vahava Paykhah. At least, not so far as the Galel knew. There were gray-robed clerics in the fortress, there to pray and tend to the wounded. But none of them were standouts in the mystic realm, so far as anyone seemed to know.

Even Conall hadn't said anything much about any of them.

Still, I found that I couldn't quite take that black pill. It was bad, certainly, but we had the Tuacha with us. None of us—Marine, Tuacha, or Menninkai—were exactly of the lie down and die persuasion, either.

All the same, looking out from the second wall at the wreckage of the first, I could understand the temptation to despair. That had been a hell of a thing. The question was, could we adjust and stop it if they tried again?

The ground on which the second wall stood was steeper and rockier than the first, the base of the wall standing nearly fifty feet higher than the lower fortification. The gate stood on a slight cant, never presenting its face directly to the first wall. Even if they managed to breach that second rampart the same way, the fight to get through the gaps was going to be a bloodbath.

In fact, the Galel were already adjusting for just that eventuality. Scorpions—essentially giant crossbows—and onagers—more traditional catapults that could fling rocks twice the size of my head—were already being prepositioned atop the third wall, just in case.

Still, what I was looking at didn't suggest that we were going to have to face an immediate assault within the next few hours. The Peruni hadn't abandoned the space between the walls the way that the Lasknut and Dovos had at Vahava Paykhah, but they weren't massing for a renewed attack, either. In fact, they were being surprisingly cautious, bringing more of the hide-covered barricades in to shield themselves even as they began to throw up earthworks just inside the outer wall.

"They're setting in for a long haul." Gurke was the first to voice it. The five of us—Gunny, Mathghaman, Bailey, Gurke, and I—were standing atop the second wall, just above the gate, careful not to expose ourselves too much.

He frowned as he watched them. "That doesn't make a whole lot of sense. If they're going to set in for a long siege, then why the hell would they have stormed the first wall? Why lose all those soldiers if you're just going to try to wait the defenders out?"

"Maybe they did it to show us that they could," Gunny mused, his eyes fixed on the growing camp below. "Maybe that's the reasoning. Smash the first wall fast, then show us just how many more men and monsters they've got, so that we surrender."

I glanced over my shoulder at the men moving furtively along the wall, watching not only the growing force down on the open ground, but also the skies. Wyverns still circled overhead, just out of bowshot. We could probably shoot them, but we might need the ammo later on.

Hold that thought. I'd barely looked up there when the first attack of the next phase began.

With a hoarse, croaking chorus of screams, half a dozen wyverns swooped down on the walls, off to our left.

Before the first one reached the battlements, Gunny was already moving, roaring out, "Gunners up!" Just about every Marine, Tuacha, and Menninkai headed toward that part of the wall in the next moment.

I didn't, but only because I had turned back to grab my M107, which I'd been grateful to see Bearrac had brought back with him. If I was going to shoot at one of those monsters, I wanted something with some punch.

The cacophony was getting louder by the time I came out of the tower, lugging the heavy rifle. I came out of the door just in time to look up and see one of the fanged creatures swooping down at me, its wings high and its talons spread, its jaws gaping wide.

It's not easy to shoulder a thirty-pound rifle like a carbine and take a snap shot at a flying target that's getting closer to biting your head off with every passing second. The urgency of the matter sometimes makes up for the difficulty though.

It took a precious second to get the sights on, and I overcorrected just a hair, heaving the rifle up over the top of the wyvern so that I had to drop the muzzle to get on target. By then the monster's toothy maw filled the entire scope, so I leaned into the weapon and pulled the trigger.

It wasn't the best shot I've ever made. I kind of slapped the trigger and my stance was hardly the best for firing a .50 from the standing. The recoil knocked me back a step, and I completely lost the sight picture.

Feeling the edge of panic, I came off the weapon to search for the monster, only to see it veer off, fluid and smoke pouring from one eye socket. I hadn't killed it, but I'd hurt it. It twisted its head around to hiss at me as it banked past, then it flapped higher and began to come around for another pass.

Dropping to a knee, I hauled the .50 around to track it, wishing I had a moment to dial the scope's magnification down. Right then it was like looking through a straw.

That steam boiler hiss came at me, audible even over the thunder of gunfire, the clash of weapons, and the roars and screams of men fighting and dying elsewhere on the wall, as the wyverns continued their assault. I missed the thing in the scope and desperately searched the sky, until I thought I could almost feel its breath and the wind of its wings, at which point I came off the scope.

It is possible to aim without the optic, but while I've known guys who swear by point shooting, I've never been a fan. Still, as that toothy maw swept down toward me and I opened both eyes and lifted my head over the scope, I was close enough that it almost didn't matter.

If you've never done a mag dump with a .50 cal, allow me to give you some advice: Don't.

Even as braced as I was, I got rocked. The recoil hammered at my shoulder and my cheek, and by the time the mag was empty, I felt like I'd just gone a couple rounds with Mike Tyson. My jaw hurt worse than my shoulder, and a headache was setting in fast.

Fortunately, I'd done a lot more damage to the wyvern than I'd done to myself.

Blood streaming from multiple wounds, it thrashed and twisted in the air for a split second before it smashed into the wall almost right at my feet. I stepped back as its head slammed down on the battlements only a few paces away, and got a glimpse of at least two terrible wounds torn through its skull, and a third that had gouged a bloody furrow down its neck, before it fell away, the massive head sliding off the walkway to disappear over the edge and down toward the rocks below, where it crashed in a tangle of broken bones, scales, and leathery wings with a resounding *boom*.

Lifting my head, I ripped the empty magazine out of the Barret and looked for another target, only then realizing that I didn't have another mag handy. I'd been in enough of a hurry to get out on the wall that I hadn't grabbed a reload.

I didn't need one, as it turned out. I watched a stream of tracers intersect another diving wyvern, tearing one eye out before tracking along its neck to rip through its wing. Screeching with rage and agony, the creature dipped its wing and tried to fly away, only to get hammered by another burst that sent it spinning into the ground, wiping out two of the Peruni's barricades as it fell.

A booming call went up from somewhere beyond the outer wall. It was a command, there was no doubt about that. I was reminded of the sound that had ended the Dovo assault on the tor where we'd first taken refuge, far to the north in the Land of Ice and Monsters.

The last of the wyverns turned aside and winged for the clouds, letting out croaking calls of hatred as they flew higher into the sky. Something told me we shouldn't relax, though.

"Get to cover!" I felt the hair rise on my arms even as I shouted. The tension in the air suddenly redoubled. Something was about to go down, that was for sure.

None of our guys hesitated. Few of the Galel hesitated. Those who did, paid for it.

A flickering curtain of lightning blasted down out of the clouds a second later. Stone exploded under the bombardment, sending glowing shards of rock flying like shrapnel, some of those fragments whickering through the opening I'd just ducked through to get back inside the tower. A crenellation on top of that tower was smashed by a lightning bolt and crashed to the battlements below, right about where I'd been standing a moment before.

Three men right outside weren't quite fast enough. One was struck dead in a flash, stiffening as the bolt stabbed down through his shoulder. He dropped as if he'd been stabbed, going limp just before he vanished over the edge of the wall.

Another man burned like a torch as the bolt slammed down through the top of his head. I knew that the lightning wasn't natural, but that took it a step beyond.

The sorcerous thunderstorm didn't last, fortunately. The bolts strobed along the top of the wall for another few seconds, then ceased, the echoes of the thunder rolling across the mountainside and out onto the plains.

When it finally stopped, the wyverns were far enough away that none of us were going to risk wasting ammo on a shot.

I stepped out of the tower and looked around for my team. At least a dozen dead men were sprawled on the wall or the ground beneath just within a hundred yards. Several had been struck by lightning, others appeared mauled and torn by wyvern claws and teeth.

"Team One!" I roared, even as Bailey, Gurke, and Orava echoed me.

"I'm up!" Farrar leaned out of the door of the next tower over.

Santos just stepped out onto the battlements and gave me a thumbs-up.

I let out a breath I hadn't realized I'd been holding. In the chaos of the attack, I'd lost track of where my teammates were, and I'd had visions of being the only one left. Rodeffer's loss had shaken me, deeply.

Gunny appeared from behind Santos, putting a hand on his shoulder to usher him out of the way. "Bring it in to the gatehouse. Two minutes."

* * *

It took a little longer than two minutes, since there were Ammo, Casualty, Equipment reports to take, and we had to give the Galel some space to reset, too. They'd lost about two dozen men in the attack. It was a paper cut compared to a full-fledged assault on the wall, but every man dead was a precious resource lost.

"They're definitely settling in." Applegate was watching through one of the arrow slits. Now he turned back toward the room that we'd been allowed to use as a team room, especially since we had the firepower to put some serious hurt on any assault force trying to come at the gate. "This is weird."

"I think that Gunny has the right of it." Mathghaman tapped his chin with a thumb, watching the barricades and earthworks in the open ground between walls go up. "They have demonstrated what they can do, now they want to take the time to let it sink into the minds of the defenders. Let despair set in." He shook his leonine head. "They are not fools. They know the cost they will likely have to pay to destroy every Galel hold. They will seek to preserve as much of their force as they can. If they can force a surrender of this fortress through fear…"

"Then they've got all this army to go in and steamroll the rest of the country, one hold at a time." Bailey nodded. "Things might not fall apart as thoroughly as they hope with Uven dead or captured—at least, not after the fun and games of the last couple months—but it'll take time for word to get to the rest of the lords, by which time the Peruni will already be at their doorstep."

"So, what do we do about it?" Santos asked.

"Perhaps, if they are sitting out there and waiting, hoping to let the threat of their presence weigh upon our minds, then an opportunity might lie before us." Bearrac was watching the enemy lines thoughtfully.

"You're thinking that we do what we were going to try to do before? Slip out into their rear area and wreak some havoc?" I asked.

"How?" Gurke was understandably skeptical. "Even if they hadn't found the secret passages, we kinda caved 'em in."

"It will be riskier, but there are places we might go over the wall. Perhaps while our allies perform some demonstration elsewhere." Bearrac's eyes moved toward the northern end of the fort. "They do not have the entire fortress surrounded on the inside. They cannot. The walls go to the cliffs on the sides of the mountain. There are places there where we might get over under cover of darkness."

Gunny was nodding, even as he moved to peer along the length of the wall itself. We couldn't see the outside of the north end from where we stood. The curvature of the wall meant that we could only see the inside for most of its span. But we could see the sheer, jagged cliffs that rose above it on the flank. Without air support, nobody was climbing that, especially not with Galel archers and slingers in place to shoot them off the rock face. With ropes, however, we could get down. *Provided* we got all eyes looking elsewhere.

"We'll need to identify specific targets and plan this down to a gnat's ass." He turned, his unblinking stare sweeping across the lot of us. "This can't be a seat-of-our-pants op. We find our target, plan our diversion, infil, and exfil down to the second. I don't want to lose anyone else out there." His gaze moved to Bailey, then me. "I'd stick with rifle and machinegun fire from up here on the wall, but somehow I think that you boys are going to be the main effort, with those holy pigstickers of yours."

He turned back to the arrow slits, and the vast army of the Empire of Ar-Annator beyond, inside and outside the wall. "Let's get to it. No time to waste."

CHAPTER 14

WHILE the ATLs figured out the logistics, the team leaders scanned our enemies and looked for targets.

There were plenty of them. We had gotten to the point that we could pick out the sorcerers, even as armored as most of the Peruni's wizards were, without much trouble. Some of them were still dressed out in robes and headdresses, looking like some kind of heathen priests, but many of them were as armed and armored as their fellow warriors. A couple even carried spears. Yet there was an aura about them that was strangely easy to spot. Maybe it was the open fear that their followers tried to suppress whenever they were near them. Maybe carrying one of the Two Swords meant that I could see things that most men couldn't. At any rate, I could usually pick them out even when they tried to hide in the crowd.

It's funny sometimes, the weird presuppositions you develop. Gurke had expressed his surprise that the sorcerers here wore armor and carried ordinary weapons. It can be difficult to get past the reality that while fantasy books, movies, and games might have echoed this place, they hadn't even come close to preparing us for it.

The wizards weren't the real high value targets, though. We could shoot them from the wall. There was zero need to drop down and go hands-on with them. We could pop sorcerer and warlord skulls all day—at least so long as our ammo held out.

No, we were going to have to go after the Dullahans. And that was a daunting prospect, let me tell you, *especially* as the only man in living memory to have actually killed one.

I still have nightmares about that duel. The prospect of doing it again, so soon after the fight in Cor Legear, was chilling.

That was the mission, though. I found myself whispering pleas to Iudicael to give me strength as we moved up and down the wall, looking not only for the Dullahan we intended to challenge, but the best way to get to it.

It was important to avoid looking like we were scoping them out, for a couple of reasons. The most obvious was that the Peruni commanders would notice and shift their forces to cut off any weak points we found. That's always been why Recon has remained clandestine.

The less obvious factor to someone unfamiliar with this world and its rules of warfare was that we *really* didn't want to attract the Dullahans' notice. I had no doubt—and I'm sure Bailey was thinking the same thing—that the lightning storm that had killed over a dozen men on the wall as the wyverns had retreated had been a parlor trick to those things.

I'd already spotted two of them as we'd scanned the encampment and fortifications inside the wall. One was incredibly skinny, seven and a half feet tall even without its head, swathed in black robes that trailed on the ground as it moved, seemingly without moving its feet. It carried a staff from which its head, as gaunt as the rest of it and with eyes that burned with blue fire, hung from a strap. In its other hand it carried that awful whip of human vertebrae.

That one seemed to be hanging out near the gate, supervising several of the sorcerers and warlords. Not an actionable target. There were simply too many bad guys and too much open ground to cover to get to that one.

The other one, however, looked like a possibility. It—most of these creatures appeared to have been men, once upon a time, though at least one, way out there in the east, outside of Myrgarak, had looked like it had been a woman, but they weren't really human anymore, so I never thought of them as either men or women, but rather as monsters, *things*—was elusive, only appearing from time to time, and then mostly off toward the edges of the enemy forces. It was smaller than the black-robed one, and broader. It looked almost as if it had been a Menninkai before its unalterable corruption. Maybe an Avur.

This one didn't wear the heavy armor of some of the Dullahans we'd seen, including the one I'd killed in Cor Legear. It still wore armor, but it was strange, unlike anything I'd seen in this world before. It almost looked like it wore an ancient brocaded jacket, embroidered and studded in faded red, green, and gold, but with plates of verdigrised metal sewn in over its collarbone, chest, thighs, and upper arms.

It carried its head, glowing faintly with a grayish sort of light, by its topknot. Its eyes were utter blackness.

We might be able to get to that one. It appeared to avoid the others and stay on the periphery, though it was still one of the few that had appeared within the outer wall. If we timed things right—and that was going to be tricky, because it was hard to keep track of that creature—then we might be able to corner it near the end of the wall, kill it, and then get back to friendly lines in the confusion.

There were a lot of "mights" in that plan.

I shook my head. I'd lost it again. "We're going to have to split up. One team on one end of the wall, the other opposite. That way at least *one* of the Swords will be in action."

"I don't like it." Bailey didn't have to say why not.

I eased back from the glass and rubbed my eyes. "I don't either, but this bastard is slippery."

Bailey sighed, looked down at the floor, then turned to me. "I talked to Conall. He said he's willing to help us with a bit of a vigil. Might not be long enough, depending on the tactical situation, but…"

I raised an eyebrow at him. "I've got to admit, I'm a little surprised that you brought that up first."

He shrugged, still looking a little uncomfortable. "Got to acknowledge reality as it is. We both would have been dead—or worse—in Cor Legear if we hadn't asked Iudicael and Categyrn for help." He glanced upward, the look taking in not just the ceiling overhead but the sky and the implied heavens. "Life ain't like we thought, back in the World. There's more to it than just what we can see and touch. I never really figured that out, back there, because we could sort of ignore it. Not here."

I nodded as I stood up and stretched. "It's a good point." I looked down at the Sword by my side, identical to the one Bailey carried except that mine was inlaid with gold, his with silver. "I think it's something we've all been thinking about, at least since we came here."

"Either we've been thinking about it, or we've been some particularly dense, obtuse sons of bitches." He might have started thinking along different lines in the metaphysical sort of realm, but like most of us, that hadn't taken the edge off Bailey's language.

Some habits die hard. None of us can just flip a switch, not without some extraordinary help.

"Well, let's go find Conall." I glanced out at the enemy again, and the lowering darkness of the sky. "I don't know how much time we're going to have."

* * *

As it turned out, we had considerably less time than I'd hoped.

I didn't wear a watch anymore; I was pretty sure the batteries were dead by then, though the biggest reason was the fact that days were a little longer than twenty-four hours here. Having spent much of the time since Bailey and I had left the wall in meditation in company with Iudicael—I'd seen him, though I'm pretty sure no one else in the chapel did, and he'd said nothing—I really didn't know how much time had passed. I just knew that it wasn't enough.

A rumble of thunder and a booming voice calling out Uven's name heralded the end of our vigil. I'd had my eyes closed for the last few minutes, and when I snapped them open, Iudicael was gone, and Bailey was already getting to his feet as the candle flames flickered and wavered around us.

It didn't take long to get back up to the battlements, charging through the still-open gate in the third wall and running across the killing ground to the second, pounding up the stairs as that thunderous, stentorian voice continued to call for Uven. It was coming from somewhere out on the other side of the wall.

When I reached the battlements, I stopped dead.

The glowing golden figure looming above the first wall could only be the Emperor of Ar-Annator, or at least an idealized image of him. Tall, entirely clad in glittering mail, with a masked helm worked in gold and topped by an elaborate crest that looked much like the horsehair fringe of a Corinthian helmet, he would have struck an imposing figure even if he hadn't been a hundred feet tall.

I knew it was a projection, but it was still a hell of an impressive projection. The fact that it managed to appear golden and majestic instead of horrifying and dark said something about the power behind it. Most of the evil we'd encountered here—the open, unapologetic, power-hungry malevolence, anyway—had been dark, twisted, easy to recognize on some level, though it seemed that the ability to instill fear in one's enemies or those one wished to rule wasn't exactly a deterrent.

That shouldn't have surprised me, given some of the ugliness I'd seen the powerful and immoral embrace back in the World.

Some of the most dangerous evil, though, was gentle and inviting as long as possible. Subtle, even. Something like that was doubtless behind this image. I doubted, even if he wasn't dabbling in sorcery himself, that the emperor looked like that in real life.

"Uven! Come, kinsman! Let us talk together!"

The projection of the emperor had been saying that for the last several minutes and had, so far, gone unanswered. Now, however, as Bailey and I gained the top of the wall, King Uven stepped out atop the gatehouse, in full armor, a golden circlet around the rim of his helm, the crimson horsehair atop its peak waving in the wind.

The king was still gaunt and slightly pale, and some of the fiery aggressiveness seemed to have gone out of him, beaten out by sheer weariness. Yet his face was set, his mouth a hard line beneath his beard, as he stared out at the projection of his enemy.

"I have naught to say to you, Enmenunon, slayer of the innocent and breaker of the peace!" As strong as Uven's voice was, even after his wound, he still sounded hoarse and muted compared to the otherworldly thunder of the emperor's words.

"*Truly?*" The emperor sounded hurt and disappointed. Which was probably a carefully rehearsed act, to my complete lack of surprise. "*I weary of this, Uven. What has your defiance bought you and your people? Need we continue this any longer? I assert my rights as emperor of these lands because such has it always been, since before even the fall of great Commagan. You know this as well as I.*"

Uven spat over the wall. Given the generally fairly fine manners of the Galel, that was a deadly insult, and I was sure that the emperor understood that even better than I did. "The Commagan never ruled the Galel, as well you know. And to tie your own thirst for power and bloodshed to that doomed race is folly. These are not your lands, and even if they had been at some time in the distant past, your murders and your robberies have forfeited all claim to them. Turn your army around and go back from whence you came, lest they break themselves against this Rock!"

A bellowed cheer went up from the wall at that. No, not a cheer. A full-throated battle roar. The Galel, knights, men-at-arms, and archers alike, were telling the Peruni and their allies what they thought of the emperor's words.

Enmenunon—or the image that was supposed to be him—shook his head and looked down at the ground, as if disappointed. "*If you truly cared about your people, Uven, you would surrender now.*" He waved a hand to indicate the ruin of the first wall. "*See how easily your first line of defense fell before my armies? Such should be an object lesson to all who defy me. Come, kinsman. See reason. Do not sacrifice your people on the altar of your own pride.*"

Leaning on the battlements, Uven bowed his head. For that brief moment, he just looked deathly tired. But when he looked up again, the fire in his eyes had not gone out.

"You are an oathbreaker, a murderer, a liar, a trafficker with devils of the Outer Dark, and in every way damned, Enmenunon." He drew his sword and pointed it at the projection of the emperor. "Were I the fool you think me to be, perhaps I would surrender, to be tormented by your monsters and turned into a broken man, your pet for the rest of what little would remain of my time in this world. Anything to buy a few more precious instants of life." He laughed then, a booming, derisive sound. "I do not value my skin highly enough for that, you pathetic worm! I have fought the monsters you sent into our kingdom, to corrupt and devour my people, to make your conquest all the easier. Should we *all* die within these walls, our sacrifice will bolster our people's spirits, and Cor Chatha will be a monument to those who would keep faith with Tigharn and defy your dark masters. So come, Enmenunon!" His voice rose even more to a thunderous bellow that reverberated off the mountain behind us. "*Come meet our steel! Break your army upon the Rock of Battle and learn what true men are made of!*"

The roar redoubled in its fury. The echoes rumbled from the mountain behind us and washed over the imperial army below.

For a long moment, the emperor's image bent its head as if disappointed and thoughtful. When he looked up again, however, his eyes burned a lurid red. The gold seemed to fade and tarnish. I was sure that behind the mask, the emperor's face was twisted with rage and hate.

"*True men? Your 'true' men are animals, beasts of burden to be used or discarded. They are dogs yapping at the heels of those who could crush them like insects.*" He stabbed a finger at the walls. "*Bark while you can, dog. I will bring you to heel.*"

Most of that response I saw and heard on the move. While Uven had been issuing his challenge, I'd looked around and found the rest of the team close at hand, and now we were making for the end of the wall as fast as we could move without attracting too much attention.

All eyes were on the emperor and the king. We had our diversion.

Now we had to get down there and close in with the Dullahan before the enemy figured out we were in their backyard.

CHAPTER 15

WE covered the last bit of distance at a run. I'd led the way to the nearest tower, at which point we'd headed down the steps to the ground, then hustled along the inside of the wall to the last bastion, where we regained all the elevation we'd given up.

The Galel guards already had the ropes ready. We'd set that up before Bailey and I had begun our vigil. Now, even as the emperor raged and cursed at King Uven—he'd been going for a while—we quickly tied our Swiss seats around our hips and got ready to descend.

We were going to need to climb a lot faster than a Swiss seat would allow on the way back, but we could get down by rappelling a lot faster than climbing hand over hand.

It was a good thing that we'd still had our sling ropes and carabiners in our rucks when we'd come through the mists. They were about to be extremely handy.

Clipping in, I looked skyward and silently asked Iudicael to help us out, then, with my rifle across my back, my pistol on one side and the Sword on the other, laden down with enough ammunition to kill a company, I swung out over the battlements and kicked off.

It's often preferable to have a man on belay on the ground beneath you when you rappel down a cliff—or a wall—but it's not always possible. So, I went down awfully fast, relying almost entirely on the tension I could put on the rope. Santos still almost beat me to the ground.

The darkness was the only reason we went unnoticed, at least at first. The clouds had gotten so thick that it was always twilight or night, except for the brief moments when lightning split the sky. So far, the overcast hadn't shed a single drop of rain or hail, which only made it all the more eerie. It made for better footing, but it was still weird and unnatural.

It took seconds to shed the ropes and get into a tight half-circle, weapons pointed up and out. Nothing moved near us, and we were right in the shadow of a shoulder of the mountain that jutted out a few yards into the killing ground. Not far enough to provide us with a good covered and concealed position, but far enough that we were lost in the murk to anyone with normal human eyes.

I just hoped the Dullahans weren't looking this way yet.

With Rodeffer dead, I didn't really have a pointman anymore. Farrar would have done it, but I was to the point that I was going to take it on myself, if only because I had the Sword of Iudicael, and if we ran headlong into a Dullahan, I was the only one who had a snowball's chance in hell of standing against it.

That wasn't the only reason I took point, even though I knew that either Mathghaman or Bearrac would have done it if I'd asked them. They had both come along, naturally. Conall and Diarmodh had accompanied Bailey on the other end of the wall.

No, I was out there because I felt guilty over Rodeffer's death. Rodeffer's, and everyone else who'd died while I'd kept breathing. It wasn't even a matter of feeling responsibility for his death, though that certainly played a role, since I'd been his team leader. It was survivor's guilt, plain and simple.

I knew it then, and I know it now. It doesn't get any better with time.

Still, bearing the Sword of Iudicael was a rational reason to be out front, the emotional turmoil in the background notwithstanding. True to what I knew I had to do, I quashed the emotional part into a deep, dark hole and pushed out along the cliff face toward the smashed remains of the first wall.

There were still more Peruni at that end of the wall than I'd hoped. The encampment had spread to the entire inside, and there were barricades and tents going clear to the cliffs. Not ideal for an infiltration, but they were there, and we were going to have to deal with them. Either that or turn around and climb back up.

That wasn't an option. I wanted a crack at that headless abomination with its whip of human bones.

Maybe I'd gotten a bit too much confidence after fighting that one in Cor Legear. I didn't think so, though. It was weird. I was scared stiff, but I still didn't want to turn around and go back, not without at least hurting that thing.

So, we kept going, creeping across the killing field toward the barricades.

It was fortunate that the enemy was worried about the archers up on the second wall. They were worried with good reason. Those boys with the war bows could put a heavy shaft right through an unarmored throat at a hundred yards almost. Especially when they were shooting downhill. That was aiming at a point target, too. Their range got a lot longer if they were shooting at an area target.

That threat was what was keeping the Peruni's heads down, behind the barricades they'd brought across the plain and the shallow earthworks they'd thrown up since they'd penetrated the wall. It kept them from noticing us as we slipped across the open ground, concealed by the very darkness their masters had summoned to oppress and demoralize the defenders.

I moved up carefully, staying low, hoping that I didn't have to shoot any of the enemy just yet. We might all have been running suppressed, but supersonic bullets still make a hell of a *crack*. Someone would notice, even if they didn't quite understand what the noise was.

There was a gap between the hide-covered barricades and the cliff, which made sense. They only had so many of the wicker and hide shields, and it must have taken a lot of work and effort to get them across the plains from Ar-Karum the Great, the nearest Peruni city. Since this end of the line was shadowed by the same finger of the mountainside that we'd used to cover our descent, it made sense that they wouldn't worry so much about covering this distant flank.

I still got down in the prone and crawled as we got closer, pausing every yard or so to check that I wasn't about to stumble on a sentry or catch the eye of an archer or worse, a sorcerer. I made it all the way to the barricade without even seeing movement.

Once I reached the angled shield of wood, wicker, and hastily tanned leather, I could hear voices. They sounded like Avurs. I hadn't heard the Peruni speak nearly as much as I had the steppe horsemen, but I could tell the difference between their languages.

I eased around the edge of the barricade behind my rifle, keeping it canted so that I could look through the red dot. We were too close for the scope even if it hadn't been dark enough that I had my NVGs down.

Somewhat to my surprise, the earthworks right in front of me were abandoned. There was no one in sight, at least not until I moved around a little farther, so that I could see deeper into the enemy's encampment.

This is bad. I knew a marshalling area when I saw one. They were getting ready for a push. There were probably over a hundred forming into a tight square behind another barricade, about a hundred yards away.

The Dullahan stood a lot closer, atop a mound in the middle of the earthworks, about ten yards behind the line of barricades. It was not lost on me that the formation of Peruni soldiers was as far away from the headless sorcerer as possible.

They weren't dumb.

Unfortunately, I knew as soon as I'd laid eyes on it that our planning had just gone to crap. Unless the black-eyed one in the brocade was over where Bailey had inserted, we weren't going to get a crack at it.

This one was a giant, dwarfing even the tall, skinny one in robes that we'd seen during our initial pre-mission reconnaissance. It had to stand ten feet tall at the shoulder, and it was built like the biggest, least natural, mutant bodybuilder I'd ever seen. I could tell, because it wore only a short cape and wide breeches, its chest and shoulders exposed, its brawny arms holding its whip in one hand and its head—heavy-browed and with a prominent underbite to its thick jaws, its eyes milky and glowing with an unwholesome, pale light—resting on the up-raised palm of the other.

That thing was even more horrifying than our original target.

It also wasn't as complacent as we might have hoped. While the body didn't move a muscle, the head turned in its hand, fixing those pale, glowing orbs on us.

"*Daring. Futile, but daring. While those others cower behind their walls, you have the temerity to walk right into the dragon's mouth.*" The head grinned then, a horrible ex-pression, revealing jagged, bloodstained teeth. "*There is no prey here, though. Only something worse than a dragon.*"

That I doubted, having faced one of those ancient evils before.

Since we were made, I stood, slinging my rifle to my back while Santos, Farrar, and Bearrac set in to cov-er the Peruni—who were now on the wrong side of the Dullahan to really support it, especially if they were as reluctant to get near the monster as they seemed—and Mathghaman drew his own blade and stepped up next to me. The Tuacha's rifles were wonders in and of them-selves, but even they wouldn't scratch a Dullahan.

I drew the Sword of Iudicael, kissed the cross guard, and sent a wordless prayer for aid toward the sky as I dropped into a guard.

The Dullahan *laughed*.

That sound was even worse than its grin. It grated on my ears, and I could hear the corruption and malev-olence in it. It cracked that awful whip, and then leaped backward.

"*There is no easy victory here, either. I know what it is you carry. Think you I am so foolish as to come close enough to suffer the fate of the Soulgrinder?*" Its grin, if anything, got even wider and more insane, and then it started to chant, a guttural, mind-shredding sound that sounded like the gnashing of the teeth of Hell.

As it chanted discordantly, things like black plants started to sprout from the ground between me and it. They weren't plants, though.

Easily a dozen of the same sort of inky black, six- or eight-legged, red-eyed lizard-dogs that we'd confronted inside of Cor Legear writhed out of the ground and came for us, moving fast and snapping their distended, mis-shapen jaws as they leaped through the air.

Santos cut one in half with a short burst of machine-gun fire, then they were on us, and there was too much risk of friendly fire.

I brought the Sword of Iudicael up in a sweeping cut that took the closest in the throat as it sprang at me. The smoky blade clove through unnatural flesh almost as easily as if it hadn't even been there. The thing's head nearly came off and it went limp for a moment as I punched it with my buckler, knocking it offline and away from me. Its body slammed into the next one, tangling the two of them up, but I couldn't even take advantage of that momentary breather, because three more of them were coming at me a split second later.

Mathghaman was right at my shoulder, hewing at the monsters as only he could, his sword moving so fast it was a blur. Wherever that blade struck, sparks flew, and unnatural black ichor flowed. He wove a web of steel before him, and the creatures fell lifelessly to the dust with every blow.

I wasn't nearly as fast or as graceful as Mathghaman, but I was holding my own. No small part of that must have been because I was wielding the Sword of Iudicael. I was long over any thought that the Sword might make me invincible, but it *did* give me a bit of an advantage against things of the Outer Dark. Any sorcerous beasties, really. There had been a five-eyed, frost-encrusted, skeletal giant in the mountains of the Land of Ice and Monsters that had only gone down when I'd started cutting it up.

Still, there wasn't a lot of grace in my movement. I was swinging and hacking as fast as I could, basically trying to keep the blade moving in something like a figure eight in front of me, just trying to cut or stab any of the ravening beasts that got too close.

There were a *lot* of them, and for every one that Mathghaman or I cut down, it seemed like three more sprang up out of the ground. The rest of the team had pushed up to join us, slamming rounds into the slavering horrors wherever they could be sure they weren't going to shoot one of us, and now we fought shoulder to shoulder, cleaving unnatural black flesh and chitin as fast as we could.

Mathghaman put out a hand and began to draw me back, step by step, as we closed our ranks and the lizard-dogs swarmed us. I could hear grunts and the smack of weapons over the snarls behind us and knew that we really were surrounded.

The Dullahan was laughing at us. For a moment, I desperately wanted to cut my way through those monstrosities and plunge the Sword through that grinning Neanderthal head. There was no way I could reach it, though, and it knew it. It wasn't dumb; it wouldn't come near the Sword as long as it knew that I wasn't quite the aggressive idiot who had nearly gotten torn apart in Cor Legear anymore.

I almost reverted, though. As that thing laughed and the demonic lizard-dogs tried to eat our faces off, I almost threw caution to the winds and tried to just carve my way through—to hell with defending myself or my team—to try to get to it and split its terrible face. The rage at its mockery burned in my chest, and only years of harsh discipline kept me in formation as Mathghaman drew us back toward the wall.

My lungs ached and my limbs got heavy as we moved and fought. I split one skull, then ripped the glowing guts out of another monster, then stabbed a third through the mouth, but there were always more. They disintegrated rapidly to a sticky, smoking, black tar when they died, but more crawled up out of the dirt, almost as if we weren't killing them but multiplying them, sort of like cutting the heads off the Hydra.

Still, we held tight and kept moving. They weren't sprouting out of the ground behind us, at least, but only in the one spot where the Dullahan had first summoned them, so the farther away we got, the less the pressure, though we were still fighting so hard we could hardly tell at the time.

A hiss sounded from above, and I heard flapping wings and the rattle of dislodged rocks as a wyvern alighted on the clifftop above us. I was too busy fending off another hellhound as it snapped at my legs to look up, but I knew that thing was up there, and I had to fight the urge to turn from the present fight to try to face it. A moment later, I heard the heavy *boom* of my .50, and then, with a catastrophic crash, the wyvern fell from the clifftop, scraping a couple tons of rock off with it, and smashed to the ground right next to us.

The impact flattened a couple dozen of the hell-hounds, one of them vanishing with a sickening *pop* beneath a snakelike head that was missing a chunk of its skull from the Raufoss round that had killed it. I didn't know who had commandeered my rifle, but right then, I was grateful to them for it.

The shock of that fall gave us a moment to catch our breath. I looked up to see the Dullahan, no longer laughing, staring at us. The flow of hellhounds seemed to have slowed. I didn't know how; their malice seemed bottomless, and even as we'd sliced them up, the following monsters had shown no hesitation as they'd thrown themselves at our blades.

We had come just around that shoulder of the mountain by then, and even as Bearrac bellowed, "Run!" the first *pop*s of mortar fire began.

I hacked down another inky black cross between a Doberman and a caiman, scuttling at me on eight legs, and then turned and sprinted toward the wall. A stream of tracers crackled over my head, hammering into unnatural, tarlike flesh and giving us just a little bit more space.

The .50 *boom*ed again, the round going above and behind us with a thunderous *crack*. I didn't bother to try to look and see what the target was; I was too busy trying to get to the ropes already waiting for us at the wall.

I didn't need to look, anyway. I heard the roar of hatred and rage. I hoped that the Dullahan had to run a good distance to pick up its head.

The straight dash for the wall and the ropes didn't last long, though. Mathghaman suddenly stopped and turned, swinging his own leaf-bladed sword in a short, hard arc to intersect one of the hellhounds as it went for Farrar. He cut it in half, sending its front spinning to the ground behind him with a shower of ichor.

Even with the Sword of Iudicael in my hand, I didn't think I could have done that.

I still had to stop and turn, though, at least to cover his flank. I pivoted and found that I didn't have the time or the room to swing, so I just stabbed straight out, and the thing that looked like it was all teeth from the hinge of the jaw forward impaled itself on the blade, already turning into bubbling tar before I could even haul the Sword clear.

Two more went down in two fast chops. I *know* that even though I didn't see the glowing figure, or even feel that hand on my shoulder, Iudicael was there with me. I doubt, as tired as I was by then, that I could have managed two such perfect cuts otherwise.

"Conor, get on the rope!" Bearrac was suddenly beside me, grabbing me by the shoulder and physically hauling me around so he could shove me toward the wall. At the same time, he brought his own sword up with a grunt, disemboweling yet another monster as it reared up to leap at him.

I was about to fight him. It's not a good idea to fight Bearrac on general principles, but I suddenly thought that he'd just torn me away from the battle while my team was still in danger. It was only after he yelled at me again, while splitting another hellhound from gullet to gizzard, that I realized Farrar and Santos were halfway to the top already.

Then it made sense. Bearrac and Mathghaman stood a better chance down there than I did, blessed Sword or no, and they could probably jump the whole wall if they really felt like it. So, I did as I was told. I sheathed the Sword, grabbed the rope, and started to haul myself up hand over hand, while I felt the line go taut and rise with me, as someone up on the battlements pulled me up.

I got about halfway up before Mathghaman and Bearrac finally disengaged. Under different circumstances, they might have ascended normally, just like I was doing. They didn't like to show off. Here and now, though, they both leaped a good twenty feet in the air, seizing ropes partway up the wall, and held themselves there just long enough to sheath their blades before beginning to climb past me.

I reached the battlements right behind Bearrac, and he and Gunny hauled me over the crenellations. Suddenly exhausted, I slumped to the catwalk and leaned back against the stone.

So much for that idea.

Then the horns sounded down below, and the first catapult stones struck the wall not twenty feet from me. The next assault was about to begin.

CHAPTER 16

WEARILY, I turned back toward the wall, bringing my rifle back around. Gunny leaned into the .50 next to me, searching for targets.

I felt a flash of resentment, right then. I was exhausted, drenched in sweat despite the faint chill of the wind and the fact that the sun had been hidden for the last couple of days. Every bone seemed to ache, and my mouth was dry, my eyes gritty. I'd just been through a hell of a fight, and here came another one, one that promised to be worse.

That's combat, though. If I'd wanted to be bored and comfortable, I should have chosen another profession.

Maybe that wouldn't have made that much difference. Maybe I was *supposed* to be here, now. I sure hadn't ever expected to travel the mists to a time and place as far removed from the world I'd grown up in as this.

So, I got on my sights and joined Gunny in looking for targets of opportunity.

The advance was slow and cautious, even as the enemy's catapults hurled rocks and gigantic spears at the battlements. Boulders that had to weigh nearly a hundred pounds slammed against the face of the wall or soared over it, shaking even the massive barricade with their impacts. Dust and rubble sifted down toward the ground with each blow, adding the rattle of falling stones to the tramp of feet, the calls and chants of the enemy warriors, and the horn calls and drums that directed them.

Not far to my left, a six-foot, iron-tipped bolt from a scorpion struck a Galel man-at-arms in the head. His helmet flew away as his skull simply *disappeared* in a mist of blood, bone, and brains. His body crashed onto its back on the catwalk, blood pulsing from the ragged stump of his neck.

I was looking for the scorpions. If I could pick off the operators, that might take some of the pressure off. It wouldn't stop the sorcerers, but they were insta-kill targets, too.

The giant crossbow-style weapons were set back against the remnant of the first wall, shielded behind more of the tall wicker-and-hide shields. I spotted one of them, shifting my sights to it, and found one of the Peruni eyeballing the siege engine's aim, unavoidably exposed behind the bolt as he lined it up.

I let out a breath and squeezed off my shot. I hardly needed to worry about the hold. We were too close for that. Just point and shoot.

I was braced against the stone crenellation solidly enough that my scope hardly moved with the shot. It was still slightly too dark to tell exactly where I hit him, but he dropped out of sight with a finality that told me all I needed to know.

There was a pause, then another Peruni tried to dash for the scorpion, and got the same treatment. He probably fell on the body of the first one.

When no one else stuck their necks out after the next few seconds, I dumped several rounds into the engine itself. The M110's 7.62 rounds weren't nearly as destructive as the .50's, but I still must have cut the bowstring, because the arms suddenly snapped forward without the bolt moving except to bounce in its trough. One less siege engine to worry about.

Gunny fired again as I came off sights to scan the approaching front. Some of the incoming had slackened a little, while our rifle and machinegun fire had stepped up. Another volley of mortar fire whistled overhead to slam down into the midst of an advancing square of Peruni infantry, tearing through armor and flesh and throwing men to the ground like broken, bloody rag dolls.

Then the sorcerers started up.

More lightning flickered along the battlements, and I ducked away from a small explosion as a strike hit the stone only inches from my face. Gunny had dropped with a curse, blood welling from a cut on his forehead, and I realized that we needed to get off the wall and into cover, fast.

I grabbed Gunny by the chest rig and hauled him toward the nearest tower. Farrar and Santos were already moving, Santos pushing Farrar ahead of him. Mathghaman stood defiantly atop the wall, ignoring the rocks, scorpion bolts, and lightning flying through the air, his rifle in his shoulder, searching for a target. He fired just before a lightning bolt came so close that, for a moment, I thought it had hit him. I blinked against the green and purple afterimage, to see Mathghaman still standing tall, unscathed. He turned with a faint nod, as if satisfied with his shot, and jogged to join us in the tower.

Gunny shrugged me off as we got inside, wiping the blood away from his eyebrows. He had held on to the

.50, and when I looked down at it, he caught the glance and glared at me. "You left it, Conor. It's mine for now."

"I wasn't exactly going to take that thing for close-quarters combat, Gunny."

He grinned wolfishly. "Don't matter." He pointed at the arrow slits. "Come on, the fight's out there. Don't worry, I'll take care of it."

There wasn't time to argue. I made sure Farrar and Santos were all right, but both of them were already at firing positions and pouring high-velocity hate at the enemy. I found an arrow slit and moved in to go to work.

The lightning stopped abruptly just then, and the darkness deepened. Within seconds, it became almost impossible to see the first wall at all. The squares of Peruni infantry continued their advance, though more slowly. It had to be hard on those guys, too. They were still men, not otherworldly monsters that shunned the sunlight and could see in the dark. Given the fact that they were trying to storm the walls and kill us all, I didn't have a lot of sympathy, but I imagined they were stumbling over each other and cursing the sorcerers and the Dullahans—quietly, so they wouldn't get in trouble and be sacrificed—with every step.

Ten squares of infantry, huddled in tight shield formations and moving in way that suggested they were carrying ladders, were moving toward the wall, but as I scanned them, I dismissed them. They were a threat, certainly, but it would take a few more minutes for them to reach the wall at that pace. No, the bigger threat was behind them.

I really, really wished we could reach out and touch those Dullahans. Especially as a deep, angry groan seemed to reverberate through the ground in the next instant, and I thought I saw that heave begin again, somewhere back near the first wall, climbing the slope toward the second.

There's a particular sort of helplessness, watching something like that. It's every bit as bad as being under an artillery strike. There's simply nothing you can do but hunker down, brace yourself, and hope the Man upstairs is looking after you.

In some ways, though, the sheer weirdness of what was happening made it worse. I'd been under rockets and mortars in Syria. But rockets and mortars don't make the ground itself groan with the unnatural horror of their very existence. Whatever the Dullahans were doing, it made the very rocks of the mountain shudder.

I had forgotten about the guardian, though. So had the enemy, apparently.

A faint luminescence caught my peripheral vision, and I turned aside for a moment, searching for it. The glow drew my eyes to the top of the gatehouse, halfway down the wall.

That same glowing figure that we'd seen down in the tunnels beneath the mountain now stood atop the gate, though he seemed to have grown since we'd first encountered him. While not nearly as huge as the emperor's image had been, he must have stood twelve feet tall, his feet spread apart and his sword held point-down in front of him, facing the enemy.

For a long moment, the figure didn't move, but simply stood there. Only after a handful of heartbeats did I realize that the heave in the ground had stopped, though the tension in the air built and the entire world seemed to groan and creak, as if immense forces were striving with each other deep beneath the ground.

Then the figure lifted that sword and pointed it out over the wall.

He said nothing. Just made that gesture of denial and defiance. But the ground shook and that awful groan got louder and louder, until it was downright painful. Then, as if something deep underground had snapped, the quake stopped and the earth fell away where it had heaved up, leaving several deep grooves in the rocky ground between the walls, stopping still a good twenty yards short of the second wall.

I could have sworn the darkness eased then, just a little.

The oncoming infantry stutter-stepped. For a few moments, they just sort of milled around, though they didn't break formation, which saved a lot of their lives, as they were still being pelted with arrows and sling stones from above. Iron-tipped shafts hammered into shields, a few of them slipping past to gouge their way into the men carrying them. Every few moments, a shield would disappear as its bearer fell, only for the gap to be quickly closed.

Confused and frightened they might be, since the Dullahans' sorcery was probably supposed to be invincible, but they were disciplined. They knew that a rout would only get the lot of them slaughtered, so they held formation, even as strident voices were raised to urge them forward once again.

They came on, perhaps more cautiously, but still they came.

It looked like we didn't have to worry about the walls being blown open, at least not for a while, but the ladders were still coming, and the catapults were still launching their payloads at us.

Santos broke the pause by leaning into the Mk 48 and sending a long burst into the lead ranks of the nearest formation. He was answered quickly with a torrent of sling stones from the rear, forcing him back from the arrow slit as the flying stones rattled off the wall in front of him.

They were adapting faster than I might have hoped.

I stayed a step back from the slit. It meant I had to shoot from the standing, but while the distances were pretty long for arrows or slings—by design—they weren't half bad for a 7.62 marksman's rifle. Or battle rifle, the way I was generally using it.

Searching the rear of the formation in the dimness, I spotted one of the slingers. They had to step back from the fortress of shields to get a shot, the men in light tunics and leather caps rearing back as they spun their slings to get the stones up to speed.

My first shot was low, and the slinger doubled over, letting go of the sling at the wrong time and smashing the rock into the back of the man's head in front of him. That one went down, crashing into the man beside him and sending a ripple through the formation, a disruption that Santos immediately took advantage of, raking the oncoming enemy infantry with more fire and dumping a dozen more to the dirt.

They still kept coming. And we couldn't be everywhere on that wall.

The horns got more insistent, and another swarm of the dark flying things raked the wall, forcing most of the Galel defenders behind cover and disrupting the hail of arrows that was still pelting the assault. That gave the attackers a bit of a breather, and with their officers and wizards urging them on, they took advantage of it.

The first ladders hit the top of the wall, and as lightning flickered and reached for any man who was exposed—except for the Peruni, strangely enough—the first attackers began to climb.

There were a lot more ladders this time than there had been the first time. The ram was starting to move toward the gate once more, apparently having been hastily repaired after the assault on the first wall. It wasn't alone, either.

They must have trailed behind the main body by some distance, possibly because they couldn't keep up, given their size and weight, but half a dozen siege towers were now being rolled through that gap in the first wall. They weren't quite what I pictured when I heard the term "siege tower," but they looked solid, covered in so many hides that they must have slaughtered entire herds to shield the engines from arrows and fire.

There was no way we'd keep all of them from getting to the wall. But we could sure try.

I keyed my radio. "Four, this is one, requesting immediate fire mission."

"This is Four." Orava sounded a little harried.

"From your position, seventy-two degrees, four hundred fifty yards." It was anything but an orthodox call for fire but, given the constrained environment we had to work with, it was better than nothing. There were ways of direct-laying mortars, and while the mortar teams, up on the fourth wall, couldn't quite do that, they could follow a simpler call for fire.

"Copy. Shot, out." They hadn't had far to adjust, since they'd been dropping mortar rounds on the inner killing ground, anyway.

The first rounds came whispering down out of the clouds and slammed into the ground just in front of the first of the trundling siege towers. They'd missed short, but they were close enough that I didn't bother to send a correction. Unless the tower stopped dead, the next salvo should be dead on.

In the meantime, though, we had our hands full.

While the defenders were isolated in the towers by the lightning and the flying shadows, the first Peruni soldiers had gained the top of the wall, and there were a lot of them. This was a full-scale assault, rather than the end run to try to get the gate open that they'd tried on the first wall. They'd learned from that experience.

Santos turned from his firing port, leveled the Mk 48, then cursed and dropped it to the floor, drawing his axe. I hesitated briefly—there were bad guys on both sides of our tower—then moved to join him. Mathghaman, Bearrac, and Gunny had already stepped to the doorway behind me.

Neither of us stepped right into the doorway. The lightning still flickered right outside, hammering into the stone of the wall in a constant, strobing curtain of electricity, blasting glowing bits of rock into the air at each impact like red-hot shrapnel and battering us with the thunderous shockwaves. It was worse than getting shot at, and neither one of us was willing to risk getting hit by one of those bolts. Fortunately, that wall of sorcerous electricity also stood between us and our enemies.

Not for long, though. Almost at the same moment I thought it, the lightning storm ceased, and the first Peruni swordsmen charged us.

They all wore coats of scales and peaked iron caps with heavy leather strips hanging over their necks. A couple of them had similar aventails covering their faces. Their shields were oval, with the rather ironic sunburst of Ar-Annator being the most prominent emblem painted on them. Their swords were short and broad, their hand-guards thick discs of bronze.

They didn't rush us like savages. That would have been suicide, anyway, since we held a choke point. These men weren't amateurs. I didn't doubt that they'd done this before.

Crouched behind their shields, only their eyes and their blades showing, they advanced on the doorway. They didn't present much in the way of targets.

At least, they didn't to an enemy who was going to get in close with blades.

I didn't have time to sheathe the Sword. I took a second to set it on the floor, leaning against the stone wall, as gently as I could, then drew my .45.

Their shields and armor might be proof against swords and armor, but let's see how they do against .45 ACP.

Somewhat to my surprise, the first shot didn't penetrate the closest man's helmet. It still knocked him out from the sheer force of its impact, and dented it so deeply that it *might* have cracked his skull, but it wasn't the kill shot I'd been going for.

Still, he crashed backward, and the man behind him wasn't ready for it. They both went over the side of the wall, falling toward the rocky ground below.

I'd already shifted to the next one back, who had ducked beneath his shield. After that first shot, I wasn't sure how well the bullet was going to go through that, but I shot it three times anyway. It was just wood and hide, and I was shooting ball rounds, so they *should* penetrate.

He howled and dropped to a knee as a gush of blood painted the stones beneath him red. I shifted to the man behind him, who had just figured out that he needed to close the distance fast.

Santos shot him in the temple, just beneath the rim of his helmet. Blood spurted and he fell on his face.

Then the rest of them rushed us, trampling the bodies of the fallen to get in close. It wasn't a breakdown in discipline, like we'd seen with the Dovos. It was the recognition that if they left us any breathing room, we'd gun them down two by two.

Unfortunately for that first one, I still had five rounds in the gun. I punched his short, broad-bladed sword aside with my buckler and shot him over the shield rim, practically a contact shot to his eyeball. It was definitely close enough that I'm sure I flash-burned his eyelid just before the two-hundred-thirty-grain bullet smashed through it and cored out his brains.

I had to shove his corpse into the next man's way, just before Santos shot him, then I nailed another one through the neck. I wasn't doing my best pistol shooting, considering I was shooting strong hand only and barely looking at the sights, but we were so close that I'd have to get *really* sloppy to miss altogether.

Then the slide locked back on an empty mag, and I had to drop the weapon and scoop up the Sword. If I'd had the time to think about it, I might have winced at treating a 1911 that way, but survival was at stake.

Our allies hadn't been idle, however. Before I could do much more than parry the thrust that came for my eyes over the top of the next man's shield, a Galel bellow of, "Stand clear!" sounded behind me.

Two burly knights, backed up by enough men-at-arms to make the tower pretty crowded and armed with big axes, shouldered into the breach. The first one, his tunic and crest a brilliant, vermilion green, brought that curved axe crashing down atop the shield rim of the man I'd been fighting, hooked the shield and pulled it back, then rammed the upper horn of the axe blade up under the man's chin.

Then, as I fell back into the tower to give the Galel room to swing, they got to work.

CHAPTER 17

THE rest of that day turned into a blur of sweat, herculean effort, and pain.

Those ladders were only the first wave. The Galel who had relieved us fought them back from our portion of the wall, though it was touch and go toward the south end. At least two towers were seized and had to be taken back, slowly and bloodily, before the Peruni could get men on the ground on the inside of the wall, in an attempt to get the gates open.

With our tower somewhat secure, I was able to retrieve my pistol, reload, and get back on the firing slits to worry about the rest of the oncoming forces while the Galel retook the battlements.

The mortars had severely damaged one of the siege towers, but the others were still coming on, spreading out between the gaps in the wall and trundling across the rocky killing ground beneath the second wall. They were having a rough go of it but, all the same, it looked like they'd been built with rough terrain in mind. Between their wide wheelbases and forward lean, it was clear that the engineers who had built them had expected that they wouldn't make it all the way flush with the wall.

Another one went up in flames somewhere off to our right, even as I tried to get a shot on the men and animals

pushing the nearest toward the wall. They were well-pro-
tected, though, almost all behind the engine, where even
with a rifle I couldn't get to them. We could only lob what
grenades we had at the advancing monstrosity, knowing
that sooner or later, it was going to get to us.

The engine wasn't alone, either. Even as it creaked
up to the wall, more ladder carriers came running up,
while the massive drawbridge on the front of the tower
rattled down toward the battlements.

We held our position while the Galel fell back toward
the tower, their shields interlocked, preparing for the
onslaught. There was only so much we could do about
the ladders, and I expected that the greatest threat was
probably going to come from the towers. Sure enough,
as soon as that drawbridge hit the wall with a *boom*, a
platoon of howling berserkers came charging across the
bridge. They were bare-chested and wearing little more
than buckskin trousers and knee-high boots, their brown
and blond hair pulled to one side, most with an axe in
one hand and a long knife in the other. They were only
the vanguard, though. The heavily armored Peruni infantry, crouching behind oval shields, advanced in a tight
formation behind them, short spears leveled over the
shield rims.

Santos raked the berserkers with a long burst of machinegun fire, killing half of them in the first couple of
seconds. True to his 0331 machinegunner roots, he kept
the line of his fire right about at knee height, chopping
the imperial auxiliaries' legs out of from under them and
sending them crashing down into the stream of high-velocity metal, bullets smashing through stomachs, lungs,

hearts, and heads. Even if they'd been as armored as the Peruni, at that range they wouldn't have stood a chance.

Things were actually starting to look like we might be able to hold without too much more difficulty, but then the wizards had to stick their oar in again.

A roll of thunder rumbled across the sky, though it sounded strange, off. The very world seemed to tilt for a moment. I felt a flash of nausea as a stabbing pain built in my head. Then the first of the oily black horrors dipped down out of the sky.

I'd fought these things before. They were so black that they seemed to drink the light except where eyes sprouted from odd places. Vast wings beat at the air, though they were so unnatural that it hardly seemed as if they should interact with the real world in any meaningful way. Their shapes were hard to make out, seeming to shift every time you looked at them.

They ignored the Galel on the walls, some of whom had reacted to their presence by curling up in the fetal position or puking their guts out where they dropped to their knees. Those horrors were meant for us.

The first one slammed into the tower right at my arrow slit, a long—and growing—limb tipped with talons the size of my forearm speared through the slit and grabbed for my head. If I believed in fortune anymore, I'd say it was only sheer, unadulterated luck that allowed me to throw myself aside just fast enough that those talons closed on empty air.

Another one of those flying nightmares had alighted on the roof and I could hear it tearing the defenders up there to shreds, even over the sounds of battle all along the wall and Santos's continued fire. It only took seconds. Then it was ripping at the timbers of the roof, even as the one at the window clawed at the stone, that long arm stretching still farther, more eyes sprouting along its length as it searched for its prey.

We weren't prey, though. I already knew how to fight these things.

Letting my rifle hang, since there was no time to move it around to my back, I drew the Sword of Iudicael, sending a wordless plea to its original owner to stand by me and give me a hand, and waded in.

But when I took a swing at that arm as it darted toward my face, it suddenly sucked back toward the window, shrinking even faster than it had speared its way into the room. Whatever that thing was, whatever hellish place it had come from, it knew what that Sword was, and it knew what I could do with it.

I advanced on it anyway, as much as every fiber of my being screamed at me to get as far away as possible. Thrusting the Sword out through the arrow slit, I stabbed it right in a mouth that seemed to open in the center of its chest, long, translucent fangs dripping with ichor that dissolved into smoke as it fell.

Blue flame erupted around the blade, tearing through the thing as it thrashed and shrieked, the noise stabbing through my eardrums and driving me to my knees. I held on to the Sword as if it was a lifeline, and it slid out of the rapidly dissolving nightmare as if it weren't even there.

Rolling back to my feet, though somewhat unsteadily, I looked up just as the next abomination tore a hole in the ceiling above us. Shattered splinters of ancient wood rained down as timbers and boards cracked and split, and then the thing was swarming down through the opening.

Its wings had disappeared, and now it had sprouted a myriad of legs, scrabbling along the ceiling like a horrifying cross between a spider and a centipede. Farrar shot it, though the bullet did nothing but draw its attention, and it twisted around with what might have been a glare of hatred and sprang at him.

I threw myself at it, trying to get between it and my teammate, swinging the Sword at the nearest whiplike tentacle that lashed out toward Farrar's throat.

It tried to evade, almost as if it had only just then noticed that a Sword Bearer was in the room, despite what had just happened to its fellow clinging to the wall. Maybe these things didn't have the best perception of their surroundings in the physical world.

While they could be touched, these sorcerous monstrosities could still defy physics. It seemed to change course ninety degrees in midair, darting aside to get away from the Sword of Iudicael and landing on the opposite wall.

I went after it. It might sound heroic and everything, but let me assure you, chasing something like that is a horrifying prospect that any sane man would quail at. Every part of me wanted to run. Only the fear of losing yet another teammate drove me to attack it.

If I'd stopped to think about it even for a fraction of a second, I never would have dared. But I was committed, and I kind of made a point of not thinking about it. I just went at it like a monkey with a meat cleaver.

While those abominations might have been not entirely of the physical realm, they had still physically manifested enough that they couldn't simply slip through a solid stone wall. It slithered rapidly toward the nearest arrow slit, but not quite fast enough to entirely evade the slash that would have laid it open had it been a creature of flesh and blood.

As it was, it burst into violent blue flames, melting to black sludge as the scream shook the very tower itself. I think I blacked out for a moment from not only the force of the noise, but the sheer hatred and despair behind it.

If I did, it was only for a moment. I shook my head, regretting the movement immediately, and looked around to see that the Galel had been pressed back still more, and while we'd broken the berserker charge, the armored infantry were pushing hard, and more of them were coming up through the tower. Unless it was set ablaze immediately—which would present some problems for us up on the wall, too—then the enemy had a semi-permanent foothold already.

Fighting through the throbbing pain in my skull, I hauled myself back to my feet and got back into the fight.

* * *

The day dragged on. We switched out with the Galel as the fight ebbed and flowed along the wall. Reinforcements kept coming up, but they were limited. Uven and Tarvedum still had to maintain a reserve, though there was a balance to be struck there. Let the wall fall, and the eventual fall of the fortress and the loss of the kingdom was that much closer. Spend all their forces defending that wall, and the entire fortress might fall when the next blow fell. We were outnumbered. Defense in depth was our only advantage.

The waves of Peruni infantry were interspersed with auxiliaries and once with something that looked an awful lot like a troll. None of the Peruni or the auxiliaries seemed to want to get close to it and, considering that it had to weigh five hundred pounds, had jaws like a hippo, and smelled like a sewer, that was understandable. Our gunfire only seemed to make it angrier, and only when Bearrac grappled with it and got his blade up into its guts did it finally go down. He heaved it past him and let it crash down onto the ground at the base of the wall.

A few hours later, a Galel knight named Gurum led a charge that almost succeeded in taking the siege tower. He got all the way across the drawbridge before running into a phalanx of dismounted cataphracts that he and his swordsmen couldn't break. They crashed to a halt against the wall of short spears, and Gurum was pierced through the throat and groin before being thrown to his death outside the second wall.

Machinegun fire forced the cataphracts back, but the enemy still held the tower.

The siege engine had held up to a hell of a battering. It was now too close to the wall to risk mortar fire, but 40mm grenades were taking bites out of it. Just not big enough bites to matter. Splinters lay scattered on the ground below, and some of the hides were blackened and shredded, but the tower still stood.

We had to bring it down somehow.

Yet no one could get close enough to even try to set it alight. Archers were now perched atop the thing, though they stayed behind cover and concealment most of the time until someone on our side tried to get close. Then they'd pop up and shoot him full of shafts before dropping down again. We'd perforated their barriers with quite a few bullets, but wherever they were hunkering down, it was below the barricade, because we never seemed to hit any of them. Or at least not enough of them to matter.

Some of the Galel came up to the wall a short time later with fire pots. They didn't have a lot of range, essentially being small clay pots filled with pitch on the end of a rope, so they could only fly so far as a man could fling them. That was a problem when there were archers in an elevated position.

But we had rifles and machineguns, and Tarvedum was hoping we could cover for them.

The men lit the pots and ran forward during a lull in the fighting. One immediately took an arrow through the eye and fell, the pot dropping off the edge of the drawbridge to shatter in a burst of sparks and flames on the rocks below. Two more went down almost as quickly, one to an arrow, another to a javelin hurled from inside the tower.

We opened fire on the top of the siege tower then, punching rounds through hide, wicker, and wood. Several archers dropped, shot through the vitals or the head, and the remaining Galel charged forward.

The Peruni infantry saw the danger and counterattacked immediately, moving out onto the drawbridge to head off the attackers and the threat of the fire that they carried. These guys weren't dumb.

But the Galel were desperate, and entirely willing to sacrifice themselves to bring that tower down. Most of them didn't get close enough, flinging their fire pots just before they were stabbed or cut down, still far enough away that the pots were either deflected off to the sides or, if they hit and broke on the drawbridge, the flames could be quickly stamped out.

Then one brave man, an axe in one hand and a fire-pot in the other, threw himself on the Peruni spears as he hurled his firepot, hard enough that it shattered on the shredded hides above the opening at the back of the drawbridge. Burning pitch sprayed over the topmost story of the tower, and in a few moments, the fire had caught and was taking hold.

The Peruni retreated, though we shot a few more before they got through the flames and down below. Between us and the archers, we managed to keep anyone with water or sand at bay until the entire top of the tower was fully involved. Then several men got to work on the drawbridge with axes, hoping to break it and throw it down before it caught fire and brought the conflagration clear to the battlements.

That seemed to be the final straw for the assault on the second wall. A braying, angry-sounding horn called out, and the Peruni began to withdraw, in good order, holding their formations of shields up as they drew back.

There were considerably fewer of them now, but still far too many.

Even so, the wall had held.

For now.

CHAPTER 18

THE view from the third wall was different.

Tarvedum had prevailed to switch out as many of the defenders on the second wall as possible, and Gunny had been way ahead of him already. It had been a grueling fight, though I doubt any of us knew exactly how long it had dragged on. We were all completely exhausted.

Fortunately, none of us had been killed. Hundreds lay dead on and beneath the wall, but the platoon had weathered it. For certain values of the word, anyway.

We slumped against the walls inside the tower, most of us too tired to do much of anything, but too shell-shocked to sleep. I know every time I closed my eyes, I saw blood, and death, and monsters out of the deepest pits of the Outer Dark.

For a long time, we just sort of sat there in a haze. Silent. Staring at nothing. Trying not to think too hard of what we'd just been through.

It wasn't our first rodeo. Not even our first siege. We'd faced nightmares at Vahava Paykhah, and even that bloodletting hadn't quite equaled this. Even massacring the entire Lasknut and rogue Dovo army when Vaelor—or whatever Outsider had really sponsored their assault—had gotten tired of them and ripped their sanity away hadn't gotten quite to this level of bloodshed.

I knew that there had been engagements in Syria that had come close to the last day. There had been a distance to it, however. There's a difference between seeing airstrikes and artillery hammering a city and being up close and personal as the blood is flowing down the walls like waterfalls, and smashed and mangled bodies are packed underfoot or falling to smack messily on the rocks below.

The stench rising from the wall was even reaching us there in the tower five hundred yards above. Either that, or it was so thoroughly impregnated into my sinuses that I'd never get rid of it.

Gunny had gone higher up to consult with Tarvedum. Now, after what felt like either too long or too short a time, he came back in, slumping down against the wall after carefully leaning his rifle on the stones next to him. "Looks like they're not ready for the next push just yet. They've hunkered down behind the barricades. Licking their wounds."

Gurke snorted. "Just means they'll turn to sorcery again. The guardian might have saved our asses back there, but I'm sure the Dullahans have plenty more tricks up their sleeves."

"Maybe." Gunny ran a hand over his face. He ignored the spatters of blood on his hand. I was sure I was just as rough. "I think they got a hell of a shock from that, though. I can't say why, but something seemed to set them back." He looked over at me. "The Sword of Iudicael might have dealt with the things they summoned here, but those monsters didn't have much better luck elsewhere. The guardian showed up again."

"Well, that's something." Bailey's voice was more muted than usual. He was a quiet man most of the time, despite his innate aggression, but exhaustion had him more subdued than I think I'd ever seen him.

"So, what do we do now?" Chambers looked absolutely drained, and there was a note of what might have been trepidation in his voice. He was no slacker, but we were all tired enough that the prospect of getting right back up and back into the fight after what was probably close to a full day of the most brutal, grueling combat we'd ever seen wasn't appealing to anyone in that room at the moment.

"For the next few hours at least, everyone's racking the hell out." Gunny grinned like a skull at the muted sighs of relief that everyone in the room was trying not to show but was obviously feeling anyway. "Things are quiet right at the moment, and we're not on the front line anymore. Furthermore, any forays beyond the wall aren't all that likely in the near future." He stood up, stifling a yawn as he did so. "So, make sure your weapons are clean, ammo's topped off—as much as possible, anyway—and that we're ready for when the next wave *does* come, and get some sleep."

Most of that we'd taken care of through sheer force of habit, before we'd even sat down. I heaved myself to my feet to check Farrar and Santos anyway, just to be on the safe side. I was so dead tired that I couldn't entirely trust that I hadn't missed something. Santos, for his part, was already checking on Farrar, though he was still sitting as he did so.

Conall came in. Most of the Tuacha had headed up to the keep to consult with Brother Domech, Tarvedum's chaplain. It must have been a brief meeting. Either that, or I was already drifting and had lost track of time.

All the Tuacha had a bit of an otherworldly aura about them, but it was even stronger with Conall. I couldn't say that he was an out-and-out mystic, but if he wasn't, he was awfully close. We hadn't seen him for a while before we'd come to Cor Chatha, since he'd stayed with the people of Cor Wudrun, helping against a sorcerous plague that had struck that place just prior to King Uven's arrival, and the ambush that had laid him low for nearly two weeks. As events had converged on the Rock of Battle, however, he'd returned, though he'd shown up more quickly than could have been explained by a messenger finding him at Cor Wudrun.

He crouched next to Gurke and put a hand on his shoulder. "Let some modicum of Tigharn's peace rest upon you and give you rest, even if only for a little while." Gurke visibly relaxed a little, and his eyes closed.

Conall went around the room then, laying a hand on each man in turn and murmuring much the same prayer, sometimes in the *Tenga Tuacha*, sometimes in the more ancient language they use for prayer and invocation.

He came to me near the end. I almost drew away, but he nodded to me, gripping my shoulder firmly. If I'd been worried that he'd put some sort of spell on me, that it would feel like I was being drugged, I needn't have. A sense of peace settled over me, despite the horrors of the last few days, and I relaxed, closing my eyes and letting exhaustion take me.

* * *

My sleep was dreamless and deep. I was still tired when I came awake, I didn't know how many hours later, but I wasn't achingly exhausted the way I had been.

I sat up to find that most of the platoon was still out. The windows were still dark, too. That pall of unnatural storm clouds still blotted out the sky. Even as I glanced up through the narrow slit in the stone wall, another bolt of lightning forked across the clouds above, lighting up the inside of the room starkly, in contrast to the single candle that had remained lit as we'd gone to sleep.

I wasn't the only one up, though. Gurke was sitting up, his arms wrapped around his knees, staring at the floor. He looked up at me as I sat up, and his eyes were haunted.

"What's up, Ross?" I kept my voice low, almost a whisper.

He looked down again, his face screwing up slightly as he thought through what to say. I'd never been close with Gurke. He was a bit of a contrarian, but some of that seemed to be only intended to make his mark. He wasn't like Zimmerman, who had been so committed to being that contrarian that he'd sided with Captain Sorenson, and eventually Dragon Mask. Gurke was just kind of the odd man out.

"I…" He hesitated. He was also one of those who'd had the hardest time adjusting to the mystical side of things here. He was a concrete sort of guy, the one who didn't *want* to believe in anything he couldn't see, hear, or touch. "I saw Cairbre."

I had to raise an eyebrow at that. Cairbre had been one of Mathghaman's companions, one of the group who had joined the platoon out of loyalty to the King's

Champion, rather than any affection or attachment to the foreigners from beyond the mists. He hadn't thought much of us, and while he'd certainly pulled his weight, finally sacrificing himself to save Gunny from Vaelor's wrath as the Outsider had threatened to break free of his stony prison, he'd always been aloof and impatient with us, barely saying a word unless directly addressed. He hadn't been a likeable man, and it was even more odd that Gurke of all people should have dreamed about him.

"Sometimes we dream about some weird stuff." I didn't really have much more comment to make than that, especially since it was Gurke. He could get prickly sometimes.

He shook his head. "I don't think this was a dream." His eyes lifted to mine again, and even in the dim light of the candle, I could tell he was uncertain about elaborating. He was worried that I might think he was crazy, that he was buying into all this mystical, magic stuff.

I could have given him some grief about it. After all, after the nearly two years we'd been there, we should all have seen enough to accept what was right in front of us. I just inclined my head to encourage him to proceed, though.

"It was vivid as hell." He wasn't looking at me anymore, his eyes fixed on something only he could see. "I was standing in a great hall, kinda like at Cor Legear, but bigger. Way bigger. I couldn't even see the ceiling.

"He was waiting for me. Still in his armor, but it seemed shinier. He didn't smile, but he seemed like he was... I dunno. Like he wasn't as pissed off as he always acted. Like he was actually glad to see me." Gurke sounded a little perplexed and given Cairbre's attitude

while he'd been alive—and Gurke's—that was understandable. "He even called me Ross.

"Then he told me that we all have to be ready to die."

He fell silent at that, staring into the distance with a
faint frown on his face. "He didn't say it like a threat, or
anything. He said it like, I don't know… dad advice. He
said that it's not something to be afraid of if you're ready
for it. If your… he said, 'If your honor is clean.'"

At that, Gurke finally brought his gaze back to the
here and now and locked eyes with me. "But at the end
of it all, he told me that we *had* to get ready to die."

I didn't have a reply at first. How do you answer that?
The truth was, on some level, we'd needed to be ready to
die from the instant we stood on the yellow footprints at
boot camp. Not everybody thought that way, because the
human impulse is to think, "It's not going to happen to
me." And the longer you work in a high-risk profession
without getting messed up or killed, the stronger that impulse gets.

It wasn't something most of us thought about, especially in the materialistic world we'd grown up in. But
if there *is* something after, what does it mean if you've
lived a life that you know is finite as if it's never going
to end?

"Well, he's not wrong when you think about it." I
looked up at the arrow slit again, as another lightning
bolt strobed above us. "How many of us are left, after not
even two years? We've all got to die sometime."

Gurke nodded, though I could tell he was withdraw-
ing again, thinking over the vision of Cairbre. From his
description, I was now fairly sure that he was right, that
it had been a vision, not just a dream. Our fallen com-

panion had come back to warn us, through Gurke of all people, to be ready for the end.

Whether that was a prophecy that none of us were going to get out of this place or not, I didn't know, and if Cairbre's spirit had told Gurke, I was sure he would have said something about it.

I wished I could ask Iudicael. Realizing that I'd spent some time in meditation with him present before, I adjusted myself so I could lean back against the stone wall and closed my eyes.

He didn't come, though. The messengers of Tigharn are not at our beck and call, not all the time. They will come when they are needed, but while it hadn't been said outright, I had gathered from our interactions that there was a degree of hands-off involved. We still had to work out our own destiny. They'd help, but they wouldn't do all the work for us.

That was probably why the guardian didn't just send the entire army of Ar-Annator packing, too.

There were no easy answers. So, sitting there in the quiet and the dark, as thunder rumbled outside, I prayed like I don't think I ever had before.

CHAPTER 19

IT might have been day. It seemed slightly less dark. That made targeting easier.

The next assault still hadn't materialized yet. There was a lot of activity back there beyond the barricades they'd erected inside the wreckage of the first wall, but they hadn't advanced again. That gave us an opportunity to sow some more chaos and disruption in their ranks.

I had taken my M107 back from Gunny before we'd headed back down to the second wall, though he'd handed it over with exaggerated sorrow. It had a lot more range than I necessarily needed, but I wanted the punch. It might not harm one of the Dullahans, but I was banking on the wizards to have some nasty tricks up their sleeves too, and I wanted something that was going to ignore those tricks like only a six-hundred-seventy-one-grain bullet with a small explosive charge behind a tungsten penetrator can.

So far, though, I hadn't found a target, and I'd been scanning the enemy lines for over an hour. The mortar fire had taught them to avoid giving us something to shoot at. The wizards and generals were keeping their heads down.

There. I caught a glint of gilded metal and shifted my sights to find it again. The man in the high, crested helmet with a scale aventail had forgotten to keep his head down.

For a moment I just watched him, my finger resting on the receiver above the trigger, my breathing even and steady, ready to hit that natural respiratory pause and squeeze off a shot at any time. It had taken some doing to get a table up into the tower and a bench set up behind it, but I now had a good, solid shooting position from which I could engage almost the entire center of the enemy encampment through one of the arrow slits.

The concussion inside that tower when I corked off that .50 was going to be brutal, but sometimes you've got to make sacrifices.

I wasn't worrying about the muzzle blast as I watched this guy, though. I was wondering if he was worth one of our dwindling supply of Raufoss rounds.

The longer I watched him, the more I was convinced he wasn't. He was important, that was certain, pointing and gesturing as he directed his underlings on some task doubtless aimed at our eventual overrun and extermination. But he was an ordinary man in shiny armor, nothing more. I saw no signs of sorcery or unnatural protection.

He merited a 7.62 round, not one of our precious .50s.

I resumed my scan.

It didn't take long before I had another target, one that might just merit the big .50.

He was talking with one of the Dullahans. That alone was an indicator. Most of the Peruni—the sane ones, anyway—stayed as far away from those horrors as possible. That this guy was apparently having a chat with one meant he was either insane or he was a wizard. Or both. At any rate, that probably meant he rated a Raufoss round.

He was armored almost just like the man I'd been watching a moment before, though less ostentatiously gilded. A dark cape covered his shoulders, though it didn't go past his waist. A curved sword sat at his hip, more of a cavalry weapon than the short, broad-bladed stabbing swords that most of the infantry carried. I couldn't see his face; he had his back to the wall and was facing the Dullahan, the one that wore strange gear that looked an awful lot like black fatigues and a plate carrier. With a bit better view, they weren't *quite* the modern accoutrements they resembled, but this Dullahan was decidedly different from the rest of the Thirty.

I wondered at that. The Tuacha had told us that the Dullahans were believed to be the Summoner's first disciples, and that the Summoning had broken a world already civilized and slouching into depravity and decay. Was that why things had been getting weird back in the World just before we'd passed through the mists? Was that why this creature appeared to be wearing modern-looking gear while everyone else looked like they'd just come out of the tenth century?

I sure wasn't going to go down there and ask.

Under different circumstances, I might have waited until my target was a little more isolated, but there was no point. It wasn't as if the enemy didn't know we were up there. It was his fault if he wasn't paying attention to cover and concealment, after we'd shot dozens of his fellows from up on the second wall.

I already had the scope dialed in. I'd gotten used to using holds, simply shifting the scope to compensate for the wind and the elevation rather than dialing the turrets, especially since the scope the *Coira Ansec* had provided us had come complete with a mil-grid reticle. For this, though, I'd gone ahead and adjusted the elevation, so the center crosshair would provide point-of-aim, point-of-impact shots at the distance between the walls. The wind was negligible at that point; the storm seemed to have left the ground level winds dead while the black clouds slowly turned overhead.

So, I put the crosshairs on the center of my target's back, flipped the selector to "Fire," and started to squeeze the trigger as I let my breath out.

The trigger broke right as my lungs emptied, and the shock of the shot rocked me back on the bench. The *boom* echoed out over the wall, and the shockwave from the angled muzzle brake hammered the inside of the tower, blasting dust off the tabletop and giving everyone inside—myself included—an instant headache.

I'd called the shot as soon as the trigger had broken. It was an old habit instilled by years of Marine Corps marksmanship training. Always note where the sights are when the shot breaks. I knew it was good even before I recovered from the recoil and got back on the scope.

Sure enough, the armored wizard was down, the mangled remains of his corpse just barely visible on the ground at the Dullahan's feet. I'd had a narrow window between barricades to work with.

The Dullahan had lifted its head, the eyes glowing a pale orange, and stared toward the tower. I didn't doubt that it could look right through the arrow slit and see me up there behind the rifle, ready to knock that head through the gap in the wall behind it, just because.

It didn't react, though, except to step to one side, disappearing behind the wicker-and-hide barricade. I could have blasted a few more rounds through that barricade after it, but it didn't seem that useful, especially when we only had so much ammo left. Had to make every shot count.

I waited for a few moments, for either the Dullahan to show itself again, or to retaliate with a curse or a summoning that we'd have to find a way to deal with. Nothing happened. It had slipped away and left things as they were.

With a faint shrug, I went back to scanning for other targets.

As I did, however, the darkness seemed to deepen again. I heard an exclamation and came off the scope to see one of the Galel facing the door onto the top of the wall, his sword drawn and pointed over his shield. "What is it?"

He didn't respond right away, but slowly lowered his weapon. "I thought I saw something move over there."

I watched him for a moment, letting my gaze slip out onto the top of the wall. I had my NVGs mounted but flipped up. It was dark and dim out there, but PVS-15s don't play well with magnified optics. Something about the *Coira Ansec*'s glass seemed to amplify light and make it easier to see in the twilight, too. The middle of the section of wall between us and the next tower was shrouded in shadow, but I should have been able to see anything silhouetted against the dim glow of the lanterns in the next tower.

There was nothing there.

Dismissing his nerves, I turned back to the open ground between the walls, but before I could get back on sights, something made me stop, flip down my NVGs, and scan the no-man's-land below.

I had to stare for a moment to be sure I was seeing what I thought I was seeing. There was movement out there, but it wasn't an enemy advance. At least, not the Peruni, Avur, or any other human enemy.

Shadows flitted and flowed along the rocky ground. They moved like snakes, spiders, and scorpions, and disappeared whenever I looked directly at them. They were always there, though, just visible at the edges of my vision.

I flipped up the NVGs and got back on the scope. If things were getting weirder, then that told me that something big was coming. And the Dullahans were probably behind it.

I couldn't kill them with bullets, but we'd seen at Gremman that we could at least make them uncomfortable enough to disrupt whatever they were trying to do.

None of them were in sight, though. In fact, it looked like everyone and everything down in the enemy's camp had gone to ground. Even the movement we'd seen before had vanished. Everything but the shadows creeping and slithering toward the second wall was still.

The pressure in the air got heavier. I could have sworn I caught a whiff ozone.

Another yell sounded out on the wall somewhere, answered by a tormented moan. A flicker of movement in my peripheral vision drew me away from the M107 suddenly, as I snapped my head around, my hand dropping to the .45 at my hip as I thought someone had just lunged at me from my left. There was nothing there.

Lightning forked across the sky once more, and that thunderstorm tension got immensely worse. A faint droning started out in the Peruni camp, a chant that got into your head and scratched at your eardrums. It was eerie, guttural, and discordant. It sounded more like the chants Dragon Mask and his renegade Dovos had used than anything we'd heard from the Peruni so far.

A thin, high wail went up to the sky, and I heard Santos yell, even as pandemonium broke out in one of the nearby towers. I came entirely off the rifle then, kicking the bench over as I surged to my feet, grabbing the Sword of Iudicael and the buckler that I carried affixed to its scabbard. I might have drawn my Bowie in my off hand, but my family's knife—that my grandfather had carried in World War II, my father had carried in Vietnam, and I had carried in Syria—had been snapped at the hilt during my duel with the Dullahan in Cor Legear, only weeks before.

I turned toward where Santos stood with his Mk 48 pointed, to see a translucent figure standing in the doorway, pointing at us and screaming incomprehensibly in a voice that sounded far, far away.

If we were supposed to recognize the figure, the enemy had slipped. I had no idea who or what this thing was supposed to be. I advanced on it with the Sword of Iudicael held in a high guard, just in case it was more formidable than the last phantom I'd encountered.

Before I could reach it, though, it completely freaked out, whirling like a dervish before it vanished into the stones beneath our feet.

I stepped out onto the wall, looking around with the Sword in my fist. As I did so, the wind, which had been dead for some time, suddenly picked up, plucking at me where I stood, and something hit my helmet with a *tap*. Seconds later, a torrent of icy hail lashed the battlements. The lightning increased in violence and frequency, and thunder rumbled continuously overhead. Shadows crept over the ramparts to slither along the top of the wall, though they quite noticeably avoided getting too close to the Sword of Iudicael.

We retreated back into the tower. The hail pelted us like falling nails, and the wind had intensified, blasting it into our faces. If the Peruni hadn't also faced the same conditions, I would have expected them to push the next assault while we were hunkered down hiding from the weather.

In fact, as that occurred to me, I moved quickly back to the M107 and got behind the big rifle, looking over the killing ground before the second wall as best I could through the windswept sheets of hail. I frowned. Still nothing moved.

Yet the sense of trepidation and impending doom deepened. *Something* was coming. Something big. The weather, as unnatural as it was, wouldn't have taken this turn otherwise. If they weren't going to try to storm the third wall, what were they up to?

Then a titanic lightning blast, bigger and brighter than any of the bolts yet, split the sky. It seemed to flicker from horizon to horizon, and almost lingered there, hanging like lightning just doesn't do.

And through the thunder, a roar sounded that shook the very mountain beneath our feet.

Then, with a rattle of leathery wings, a black dragon that looked almost as big as an aircraft carrier dove out of the clouds toward the fortress.

CHAPTER 20

ITS wings kicked up whorls in the clouds and the hail, and the purple-tinged lightning seemed to cling to it as it flew in a lazy circle around the fortress, momentarily disappearing behind the peak that loomed above the citadel. It let out another roar that drowned out the thunder as more lightning flashed, one bolt slamming into the peak itself hard enough that shards of molten rock flew from the impact.

The dragon loomed out of the dark again, coming around the peak with another croaking roar. Lightning flickered around its jaws. Every stroke of those mighty wings stirred up the wind and battered at the walls beneath it.

That thing was enormous. I'd thought the red dragon we'd fought in Gremman had been big. This was easily twice its size, its scales jet black yet gleaming even in the twilight under the clouds. Its head was slightly more triangular than the red's, too.

There was something about that thing that fueled a deep sense of dread. It was more than its size. More than the fact that it was a dragon, several hundred feet long. There was a weight of evil in it that I hadn't experienced since the Throne of Vaelor.

This thing was an Outsider, an eldritch abomination from the Outer Dark. I suddenly knew it as clear as day. One of the enemy's "elder gods" had just entered the fray.

I'd expected one of the greatest enemies of all that is natural and good to be more like the shadow demon we'd fought in Cor Legear. Formless, always shifting darkness. This thing seemed entirely solid, yet I couldn't shake that sense of tangible *wrongness* to it. I had no doubt that we were now facing the most dangerous foe we'd ever even heard of. Vaelor had been imprisoned. This thing was flying right over our heads.

It continued its circle, flapping its wings almost languidly, its baleful eye roving over the defenses as it flew through the storm.

Then it laughed. It was a terrible sound, worse by far than all of the screaming and roaring that we'd heard from the otherworldly horrors that we'd fought since we'd come through the mists. It was a sound of madness and hate wrapped up with derision and uttermost pride. There was no humor, no mirth in that blast of noise. Only an invitation to despair.

"*Such defiance. Such bravery. Such useless pride. Look upon my majesty, thou puny worms, and throw thyselves to thy deaths! Canst thou stand against such as I?*" The blast of its voice hit with almost physical force, rattling hail against the walls and blowing through the arrow slits. "*I have withered entire worlds with but a glance, burned whole civilizations with a gust of my breath. Thy resistance is laughable. I shall rip thy souls from thy fragile shells and thrust thee naked, one by one, into the Outer Dark, to writhe and scream under the pitiless gaze of the infinite nothingness for all eternity. I am Death such as thou hast never imagined. I am the End."*

Just the words don't do justice to their effect. There was such a depth of malice in them, such a weight of pure, unalloyed malevolence, that they were far scarier to hear, to experience, than can ever be put into any mere words. And it was having its effect on the men on the wall.

That thing hadn't even finished speaking before a man in our tower completely lost his mind, screaming as he clamped his hands over his ears and tried to break for the doorway leading out onto the battlements. Two of his companions grabbed him and wrestled him down to the floor, but he kept screaming until one of them hit him over the head hard enough to leave him dazed.

"Tie him up and gag him." Lord Talore was a younger knight, his hair and beard black, his skin pale. "If he recovers, we will send him back to the higher wall." He looked up at the arrow slits. "Were there any way to block out that thing's speech."

That hateful, mocking roar of a laugh drifted down from the sky again, as more screams and wails rose from the walls, as men who were perhaps weaker in mind—or less prepared for death—started to lose it.

"Yes! Wail and mourn, for fate has come for thee! Forget all sweet tales of light and comfort! Night has come upon thee, and the morn shall never again dawn! The pathetic little spark of light thou didst enjoy has gone out, as was always inevitable!"

It slithered across the sky, and for a moment, it almost seemed as if its wings were more of an affectation than a necessary means of flight. Then it was all too physical as it alighted atop the broken gate of the first wall, its tail reaching nearly all the way across the wall to the south side and its neck and head rearing high over the rampart. The impact of its landing shook the very ground beneath us.

"*I see thee, 'dragon slayer,' even as thou dost cower amidst the rubble and behind the pathetic excuses for warriors whom thou callest friends.*" It glared across the no-man's-land between walls. "*The red thou didst kill in Gremman was but an insignificant worm, hardly worthy to be called a dragon. Think thee that thou shouldst take pride in such a feat?*" It spread those vast wings, and they stretched for nearly two hundred feet in either direction, intensifying the shadow around it, while that purplish corposant once again crackled around its fangs and in its eyes. "*I shall teach thee the price of thy temerity. Even such a miserable little one as that was still far beyond thee.*" Its head slithered forward, its neck stretching a good way across the open killing ground. "*Come out, 'dragon slayer.' Come out and face me. Prove what a great warrior thou art!*" Its voice shook the tower where we stood.

I could almost see Bailey staring at it from the tower where he'd set up about two hundred yards over. For a moment, knowing my brother the way I did, I was afraid he was going to take it up on its challenge. Even with the Sword of Categyrn, I feared he wouldn't have a chance against *that*.

Then I realized that my hand had dropped to the Sword of Iudicael at my side.

"*Come, bearers of the Swords of those messengers of false hope! Face me, or I shall blast this fortress to slag and tear your wailing spirits from your ashes to fling them into the endless nightmare that is all that awaits you!*"

"Conor." Mathghaman was at my elbow, his hand on my shoulder. "Hold your ground."

I looked down at the Sword. "It held that other one in place."

"Not this one. Not now, not here. You are not ready." His voice was terse and more urgent than I think I'd ever heard it. "Even if you faced it, it is a liar and murderer from the day it was born. It would turn you to ash from the air and then burn whatever it could in the fortress anyway."

Turning to look at him, I saw he was watching the dragon, his jaw set and his eyes like points of steel. "Then we're lost, anyway."

He shook his head. "Remember, it is a liar. Nothing is lost yet." He turned those steely eyes on me. "Do not throw your life away on the word of a demon of the Outer Dark."

I took a deep breath at that and relaxed my grip on the Sword. He was right. Every one of these things we'd faced so far had been a liar, and if it really was afraid of the Two Swords, then it stood to reason that it would try to draw us out.

So, I got back on the .50 and started looking for a weak spot. Bailey had hurt that red dragon at Gremman with it. This thing was hugely bigger than that one, but hopefully I could at least hurt it.

"*Still thou dost hide.*" The contempt in that thing's voice might have dropped another man, and despite knowing just what it was and what it was trying to do, I felt a sinking feeling in my gut. Its powers were immense, and I knew it could get into my head if I let it. Keeping it out was a bigger task than I might have thought, too. "*Puny insects. I will burn the world down around you.*"

I answered with a Raufoss round.

The *boom* echoed almost as loud as the dragon's voice, and the blast scattered hail away from the arrow slit. The round struck with a flash and a puff of smoke, hammering into the dragon's neck just below its jaw. It had moved just as the shot broke, or else I would have hit it in the nose.

It reared back then and roared at the sky. Purple-tinged lightning stabbed from its jaws into the clouds, and when it brought its head down to glare at the wall, more lightning flickered and stabbed from its eyes.

"*So be it.*" The words came in a low hiss, but they echoed and reverberated over the fortress, nevertheless.

It flapped into the sky in a whirl of hail and smoke, crumbling more of the ruined wall as it shoved off. I twisted in my seat, trying to get a second shot at it, but I already knew it was a fool's errand. Single shots of .50 cal wouldn't hurt a B-52, let alone an eldritch monstrosity of such an otherworldly nature like that dragon. It was going to take something a lot bigger to bring that beast down.

Probably something with a lot more metaphysical heft than a .50 caliber Raufoss round, too.

It climbed into the sky, moving faster than it seemed something of that size without jet engines should be able to. Higher and higher it rose, until it had to be at several hundred feet above the tower atop the citadel.

Then it dove.

Tucking its wings, it arrowed down toward the earth, its jaws agape, ignoring the few arrows that darted up toward it. Even the ones that might hit couldn't hurt it.

With an eye-searing blast of lightning, it blew the second gate apart.

Burning splinters the size of my arm were blasted across the gateway as stones that had stood for over a century exploded, launched high above the top of the wall and the towers before arcing down toward the rocky ground below. The wind and the storm blew the dust away quickly, revealing that the top of the gatehouse was simply *gone*.

Spreading its wings once more, the dragon rose higher again, though it dipped its long neck to send another ravening bolt of lightning into the wall just off to our left, shattering stone and sending molten shards whickering through the air on the heels of the thunderclap that nearly drove us to our knees inside the tower.

The wall was breached. Horns sounded below, and the Peruni began to move, advancing in tight formations with their shields interlocked around and overhead. They'd been waiting for this, preparing behind the barricades while the dragon approached.

I wondered how many men had been sacrificed to the dragon to draw it here.

Twice more it struck before the first squares of Peruni infantry got even a quarter of the way across the open ground before the second wall. Santos was firing into the advancing formations, but a moment later I grabbed him by the shoulder.

"This wall's done. We've got to go." It was obvious even before the dragon had hit the other parts of the wall itself. As soon as it had blasted the gate open, we weren't going to be able to hold the second wall any longer.

With that thing overhead, I wondered if we'd be able to hold at all. It could simply blow holes in every defensive bulwark we had and let the enemy flow through, provided it wanted to let them have any of the glory.

We headed for the stairs, sending a few last shots at the oncoming foe, as the dragon rattled the walls around us.

CHAPTER 21

THE retreat to the third wall wasn't quite a rout, but it was awfully close.

With the second wall breached, Tarvedum had ordered the recall sounded. There was nothing to be gained by trying to hold the remaining fragments of the rampart. We would only lose hundreds more, men we would need when they came at the third wall.

Whether or not they'd last much longer at the third wall, with the dragon in the mix, was another question.

The Peruni and the Avurs were still too far away to engage any of the surviving Galel as they drew back off the wall and headed for the next gate, offset from the second by nearly three hundred yards. That gave us a bit of breathing room, especially since the ground between the walls wasn't exactly even or flat, but the dragon made that a mixed blessing.

It wasn't alone, either. More of the wyverns flapped and screamed in its wake, stooping on fleeing men and seizing them in their talons, lifting them screaming into the air as they tore at their prey's necks and guts. Some of the archers paused to try to shoot at the flying monsters, and several scored hits, but the arrows didn't seem to do enough damage to slow them down. Bullets did better, but again, it took a lot of concentrated fire to knock one of those things out of the sky, and we couldn't exactly go to ground out there in the open.

I glanced over my shoulder as we ran up the hill toward the third wall. The smashed and broken bodies of men in the multicolored livery of the Galel lay amid the blackened and dust-covered ruin of the nearest breach, men who had been thrown there when the dragon had struck. The dead from the fight at the wall the day before had all been carefully taken up and prepared for burial, even the enemy.

The dragon swooped down again, blasting a glowing furrow in the rock with another flickering bolt of lightning and sending the shattered and smoking bodies of our allies flying. It dipped even lower and snatched a man up with one taloned paw, crushing him as it climbed back into the sky, making his blood rain down on the men below.

I shot at it out of sheer defiance, then kept running. There was no way to stand and fight it then and there.

It was a struggle to get up that last few dozen yards to the wall and would have been even if I hadn't been hauling the .50 in my hands. A hail of arrows and sling stones were being shot at the dragon and the wyverns, but a lot of the men up on the battlements were a little too focused on trying to fight the monsters, and in their fear, they had forgotten that what goes up must come down. We were dodging iron-tipped shafts, rocks, and lead shot as we ran, and I saw several Galel men-at-arms go down to their own people's arrows.

The gates were already swinging shut, but I could just barely hear, over the cacophony of battle and terror, Tarvedum himself bellowing at his men to keep them open. The enemy infantry had not yet reached the second wall, and he would not have the rest of us shut out just because his men were afraid of the dragon.

A man just ahead of me stumbled, and I could see the fear in every move as he scrambled to get back up before the monsters swooped down on him again. A wyvern hissed as it dipped through the air toward him, and I shot it in the head from only a few yards away. It snapped its head back and flared, its wings flapping violently, and turned toward me, but I had the Sword of Iudicael out as I dashed as best I could up the hill to stand over the fallen Galel warrior.

The wyverns were more beast than malevolent intelligence, but even they feared the Two Swords. It let out a rattling screech and twisted around as it landed short, turned its tail, and flapped back into the air.

I grabbed the fallen Galel and heaved him to his feet, helping propel him toward the gap in the gates ahead.

My lungs were burning, and my exposed skin stung from the pelting hailstones as we reached the gate. I stopped short, turning to make sure that the rest of the team got through first, swinging the M107 to my shoulder and looking for a target. The dragon came out of the clouds again, diving toward the knot of knights and men-at-arms who had formed the rear guard at the gate, and I struggled to bring the heavy rifle to bear and leaned into it as I fired.

The muzzle blast was almost as punishing as the shock of the bolt hammering back into the receiver right next to my jaw. The shot hit, more through luck—or the hand of Iudicael, maybe—than my good marksmanship, but while it might have cracked a scale, it didn't do much more than irritate the monster. It sent a lightning bolt at us, but for whatever reason it missed, blowing a rock apart about a yard away. I felt the sting of the shards of rock punching into my cheek, but that was all.

Santos propelled Farrar through the open gate, Mathghaman and Bearrac on his heels. That alone told me that the other teams were already on ladders or ropes and getting over the wall. The King's Champion would be the last man through the gate. Always.

He nodded to me then, in the brief moment of almost calm in the aftermath of that missed lightning strike. I took that as the signal and ducked through the gate.

We gathered in the shelter of the wall as the dragon raged in the sky above, and the last stragglers from the second wall rushed through. Minutes later, the gate shut with a hollow *boom*.

Whether it would keep the enemy out for long was the question.

* * *

The Peruni swarmed over and through the second wall, bringing more of their engines up. The Galel artillery on the third wall pelted them with stones, firepots, and scorpion bolts, but they weren't camping on the inside of the second wall the same way they had the first. The only openings where we could lob projectiles at them were the shattered gaps in the wall that the dragon had blasted open.

Somewhat to everyone's surprise, the dragon backed off. It was still up there, circling in the clouds, but it hadn't pressed the assault on the third wall. When we gathered in the third wall gatehouse, I wondered about that.

"It is not that it cannot, though I wonder just how much it fears the Swords and the guardian." Mathghaman stood on the wall just outside the tower, his arms folded, watching the enemy through the gaps in the fallen second wall. "It is still limited, and it fears Tigharn as much as it hates Him." He turned and joined us inside. None of the Galel were out on the battlements at the moment, either. The wyverns were a threat that could sort of be dealt with. That dragon, though, was on a whole different level.

"Notice that it never named Him. It fears His name, in contradiction to its claim to be a 'god.'" He snorted.

"I don't think that means there's nothing to worry about, though," Applegate put in. The gatehouse on the third wall was a small fortress in and of itself, so there was plenty of room to get the whole platoon together, probably for the first time in days.

"No, it does not." Mathghaman gripped the big man's shoulder. "Yet that is part of the creature's plan. It is as insidious as it is brutal. It cares little for the Peruni who will die in the storming of this place. In fact, it cares not at all. It wants destruction, complete and total. Spiritual as well as physical."

He turned to look out one of the tall, arched windows. They were a little wider, as arrow slits went, but we were high enough up that it would take a particularly talented and committed archer, with one hell of a bow, to get a shot through it from below. "It will draw out the agony as long as it may. It wants the suffering to continue, in bodies and minds. It wants to bring despair. If it must let tens of thousands of its servants die, so much the better. It will feast upon their despair and lay claim to their souls for their service."

"So, it was lying when it threatened to just burn the whole place down." Bailey didn't sound entirely convinced.

"Perhaps. More likely it did not specify *when* it would burn it down." Mathghaman laughed softly, though there wasn't a lot of humor in it. "I am sure it still intends to."

"So, we've got a dragon the size of a naval vessel, twenty-nine Dullahans, a whole lot of wyverns, a bunch of lesser wizards, and still most of half a million men to worry about." Gunny rubbed his jaw. "Any ideas?"

"Kill as many of them as we can until the fortress falls?" Gurke didn't quite sound like himself. He sounded half-dead, beaten.

No, not beaten. Resigned. Tired. That vision of Cairbre's spirit had really gotten to him, and I wondered if it had gotten to him in the way that Cairbre had intended. He was convinced he was going to die here, and since he was still Ross Gurke, he really wasn't convinced that he was ready for it. He was starting to draw inward, to close in on himself.

It wasn't a good thing. Not when we still had a battle to fight. Certainly not when that dragon was gleefully, eagerly looking for us to despair.

"We're not dead yet." My voice might have been harsher than I'd intended, but my throat was raw after too long without water, and I was every bit as tired as Gurke was. "I won't lie down and die for that thing."

"Nobody's saying that, Conor." Gunny was a little punchy, too. There wasn't any normal, ordinary man in that room who wasn't. Mathghaman and his Tuacha were in much better shape, but even they weren't un-touchable. It was rare that we saw it, but I'd seen the nightmares in Bearrac's eyes after their imprisonment in Taramas's catacombs. "We need a bit more of a plan than just 'hold out until we all die,' though." He looked around the room. "We've tried an end run a couple of times already. It didn't work either time."

"We still have to kill or scatter the Dullahans." Bailey was thinking, ignoring the rest of us, his eyes fixed on the window. "Going to them hasn't worked. They're ready for us to try that. Especially since we've already tried it three times." He turned back toward the rest of us, looking around at each team leader in turn. "Maybe we get them to come to us. Give them a target they won't be able to resist. One that only *they* can really go after, not their lackeys."

Quiet fell as we thought that one over. "It might work. At least once." Gunny glanced out at the wall with nar-rowed eyes. "It'd have to be one hell of a target, though."

"It would, indeed." Everyone stood as King Uven came out of the stairwell and joined us, flanked by Tarvedum and Vepogenus. All three men looked drawn and haggard, and all three were spattered with mud and blood. I could only imagine how desperately Uven's men must have fought to keep him safe. As newly recovered from the wounds taken outside of Cor Wudrun as he was, he had thrown himself into the battle, ferociously deter-mined to be the warrior king his people expected and de-served. "I think I know what sort of bait might suffice."

"My lord king..." Tarvedum's protest was evident in his voice even before he could finish his sentence, which was cut short by Uven's upraised hand. Vepogenus just looked grim and resigned. He knew better than to try to stop Uven when the king's mind was made up.

"I fear, however, that I alone might not be sufficiently delectable bait to tempt them." He turned to Bailey and me with a slight bow.

There had been a time when he would have been apologetic about asking us for help. I think it had stuck in his craw a little bit, as much mutual respect as seemed to have been built between us Marines and the warrior sovereign of a warrior people, to ask us to take the primary position on the quest for the Sword of Categyrn, and again to help ferret out the traitors and sorcerers who had infiltrated the kingdom for the Empire of Ar-Annator. Yet now, while he was definitely making a request, albeit without saying as much at first, there was none of the attached apology.

I returned his bow. "I'll go with you."

Bailey sighed. "Me, too."

It might not have been the formal way you were supposed to talk to a king, but Uven wasn't the sort of king we'd grown up with in books, movies, and video games. He bowed more deeply, gratified that we had agreed and offered before he'd needed to ask.

We were committed. We had been committed since we'd agreed to ride to Cor Chatha. Hell, we'd been committed since we'd agreed to join the quest for the Sword that Bailey now carried at his side. Really, if we looked at it a certain way, we'd been committed since we'd taken sides against Dragon Mask, far away in the north.

The Outer Dark was our enemy. That would have made the Galel our friends, even if we hadn't come to think of them as the closest people to us except maybe the Menninkai.

"We shall also stand with you." Mathghaman spoke for the Tuacha, as he always had. Even Cairbre, as aloof and irritable as he had been, had always deferred to Mathghaman Mag Cathal without question.

He stood half a head taller than any of us, his arms crossed, and looked around the room. "Now is not the time, however."

King Uven turned to him, his eyes flashing ever so slightly. Knowing Uven as I had come to know him, he had probably planned to go right out onto the battlements from there and issue his challenge, just as he had challenged the emperor. He was still a young man—younger than me, if I was judging things right—and therefore impatient, aggressive… and eager to finish this, one way or another. He was already haunted by the number of men who had died, and how quickly the first two walls had fallen. I could see that in his eyes.

Mathghaman headed off his protest before he could speak. "You would challenge the first disciples of the Summoner and one of the princes of the Outer Dark. Such is not a fight that it is wise to go into unprepared. This will be fought as much in the will and the spirit world as with weapons. Moreso, even." He looked up into the dark beyond the tall window. "Time is short, yes, but it will be shorter if we go out there now. Come aside and hold vigil with us. Purify and prepare, for any weakness *will* be exploited."

King Uven nodded, albeit somewhat grudgingly. Conall started below to fetch one of the cloaked brothers who served under Brother Domech. The rest of us settled in to wait.

CHAPTER 22

THE chant swelled through the room, the candles flickering in the darkness, seemingly insignificant next to the titanic lightning flashes outside, but still holding back the unnatural night in a way that the lightning couldn't.

After a few minutes, I closed my eyes as I knelt on the wooden floor, my weapons laid next to me, still in my armor and chest rig. I let the chant roll over me as I tried to lift my mind and my spirit out of the darkness and horror that was this nightmare of a siege.

For what felt like a long time, I just saw the dimness behind my eyelids, heard the chanting, and felt the growing chill of the wind through the windows and the hardness of the floor beneath me. I felt alone, lost and scared, knowing that death was closing in all around us. I tried really hard to maintain that hard-as-woodpecker-lips exterior, but there's only so long a man can lie to himself. I knew what was coming. I had no illusions that being a Sword Bearer made me immortal. Too many other men had carried those blessed weapons and fallen into darkness.

Sure, the guardian had intervened before, but that hadn't kept the first or second walls from falling. Iudicael and Categyrn had assisted us more than once. There's something about the way the human mind works, however, that made those times seem to pale in comparison to the vastness of the threat that confronted us. The sheer weight of evil out there—and the knowledge that there were seeds of evil amongst us, a conclusion that was inescapable after the fight we'd been through only a few weeks before—seemed overwhelming.

I was sure that the dragon's influence had a lot to do with that perception. Its size and power were immense, and I had little doubt that its physical form was only a minor manifestation of what it really was. A reflection, as it were. I remembered the dream I'd had on the way to Vaelor's Throne. I knew that the princes of the Outer Dark could reach into our minds, planting thoughts of fear, despair, misery, and worse. I was sure they'd lent the Dullahans much the same power.

That didn't make it any easier to separate my own thoughts from those possible intrusions from the Outer Dark.

Over time, however, the chant seemed to work its way into my soul, and even with my eyes shut, a faint glow began to surround me. A moment later, even though I still didn't open my eyes, Iudicael came out of the darkness and stood before me.

I have never been able to really describe him. I can't remember facial features, or anything other than a figure of such brilliance that it was hard to look at him. There was always the vague impression of a great stature and power, such that he made the Tuacha look small and stunted by comparison.

He did not speak. He didn't really need to. His presence alone could sometimes be enough. It had happened before. He hadn't spoken to me, truth be told, until after the battle for Cor Legear, when, with his help, I'd killed the Dullahan.

He looked down at me for a moment, then stepped around to stand at my shoulder. He didn't have the last word here. He had made it clear, the first time he'd spoken to me, that he was only a servant.

With him standing there beside me, the weight of my thoughts changed. I saw less of the overwhelming threat outside, and more into myself.

Not all of it was pretty. Yet whereas the Outer Dark's influence would lead me toward despair, having Iudicael at my side, I was able to see those darker parts of myself and my own past in a different light. See them as times when I had gone astray. I could mourn for them, repudiate them. It was a purification, as incomplete as it might be in such a short time. Necessary, nevertheless.

Warfare against such things as dragons and Dullahans must occur on more than one level. They don't just want you dead. They want you destroyed, body *and* soul. The war is as much in the mind and soul as it is with guns, explosives, axes, or swords. If the monsters find *any* weakness, they'll exploit it.

Even a man as pure and noble as Mathghaman has weak points. That was why I was more than glad that Iudicael stood by my side.

It wasn't all comfort, however. Though, again, no words were said that could be heard, I began to understand Gurke's vision of Cairbre a little better.

This life is limited. Short. The one inevitability in all of it is that it ends. That part I'd figured out. But Iudicael showed me more.

I saw, once again, in excruciating detail, Cairbre's death. Gunny had been in front of us, in a desperate and doomed attempt to stop Vaelor from breaking free of his prison. The Outsider had already begun to shake off its shackles, and a great spike of a limb had been poised to spear our de facto platoon leader through the skull.

Cairbre had willingly and knowingly thrown himself into the path of that great, otherworldly talon, and had been briefly nailed to the floor before his corpse had been flung against the far wall, his noble visage smashing against black rock carved into the likeness of atrocity and madness.

Yet his sacrifice had fettered Vaelor once again.

My vision shifted to the hills above Gremman, as the great red dragon swooped down on us once again, after having killed men outright or poisoned them, shrugging off every round we fired at it, sailing through the air over our heads, out of our reach. I watched once again as Galan caught the spear that Cailtarni had tossed him and issued his challenge, roaring out his defiance against the dragon. Saw him speared through with one long, poisonous fang, even as the weight of his body suddenly seemed too much for the dragon to lift, giving Bailey and I a chance to strike at it.

And it had been the very spear that Galan had wielded that had pierced the dragon's heart.

I began to understand. There was more to it than just a readiness to face death. There had to be a purposefulness to it. It wasn't just those men's deaths that had turned the tide against the monsters.

It had been their own willing abandonment of their lives. Self-sacrifice was something we never saw from the monsters or their minions. If I thought about it, I could remember the looks of horror and fear that I'd seen on the faces of every Fohoriman, every monstrosity that had once been human, including the vampire Unsterbanak, at the moment of death. They feared being ripped out of this world to face their judgment more than anything else.

To willingly lay one's own life down to save others was the antithesis of everything they were.

Words echoed in my mind then. *No greater love hath a man than he lay down his life for his brother.*

I knew then just what Cairbre's warning had really meant. And what might be demanded of us in the dark hours and days to come.

I was afraid that I wouldn't be ready. That the fear might overcome me, or worse, that I wouldn't be strong enough. That my sacrifice might be too little, too late.

Iudicael's presence lent me strength, but I didn't know if it would be enough.

I still wasn't sure by the time the chant ended and I opened my eyes. I'd just have to hope.

CHAPTER 23

THE candles were blown out, and we gathered our weapons and rose to our feet. No one said anything. The quiet seemed almost unshakeable, just then. Even the thunderclap that sounded outside as another purple-tinged lightning bolt slammed across the sky didn't seem to disturb anyone.

Now, that's not to say that we were all perfectly calm, serene warrior monks at that moment. We weren't. I could see the trepidation in men's eyes, almost especially in Uven's. We were on a better footing, but that didn't mean any of us were entirely self-assured enough to have no doubts or fears left.

Despite his fears and misgivings, though, King Uven was committed. And that meant so were we.

Drawing his sword and hefting his shield in his other hand, he led the way up the ladder to the top of the gatehouse. Vepogenus followed him immediately, while the rest of us waited to file our way up.

The gatehouse stood high above the killing ground, thrust out on a rise from the main line of the wall, giving us a commanding view of that part of the fortress that had already fallen, as well as the plains beyond. Or it would if there was more light to see by.

Our vigil had ended just in time. The enemy was on the move.

Too many of their siege engines had been destroyed at the second wall for them to move up to the third. That didn't mean they were giving up entirely, and the evidence of more ladders and catapults being brought through the gaps blasted in the wall told me that the dragon definitely *was* hanging back.

A part of me hoped that, despite the plan, it continued to do so. I didn't really *want* to die right then and there, and I couldn't shake the feeling that what Iudicael had showed me had been a forewarning of what would *definitely* be asked of me.

I wouldn't mind putting that off a little longer.

Taking chances in combat is one thing. It was something we'd been doing our entire careers. Even training for this profession is risky, and all of us knew someone who'd died in training. I'd known a guy who'd drowned in MART—Marines Awaiting Reconnaissance Training. Another had rolled a vehicle and been killed that way. Yet another had burned in on a jump.

But you didn't think about that most of the time. Detachment was a useful combat multiplier. While we would all have asserted that we were ready for death, some pointing to Ronald Spears's speech in *Band of Brothers*, it still wasn't something we contemplated all the time.

Possibility is something far different from certainty.

Still, we were up there, the King, the Tuacha, and the Sword Bearers, for a reason. And I wasn't going to back down from that.

Uven looked down at the formations of Peruni and Avur infantry coming through the gaps and the shattered gate in the second wall and lifted his sword. He didn't address the enemy. Instead, he turned his back on them and stepped up to where the Galel could see him, both on the third wall to either side of us and on the fourth above and behind us.

"My brothers! We stand against the greatest evil to face our people since the fall of the Commagan Empire!" His voice rolled out over the walls, loud enough that even the wind couldn't drown him out. It almost sounded like someone up above was lending him a little mystical help.

He stabbed a hand out toward the advancing foe. "The enemy's shriveled emperor can use the arts of sorcery to project his image above our walls, to urge us to cowardice and surrender, all while wrapping his degenerate form in false light! Yet *he* does not dare lead his own armies against us! Such confidence he has in his cause!"

Raising his sword higher, he looked around at the faces that turned up to watch him from beneath iron helmets topped with horsehair crests. "This sword has been borne by my family for four generations! It will drink the enemy's blood once again, for I will not cower and let you face our foes on your own! I stand here, on the front line of defense, with you!" He turned to face the advancing blocks of Peruni then. "After all, I am the one they want, the one they fear! They tried to assassinate me before their army had even neared our borders! Let them look on their fear and cower before our walls!"

The Galel let out a great roar at that, though when I glanced at Gunny, I saw the same bleak look in his eyes that I felt. There was a hollowness in that sound. They cheered and roared and challenged the imperial army because they needed to. They had seen the devastation wrought on the first two walls. They had seen and heard the dragon. The emperor's generals might have feared King Uven, but it seemed unlikely that the dragon and the Dullahans did.

A deep, braying, mocking laugh rumbled from the sky above as another shaft of lightning flickered through the clouds. "*Such hubris. Young fool. Thou shalt receive the reward thou dost ask for.*"

And then the assault began.

The wyverns came screaming down out of the clouds, as if they'd been clustered in the dragon's wake the entire time. A phalanx of about twenty of them swooped on the gatehouse, and we suddenly had our hands full.

I'd brought the .50 up, and while ammo was still scarce, I figured a wyvern was worth a few rounds. I heaved the big rifle to my shoulder, thankful that all the moving and fighting in a world without the internal combustion engine over the last couple of years had left me stronger and meaner than I had been before. I still barely stabilized the weapon before I blew a hole in the nearest wyvern's throat, sending it thrashing and twisting to fall below the top of the wall, hitting with a powerful impact that shook the gatehouse. It still hadn't been that great a shot. I'd been aiming for its open mouth. I'd take the kill, though.

Santos was leaning into his Mk 48, pouring fire into multiple wyverns in turn, as were Huuhka, Applegate, and Chambers. They were hurting the monsters, but the entire furball was so chaotic that I didn't think they'd actually dropped one by the time they were right on top of us.

One of them dropped toward King Uven and I rushed forward as its talons darted toward him. A contact shot with a .50 is hard to imagine, especially since the rifle's so big, but I was still almost touching the wyvern's skull when I pulled the trigger. Blood, shattered scales, smashed bone, and smoking debris sprayed several yards from the creature as it was knocked sideways by the force of the shot, though not before Uven dove in the opposite direction. That probably saved his life as much as my bullet had. If that monster had hit him, dead or not, it would have crushed every bone in his body.

Mathghaman was everywhere, seemingly switching smoothly between rifle and blade, getting contact shots to wyvern eyes where he could, carving into wings and limbs where he couldn't. The full grace and power of a Tuacha warrior in his prime was there for all to see. And it wasn't just him. Bearrac, Fennean, Diarmodh, Conall, and Eoghain all fought with nearly the same intensity and ferocity.

It would have been awe-inspiring if I'd had the time to watch.

I took one more shot at a wyvern before they got canny and the next one took a swipe at me with its tail. I ducked, but it had only been a diversion.

A whip made of human vertebrae wrapped around the M107's barrel and wrenched it out of my hands.

The Dullahan wore long black robes and rode a flying horror out of nightmares. The creature was black as pitch and seemed to be made out of smoke and burning tar, with the body and wings of a bat and the head of a toad. It dripped smoking black ichor as it swooped down and alighted on the battlements, even as the Dullahan flipped my precious .50 caliber rifle over the side of the tower, sending it tumbling toward the ground below.

For a second, I raged at the loss of the weapon, but then I reminded myself that it was from the *Coira Ansec*, so it would probably survive the fall, and even retain zero. Fortunately, it had tossed the rifle on our side of the wall, but then I was in a fight and couldn't think about it anymore.

It brought that whip back around and aimed it at my eyes, but when I swept out the Sword of Iudicael, it suddenly withdrew the whip, pulling it short so that I couldn't reach it. Remembering what had happened to the other Dullahan's macabre lash when it had tried to pull the same trick with the Sword, I could understand why it had done so.

Checking to make sure I wasn't about to expose not only myself but one of my teammates, and confirming that the Dullahan was indeed alone, I broke ranks and pushed toward the battlements, toward the headless horror and its nightmare mount.

It wasn't playing that game, though. With a hollow, derisive laugh, it urged its mount into the air again, leaving me out front and swinging in frustration at empty space.

That almost got my head taken off. Another wyvern dove down and snapped at my skull, its jaws closing with a *clop* only inches away from my helmet, and that only because something—or some*one*—had warned me without words or vision a moment before, and I'd thrown myself flat. I rolled as I hit the roof and slashed upward, the point of the Sword catching the wyvern under the jaw.

Scales split and black blood sprayed from the wound as the Sword of Iudicael clove through the creature's jaw, carving a furrow through unnatural flesh and bone. The monster screamed and twisted in midair, flapping higher and battering me with its wings as I tried to avoid that lashing tail.

Then it was gone, and I surged to my feet as King Uven and Gunny moved up next to me.

The wyverns continued to swirl around the top of the gatehouse, keeping us tied up fighting them or defending against them. The Galel artillery was lobbing rocks and scorpion bolts into the oncoming enemy forces below, but we were too busy to see if they were doing any substantial damage.

Warier now, the wyverns kept their distance from our blades and flew erratically to avoid our bullets. Perhaps those creatures shared the same horror of being cast out of this existence that their eldritch masters did.

The dragon roared again, a blast of angry noise that actually seemed to make a few of the wyverns flinch— and renew their assault even more ferociously.

Two of the Galel men-at-arms who had refused to be separated from Lord Tarvedum were seized and hauled into the air, one ripped in half between the monster's claws, the other swallowed nearly whole as he screamed, and the wyvern hauled itself higher into the sky.

The Dullahan was circling, riding that awful bat-thing, and when King Uven roared his frustration and defiance at it, it only laughed. Its head was cradled in a basket at its saddle bow, its eyes trailing yellow flames, its mouth leering a little too wide, as if its cheeks had been split.

Then it lifted one hand and uttered a word that made reality itself seem to ripple. We all shuddered, and one of the Galel retched.

The air swirled not far from the Dullahan, and then it *split*, opening on some other place, a place of chaos, darkness, and suffering.

Like a swarm of flies, the winged horrors of the Outer Dark spewed from that unholy portal, screeching their madness.

Things had just gone from bad to unmitigated disaster. Even with the Two Swords up there atop the gatehouse, there was no way we were going to hold all those horrors *and* the wyverns off, even if the dragon and the Dullahans continued to keep their distance.

We had forgotten about the guardian, however.

His entrance was hardly noticeable, without flash or fanfare. He was just suddenly there, in our midst, spear in one hand, the other held up in a gesture of denial. Still translucent, he glowed slightly more brightly than before, which is probably the only reason any of us noticed his presence at all.

The screaming, oily horrors scattered like quail, then dissolved into showers of black ichor and smoke.

The guardian had just essentially said, *Not here.*

The Dullahan reeled, hauling its mount hard to the left to bank away from the gatehouse and the guardian. The wyverns screamed and the dragon roared, finally swooping down out of the clouds to send a scorching blast of lightning over our heads. The thunderclap drove everyone on the roof—except for the guardian, who wasn't physically there—to their knees.

Somewhat to my surprise, the dragon didn't taunt or otherwise threaten us. It only roared, an earthshaking blast of noise as it went overhead, its wings battering at the wall even as the first of the Peruni's ladders reached the battlements.

The guardian hadn't moved as the dragon went over. He simply stood there, his spear in his hand, watching impassively.

The wyverns didn't seem to want to get near him, and we suddenly had a bit of a breather. It wasn't much of one, though, because then the assault on the third wall started in earnest.

CHAPTER 24

WE were not in a good position. With the entire platoon along with King Uven and his bodyguard all gathered on top of the gatehouse, we couldn't support any part of the wall that wasn't already within line of sight.

Nothing against the Galel as fighters. Those boys could lay the hate. We could just hit harder and farther away than they could.

"Bring those wyverns down!" Now that we had the space, Gunny was determined to put the hurt on our enemies. If we couldn't stop any of the Peruni climbing the walls, we could eliminate a chunk of their aerial support.

Santos was already on it, moving to the battlements and dropping to a low knee where he could steady the bipods against the rampart and keep his bursts tight. He clamped down on the trigger, sending a stream of tracers spitting at one of the nearest wyverns, correcting his fire as the first burst went just ever so slightly ahead of it, the second tearing into its jaw and then its wing. It thrashed and hissed and screamed as the wing collapsed, Santos leaning into it and pouring on the fire, his suppressor smoking as he held the trigger down.

I almost headed below to try to retrieve the .50, but a moment later, King Uven decided he wasn't going to wait around atop the gatehouse. He ran to the ladder, slid down with his hands and feet clamped to the rails, and ran toward the wall.

Vepogenus had clearly been caught off guard, though Tarvedum started after the king with a bitten-off curse. I hesitated for a moment, then grabbed Farrar. "On me."

Gunny looked over and just nodded. King Uven was a High Value Individual. While the fortress might not crumble if he was killed, after everything else, we really didn't want to lose him. It might just be the shock that drove us back to the fourth wall.

The rest of us didn't get down the ladder quite as fast as the king had, if only because Tarvedum was older and heavier, and didn't seem to trust himself to not fall off the ladder if he tried to slide down the way the king had. By the time we made it down, Uven was already in the thick of it, while the men-at-arms on the wall, led by a knight in orange and yellow named Onnist, desperately tried to surround him and keep him safe.

It says good things about a sovereign when he's so aggressive that his men will throw themselves at the enemy to try to keep him from getting himself killed. I sure couldn't think of any politicians back in the World who would even think of doing that. Still, if he did get himself offed, it was going to be devastating for the defense.

So, we waded in after him, moving as fast as we could without getting tangled up on each other.

His fury had already staggered the oncoming enemy, and their foothold was faltering. He'd already driven them back to the ladder, and even as I came out on the battlements with Farrar, I saw him bull-rush a big Peruni captain, the man's onion-dome helmet topped by three black feathers, and shove him over the side, sending him screaming off the wall to crash onto the rocks below. Then the king himself leaned on the ladder, stabbing his sword down at the next man who was trying to climb it, even as he tried to shove it away from the ramparts.

One of the Galel knights, a man I didn't immediately recognize in the press and the chaos, got half a dozen men-at-arms to rush the ladder, pushing on it with their spears. There were too many men already climbing to just lever it straight away from the wall, so they shoved it sideways until it tipped over and crashed into the next ladder to the north, bringing them both down in a smashing pile of wreckage and shattered bodies.

By the time I fought my way to the king's side, we found ourselves in a bubble. The fight continued farther down the wall, and on the other side of the gatehouse, but the king had cleared a section of it almost by himself.

It was true that he'd had help, but if he hadn't thrown himself with reckless abandon into the middle of the fray, the fight might have gone much more slowly.

King Uven wasn't going to leave it at that. He paused, his head high, almost as if he was smelling the air, looking for where the fight might be thickest.

Or where the Dullahans might make an entrance. I was sure he hadn't forgotten the plan. I pushed up to stay close to him. Better to present the enemy with the best lure possible, plus we had a better chance of keeping Uven alive if he had the Two Swords fighting alongside him.

He pressed toward the end of the wall and the cliff beyond, almost before Bailey and I could reach him. He was angry and nearly lost in his own aggression, his fury burning red hot at what was being done to his kingdom and his people. The flame of that rage was an advantage for now, but I hoped it didn't burn out of control to the point where we lost him.

With a roar, he slammed shield-first into the ragged wall of Peruni swordsmen on the wall, still trying to establish their foothold after gaining the battlements against stiff Galel resistance. Uven nearly ran over several of his own men to get at the enemy, and if he hadn't been still fighting smart, I would have thought that he'd given in entirely to his rage, becoming little more than a berserker.

He wasn't simply hacking and slashing mindlessly, though. There was method to his ferocity, and I saw him smash the rim of his shield against the top of an oval Peruni shield, knocking it into its bearer's teeth before dipping low with his sword, slashing the man's leg open just above the knee, where the armor didn't quite cover him. A moment later, as that one began to crumple, bright red blood pulsing out onto the wall from a severed femoral artery, he battered aside a thrust from one of those short, broad-bladed Peruni swords and stabbed its wielder through the mouth. He had to lift a foot and kick that man off his blade as the body dragged his weapon down, but Bailey and I were at his side, keeping the others off him. There was just enough space for about three men abreast atop that wall.

The man I found across from me was tall and spare of frame, armored from his chin to his knees, and keeping his shield solidly in front of him as he held his sword in a high guard near the crest of his helmet. He was in a much better position with that shield than I was, since I still just had my buckler in my hand, and with the Sword of Iudicael in my fist, I had no way to quickly get my pistol out.

So, I kicked his shield, knocking him backward, and lunged as he staggered. I kept the Sword held back and ready as I punched my buckler into his head, knocking him back again and rattling his brains. He relaxed ever so slightly then, and I brought my blade crashing down on his helmet. Any other sword would have skipped off the curve of the metal, but I hit it just right so that the Sword of Iudicael smashed right through the iron plates and sank into his skull.

He froze, twitched ever so slightly as I drew the blade out, and then crashed into a heap at my feet.

King Uven had wrenched his own sword free and stabbed another Peruni swordsman who had lifted his own shield and sword to try to fend off Bailey's brutal swings, ramming the royal blade beneath a lamellar breastplate and deep into the man's guts. Blood gushed over his hand and then he lunged forward and upward, propelling the impaled corpse ahead of him like a battering ram.

He began to sing as he fought. I couldn't make out the words, but it was unmistakably a battle hymn, an ancient song with a tune that fired you up just by listening to it. Soon the other Galel around us took up the song, and it soared over the battlements, quickly traveling across the wall until it seemed all the Galel on the third and fourth walls had raised their voices, bellowing their defiance of the darkness and their joy in the battle.

I held my peace. I didn't know the song, and I've never been much of a singer anyway, but I could certainly appreciate it, and the effect it had not only on the friend-lies but also the enemy wasn't anything to discount.

The Peruni on the wall didn't break, but they got more defensive, and I could see the trepidation in their eyes as we advanced on them. Spears were starting to lance over our shoulders as the Galel got more organized and more were aimed at the ladders, though our line was still too far away to repeat the assault that King Uven had led only a few minutes before.

Sword blows battered shields, helmets, and armored limbs. The crash of steel on steel, wood, and hide rang and boomed, even as hoarse voices continued the battle song. Step by step, we were forcing them back, though only one or two fell as they tightened their formation and tried to hold.

If anything was going to bring the dragon or the Dullahans within reach, it had to be this. King Uven and the Sword Bearers were about to drive their northern foothold over the edge.

And the dragon came.

It swooped down out of the clouds with a roar, bat-tering the wall with the wind of its wings, more pur-ple corposant crackling around it. The entire monster seemed wreathed in purple flame, though it didn't send the expected blast of lightning at us. It just overflew low over the wall, though the shock of those massive wings slammed men down onto their faces, and even threw a few off the wall altogether, sending them tumbling to their deaths. Then it climbed away with another roar.

King Uven stopped singing, pointing his sword at the dragon. "Come, you crawling worm! Or do you fear to face men who do not fear you?"

"*Crow, little insect king. Rattle thy puny weapons and sing thy insipid songs, as if death doth not hover at thy very elbow.*" It surged higher with only a few strokes of its powerful wings, then banked and tipped back over in an Immelmann turn to dive back toward the wall again. Its jaws gaped. "*Oblivion awaits thee, through fire and pain.*"

It dipped straight toward us, and for a moment, it looked like the clash we'd tried to engineer was about to happen.

At the very last second, though, it banked aside again, though as it swept past the gatehouse, it struck, its head darting in on that long neck like a striking rattler.

There was a scream, and while it quickly disappeared into the murk, I caught a glimpse of legs sticking out from between its jaws. I thought I recognized the boots. Whoever had just died, it had been one of ours.

Then a Peruni horn sounded the recall, and they began to retreat from the wall again as the dragon climbed back into the clouds.

King Uven continued to press the fight even as the Peruni fell back to the ladders. He battered at them, getting a strike in that cut one man's ankle deeply enough that he fell howling to the battlements where he was quickly finished off with short sword thrusts as the line moved over him. Another fell with blood spurting from his neck. Yet another lost an eye and threw himself over the wall as he staggered back and was cut off from the rest.

One man still held his ground, his shield held high, crouched so that almost all his body was hidden behind the barrier of wood and hide, his shoulder against the inside to keep one of us from battering its edge into him.

He twisted and turned as we closed in on him, his blade licking out at any exposed target, lightning fast.

I looked into his eyes as I parried a thrust and searched for an opening. I saw the knowledge of imminent death there. He was sacrificing himself to save his comrades.

I could respect that. It was slightly heart wrenching, really, seeing what he was doing. He was about to lay down his life, just as we knew we might have to do, to save men fighting for absolute evil.

I moved in to kill him anyway. There was too much at stake, and I didn't think for a moment that he'd return the courtesy if we tried to let him live. I'd seen too much of the Peruni's dedication to killing for their dark masters.

He was good. He had that shield braced just right that I couldn't get over or under it, and by the time we were able to close in on him altogether, he had his back to the battlements, covering the men clambering down the ladder behind him. He kept the shield between me and him and kept stabbing and parrying with that short sword against King Uven on the other side.

He couldn't hold us both off for long, though. I feinted, and he lifted the shield to block it, at which point I stepped in close and kicked his knee in.

I had put all my weight behind that strike, and his knee snapped, folding backward with a sickening *crunch*. He crumpled with a scream, silenced an instant later as Uven battered the Peruni sword aside and plunged the point of his own blade down under the scaled aventail and into the man's neck.

Then it was over. At least for the moment.

The Peruni and Avurs streamed back toward the second wall, though in good order and keeping their shields between them and the Galel's arrows and sling stones. Those were unfortunately few, as the exhausted defenders caught their breath and tried to fend off the wyverns that were even then stooping on the walls once more.

We'd held, but the dragon and the Dullahans hadn't taken the bait.

CHAPTER 25

I found myself sitting atop the wall, leaning against the battlements, next to Gunny. I didn't think I'd ever seen the older man look so tired. We were both weary and blood-spattered, but Gunny looked beaten down clear to his bones. He'd taken his helmet off, and as I painfully eased myself down to rest, he leaned his head back against the stone and closed his eyes.

Under different circumstances, that might have been cause for worry. Gunny had been a rock, seemingly unshakeable, through the workup with Captain Sorenson—which had been a trial all of itself—across the Land of Ice and Monsters, through the fight with the vampire, the siege of Vahava Paykhah, the quest for the Sword of Categyrn, and the first phases of this war with the Empire of Ar-Annator. Through all of it, he'd been steady and certain, never flagging or even losing his temper.

To see him so thoroughly and visibly exhausted was almost shocking. I'd never fallen for the illusion that he was somehow superhuman—he would have disabused me of the notion quickly had I said anything to that effect—but I knew that as a leader, he'd always believed that he had to maintain a certain aloofness, a certain aura of indestructibility, just for the sake of the men under him. By his school of leadership, he *had* to be that rock, just like a good father was to his kids.

When I thought about what we'd been through over the last few days, though, it became more obvious that every man had his limits, and Gunny was getting close to his. When he turned to me and opened his eyes, it became even clearer.

"You know, I always tried to be a moral man." His voice was low, tired, and probably didn't travel far. I was most likely the only one who could hear him, except for the Tuacha, and they wouldn't listen in. "Looking back, I don't know that I was ever all that good at it." He turned his face toward the cloud-shrouded sky again. "I was always too busy to give it all that much thought. Just did what seemed right."

He sighed. "Now I wonder."

"Wonder what?" I wasn't entirely sure how to proceed. Gunny was the man whom I'd always gone to for guidance. I wasn't used to being his sounding board. And I wasn't sure I was the right man to voice any sort of opinion on the subject, whatever it was, either.

He laughed, a silent, single chuckle, without looking at me. "Cairbre appears to Gurke and tells him that we've got to be ready to die. The first two walls fall like nothing, and we've got a dragon twice the size of that monster that Sean killed in Gremman circling overhead, one that we can't seem to touch." He shook his head, his eyes closed again. "I can feel it. The end closing in. Maybe the Man Upstairs *is* watching over us, and we'll somehow manage to win here. I'm still far from sure that I'll live to see it.

"And that makes me wonder if I did a good enough job of being that moral man, or if I just went through the motions because I wasn't going to die *yet*."

I didn't have an answer right away. Wasn't sure if I had an answer at all. I couldn't judge the state of Gunny's soul. I wasn't even sure about mine.

He'd fallen silent then. Maybe he wasn't looking for an answer, but just unburdening his mind and soul a little. It said something that he'd said it to me. It was a mark of respect that I hadn't ever expected—I wouldn't have dared to.

Finally, though, I couldn't just leave the question in silence. "I wonder if that vigil we held was enough to get us ready. I mean, I don't suppose anyone's ever *really* ready for it. Self-preservation is too strongly wired in the human mind." I took a deep breath. I was in uncharted territory, and a part of me kind of hoped that we'd come under attack soon, so I didn't have to keep thinking about this. "I don't think Cairbre was allowed to come back just to point us to despair."

"Presuming it was really him, and not just some weird dream Gurke had." Gunny still hadn't opened his eyes, but he didn't seem to believe it, even as he said it.

"Presuming it was a real vision, yeah." I squinted up at the roiling black sky as something occurred to me. "You know, maybe there's some hope here. Just from that vigil alone, if nothing else."

"What do you mean?" He still didn't look over at me.

"The dragon has been keeping its distance, despite all its shit-talking. I doubt that it's afraid we're going to kill it. This thing is obviously more formidable than the red in Gremman. Even with the Swords, I wonder if we'd even be able to scratch it." It felt a little like blasphemy to voice the doubt, but there it was. "So, why hasn't it just smashed everything and killed us all?"

A frown deepened that permanent cleft between Gunny's eyebrows. "What are you thinking?"

I was still forming the thought as I spoke. "It keeps talking about destroying our souls as well as our bodies. Not sure it can do that, but what if it's waiting to let despair set in? As if that's going to somehow make us less ready for death? Not less ready to die, strictly speaking, but less ready for any judgment that might come after?" I was increasingly convinced of an afterlife from our time here, even if Cairbre hadn't appeared to Gurke.

He opened his eyes at that, tilting his head as he thought about it. "Interesting thought." His frown deepened a little. "Hard to believe, but you're right. It should have just blasted us all to glowing slag. We know it *can*. So why hasn't it?" He rubbed his chin. He'd started growing the beard out while we'd been on the quest for the Sword of Categyrn but had shaved it again once we'd returned to the Kingdom of Cor Legear. Now the stubble was coming back, since we hadn't exactly had a lot of time for grooming since reaching Cor Chatha. "If it really wants to destroy everybody's soul, maybe it is waiting because we're a little *too* prepared to die for its liking." He smiled faintly. "That's comforting, in a ghoulish sort of way."

The scrape of a foot on stone drew my eyes. We were all too keyed up not to react to any movement near us, even though the enemy had fallen back behind the second wall. Maybe I'd instilled some caution in them, knocking down a few of their officers with the .50.

King Uven stood next to me, Tarvedum and Vepogenus standing a few paces behind him. He looked even more ragged and weary than I felt, though he was trying hard not to show it. There comes a point where you can't disguise the exhaustion anymore, though. He was about ready to collapse, but this soon after the battle, he knew he couldn't just disappear. He had to stay visible, as a sign to his men—all of them—that they were not abandoned. That he wasn't expecting them to die for him while he went and cowered in a hole somewhere.

It was commendable, but it might backfire if he fell on his face in front of half the fortress because he was too tired to stand anymore.

"Lord Conor, will you walk the wall with me?" His voice was a hoarse rasp. "I must see to my men, and it would lift their spirits to see the Sword Bearers with me."

I glanced and Gunny and he nodded shortly. I'd already seen to what was left of my team. I wouldn't have sat down otherwise. So, I heaved myself to my feet—which was a lot harder than it should have been—and joined the king.

We picked Bailey up on the way through the gatehouse, and while there were few words exchanged, when Mathghaman stepped forward to join us, the king actually bowed to acknowledge him.

None of us said much as we proceeded south along the wall, the king stopping every few yards to speak with the bone-tired men-at-arms and knights on the battlements. The wyverns had retreated, so men could venture out onto the wall again.

It was interesting to watch him. As tired as he was, he took an interest in every man, checking that they were holding up, praising them for their exploits, whether he'd seen them or not, and commiserating with them about their weariness and their hurts.

Yet it was a struggle. Not only because of King Uven's own exhaustion, but because of the bleak despair we could read in so many men's eyes.

Despite the fact that we had, apparently, beaten the enemy back from the third wall, there wasn't a man on those battlements who wasn't aware that the dragon *could* have blasted them all to hell and gone. Even if they might not be able to put it into words—though I was sure most of them could, and refused to—they had to suspect the same thing I did.

The Dullahans and the dragon were playing with us like a cat with its prey.

I knew that King Uven saw it and understood, but he refused to let it color his actions or his attitude. He maintained his weary determination, since I don't think he was capable of actual optimism at that point. He wouldn't let the enemy tear him down in front of his men.

By the time we reached the southern cliffs, though, I wondered if the tour had had the desired effect. From the look in the king's eyes as we stopped in the tower, the guards within dismissed for the time being, he was wondering the same thing.

He passed a hand over his eyes, then turned to lean against the wall, peering out the tall windows. "Do we truly have a chance, Lord Mathghaman?"

I couldn't help but breathe a little sigh of relief that he hadn't asked Bailey or me. Mathghaman was definitely the one to field that question, Sword of Iudicael or Categyrn notwithstanding.

Mathghaman didn't look out the window with him, but stood at the rear of the room, his arms folded. "All things are possible in Tigharn."

It wasn't exactly a sterling vote of confidence, and as the king's eyes tightened into a faintly pained squint, without taking his eyes away from the fallen second wall, he fully grasped it.

I joined the king, drawn to the window and the sight of the enemy out there. The dragon was briefly visible in the distance, dipping just beneath the clouds. Something was nagging at me, growing in the back of my mind.

"There seems to be little hope at this juncture," Mathghaman allowed. "Yet the enemy's determination to drive us to despair may yet be their greatest blunder."

I frowned. From where we stood, I could just see the jagged, broken line of the first wall beyond the wreckage of the second. I remembered the glowing, golden image of the emperor standing above it, when he had demanded the fortress's surrender.

"The Dullahans and the dragon don't really care about the Empire of Ar-Annator, do they?" That idea was still coalescing. "I mean, they didn't come out of wherever they've been lurking for all this time because they believe in the emperor and his destiny to rule the whole continent, or whatever."

"No." I could feel Mathghaman's eyes on me as he spoke, though I kept staring out into the dark beyond the walls, trying to bring this idea into focus. "The dragon is an Outsider, a thing altogether of the Outer Dark. The Dullahans, the Thirty, were once men, but they are now something between men and Outsiders. The politics of mere men and empires do not interest them."

"So, if they're fighting for the emperor, then he must have made a deal with them. Offered them something or bound them in some way."

"Most likely." I could hear the thoughtful frown in Mathghaman's voice as I kept trying to work this out.

"So, what if the emperor was suddenly removed from the equation?" I turned around finally, to find all eyes in the tower on me. "If he was the one who bound them, is it *possible* that killing him might scatter them?"

Another thoughtful silence descended. "I cannot say that it would work. The Outer Dark is powerful and capricious, and such monsters as the dragon will not easily be denied. Should its chosen price not be paid, it will find a way to extract it, unless stopped by the power of Tigharn himself."

"Or slain." Bailey was tapping the hilt of the Sword of Categyrn with his fingers.

"Or slain," Mathghaman allowed. "Though it will take considerably more to kill such a beast than it did the dragon of Gremman."

King Uven glanced out the window again. "Do you have any idea what it would take to get to the emperor?"

I grimaced. "Given how every other attempt to get behind enemy lines since they hit Cor Chatha has gone, yes, I've got some idea. I never said it would be easy, and it might not even be *possible* short of Olgudach getting here with reinforcements. Even then, it'll probably be a bear."

Bailey made it worse. "And if he's a sorcerer—which it kinda looks to me like he is—then we've got a whole other set of problems on top of just trying to get through enemy lines."

"What other choice do we have?" I spread my hands. "They're going to keep whittling us down until the dragon gets bored or decides that we're about as down as we're going to get. Then it's going to be over." I looked around the room at somber, weary, haunted faces, few meeting my eyes. "I'm not the type to lie down and die, no matter how inviting the rest might seem. And waiting for the fortress to fall seems like lying down and dying to me."

For a long moment, no one said anything. King Uven, finally, with his jaw set, met my eyes. "I do not have a better idea, Lord Conor, so let us talk of what we might do to draw the emperor out into the open."

CHAPTER 26

WE still didn't have a workable plan a day later, when things really started to get bad.

The Dullahans had buzzed the wall several times atop those burning-tar flying horrors of ever-shifting shape, though they hadn't closed in to engage. The terror of their passage deterred all but the toughest of the Galel from even launching an arrow or slingstone at them.

But the real threat started to make itself felt later, after the headless riders had vanished back into the lowering dark of the storm.

I had been dead asleep, thankfully without dreams, catching the short rest that Gunny had insisted we all try for. I was jerked out of my near coma by a bloodcurdling scream.

Most of the defenders had moved back into the towers and the gatehouse after the Dullahans' flyby. As the pause between assaults continued to stretch out—possibly in no small part because the Peruni, sorcerous leadership or not, needed to lick their wounds after the bloodbath of the last assault—the exhausted defenders began to rotate through a watch schedule, as the others ate or tried to sleep.

Now one of the Galel, a man-at-arms wearing a badge displaying Lord Virguist's blue and gray, had suddenly surged up off his sleeping mat, his eyes wild, screaming like a banshee. He looked around him with quick, pan-icked, jerky movements, and there was no recognition in his eyes.

Barely taking a breath between screams, he snatched up his axe and went for the man on watch.

If Virguist himself hadn't been awake, barely an arm's length away from the man, things might have got-ten very ugly, very quickly.

The knight, still in his armor though he had doffed his helmet, threw himself at the man-at-arms, tackling him to the floor with a crash before he could get more than half a step from his mat.

"Uoret!" Virguist's bellow sounded even over the high-pitched squeals now coming from his man-at-arms. "Uoret, wake up!"

The man just kept screaming incoherently. There might have been words. Maybe a name, a name that didn't bear repeating. I didn't think he was still asleep.

I also didn't think he was going to live through the next hour.

Sure enough, he didn't calm down. His eyes were rolled back in his head, and even after the axe was wrenched out of his hand, he kept fighting, trying to strike his lord while he twisted and screamed. He was completely out of his head.

Finally, Virguist struck him in the head, hard. It didn't stop him, so he hit him again and again, until finally he went limp and fell silent.

When Virguist got up, the look of horror on his face spoke volumes. He looked down at Uoret with a mix of shame and grief in his eyes.

The blood seeping out from beneath Uoret's skull told the rest of the tale. He wouldn't be getting up again.

"Take the body below and burn it." Lord Luthren, who commanded the north part of the wall, at least when the king, Tarvedum, or Vepogenus were elsewhere, stood near the door. "Say the prayers over him, but he must be burned within the hour."

Two men, both wearing Virguist's colors, quickly stood and took up Uoret's limp body. The knight went with them, his face still a mask. There were always exceptions, but I'd noticed that many knights and their men-at-arms among the Galel were, if not family, close as kin. They were fighters, all of them, and they'd trained, fought, and bled alongside one another most of their lives. A bond comes from that, no matter the difference in station.

Were I Virguist's lord, I'd be keeping a very close eye on him for a while. He'd just had to kill one of his own men to keep him from murdering the rest of us. That was going to weigh on him, badly, for a long time.

More screams echoed down the wall. The madness wasn't limited to the gatehouse.

Perhaps the Dullahans had done more than just fly by the wall. Still, there wasn't much we could do but watch, and pray, and lose more sleep worrying about whether the man next to us might be the next one to lose his mind.

Or that one of us might be next, and have to be put down.

It was some time later, after my watch, that I was finally able to sleep again, my hand wrapped around the hilt of the Sword of Iudicael.

* * *

I didn't escape the dreams that time.

They weren't especially new. I'd seen horrifying things in my sleep before, things that had crept into my dreams from the influence of the creatures of the Outer Dark. The visions I'd had in dreams on the way to Vaelor's Throne had been horrifying, haunting my memories for months afterward.

These weren't much different.

I won't go into detail. The memory is muddled, anyway. There wasn't a whole lot of rhyme or reason to any of it. Flashes of images and disturbing noises that lingered even after waking, as if the echo had reverberated into the waking world.

All of it was some manifestation or another of madness, hatred, torment, and violent death.

I was shaken when I got up, and that took some doing anymore. Worse, I felt even more tired and worn down than I had when I'd gone to sleep.

The men in the gatehouse were grim and quiet, eyeing those who were still sleeping from time to time, as if waiting for the next eruption of violent madness. Our guys were off in one corner, keeping to ourselves, but we weren't immune to the same fears.

We'd all been through hell over the last couple of years, but again, every man has his breaking point.

Several of the watchstanders, Galel men-at-arms, were gathered near one of the windows, occasionally turning to check the men sleeping or sitting and staring into space behind them. They murmured amongst themselves, and while I wasn't trying to listen in, I still heard snatches.

"A curse…"

"They cast something."

"Of course they did."

"Cursed…"

"Doomed…"

I wanted to say something. Kinda felt like I had to. But what was *I* going to say? I might have fought beside these men for the last several days, might have fought to try to head this siege off, might even be a Sword Bearer, but I didn't *know* these men, and I feared that anything I said would sound in their ears like insincere platitudes from higher.

I knew *I* sure hated insincere platitudes from higher-ups. I'd been hearing them all my career, at least up until we'd joined the Tuacha, beneath Taramas's citadel.

So, I held my peace.

Maybe I should have said something. At least tried.

Considering what was about to hit.

* * *

Tarvedum came into the gatehouse, his eyes hooded, his face impassive. He came quietly enough that I didn't notice until Santos smacked me in the shoulder.

Something was definitely wrong. He kept his voice low as he said, "The king requests the Sword Bearers and the King's Champion of the Isle of Riamog."

I traded glances with Bailey, and we both stood slowly. I think we were both trying to appear casual, so as not to panic the already shaky defenders, but I, at least, was stiff as a board, and it hurt to get up. I hadn't felt this beat up in a long time.

We followed Tarvedum out onto the wall and down to the open ground between the third and fourth ramparts. My frown deepened as we moved out there, joining King Uven about halfway to the fourth wall.

In the dark, it was hard to see his expression until we reached him. His face was impassive, but he was pale, drawn, and his eyes were haunted.

"Have you seen Lord Vepogenus?" That he didn't even bother with a greeting of any kind was sign enough that he was deeply shaken.

We looked at each other. "Not since the planning session up on the wall a few hours ago," I said. "I thought he was with you."

"He was." The young king sounded almost scared. "He watched over me as I went down to rest, in the southmost tower with the knights. When I awoke, he was gone, and none knew where he went. The men on watch recalled nothing but darkness and could not even be sure of how much time had passed."

"Vepogenus, a traitor? A sorcerer?" Bailey was the one to give voice to it, though I think everyone present was thinking it, as unthinkable as it was. That hard old man had held things together as best he could when King Uven had been downed by his wounds, and he had been the backbone of the resistance to Tharain's Imperial-backed bid for the throne. For him to turn his coat didn't make sense.

The watchstanders with lost time might be a clue, though. "Did anyone elsewhere on the wall see anything?" I ran a hand over my face. My beard was filthy and greasy, though I'd done my level best to at least wash all the blood out of it. No one wanted to remain covered in the blood of our foes, let alone our friends, and in the press of the melee, there was no way to be sure which was which. "If he went over the wall, *somebody* had to have seen *something*."

Uven shook his head. "No one. At least, no one who is speaking about it."

Bailey's face was stark. "I think we must have gotten another visit from the Dullahans. They just didn't want us to know about it this time."

A red glow suddenly lit up the underside of the clouds from somewhere beyond the wall. All eyes turned that way as another blast of lightning forked across the sky. "I think you are right, Sean." Mathghaman stared grimly at the lurid glare. "Except now they do want us to know."

We hustled back up to the wall. Before we'd even reached the stairs, a hollow voice was calling out Uven's name. It didn't sound like the emperor this time.

It sounded like a Dullahan. And so it was.

We reached the battlements to see one of the Thirty, in gothic armor and, unlike the others, not carrying its head under its arm, or in a sling, or even on a pole. This one had its bald, leering head suspended in a column of green fire that rose from the gorget of its armor. It sat astride one of the burning-tar horrors, a thing that looked vaguely like a lion, but with a multitude of horns sprouting from its head.

It held Vepogenus up over its head by the throat.

"There you are, upstart king." Its voice was loud as the thunder, but still somehow sounded dim, as if it was coming from a great distance. "I would not have wanted you to miss this."

I'd known for some time that Vepogenus was tough. That he held his tongue and didn't make a sound as that thing proceeded to flay him alive, invisibly, from the toes up, an inch at a time, showed just how tough he was. Only near the end, when he was probably almost dead and insensible, did he start to make noise.

King Uven might have raged. From the way he gripped the stones of the battlements, staring with every muscle taut as his uncle and right hand was slowly tortured to death by sorcerous means, I could tell that he wanted to. He wanted to scream, to curse, to lash out and tear that abomination to pieces.

But he was the king. Every eye on the wall was focused on him. He *could not* lose control.

A lesser man would have. I think *I* certainly would have. I couldn't have stood there in silence while Santos or Farrar was murdered so gruesomely.

With one single, final, strangled cry, Vepogenus gave up the ghost. The Dullahan held his corpse aloft for a few moments more, letting his blood drip to the ground, grinning that ghastly grin, before it tossed the body into the air to be snapped up like a dog treat by the thing it rode upon.

Uven flinched, ever so slightly, as that thing *crunch*ed down on Vepogenus's body. We could hear it from up there.

"You think that by forcing me to watch such a thing I will despair, and hand my people over to you as sacrifices." His voice was low, but it carried. "You know little of the Galel, if that is what you believe. I loved my uncle like a father. Yet even his murder does not abrogate my responsibility to the living." He pointed at the Dullahan, and his finger was rock steady, though every vein in his neck stood out. "Make no mistake, abomination. I *will* see you cast from this world, thrust into the place of eternal torment to be justly punished for all the evil you have done. I am sure that my uncle's murder was only the least of your crimes. But I will not let you draw me into a foolish act of passion. Not yet."

He turned and stalked from the battlements before the monster could reply. Yet I saw those dead eyes follow him, while the leer behind the green flames remained unchanged.

CHAPTER 27

I watched the phantom flicker its way along the battlements toward the gatehouse. It looked almost like one of the shadow men we had seen near Myrgarak, but this one wasn't as well-defined. Its movements seemed aimless, and it seemed to fuzz out of sight from time to time. It was like trying to watch a badly tuned TV set, back in the day when TVs worked off radio signals.

It wasn't the first such phantom we'd seen over the last few hours. I'd thought they were sorcerous spies at first, but the longer I watched the enemy as well as the strange and disturbing apparitions, the more I doubted it.

After all, the Peruni hadn't yet reacted to the Galel's steady, quiet withdrawal from the wall, leaving only a skeleton crew on the battlements, falling back to the fourth rampart to strengthen the defenses and hopefully remove most of the men from the immediate influence of whatever curses and mental fog the Dullahans had cast over the third wall.

That had been a difficult decision, and even more difficult to sell to Uven's lords. Despite the cloud of dread and despair that hung over the walls, that Galel urge to stand and fight was as strong as ever. If anything, I thought that the sense of despair was actually hardening some of these men even more, making them even less inclined to retreat. If they were going to die anyway, better to die denying the enemy just a little bit longer.

Finally, the king had needed to invoke his authority as sovereign and war leader with a few of them. He knew what he was about. He might not have told them the whole story, but with the enemy getting into people's heads, he also didn't want the full plan out there for everyone on the wall to know.

Especially not after the bad guys had demonstrated that they could snatch someone out from under our noses. Vepogenus might have been hard as nails, never even uttering a scream let alone confessing any plans, but we couldn't trust that every one of the defenders was going to be that tough.

So, most of them just thought that they were falling back to the fourth wall to present the enemy with a shorter front, more easily defended. The fourth wall was also set up differently, in a bit of a sawtooth pattern, allowing the battlements to support each other more efficiently and putting anyone trying to scale them into a kill box.

That wasn't the only reason, however, as valid as it was.

The third wall wasn't *entirely* solid. That wasn't a design flaw. There were passages inside the wall allowing for rapid reinforcement without exposing the react forces on the battlements. The thought process had apparently been that once the third wall was under serious attack, the enemy might be able to pelt the battlements with sufficient arrows, slingstones, and projectiles from siege engines to make the battlements themselves too dangerous to move around on. Either that, or they'd just wanted to be able to surprise the enemy by shifting reinforcements around unobserved. Whichever the case, they'd decided that it was worth the slight weakening of the eighteen-foot-thick wall to put the passages through it.

Those passages were key to the real plan.

I was crouched near the entrance of one of those passages, watching the phantom flicker and blur as it moved along the top of the wall. I was trying to figure it out. That might not be the wisest idea, considering some of the warnings that Bearrac had given us in the north about phantoms in the night. Even if they couldn't physically hurt us, some of these things were far more malevolent than their seemingly aimless movement might suggest. They could get in your head, leading to madness like Uoret had suffered before his death. It was generally best to try not to give them too much attention. It could attract them to you.

Something about this one, though, was simultaneously fascinating and pitiable. It seemed lost and tormented, and while I couldn't be sure, it didn't *feel* like the things summoned from the Outer Dark. Not most of them, anyway. It didn't seem to carry the feral rage of the oily horrors pulled from the beyond to rip and tear.

That wasn't the only reason I was watching it, though. I'd learned a while ago that aimless curiosity is a good way to get messed up here. I was watching it to make sure it *wasn't* a spy, like the strange bat-things that sorcerers and shamans had summoned to watch us in the north, and again on the plains of the northern marches of the empire.

Many of the sorcerers in this world did use such summonings the same way we would have used drones. But the fact that none of the Peruni, or even the wyverns or

Dullahans, had stirred since these things had started to wander the battlements, told me that unless they'd summoned duds, these apparitions weren't working for the Peruni wizards.

That made me wonder just what they were doing there, but that didn't require a whole lot of deep thought.

Terrible forces had been unleashed on the fortress of Cor Chatha. Sorcery, like some crimes, tends to attract things that are not entirely of this world. These shadowy phantoms seemed like blind, spectral echoes of the strange creatures we'd seen in the mad, broken ruins of Tethba, a place so thoroughly wrecked by the passage of the Outsider known as Thoggudan that it almost wasn't a part of the waking world anymore, but a haunted, blasted hellscape where the sun never shone through the haze of grit that hung above the shattered rocks, stirred by no wind and never settling.

The thought brought on a shudder. If the situation had really gotten bad enough to start to let those things through the veil, we were in a lot more trouble than it appeared.

A faint croak sounded in the clouds overhead, drawing my attention upward. I might have seen a shadow pass through the murk, ever so slightly darker than the pall of cloud itself. Unless I missed my guess, a wyvern had just done a flyby, high enough that we couldn't quite see it, and sure couldn't shoot at it.

That meant the jig was up. The phantoms that had cropped up on the wall might not be reporting back, but that monster sure would.

Sure enough, a moment later the braying horn calls echoed across the killing ground between the second and third walls, and the next assault swung into motion.

It didn't happen all at once, and I didn't actually watch much of it. I stayed in the tower just long enough to see the first ranks begin to move through the gaps in the walls, then I ducked into the passage, pulling the carefully disguised stone door shut behind me.

The passage was cramped and dark, but weapon lights dispelled the darkness, at least close up. A few handheld flashlights helped, too, especially when we didn't want to point our weapons at each other just so we could see. I pulled my own out of my chest rig and flashed it down at the floor.

Most of the rest had already hustled deeper in, heading for the southern end of the wall. We expected the enemy to make their main push at the gate, up near the north end, so we wanted to stay well away from there.

It wasn't because we didn't want to fight. Far from it. That just wasn't our mission. The fight was going to be up at the fourth wall. That was why most of the Galel defenders had already retreated, leaving the haunted and still too-long third wall to the enemy, and to us.

We were the stay-behind element, there to hunker down until the front line passed us, at which time we intended to come out and wreak havoc.

None of our other infiltration plans had worked out. We probably should have stayed out in the hinterlands if we'd wanted to get into the enemy's rear area, but that ship had sailed. This might present us with the opportunity we'd lost when the Peruni and the Dullahans had found the passage through the mountains.

Fortunately, while the corridor was narrow and the ceiling low, it wasn't so low that I had to duck walk to get through it. I still had to stoop a little, but that wasn't quite so bad.

It took a few minutes to catch up with the others. These were the men who had drawn the long straws, at least those who weren't Bailey and me. We were the Sword Bearers, so we had to be there. That meant we hadn't needed to join the almost cutthroat competition not to be the ones sent back to the fourth wall.

Bailey was already waiting for me in the little chamber, reinforced with blackened timber beams, just north of the last tower. He looked up with a raised eyebrow. This deep inside the wall, no one could hear or see anything.

"They're coming. First vanguard came through the third gap to the north about five minutes ago."

There were nods all around the chamber. I wasn't sure exactly how it had worked out that all three of the remaining original team leaders had wound up here, along with Gunny, Farrar, and Synar, but there it was. Bearrac and Diarmodh had come with us, as well. Mathghaman had wanted to, but he had another role to play, up on the fourth wall, in the battle to come.

Gunny was leaning against the wall, close to the steps leading up to the hidden door in the tower that would let us back out onto the battlements. "They'll be at this wall soon." He looked around at us, skipping over the Tuacha, since every one of them was more serene and disciplined than the lot of us. "We'll have to be patient and let them pass. When we think we've waited long enough, then we'll have to wait longer." He pinned Gurke with a stare.

The smaller man seemed to squirm a little and didn't meet his eyes. "Think of it as being on rear security in a firefight."

Bailey blew out a breath. It sounded loud in the darkness. "Don't want to wait too long."

The words hung in the still, stuffy air. It was a worry. We'd seen how fast the first and second walls had fallen. We had no way of knowing when or if the dragon might decide to step in again. If we waited too long, we might come out to find the fortress fallen, King Uven and all our brothers dead, and ourselves a bit *too* far behind enemy lines.

It didn't help that none of us had watches anymore, either. We'd gotten used to telling time by the sun and the stars. Down here, inside the wall, we had nothing to go on.

"We could send one man up to watch." I knew it was a gamble. Who was to say that the dragon wouldn't spot one man peering through a secret door? Who was to say the Peruni wouldn't clear the wall and the towers, just in case the Galel tried exactly what we were doing?

Bearrac looked up. "I can tell you when they have passed. Though I doubt that would satisfy you." The faint smile in his voice took any edge off the words. Bearrac might be something of a bull, but he was as perceptive as Mathghaman. He just didn't always feel like revealing it.

No one wanted to reply to that one, though. Gurke looked even more shamefaced, and Farrar and Synar studied their boots.

The wall shuddered. It was only a faint vibration, felt through our boots more than anything else. But it was there. "It begins." Diarmodh looked up at the ceiling, as if wondering if it would hold.

It would be a hell of a thing, if we'd gone to all this trouble just for the dragon to blast the wall over our heads and collapse the tens of thousands of tons of stone and fill over our heads, entombing us forever.

The blows continued, though the vibrations never got any worse. It was probably the assault on the gate; that would make the most sense, especially if the dragon was still keeping its distance. It seemed unlikely that it would swoop in for a mostly abandoned wall. It was keeping its heavy firepower in reserve for later.

For a long time, the wall quivered around us as the Peruni battered at the gate. I knew Orava still had a handful of mortar rounds left, but if he was using them, we were too deep in the wall to hear. I knew that the assault would not have an easy time. The gate was still strong, still barred, and if they scaled the walls, our guys had them covered with rifles, machineguns, scorpions, and catapults. Some of the Galel's war bows could even reach that far.

Finally, after what felt like hours, or maybe even days, the rhythmic shudder of the battering against the gates stopped. I was still sure the dragon hadn't stepped in. That would have been a far more catastrophic blow, I was sure.

"They're through." Gurke didn't know anything more than the rest of us, but it must have felt unnatural, letting that sudden quiet go unremarked.

It was in that sudden quiet, though, as Gurke's voice faded away, that I thought I heard a footstep, somewhere in the dark above us.

CHAPTER 28

EYES, muzzles, and lights turned toward the passage I'd followed down, but only darkness met our gaze. The sound did not repeat itself.

Yet in the quiet that followed, as the Peruni and their allies and slaves pushed through the breached gates and made for the killing ground before the fourth wall, we did not hear silence.

Faint whispers seemed to hiss through the darkness, but there was no visible source. I didn't even see the flickering shadows of the phantoms that I'd seen atop the wall. Only darkness and the stones and timbers around us.

Something was definitely putting my hackles up, though. I didn't think we'd gone as undetected as we might have hoped.

I wasn't the only one who thought so. Bearrac and Diarmodh were both on their feet, their eyes searching the walls and the shadows. "We should move." Bearrac had his rifle slung and his sword in his hand. That usually happened when we were about to face something that didn't go down when you shot it.

"Which way?" Gunny didn't ask questions. Maybe he'd heard enough that he'd already made the same decision, or maybe he just trusted Bearrac's judgment.

Maybe both. I know that was about where I fell on the matter.

Diarmodh was searching every inch of the walls and ceiling with his eyes, though I doubted he could see *that* much more than we could. He was listening, and probably reaching out with the Tuacha's more preternatural senses.

"Back the way we came." Even as he said it, I thought I heard that scrape again. It almost sounded as if it was coming from above and to the south of us, in the tower. That didn't fit with the footstep I'd thought I'd heard in the tunnel behind me, but if the monsters were really at work, it was entirely possible they weren't playing by the ordinary rules.

Since I was the nearest, I turned and started on the way back up the passage. Out of habit, I began to lead with my muzzle, but thought—if the Dullahans were playing games… I shifted my rifle to my back and drew the Sword of Iudicael, keeping my handheld light in my off hand, clenched against the grip of my buckler.

Bearrac had moved up right behind me, and I could feel his presence as I climbed. His footsteps were nearly silent, but he stayed close, just in case.

The whispers were getting louder, though they were still just quiet enough that it was impossible to make out words. The tone was enough, though. I didn't want to understand what they were saying.

Still, we reached the tower where I'd been holding our final observation post without incident. Yet the sense of dread and an increasingly oppressive feeling that we were being watched only intensified.

I hesitated before opening the disguised door, as the sensation that something was terribly wrong washed over me. Was there going to be a Dullahan on the other side, leering through the opening at me with that terrible severed head? Or one of those oily, smoky terrors they'd pulled from the Outer Dark as their minions?

Bearrac's presence steadied me out a little, and I eased the door open a crack.

Darkness met my eyes, and I had to flip my NVGs down. I really did not want to shine a white light out there without knowing who or what might be on the other side. The others had already extinguished their own lights behind me.

The tower was empty and still, though my ears were immediately battered by the noise of the fight for the fourth wall as soon as I cracked the door. The clash of steel, the *thud* of stones, arrows, and other projectiles, the screams and shouts of men in battle, some of them urging others on or simply venting their rage, others wounded and dying, shrieking out their pain, and the braying of horns and beating of battle drums were all punctuated by the crackling roar of gunfire. Even suppressed, our weapons still thundered more loudly than all the rest.

For a moment, I simply watched and listened. I'd seen enough not to trust the apparent stillness in the tower, not after hearing those whispers and other strange sounds down in the tunnel.

I couldn't just stay there forever, though. I eased the door open farther, carefully scanning the opening as I moved, until I had enough space that I was committed and had to make entry.

Bearrac was right behind me as I stepped quickly but smoothly into the now-empty tower, the two of us quickly clearing the chamber, weapons leveled and eyes and ears searching for any sign that we'd been made.

I almost had a heart attack as the shadows moved near the door leading onto the battlements. It was only one of the weird shadow apparitions, though, and it faded and flickered its way across the tower floor, passing between Bearrac and me without seeming to notice either of us, disappearing onto the battlements to the south.

I sure hoped those things were as clueless and aimless as they appeared to be. We would be in a world of hurt if that one raced off to a Dullahan—or worse, the dragon—to report on the Marine and the Tuacha warrior standing in the tower *behind* the front line.

Careful not to expose ourselves more than we could help, we moved away from the doorway and started to take a look around through the arrow slits and the doors leading onto the battlements in each direction.

I looked south first, back toward where I thought I'd heard that scrape. I almost immediately wished I hadn't.

You might think that I noticed the flying horror, shaped like a winged ape or something, its oversized, misshapen lower jaw distended and dripping smoking blackness from jagged, translucent fangs, first. It was a footnote, though.

The Dullahan that rode that thing wasn't as immensely tall as some of them. It looked like it had been about six feet tall in life. It was now closer to five, sans its head, which it held by the hair, its eyes glowing green. Something about those featureless green lamps reminded me of NVGs, though that might only have been because the creature was the one that appeared to be wearing black cammies or fatigues and what looked an awful lot like a plate carrier.

It held its bearded head high, turning it back and forth to let those beams of unearthly green radiance play over the tower where the flying horror perched. The Dullahan's whip writhed in its grip, almost as if one or two of the spines that made it up were still alive and still twisting in pain.

For some reason, I was drawn to study the monster. What would bring a minion of the Summoner, a man who had sold his soul to the Outer Dark to the point where he was carrying his own head around, to dress in what looked an awful lot like tactical gear from back in the World? We hadn't seen anything like it since coming through the mists.

I shouldn't have watched it for that long. Its head turned toward me and those glowing green eyes locked gazes with mine. In an eyeblink, I found myself somewhere else.

* * *

The man who looked around at his companions as they gathered in the glass-faced tower couldn't avoid a curl of his lip. He might have long since put the sort of action that would call for the uniform he wore behind him—that had lasted just long enough to reach the next rank—but he wore it to distinguish himself from the sophists, captains of industry, and soft-clothed politicians around him. He might be little different from most of them, but his pride demanded that distinction. He was something more—even if he only had been for a moment, relatively speaking.

The bald man in the sleek black suit was speaking. "You stand on the edge of a new age, my friends. Those who would cling to the past, to outdated mores and rules, bitter in their bigotry and fear, will soon fall behind. What we will do tonight shall change… *everything*."

His curiously pointed features creased in a smile, one that even gave the man in the black uniform a momentary shiver. He wanted what the bald man promised, but that didn't mean he was always comfortable around him. There was an intensity to the man who called himself merely Julian, an intensity that sometimes became terrifying. The man in black, who prided himself on his own Machiavellian ruthlessness, refused to admit to even himself that he was afraid of Julian, but even he avoided those feverishly burning eyes when they turned to him.

"Tonight will see everything you thought you were about burned away. All that matters tonight is your commitment. Should you hold firm through tonight, tomorrow you will step into a new world." He stepped up onto the dais, backed by a soaring glass window that looked out on the city. "And you will step into that new world as its gods."

The man glanced at the middle-aged woman in the pantsuit next to him. She looked even more nervous than he felt, but there was still a spark in her eyes, a spark of sheer, unadulterated ambition.

Only five years before, he might not have been in this company. He wouldn't have believed that he ever could be, let alone that he would be looking forward to some sort of strange ritual that promised a form of apotheosis.

He wouldn't even have thought that most of the people around him would have believed in any such thing.

Passing the threshold of wealth and influence had opened his eyes to many things. Julian had opened them still further. So, while he feared what was about to happen, he still eagerly looked forward to it.

This night would change everything. After this night, he would live forever.

* * *

Bearrac's hand shook me out of it just in time. I snapped my eyes away from the Dullahan, but the damage was done. It let out a hollow laugh and kicked the flying ape-thing into the air.

We were made.

CHAPTER 29

THE beast from the Outer Dark slammed down onto the tower, having covered the distance from its perch with blinding speed. The entire structure shook with the impact, but Bearrac was already hauling me backward into the tunnel.

We were back inside the wall before the flying horror could tear its way through the roof overhead, though we could certainly hear it working on it, even as the disguised door was pulled shut.

I didn't think for a moment that it would stop that thing. The Dullahan was the size of a man and possessed of unnatural senses. Its mount was a thing of the Outer Dark that manifested in that size and shape because either it or its summoner wanted it to. I'd seen things like it grow and stretch to reach into tight quarters before.

"Move!" Bearrac didn't bother with trying to stay quiet anymore. "Dullahan!"

That got the rest moving. We'd barely covered a dozen yards, though, before the door above, thick timber faced with stones, shuddered under a powerful blow. A *crack* echoed down the passageway.

The passages weren't all that complex. If they had been, it would have risked weakening the wall too much, as thick as it already was. That limited our options. We had to run back toward the tower where the Dullahan and its mount had first alighted.

That was unfortunately predictable, but we might be able to get our shit together by then, provided the Dullahan didn't send its pet after us and tear the wall down around our ears in the process.

The plan had already gone awry, all because I hadn't been able to restrain my curiosity.

The vision I'd received from the Dullahan clung to my memory, though, even as we booked it through the tunnel and the door behind us finally broke. Was it real? Had that been the Summoner I'd seen? Had he really been speaking English, or was that just the effect of understanding what had been said, since it was in my head? And why had everything looked so much like the world we'd come from?

It wasn't the time to think it over. We were in a fight for our lives. It might even already be over, if the Dullahan figured out where we'd gone and summoned the dragon. That thing had already blown through the wall in more than one place. There was no doubt that it could do it again, and if that eldritch lightning hit one of us, we'd probably be vaporized.

We reached the chamber where we'd waited out the breach of the gate in about half the time it had taken us to get up to the tower. Bailey was already posted up on the entrance to the southernmost strongpoint, the Sword of Categyrn in his hand, ready for anything that might come at us, backed up by Synar, Diarmodh, and Farrar, who kept their muzzles on the closed door. I turned to check the way we'd coming, peering into the blackness of the tunnel, as Bearrac, Gunny, and Gurke covered me.

I waited, as the quiet descended again, hearing the beating of my heart in my ears and the rasp of my own breath, and little else. The sound of the Dullahan's mount tearing through the door had stopped, and if it was coming down the passage after us, it was being awfully quiet about it.

Considering what it was, that wasn't a reason to relax.

Bearrac peered into the shadows beyond our lights. I just watched and waited, knowing that if there was anything up there, anything coming for us, Bearrac would know before I did. I didn't turn to look, but I knew that Diarmodh was probably doing the same thing over Bailey's shoulder.

"This way." Diarmodh had picked up on something. He didn't elaborate, but right then probably wasn't the best time to get into a detailed planning discussion, anyway.

I thought I might see a faint green glow somewhere back up that passage we'd just come down, anyway, and while I was probably in better shape, physically and metaphysically, to face a Dullahan than I had been in Cor Legear, I still didn't want to get into a duel with one right then and there. That wasn't why we'd stayed on the wall, after all.

How to break contact right then was a problem, though. Our avenues of escape were rather sharply limited, and it wasn't as if we could confuse or befuddle the Dullahans, either. We'd escaped them once before, but that had apparently been because they'd decided to stick with the army of Ar-Annator. Here, where they dominated the battlefield outside the fourth wall, this was about to get hairy.

I took a deep breath as we turned to follow Diarmodh into the southern tower. I was reaching a point where I was becoming resigned to an inevitable conclusion.

Our plan had gone sideways, and now we had no choice but to confront the Dullahans and kill them if at all possible. I supposed there was a reason that the two of us Sword Bearers had come along on this mission, though getting into a fight with the Dullahans now was going to make it that much harder to get to the emperor. Might even make it impossible.

Every plan we'd tried had gone haywire. It was hard, even while focused on survival, not to start going down that grim rabbit hole. We'd been remarkably successful as a fighting force since coming through the mists, seemingly with divine intervention on our side a few times. Yet now, when it all came down to it, it looked like we might have run out of maneuvering room. It was hard not to think we were doomed.

That laborious burden of dread weighed on us all as we followed Bailey and Diarmodh into the south tower. Had we come all this way just to die in the fall of Cor Chatha?

Then we were in the tower and couldn't think about it anymore.

I'd more than half expected to find more winged horrors, wyverns, and the dragon tearing the tower apart, but there was nothing so dramatic when we came through the door. In fact, the tower appeared as deserted as it had when we'd first gone down into the wall.

"What the hell?" Bailey looked around, the Sword of Categyrn still held high and ready. "It can't just be the one."

I looked back the way we'd come. Sure enough, I could see that green glow intensifying. The Dullahan was still coming.

"Maybe it wants the kill for itself." The thought just sort of occurred to me as I spoke. "I mean, why else wouldn't it have called in the dragon?"

"That gives us a chance, though, right?" Gurke looked back and forth between Bailey and me. "Conor, you already killed one."

"Only with Iudicael's direct help, and it still almost killed me." I didn't turn away from the door, though Bearrac had pulled it closed. I was torn on that. A part of me really didn't want to lose track of the Dullahan until it popped up right in front of us, while another part didn't want to look at it even more.

Bearrac hadn't said much since he'd gotten us moving again. "There is more than one. The other is waiting for the first to flush us into the open."

I flexed my fingers around the Sword's hilt. "Maybe I should go down there and fight it, then. Better than getting picked off in the open on the wall."

Bearrac shook his shaggy head. "They know what happened to their fellow in Cor Legear. They are proud, arrogant beings, nearly as proud as the Outsiders they are thrall to, but they are cunning, nevertheless. They will not wish to come within reach of that Sword. They will seek to strike us from a distance, herd us into a place from which there is no escape, and then use their sorcery to bring us low."

"Then that's a trap." The door remained shut and still. It was eerie, just how still everything was, despite the cacophony of battle at the fourth wall, only a few hundred yards away.

"Most likely."

Diarmodh had his head cocked as if listening. Or maybe thinking deeply. "If we move quickly, we can get to the tower we just left ahead of them."

Bearrac just nodded. Gunny looked like he thought the idea was questionable, but he wasn't going to gainsay one of our Tuacha comrades. There wasn't time to ask why Diarmodh thought we should head out into the open.

With gritted teeth and weapons in clenched hands, we headed up onto the wall.

The noise was a lot worse up there. Flames licked from several places both atop the fourth wall and on the ground below. It seemed both sides were using firepots, and arrows and stones still flew back and forth. Wyverns dipped toward the battlements, though they seemed fewer than before. Maybe there were a limited number of those monsters, and we'd whittled them down.

I could hope.

We cleared the upper chamber quickly, Bailey and I leading with the Swords—since we suspected we were up against the Dullahans first and foremost—and immediately followed by Gunny, Gurke, Diarmodh, and Bearrac with their rifles.

It was just as empty as the tower below. If there were another Dullahan hunting us, it was keeping its distance.

The one below must have figured out that we'd ske-daddled. The door was struck with a *bang*, and even a floor up I thought I could hear it start to crack.

"Go." Bearrac had a hand on my shoulder, his rifle held muzzle high next to my head. Diarmodh stood in the center of the tower, his head bowed, chanting soft-ly. He would stay there until we were off the open bat-tlements, lending us spiritual cover fire, as it were, and hopefully helping to keep the other Dullahan—Tigharn willing there was just one—off us.

So, while Diarmodh prayed, we ran.

It was a hell of a sprint. The air tasted of sulfur and something metallic, burning in my nostrils as we burst out of the tower and headed over the first Dullahan's head toward the partially smashed ruin of the second tower, where the flying horror had ripped its way through the roof.

I pounded down the length of the wall, my rifle ham-mering against my back, feeling as exposed as a bug on a plate. Almost all the enemy's attention seemed to be on the fourth wall, but there were still formations of infan-try moving up from below, passing through the smashed third gate, climbing up the steep and rocky killing ground between the ramparts. Wyverns still swooped overhead, and I could see at least three Dullahans riding creatures of shadow and smoke, one shaped like a pterodactyl, an-other like a lion, and yet another looking almost like a gi-ant wasp. All but little more than impressionistic shapes made of burning tar and smoke.

That was only three, though. Counting the one down inside the wall beneath us, that left twenty-six.

That was not comforting.

I looked out toward the fallen outer walls then, just before we got to the partially ruined tower. Just in time to see another dark, bat-like thing with a Dullahan in a long coat or cloak, flapping in the wind of its flight, holding its head aloft where its eyes gleamed like red coals, bearing down on us.

"Get inside!" I still had the Sword out, and I knew that shooting either the flying thing or the monster on its back wouldn't do squat, but I felt the urge anyway. I skidded to a halt, fight vying with flight as I shoved Synar toward the opening in the tower. I wanted nothing to do with those things, but I knew that I was one of the few who stood any chance at all with them in single combat.

Iudicael, I could use your help right now.

The Dullahan might want me—or more likely, it wanted the Sword—but it didn't want to get close enough for me to swing at it. Bearrac had been right. None of them wanted to come within reach of that bitter blade. It swooped above us, its bone whip snapping down to pass close by me and take a chunk out of Farrar's shoulder.

He let out a cry as he staggered forward, then Gunny was hauling him inside. "Come on, Conor!"

I looked around one last time. I was the last one on the battlements. Even Bailey had ducked inside the tower rather than wait for that thing to try to get him with its whip.

I turned and ran into the dubious shelter of the tower, even as the Dullahan came back around, the bat-thing flaring its wings just in time to slam down on the roof over our heads with a *boom.*

CHAPTER 30

GUNNY was already hard at work. We'd brought more than just our weapons, just in case. Each man had an assault pack with some explosives, grenades, and other party favors. He was now quickly priming a satchel charge, while debris sprinkled down from the hole in the ceiling and the walls cracked and started to slump under the monster's weight.

Those weren't the explosives we were used to from back in the World. These were from the *Coira Ansec*, which meant that they weren't *quite* C4. I was sure that if we'd chemically analyzed them, they'd have the same molecular makeup, but they had a tendency to respond the way we needed them to, regardless of the actual weight of the charge.

That could come in handy. It was also still spooky as hell, sometimes.

The batlike thing glowered in through the hole in the ceiling, and Gurke shot it, just because. The 7.62 round didn't really hurt it, but it reared back from the hole, perhaps buying us a little time.

Fortunately, Gunny didn't need to do much. The initiation systems had already been built, so he just had to attach the blasting caps, push them into the charges, and pull the igniters. He did that quickly, tossing the charge next to the door to the southern passage.

"Northern tunnels. Move."

I was already pulling the hatch to the northern passage open, though I had no intention of being the first one down. There was still the possibility of a threat down there, but the more immediate threat was that robed Dullahan riding the bat-thing over our heads.

Diarmodh took point while I hung back, but Gunny pointed at me. "Conor, you're up front. Bailey has rear. Everyone else, pack it in and make it quick. That fuse isn't that long."

We hustled into the dark, even as the bat thing started to rip a bigger hole in the ceiling. I was deep in the tunnel before Bailey pulled the hatch shut, but I sure felt the blast when the charges went off.

The entire wall shuddered and rocked. Whatever the explosive weight of that charge had supposedly been, the *Coira Ansec*'s explosives had given themselves that extra bit of oomph to make sure the tower disintegrated.

I had to ignore the movement and the dust that filtered down through the air in the suddenly tight and claustrophobic tunnel. Because I thought that I'd heard something ahead of us. The echoes of the blast had continued to reverberate down the tunnel, and the wall itself seemed to shift and crack under the stresses of the explosion and the collapsing tower.

Meeting a Dullahan at close quarters in that tunnel was a nightmare scenario that I didn't want to think about. One of the horrors from the Outer Dark would be just as bad.

Shining my light ahead of me, wishing I could somehow have both my rifle and the Sword out, I moved up behind Diarmodh, who hadn't relinquished the pointman position as we'd gone deeper. He couldn't have, really. The tunnel was too narrow.

We reached the next tower in a few moments. This tunnel came out directly in the lower part of the tower, near the door leading onto the open ground between the third and fourth walls. We didn't want to go out there at the moment. It would put us in the enemy's rear area, but we'd also be exposed and in the middle of the beaten zone of friendly fire. That wasn't the mission, anyway, and I thought that Gunny was still hoping that we might manage to break contact and get a shot at the emperor.

Right then, I wasn't sure if that was a realistic hope. It's like hoping that you can lose a bloodhound in the open. The Dullahans were hunting us, and I wasn't sure we'd get clear short of killing all of them. Which also didn't seem realistic.

We quickly cleared the tower, finding it empty and no Dullahans or other monsters waiting for us. At least, not inside the tower itself.

Diarmodh and I had climbed toward the top, moving carefully and quietly, Diarmodh's rifle leveled over my shoulder as I led the way with the Sword of Iudicael. We slowed as we neared the top, and I strained my ears to hear over the awful noise reverberating from the fourth wall.

A low, sepulchral laugh reached my ears. *"Come, Sword Bearer. Test yourself against us."*

While it might have galled me a little, I immediately backed down the stairs. There was more than one of them up there, and they were waiting for us.

"They'll have some sort of trap in place." I knew it, and from the look in Gunny's eyes on the second landing as I told him, he knew it, too. "They wouldn't have ruined the ambush that way otherwise."

"I think you're right." He looked up at the timber ceiling above us with a grimace.

"How many do we think there are?" Gurke's voice was quiet, but there was a note of determination and resignation in his words.

Something about the tone of his voice drew my gaze with a frown. He was slightly pale, but his face was set, his jaw firm. "I'm not sure. At least two."

"There are three." Diarmodh sounded absolutely certain. "One sits its mount atop the tower, and the other two stand upon the battlements to either side."

Gurke nodded, taking a deep breath as he looked down at the steps under his feet. "Okay, then." He turned toward the stairs leading up. "Conor, you and Sean should probably keep your heads down until they're right on top of me."

"Wait a second." Bailey shoved past Synar to grab Gurke by the arm. "What the hell are you trying to do, Ross?"

"Look, Sean." Gurke glanced up again at the faint creak from the timbers on the inside of the tower. "I get it, now. I understand why Cairbre came to me. Why he talked to me about death and about getting ready for it. It's been right in front of my face all the time." He stabbed a finger down at the floorboards at his feet, indicating the tower and the wall. "He was warning me, telling me to get ready because I'm going to die here." He looked around at us, his eyes going to Gunny first, then to me and Bailey. "I get it. And I'm all right with it, now. I've been thinking about it ever since he appeared to me, and now I see that it's going to be here. This is why I'm here. I'll draw them in, and then Conor and Bailey can kill them with the Swords."

Gunny's frown was getting thunderous. "Ross, this isn't going to work that way. They're not going to come right to you, and as soon as the Swords appear, they're going to bolt. I'm not going to let you throw your life away like that. If there was a chance it would work, that would be one thing."

"We're wasting time here, Gunny." He started up again, pulling his arm away from Bailey's grip. "It'll work."

I looked at Bailey, but he could only shrug. Short of wrestling Gurke down and beating him unconscious, neither of us could think of what to do.

Gunny did, though. "Get ready to haul that idiot back down here. I've got an idea." He was already digging in Synar's pack for another satchel charge.

I was closest, since I'd been the first one up the stairs, so I moved up. I thought I saw what Gunny had in mind. "Farrar, get your ass back in that tunnel."

For a moment, I thought he was going to argue. Farrar wasn't the kind of Marine who did that, most of the time, but when there were so few of us, and the odds were so long, he just might. If he'd been scared enough to hang back or even take any excuse to run, he wouldn't have stayed out here with us.

PETER NEALEN

There wasn't time to argue about it, though, and he knew it. He ducked into the tunnel with Synar and Bailey, while I went after Gurke, and Gunny started priming charges again.

I pushed myself, running up the steps despite the exhaustion that had set in over the last several days. My legs didn't want to move quite the way I wanted them to, and my lungs burned, but I got to the tower just barely behind Gurke.

He had his rifle in his hands and stood in the center of the upper chamber, looking from side to side as if he wasn't quite sure which way to engage first. The Dullahan and its mount on top of the tower hadn't breached the roof yet, but the entire structure creaked and groaned as it moved around up there.

The Dullahan to the north side of the tower looked almost like an Egyptian pharaoh, sans its head, which hung from a handle in its left hand. It didn't have the headdress, but its breastplate was bronze, carved to resemble crossed wings over a blackened sun, with a mantle of bronze scales over the shoulders. The loincloth was black, rather than white, but the impression was still there. Its head was a bronze mask, its eyes glowing a sterile, electric blue.

The one to the south wore a dark robe with flared shoulders and a wide sash. The fingers that were wrapped around its whip were long and thin, its nails sharpened talons. It carried its head on the end of a scepter, wrought in black-enameled gold, and its narrowed eyes glowed a leprous yellow, a disturbing glow that, despite its shade, held no warmth.

Both severed heads were leering with grins that made my blood run cold.

Gurke decided just as I gained the top of the steps and pivoted to the south, shooting the robed Dullahan in the center chest. I saw the impact as the bullet punched through silk and brocade, and what might have been dust puffed away from the hole, but the Dullahan didn't even stagger. If anything, its hideous grin only got wider.

While he was turned away, the Egyptian-looking monster flicked its whip, and that chain of human vertebrae licked out to wrap itself around Gurke's neck. Even as I lunged forward, it started to tighten, and Gurke began to gag.

I severed the whip with a single slash, and half of it dissolved into smoke as Gurke collapsed to his knees, choking and coughing. The Dullahans continued to close in as I stood over my fellow team leader, the Sword of Iudicael leveled at the pharaonic-looking headless horror. That one drew another bone sword, not unlike the one the Dullahan I'd fought in Cor Legear had wielded, but this one had a slight forward curve, a bit like a falx. The second, which was a step behind after Gurke had shot it, also drew a curved sword, though it was more like a saber.

Outnumbered by monsters that weren't human and had the sorcerous power to make this a *very* unfair fight even without the numerical advantage. That was bad enough. Being outflanked was worse.

Fortunately, I had no intention of standing and fighting in that room. I grabbed Gurke by the strap of his chest rig with the hand that held my buckler and dragged him backward, right down the steps behind me.

I had to move fast, and I knew that the Dullahans could move faster. I was counting on their caution after Cor Legear to give me just enough breathing room.

Bearrac had been right. They closed in, but they didn't want to engage while I held the Sword of Iudicael. They might not know all the details, but they knew that *something* had happened in Cor Legear, and that I had killed one of them. That had to be a shock, after all this time. So, they hung back, their weapons drawn, and the one with its head on a scepter started to chant.

That was the threat. They might not close in to engage a Sword Bearer in one-on-one combat, but they could still summon monsters and curses. That might make things bad.

Bearrac had been ready for it, though. He was waiting on the first landing down, and he pointed his own sword up at the Dullahans. He didn't chant, per se, but that was only because his brief, clipped command in the ancient language of prayer and invocation was too short to carry a tune.

It had the effect of a slap in the face. The one Dullahan I could still see, the Egyptian-looking one, reeled back from the opening, and then Gunny grabbed Gurke and hauled him into the tunnel. I followed, Bearrac right on my heels.

We raced up the tunnel, all too aware that there might be more Dullahans waiting for us at the other end, but while that was a threat, it wasn't as immediate as the two that had been lying in wait at this tower.

There was also the fact that we were trying to outrace the time fuse.

The explosion felt even bigger than the one before. Shattered masonry collapsed with a roar behind us as the entire wall shook like an earthquake had hit. Dust sifted down from the ceiling above our heads, and I could have sworn I heard the stones crack to either side of me.

The shaking died down, and when I looked back, I thought I saw a faint glow coming from the door, as if the entire thing had cracked open and was letting in some of the light of the fires up by the fourth wall.

We slowed our rush, and I turned to face that glow, the Sword of Iudicael held in a high guard. If the Dullahans were coming, they'd come soon. Either that, or whatever they summoned to try to take us down without exposing them to the bite of the Sword.

They didn't come, and whatever they might have been working just before the charges had gone off, Bearrac's word of command had apparently stopped it. I still held what I had, even as the big Tuacha warrior rejoined me.

He didn't prod me right away. It was almost as if he were listening and waiting.

"Come, Conor. Time is short, but we have an opportunity."

I didn't ask questions. I was pretty sure I knew what he was getting at. With the Sword still held ready, I advanced on the hole in the wall.

The blast *had* been bigger. A *lot* bigger. Half the tower had collapsed, sloughing off in a landslide of shattered masonry and splintered timbers. Only one jagged, broken rampart still stood, facing uphill toward the fourth wall, a few fractured bits of the stairs and landings still clinging to the inside. The rest was a slide of scree pointing down toward the second wall.

The faint illumination from another bolt of lightning flickered off something shiny about a third of the way down. From there, it wasn't hard to see the pulsating glow of unnatural eyes in a severed head a short distance uphill from the body, that was even then starting to try to dig its way out.

Bearrac was right. We didn't have a lot of time. I scrambled down the unsteady hill of wreckage, the Sword in my fist but held high, so that I didn't accidentally stab myself. It might be a sacred artifact, handed down from on high by Iudicael, Messenger of Tigharn, but it was still a sharp blade, and I was still a mere man.

It took me a few moments to reach the head, the bronze mask torn away in the cave-in, revealing a face warped and strangely bloated, the cheekbones too wide, the chin exaggerated, the lips too large, all of it looking papery and dry, like a dead thing that had been sloppily dressed up to look like a living person. Those blue eyes blazed, turning toward me and crackling with miniature bolts of lightning.

The mouth opened, as if to speak, but I struck first. The Sword's point lanced through one of those electric eyes and the mouth froze, the lights going out as quickly as if I'd flipped a switch.

It was starting to rain. I looked up for the other Dullahan, but Bailey had come down the slide behind me and beaten me to it. I saw him wiping off the Sword of Categyrn, the scepter that had borne the other Dullahan's head in the wreckage at his feet.

Bearrac stood between us, looking up at the sky. I followed his gaze to see the third Dullahan, the one flying on the bat-thing's back, winging into the sky, even as the dragon came down out of the clouds.

That was bad. But we had a clear route down into the open ground and the enemy camp now, if we moved fast enough.

With little more than a look, we started bounding down the slide.

CHAPTER 31

WE ran for all we were worth, making for the debris at the base of the second wall, as far from the still-marching column of Peruni, Avurs, and other auxiliary infantry pouring through the open gate toward the breach in the third wall.

The dragon came down out of the clouds, but it didn't come after us, at least not immediately. It roared, lightning flickering from its jaws, but it almost seemed as if it was moving on the Dullahan riding the bat-creature.

I couldn't make out the words that boomed through the sky, but it was fairly clear that they weren't amicable. We didn't have a whole lot of time or energy to try to figure out exactly what was happening, either, because even though the Peruni seemed entirely focused on the fight for the fourth wall—if they had noticed the explosions on the third, they must have either figured they were booby traps we'd left behind or else they were simply too busy to worry about it—more of the Dullahans were peeling off to come after us.

They were being more cautious than ever, flying those tar-and-smoke monstrosities overhead and lashing at us with those long, macabre whips, but never quite getting too close. The fact that, for whatever reason, the dragon seemed to be pissed at them, was just an added advantage for us.

Just before Bailey and I reached the break in the wall that the enemy seemed to be ignoring, since the breach through the third was so far to the north, the dragon stooped on one of the Dullahans as it climbed again after trying to hit Bearrac with its whip. The dragon let out a steam-boiler hiss that shook the stones underfoot and struck like a rattler, catching the flying horror in the neck and shaking it like a dog with a small animal in its mouth.

The flying mount disintegrated into black smoke and the Dullahan, in a full panoply of knee-length mail and a ragged black cloak, leaped free, the cloak spreading out like wings to break its fall, fluttering in the wind as it descended to the ground and landed on its feet. It was far enough away that I couldn't attack it without giving it far too much advance notice, so I got into the gap in the wall and turned to face it, staying barricaded on the wreckage as much as I could, ready to move in to intercept it if it came after us. Synar wasn't quite as fast as some of the rest of us, and Gunny might be a tank, but he had one speed, which, since he was about five years older than any of the rest of us, wasn't the same as mine.

The Dullahan, however, rather than attacking, wrapped itself in utter darkness and seemed to disappear into the ground.

Not what I would consider reassuring. I was sure it would be back. It was just trying to get away from the dragon.

Gunny and Synar reached the wall, and then we were under attack again.

Two of them came in along the base of the wall, riding those horrors from the Outer Dark, except this time they weren't flying. They slithered along the ground like fast-moving serpents, the Dullahans somehow managing to ride without moving with their undulations.

Synar and Gunny barely got into the gap before they turned and opened fire. Bullets wouldn't have much effect on these things. We knew that. But we had to fight back *somehow*.

I waded forward with the Sword of Iudicael in my fist. Bailey had already pushed to the other side of the wall. He had to cover that side. Having only two of the blessed blades meant we had to split responsibilities, or we'd be quickly flanked and overwhelmed.

Rounds ripped through unnatural flesh without effect. The Sword seemed to glitter strangely in my hand as I threw myself in front of Gunny, just as one of those snake-like horrors snapped at him.

I slashed it across the mouth, and it stopped dead, recoiling from the blade but not quite fast enough. Blue flames erupted from it, and it writhed and screamed, thrashing against the ground and the wall as it burned. The shock was enough that it actually threw the Dullahan onto its back, sending it tumbling nearly twenty feet before it recovered. Then it smashed the other dark creature against the wall, and the blue flames spread. That headless rider leaped free, only to pull the same shadow-wreathed vanishing act that the first one had done.

Then the dragon came again, and we had to run. The blast of wind from its wings battered at us as we got around the outside of the wall, putting the stone rampart between us and the monster, even as it blasted a forked bolt of sun-bright lightning from its jaws at the Dullahan that had been thrown.

For a moment, no one moved. We just sheltered behind the wall, covered from the chaos happening behind us, and gasped for breath. It took an immense effort to get out of that meager and illusory cover and move again. We had only the weapons in our hands and on our backs. We were cut off from the rest of the defenders, and therefore without support, facing some of the most dangerous monsters on the face of the planet. The fact that the dragon seemed to be worse than the Dullahans wasn't a comforting thought. What could threaten the original disciples of the Summoner? It was choice between bad and worse.

But we had to move. The mission was in front of us, not behind us, and the infighting between the dragon and the Dullahans was an unexpected but welcome diversion.

I didn't know why they were fighting. Maybe they had different objectives here. Maybe the Emperor had misjudged how much control he had over the denizens of the Outer Dark, and for whatever reason they had decided to take their hatred out on each other. Maybe they were just in competition for who could claim the Two Swords.

That wasn't a comforting thought, either.

We sprinted across the empty ground, staying close together and praying that the darkness at least hid us from the Peruni and their allies. It wouldn't hide us from the creatures of chaos and old night that hunted us, but we could do without the added complication of getting swarmed by human fighters, too.

With another roar, the dragon rose above the wall. Its wings spread as it seized the battlements in its talons and hauled itself up, framed by those enormous pinions that blotted out the fires on the fourth wall.

Synar stumbled as he looked back. We were still a hundred yards from the first wall, right out in the open, as exposed as bugs on a plate. It was terrifying, I'm not gonna lie.

Yet the dragon wasn't looking for us. Not yet. It dipped its massive, triangular head and swung it too and fro, its eyes glittering in the dark, lightning playing around its fangs as its forked tongue flicked out to taste the air. It had to be able to see us. It just didn't seem to care. Not right at the moment.

It snarled a curse, though in a tongue I couldn't understand. I could feel its voice in my chest and the rocks underfoot rattled with the thunder of it. Its version of the mind speech was apparently somewhat selective. If it wasn't talking to us, we couldn't understand it.

That was probably a blessing.

I grabbed Synar and hauled him to his feet, and we kept running. We didn't make straight for one of the breaches in the wall, mainly because they were all some distance away, and we wanted *some* kind of cover, quickly. Even though that cover could easily turn into a death-trap if the dragon came across the killing ground after us.

It seemed to be focused on the Dullahans now, though. They were regrouping while it searched the shadows beneath the second wall, and I could hear their calls, hollow, inhuman hoots that didn't sound like men's voices anymore. The sound sent a shudder through me. Whatever they had become, when the mask was off, they weren't men anymore. Far from it. They might still walk the earth, but I suspected that whatever souls they'd once had were now writhing in hell, while *something else* walked the land in their bodies, toting their heads around.

That might account for the fact that they seemed to be giving the dragon a run for its money.

Those unearthly calls were answered, and soon at least a dozen of the flying horrors had begun circling the dragon. Eerie chants reverberated through the night, as they gathered their sorceries for the battle to come.

It seemed incredibly stupid from a strategic perspective. There was still a war going on, and the Peruni and their auxiliaries were fully engaged with the Galel and the rest of the platoon up on the fourth wall. The clash of battle still echoed off the mountain, thunderously loud even over the noise of the closer battle of wills between the dragon and the Dullahans. Yet these weren't men, and if the emperor had thought that they would share his goals, he was a fool. Their objectives were otherworldly, and probably included the utter ruin of both sides.

I reached the wall just ahead of Synar, and we all halted briefly, gasping for breath. It had been a downhill run, but the ground was rough and the sheer terror of what was going on was bad enough that it sucked the life out of you.

Lightning flashed and dark shadows flickered and tried to wrap around the dragon. It was shrugging their spells off like they were spitballs, but so far, they seemed to be evading most of its wrath. They were not evenly matched, though. That much was obvious. Given time, the dragon would consume them all.

For the moment, though, as I caught my breath, I just hoped that they kept each other busy while we finished our raid. Whether we'd make it back to the wall alive or not was an open question. It looked pretty unlikely. But if we succeeded in killing or capturing the emperor, it might be worth it.

The nearest opening in the wall was about three hundred yards to the south of us. The stone had run and flowed under the dragon's lightning blasts, and the ground in front of the gap looked like it had been in the path of a volcanic lava flow. Bailey was already running for it, Diarmodh close behind.

Gurke was sucking wind, and he still looked a little shell shocked, even under NVGs, that he hadn't died in the tower. He'd been sure it was over. Until it wasn't.

I gave him a punch to the shoulder as I ran past him. It wasn't much, but it was enough to jar him into remembering that we were there to do a job. Maybe he hadn't needed it, but he'd been slowing down, and he'd been sort of staring at nothing there for a second.

As we ran for the gap, I felt the hair on the back of my neck go up. Being that close to the war between the dragon and the Dullahans was like being inside a thunderstorm. It felt like we were about to get blasted at random any second.

I glanced over my shoulder as we neared the gap, Bailey slowing to a combat glide as he got closer, unwilling to just charge into unknown territory without caution. I wished I hadn't.

While nearly a dozen Dullahans clashed with the dragon, another half dozen were winging their way around the flanks, skimming the shoulders of the mountain to avoid the dragon and banking to arrow toward our position. They wanted the Swords. Of that I was certain.

The war with the dragon was probably over that very objective.

Which made us the top of the target deck. And we were surrounded by the enemy, completely cut off from support.

Under those circumstances, there was only one thing to do. Attack.

I moved up to join Bailey and Diarmodh at the breach, Bearrac stepping up to my side while Gunny, Synar, and Farrar covered our rear and flanks, at least as best they could with rifles against the otherworldly things of the Outer Dark. The Peruni still hadn't noticed us—either that, or they were being told not to—so our foes were all of the particularly weird, spooky, and hard-to-kill variety.

We couldn't be entirely sure that we'd necessarily be in the same position on the other side of the wall. We were awfully close to where we'd last seen the emperor's standard. I sheathed the Sword, brought my rifle up, and gave Bailey's shoulder a squeeze. He nodded, his eyes still fixed on the breach, and then we were moving, going through the breach with our weapons leveled, searching for targets.

CHAPTER 32

WE had plenty.

What looked like the entire imperial encampment had been set up right on the other side of the wall, probably moved there shortly after the breach. We found ourselves right at the edge of a semicircle of pavilions, seemingly set up close enough together to form a wall, as weak as such a defense would be against anything we carried. Maybe it was intended to be more symbolic. At any rate, we were standing near the open ground surrounding that palisade of tents, with hundreds more, much plainer, tents set up in squares or circles farther away.

That semicircle of tents wasn't unguarded, either, which was the first indicator I saw that it was more than just a tent city. Men in black-enameled mail and tall helmets crested with black feathers stood stock-still, spears in their hands, set about ten yards apart around the curve of close-set tents.

It had to take some serious discipline to stand that still while all hell was breaking loose above and the Dullahans were coming in from both the northern and southern flanks. I wasn't sure I wanted to know what had instilled that discipline in them.

When Bailey and I came through the gap, though, they reacted quickly. A shout went up, and in seconds, they were moving, forming a square just on the other side of the breach, bristling with spears.

These were mortal men, not Dullahans or horrors from beyond the veil. We didn't need to transition to the Swords for this fight. It was almost refreshing.

We both opened fire at almost the same instant. I caught my target just above the sternum with my first shot—they weren't using shields, but just those long, two-handed spears—and he staggered, one knee going out from under him. I shot him again as I recovered from the recoil, since he was still up, then dragged the muzzle toward the next man.

My finger was already tightening on the trigger as the reticle passed over him, the first round smashing through links and going into his high right chest, the second through his throat. I lowered my aim as I dragged the muzzle to the next man.

Bailey and I had entirely unconsciously started at opposite ends of the formation, and now we worked our way inward, hardly pausing at each dark, armored silhouette as we pivoted from side to side, riding our triggers as the suppressed 7.62 rounds hammered at our foes with a steady, staccato crackle. A dozen men went down in half as many seconds.

These guys weren't pushovers, though. Judging by the quality of their armor, as much as we could see it on NVGs, they were the elite. They might even be the imperial guard itself.

The survivors didn't stutter-step as gunfire mowed down the front rank. They didn't break and run.

They charged.

We kept shooting, pushing out to either side as we cleared the edge of the wall, and opening up the gap behind us to the rest of the team. More gunfire crashed, but it wasn't enough to stop the charge. Probably because Gunny, Synar, and Farrar were engaging the Dullahans as they swooped low, those whips snapping out at us.

We were not in what I would call a good position.

The formation split, as yet more soldiers came out of the palisade of tents, one of them lifting a brazen horn to his lips and letting loose with a hooting, braying blast. The call was answered by another horn somewhere amid the clusters of tents on the plain beyond, and soon more soldiers were coming, though they were few and spread out. The camp had nearly been emptied to assault the fourth wall.

That didn't bode well. We'd killed thousands, but when half a million men had been committed to this siege, thousands were a drop in the bucket. If they'd thrown enough of that half million at the fourth wall that they could barely muster a react force in their rear, then it was a miracle that the wall had held as long as it had.

It only meant that we *had* to press this attack, if only to take some of the pressure off our brothers up on that wall.

I shot two more as I moved, sidestepping toward the tents. They were closing the distance fast, and I had to decide quickly whether I was going to try to evade or just kill as many of them as possible. Bearrac was next to me, Diarmodh having gone with Bailey, but we had to do something quickly, or we were going to be cut off from each other.

If they'd been Avurs, the gunfire might have done it, but these guys just kept coming. Like they were Terminators or something. They didn't break ranks, didn't falter. They just stepped over the dead and dying, closed the gaps, and continued to advance. Twenty yards. Fifteen. Ten.

Then that Dullahan in full plate armor, its head suspended in a column of green fire that rose from its gorget, riding on a thing of smoke and tarry darkness, its body not unlike a lion, a crown of horns sprouting from its massive head, alit on the wall above us.

Gunfire hadn't been enough to stop the imperial guard. The Dullahan, its whip upraised, was. They halted, though their spears were still leveled at us.

Under different circumstances, we might have frozen into a Mexican standoff right then. We were not inclined to play that game, though. As Bailey and Diarmodh dashed across the gap to join us, I turned, dropping my rifle to hang on its sling, and drew the Sword. I slashed the nearest tent open and ducked through the cut, Bearrac on my heels.

Someone outside cursed—maybe a Dullahan or one of the imperial guard. Gunfire popped, probably Gunny and our other two Marines following us through the gap. I hadn't had time to say anything about my chosen course of action, so it must have surprised the rest of the team as well as the enemy. Unfortunately, we just didn't have the luxury time for discussion, so I'd gone with the old rule—*The Number One Man is always right.*

The interior of the pavilion was richly appointed, but currently abandoned. There were richly embroidered rugs on the floor, equally richly carved field furniture set around an elaborate brass brazier, and, standing against the wall, a bed that must have taken an entire wagon to haul. The door flap was across from where we'd entered, facing the inner side of the semicircle.

We had spread out as we'd made entry, though Synar and Farrar had immediately turned around to face the way we'd come, and it was a good thing, too. After a brief commotion, the first spears thrust through the opening, and Farrar answered with a mag dump through the wall. The *crack*s of bullets and *thud*s of impacts against armor and meat could be heard over the Dullahan's sepulchral bellow.

Bearrac was already moving to that flap, and I almost ran to catch up with him. We did not want to try to do a one-man clear in there. The two of us burst out into a courtyard a moment later, with Diarmodh and Bailey on our heels. We had to trust that Gunny would make sure the whole team stayed together. We couldn't spare the attention to check on the others as we continued to press the attack. That's where teamwork and professionalism come in. You've got to trust your team.

Torches flared outside the tent, so suddenly that I was sure they'd been lit by means unearthly. They ringed another pavilion, easily three times the size of the one we'd just passed through, this one hung with black and midnight-blue tapestries, embroidered in gold thread with nightmarish scenes and symbols. Some of the glyphs woven into those panels of cloth made my eyes itch, and I quickly looked away from them.

The entrance to the pavilion was framed by a triangular façade of hammered gold, embossed with more of the eye-stinging figures. Monsters and death predominated where the symbols themselves didn't devolve into utter madness. The sunburst of Ar-Annator stood above it, though the sun had been blackened.

Another line of black-mailed figures stood across that opening, except these men carried swords and shields. Their faces were covered with bronze masks beneath their black helms, the masks carved into monstrous shapes. They faced us at an angle to the larger tent, their swords leveled over their shields, and at a barked command, they began to advance.

There were at least thirty of them, but I had reloaded inside the tent. We still had plenty of bullets for all of them. How much longer that would last I wasn't sure, but for the moment, we could still fight.

The four of us mag-dumped into the advancing swordsmen, but where we'd had enough space to do that and maneuver against the spearmen on the other side of the tents, these guys were just too close.

I shot the first man on the left just above the shield rim, blowing a hole through his eye socket and knocking him back into the man behind him. That one simply tilted his shield to deflect the falling body and moved up to fill the gap.

At the same time, I'd already transitioned to the man next to him. They were so close that headshots were relatively easy, and I had my rifle canted to use the offset red dot instead of trying to look through the scope. That one took a bullet right through the noseguard and went limp as a rag doll, dropping almost straight down. His shield partially propped him up for a moment before the man behind him kicked his corpse onto its face so that he could step over him.

These guys were hardcore.

I got two more before the remainder were close enough that I had to let the rifle hang and draw the Sword. I'd gotten that transition pretty smooth over the last year, but the charging imperial guardsman still almost took my head off before I could even get the blade out of the scabbard. I blocked his thrust with the partially drawn Sword, twisting my body to divert the stab away from my face.

That almost got me shivved by the next man beside him, until Bearrac brought his own blade crashing down to split that man's helmet and the skull underneath.

We'd whittled them down in that brief fusillade of gunfire, but they'd bought their fellows time to come around behind them, and now we were getting jabbed with spears from over the swordsmen's shoulders. I kicked the first man's shield into his teeth, scraped the Sword against his greave in such a way that if it were any other blade, I probably would have cringed in actual physical pain as I completely ruined the edge, then twisted it and brought it up fast, getting underneath his mail coat and finding a weak spot where I could cut deeply into the inside of his leg. Blood gushed and spurted, and he went down to one knee, at which point I stabbed him through the eyeslit.

Hauling the Sword free, I had to batter aside a spear-point with my buckler. The spearman was keeping his distance, and there were still a few swordsmen between us and them. I wished I could draw my .45 and start blasting, but I didn't dare try to sheathe the Sword just yet.

The Dullahan hadn't gone away, but it wasn't intervening, either. It still lurked up there, watching. I could only guess that it was frustrated by the failure of its threat to hold off this fight. I was sure by then that it wanted the Two Swords. Maybe it hoped, since we were fully engaged, that we'd be overwhelmed, at which point it would swoop down and take them from our bodies.

I didn't intend to oblige it, but things weren't looking that good right then.

I heard Synar go down, though I didn't know it was him at first. I just heard the meaty *thud* and the pained gurgle, followed by a trio of shots and the sound—barely audible over the rest of the fight—of two bodies hitting the mud.

We had closed into a tight circle now, fighting back-to-back as the Peruni imperial guard cut their way through the pavilions and surrounded us. There were too many of them. We were killing them, but they were going to overwhelm us sooner or later.

I gritted my teeth as my eyes ever so briefly flicked to that golden, triangular façade. To have come so far… I knew, deep down, in a way I couldn't explain, that our target was right there. And he may as well have been a hundred miles away.

My breath burned in my throat and my lungs, my heart pounded in my ears, and my limbs got heavy and weary. I still kept fighting, kept swinging, stabbing, and parrying. What else could I do?

The number of swordsmen dwindled as we cut them down. Beside me, Bearrac had turned into a machine, his sword rising and falling like a reaping scythe. None could seem to touch him, and wherever he struck, men died. He began to sing, a thunderous, reverberating song that spoke of death, doom, and the hope that lay beyond both. It was a Tuacha battle song, the likes of which I had never heard in the nearly two years I'd been with them. It said something about where we were.

I clashed with the last swordsman in front of me. He was good, there was no denying that. I'd managed to cut down the last few, but this one always had his shield right where I was striking, and it was a constant struggle to get my buckler between his blade and my own body. I failed a few times, but fortunately, while he still cut me twice, my mail held against the more dangerous blows, the ones that might have felled me.

It didn't help that two more were trying to stab me with spears the whole time.

Under different circumstances, I might have suc-cumbed to rage. Just turned into a monkey with a meat cleaver and hoped to overwhelm them with pure fury. That wouldn't work here, though. I could feel it. Maybe Iudicael himself was at my elbow, quietly reminding me. I fought calmly, my vision clear, my movements as efficient as exhaustion would allow. Still, my opponent and I seemed evenly matched. Bearrac, as powerful as he was, had his hands full protecting my flank.

I don't know what triggered it. Maybe Bailey stum-bled. Maybe something shifted on the battlefield behind us. I had lost track of the fight between the Dullahans and the dragon; I couldn't see it and was far too focused on staying alive for the moment to listen to it.

All I knew was that suddenly the Dullahans decided to take a hand.

A whip lashed down and wrapped itself around my sword arm. It burned where it clung, and for a split sec-ond I was vulnerable, my side open to the swordsman and his two spear-wielding buddies behind him. Bearrac threw himself in front of me, blocking one of the spears with his body as he stove in the swordsman's helmet with the pommel of his sword. He bought me the brief instant I needed to deal with the Dullahan.

I couldn't swing at it, since it had my sword hand, and was starting to drag me up by it, threatening to dislocate my shoulder as it started to lift me off the ground. I still had my grip on the Sword, though, and through the pain I managed to twist it until I could scrape the blade against the whip.

The whip dissolved into smoke, and the Dullahan screamed, a sonic blast that drove me to my knees.

Bearrac had done more than just save me, though. He'd killed the swordsman and one of the spearmen.

At a terrible cost.

The second spear had transfixed his throat. He was still alive, still driving forward, though his song was stilled, and he ripped the spear from the man's hands and killed him, just before the gush of blood from his own neck finally felled him. He held himself up on his knee and one hand, frozen, looking skyward, then fell without a sound.

That I was able to drive on after watching that mountain of a man die was a testament to Iudicael's help. I'm convinced of that. The horror of it, knowing that Bearrac was gone, screamed in the back of my mind, yet I remained detached, calm enough to see what he had really done.

He had just torn an opening to the arch and the emperor's pavilion.

With the last bit of wind and strength I had, I charged.

CHAPTER 33

THE interior of the imperial pavilion was darker than the outside. Braziers smoked and candles flickered, but there was none of the blazing torchlight that had almost banished the twilight under that unnatural pall of cloud outside. It was as if I'd plunged into a temple, or something.

If so, it was the sort of temple that I'd be glad to burn to the ground.

The candles were set in an odd pattern around a central dais, with a thronelike chair sitting atop it, faced by what looked an awful lot like an altar. A figure sat in the chair, gazing down at an orb in its hand, a lurid glow coming from the head-sized sphere.

The Emperor of Ar-Annator was not a tall man. In fact, I was pretty sure, as I advanced on the dais, that he wasn't much over five feet. He wore a robe with wide, flared shoulders and dagged sleeves, but there was a mail shirt beneath it, revealed by the opening in the front of the robe, the rings gilded. He wore a golden torc above it, and a golden headdress rising to a point a good two feet above his head.

His eyes, when he looked up at me, glowed red, and his gaunt, sharp-featured face was gray.

In retrospect, I probably should have shot him right then and there. It would have saved a lot of time and pain. Something held me back, though, even though I had my red dot right on his chest as he steepled his hands in front of him.

"Conor McCall." His voice was deep and mellifluous, though somehow unlike that he'd used through the projection of his face above the walls before the second wall had fallen. It was almost as if he hadn't used his own voice then but had summoned some creature of the Outer Dark to represent him. Considering what sorcery usually boiled down to, even the "milder" form that the Fohorimans used in order to avoid directly touching the Outer Dark, and therefore exposing themselves to the Outsiders they had betrayed, that seemed likely. "The discoverer and bearer of the Sword of Iudicael has come to me."

The clash of battle was still audible outside the tent, but it was muted, as if it was a long way away, or the walls of the pavilion were thicker and more solid than they really were. For whatever reason, I still held my fire, though I moved away from the entrance, clearing my back as much as I could when the wall behind me was little more than cloth.

His eyes followed me as I moved, though he was otherwise as motionless as a statue. "Shall we talk, then, Sword Bearer? Reason together, you and I? Or will you simply shoot me where I sit, without offering you a fight?" There was a note of amusement in his voice, as if he was sure that I wouldn't shoot.

And right then, I wasn't going to. I couldn't say at the time exactly why not. But my finger stayed off the trigger, even while I kept covering the emperor with my muzzle.

Somewhere in the back of my mind, I told myself that it would go better to force the emperor to surrender than simply to kill him. Yet at the same time, I couldn't help but wonder if that was really it. I wondered if I was even capable, at that point, of putting my finger on the trigger and putting a bullet in him. There was something weird going on, despite the mental and spiritual preparation that we'd put in before we'd set in as the remain behind element. That was in addition to the fact that he was clearly using the sorcerous imitation of the mind speech—he wasn't speaking either English or *Tenga Tuacha*.

"Why shouldn't I?" I was buying time, and we both knew it. "You've certainly ordered enough death and destruction. How many murders? How many human sacrifices did it take to summon the horrors that you've unleashed on these people? How many dead defending their homeland against your invasion? Seems like an easy trade to me."

He smiled, though there was no warmth or humor in the expression. From the evidence of how far down the road to being a Fohoriman he was—provided he hadn't already crossed whatever threshold existed—there probably wasn't much of either left in the shriveled remains of his soul.

"Are you not yourself a warrior? Have you never killed your enemies? Should I simply allow this wayward people to defy my authority, my majesty? I have looked upon the mysteries of this world and the next. I have attained wisdom that these ungrateful children could never even comprehend! Wisdom which could bring order and peace to all the world! What price could be placed on such a goal? What sacrifices would not be justified?"

I snorted. That strange reluctance to shoot was still there, but it didn't seem to extend to believing a word coming out of his mouth. If he was using sorcery to try to persuade me, it wasn't working. That was a little strange, but I hoped that it was because Iudicael was somewhere nearby. "I've heard all that before, usually from people who would have done the world a favor by taking themselves out of it long before the good guys finally caught up with them."

He laughed then and stood. If he was hoping to intimidate me, he failed. Even from his dais, he wasn't much taller than me. If we'd been on the same level, I'd have towered over him. "So say all who would rage against the inevitable, against that which they do not understand." He held out a hand. "I am a merciful ruler, however. Surrender the Sword, and I shall let you live. I shall even bring you to full understanding, though it will take time."

"Remember what King Uven told you when you made the same offer to him?" I had my red dot hovering around the bridge of his nose, though I still had my finger off the trigger. "Just remember that and add a bit more vehemence to it."

His laugh faded, and his gaze sharpened. A frown creased his otherwise serene, gray features. "You have some mystical shield about you." His eyes moved to the Sword at my side. "Perhaps I underestimated the effects of carrying that artifact." His gaze grew colder, if that was possible. "No matter. It will not save you. Only to kneel before me and lay that blade at my feet might allay

my wrath, and prompt me to bring you to true enlight-
enment, though there must be some discipline to correct
your defiance." He drew his sword then, a single-edged
blade, blackened in an odd, purplish way, with only a
slight curve to its spine. He pointed the sword at me.
"Lay down your weapons, bow down upon your face,
and beg for mercy from the rightful ruler of this world."

I'd sure heard the "rightful ruler" bit before, and I
wondered just how the Outsiders would like that. They,
after all, claimed to be the "elder gods," and therefore the
"rightful rulers." Though I had to wonder just which one
was sponsoring the emperor. There was no way he'd just
come across the power to turn himself into a Fohoriman
and command the Thirty all by himself, never mind form
an alliance with a dragon.

For a moment, I almost shot him. I couldn't *quite*
bring myself to do it, though. My finger wouldn't move
to the trigger. It was weird as hell, and I started to freak
out a little. *Iudicael, I could use some help right now.* Still, I
couldn't shoot him.

I slung the rifle. There was no point in keeping it
pointed at him while I was somehow being prevented
from pulling the trigger. It didn't bode well, but whatever
strangeness was happening here, it still seemed to have
limits. I might not be able to shoot him, but I could defy
him.

*Let's see if the spell works when I've got the Sword in my
hand.*

Swinging the weapon to my back and cinching down
the sling, I drew the Sword of Iudicael and my buckler,
wishing for a moment, once again, that I still had my
Bowie. "Not going to happen."

A quick, ghostly flicker of uncertainty might have crossed his face. Only for an eyeblink, and then it was gone. His expression hardened into a mask of hatred that I would have recognized on any Fohoriman's visage. "So be it."

Then he attacked.

He was *fast*, but I should have expected that from a Fohoriman, or close enough to one. He was in my face in an eyeblink, and I got my buckler between my throat and his sword just barely in time to stop the blow before he took my head off. As it was, the blade sank deep into the rim of the small shield, and when he wrenched it clear, it twisted my wrist and almost pulled the buckler out of my grasp.

In that split second, I knew that this was going to be a hell of a fight, and the result was hardly a foregone conclusion. I swayed to the side, taking a cut at his flank that he almost effortlessly blocked as he freed his own sword from the grip of my buckler's rim and dropped it between my blow and his own side.

I kicked him in the chest, then, just trying to create some space, some maneuvering room. It felt like kicking a tree, but I got my maneuvering room anyway, since I sort of launched myself backward, shifting my weight at the last moment so that what might have knocked me onto my back turned into a leap. It still put me almost right up against the wall of the tent, which was strangely stiff, but I figured that was a side effect of whatever spell was keeping the noise of the fight outside so muted.

I couldn't expect any backup, either.

The emperor didn't allow me to take full advantage of that maneuvering room, but pressed the fight, his sword raining blows down on me in a dizzying series of cuts, slashes, and thrusts. It took every bit of skill I'd acquired from Mathghaman's and Bearrac's able instruction just to survive. He was every bit as formidable, at least with a sword, as the Dullahan in Cor Legear had been.

Circling around, I got away from the wall, but he continued to press me, his sword moving so fast that I couldn't get in a single cut or thrust of my own, I was so busy just defending my precious personal hide from his edge. We fought around the dais, the throne forming the fulcrum of our movement, as he pursued me around the interior of the pavilion, our blades clashing in a continuous cacophony of ringing steel.

The Sword of Iudicael retained its edge, like it always had, but the emperor's paramerion was starting to glint along its edge as it got ever more notched. Despite my growing exhaustion and the blood pounding in my ears, I suddenly got an idea.

With the next blow, I twisted the blade, meeting his edge directly with my own.

The stick was only momentary, but it gave me a brief opening. I twisted the swords away and lunged in close, punching the edge of my buckler at his throat.

He wasn't ready for that, and I caught him just under the jaw. He didn't recoil like a normal man would—the unnatural taint that had turned his flesh gray and his eyes to burning red coals had probably deadened his nerves somewhat—but it still knocked him back a step, and I was finally able to go on the offensive.

For a brief few glorious seconds, I got the upper hand. I drove him back with a series of high and low cuts and thrusts at his head and his legs, putting as much

controlled ferocity as I could into the strokes, so much
so that he only barely manage to parry each time. He
retreated, and as I sidestepped, he was driven back until
he came up against the back of the throne.

Then he got pissed.

He seized the blade with his bare hand, and even as
his flesh smoked and smoldered around it, he forced it
aside, dark blood oozing around the wounds. He flinched
at the pain but drove through it, bringing his own sword
around in a vicious arc aimed at my neck.

I ducked and just barely batted the cut aside with my
buckler. I was close enough in that I could aim a kick at
the inside of his knee, trying to disable him, but I may as
well have kicked an oak.

He let go of the Sword of Iudicael, a hiss of anguish
escaping his clenched teeth, and leaped backward, clearing the throne and alighting off-balance, spreading his
arms and his feet to catch himself as he landed.

I stalked him around the dais, only to face another
withering storm of blows. I was forced back another step
as I tried to keep that curved edge away from my face,
and I mostly succeeded, though he did get a cut along
my cheekbone that burned as blood started to flow down
into my beard.

It was still more than I'd managed to do to him.

Still, he seemed to have made a mistake, grabbing
the blade of the Sword of Iudicael like that. I knew that it
was a viable technique in swordfighting, so long as you
were careful, but that was against ordinary steel swords.
The emperor, a cursed sorcerer nearly as far gone as a
Fohoriman, had grabbed a blessed sword brought down
to men by a messenger of Tigharn.

The bleeding from his palm wouldn't stop. His blood was dark, sluggish, almost like molasses. The hand, moreover, was scorched and blackened, and the flesh seemed to shrivel before my eyes as it smoked, and the withering began to spread up his wrist.

He fell back, clutching that wounded hand to his chest. He was in a lot of pain, and for the first time I saw fear in those red eyes.

"I am the Emperor of Ar-Annator!" The urbane tone was gone from his voice as he staggered back, swinging his sword at me. The dynamics of the fight had changed in a heartbeat. More smoke poured from his sleeve, where he had now hidden his wounded hand. "How *dare* you stand in the way of my destiny! You will *suffer* for *daring* to wound my person! I shall strike you down and feed you to the dragon! No, you are too insignificant to insult him with your corpse! I will feed your body to the wyverns!"

I didn't answer, except to lunge again, the Sword's point aimed at his leg, where the robe was split open in front. He blocked it, but I rode the parry, bringing the Sword back around in a sweeping arc toward his neck.

He swayed back, but I pressed the attack, drawing the point back before he could parry it—he was starting to slow down—and jabbing it at his wounded arm.

He swept the single-edged sword up under my own blade, batting it away from the injured hand. He'd gotten too desperate, though. Sorcerously enhanced or not, the wound had rattled him. He was so focused on defending that hand that he left me an opening.

I almost didn't see it, but maybe Iudicael was whispering in my ear right then.

Dipping my shoulder, I twisted the Sword to change its course, bringing the blade slithering around the emperor's own saber, and rammed the point through his throat.

Then everything went dark.

CHAPTER 34

MY eyes adjusted to the darkness slowly. I was underground, and the only illumination came from the glow of firelight somewhere up ahead, around a bend in the passage. The tunnel was stuffy and hot, almost like it was a volcanic vent or something.

Strangely, though, while I felt the heat, I didn't feel myself start sweating. Looking down, I realized I couldn't see my body. I seemed to be somehow disembodied.

Through a moment of panic, I looked around, but couldn't see a way out. Had I died as I'd stabbed the emperor? Was this Hell?

I would have expected Hell to be worse, to be honest, and that realization reassured me somewhat. When I heard voices somewhere up ahead, near that flickering glow, I started toward them.

I thought I understood now. I wasn't dead. This was a vision.

Hopefully it was a vision occurring in a split second as the Sword of Iudicael clove through the emperor's throat, and I wasn't standing there frozen while the Dullahans slaughtered the rest of my team and moved in to take the Sword from me and wrap me up with those bone whips to be hauled off to whatever deep, dark hole they came from for a century of torment.

Shaking off that thought, I continued down the passage and around the bend. If I wasn't really there, I reasoned, then whoever was speaking shouldn't be able to see me.

The chamber in front of me was bigger than I'd expected, with torches and candles lining the walls and the floor. It reminded me of Vaelor's Throne. The longer I looked at the worked stone arch in the throat of the cave, though, the more it looked like the entrance to the emperor's pavilion. Perhaps the latter had been modeled on this.

It definitely wasn't the other way around. The triangular arch had clearly been there for ages, the stone crusted with mineral deposits that had run down from the cavern ceiling above. Unlike the rest of the cave, now that I was out of the shadow and in the light, I could see the arch was made of black stone. It was perfectly smooth, except for the fact that it was carved into motifs of intertwined monsters, fighting and devouring each other while they tormented screaming human beings from the top to the bottom.

Two men stood at either side of the arch, spears in their hands. They were clearly Peruni, and their armor looked like the imperial guards', except theirs was black, whereas these men wore bronze.

Their helmets were off, and one leaned against the cavern wall, looking up at the carvings on the façade before them. The other looked up from where he'd been kicking a rock. "You shouldn't look at that so much."

They weren't speaking any language I knew, but thanks to the metaphysics of the vision, I understood them anyway.

"Why would he have come here?" The man leaning against the wall still didn't take his eyes off the bass reliefs of horror and madness. He seemed transfixed, as if he didn't dare blink. "Why to a place like this?"

"His visions." The other said it as matter-of-factly as if it explained everything and needed no elaboration. "The gods have spoken to him and led him here. Who are we to question that?"

The questioner finally broke his stare, shaking himself a little as he returned his gaze to his companion. "The gods we worship are not to be trifled with, it is true, but something about this place…" He looked up at the scenes of terror and pain once again. "Would the gods truly bring him here?"

"Clearly they did." The first man was eyeing his partner with some suspicion. "Unless you think somehow that the emperor is in error?"

The second guardsman shook his head, though he didn't look at the first. "Of course not."

Apparently, it was heresy to question whether or not the emperor's visions were truly from a trustworthy source.

Granted, visions being what they were—and I had a bit of experience—it was hard to explain to anyone else whether they were legit or not. You just kind of *knew*.

Of course, if the emperor had come here, to a place so reminiscent of Vaelor's Throne, then I could guess where his visions had come from.

I moved closer, but neither guard noticed me. I walked right up to the one leaning against the cave wall, as they lapsed into an uncomfortable silence, and waved my hand in front of his face. Or, I would have, if I'd had a hand to wave.

It was weird. I *felt* like I had a body, but it was as invisible to me as it apparently was to these men.

I moved on, passing under that ominous triangular arch.

The passage got dark again as I continued downward, but it wasn't pitch black. In fact, there were lights set into the walls, though as I got closer to them, I found them even less comforting.

They were glyphs carved into the rock and glowing from within with a sickly sort of light that almost seemed to *twist* and writhe. It's hard to describe how a glow could do that, but that was what it seemed to be doing.

I didn't have all that much farther to go.

Past two more doorways, the last arch opened up on a larger chamber, lit by a massive brazier in the center. The flames rising from that huge bowl were purple, reminding me of the fire in Killaros, where we'd confronted the necromancer and the shadow demon that had enthralled him.

He'd thought he was the master there, but it was pretty evident which one was calling the shots.

The emperor stood before the brazier, looking up at the truncated, pitch-black pyramid behind it. His arms were spread wide, his uplifted face lit from below by the unnatural flames. He wore robes similar to those he'd worn when I'd confronted him in his pavilion, though lighter in color. They might have been blue, instead of black.

His skin was also of a more human shade, though I couldn't see his eyes as they were currently closed.

"Oh great elder gods of the world, I have followed the signs you have sent me. I have crossed plains and wilderness, fought the revenant of Doryvaak, and delved through the haunted ruins above us. I have come! What will you show me?"

There was a different note to his voice, too. He sounded younger, more human. Whenever this had happened, it had been long before he'd had nearly completed his slide into monstrosity.

For a long time, his words were greeted with only silence. Even the flames in the brazier didn't make a sound. His arms stayed up for a long time, but slowly began to droop. He wasn't a warrior, not really.

I was struck, then, by the difference between this man and King Uven. They were about the same age—at least, the emperor in this vision was about the same age Uven was now—but there was a softness to this man, a shiftiness, that wasn't in the Galel king. This was a man who would take the dark shortcut to avoid having to do the work.

And it really looked like that was exactly what he was doing.

After a few minutes, as his arms drooped lower and his eyes opened, searching the shadows for any sign that he had been heard, the face of the pyramid seemed to ripple and flow. Stones shifted and rearranged themselves, until a great portal had opened in the side of the structure.

Nothing came out of it. The darkness only deepened.

When I realized what was happening, my blood ran cold.

Twin sparks of purple flame appeared in the midst of that stygian shadow. The darkness spread and thickened, until an amorphous shape that seemed like hatred made manifest loomed above the brazier.

There is much to show you. You have taken the first steps. Yet more will be demanded of you. It wasn't a voice, not really. The words seemed to reverberate through everything, as if the shadow demon—I was pretty sure it was the same one we'd confronted in Killaros and again at Cor Legear—was using every surface in the cave as a diaphragm. *Kill the guards outside, and we shall speak.*

That seemed a little extreme to the emperor. "But... they are my most elite guards. Without them..."

The power I offer comes with a price. Kill them and pour their blood upon the flames before you, if you would learn what I may teach you.

Still the emperor hesitated. "They are both great and experienced warriors. I am not sure..."

I have given you the words you need. Prove your worthiness to possess the knowledge you seek.

He turned back, then, though slowly and reluctantly. It looked as though he was just realizing how much this was going to cost him and was having second thoughts.

Not strong enough second thoughts, though. He called out, his voice echoing from the stone walls. "Gemelzar!"

It took a few minutes for the man who had been leaning against the cave wall to appear in the doorway. He knelt, bowing his head to the stone floor. "You summoned me, Your Imperial Majesty."

"Come here." The emperor had had time to gather himself while he'd waited, and now he appeared assured, confident. *Almost* regal. There was still that underlying weakness, though, that he couldn't quite cover over.

Gemelzar stood and stepped up to his sovereign. "What would you have of me, my Emperor?"

The emperor held up a hand before the guardsman's face and spoke a single word. Even as disembodied as I was, I felt a flash of nausea at that unnatural sound. I was sure no human throat could make that noise all by itself. From the way it reverberated around the chamber, I suspected that it had required a certain degree of sorcery just to pronounce it.

A ripple seemed to go through the air and the rock, and Gemelzar shuddered, then stood stock still, his eyes vacant.

No, not vacant. Fixed on the shadow behind the emperor, and those two blazing points of purple light that marked the demon's eyes. He knew, then, what was happening, but it was far too late.

The emperor drew Gemelzar's own knife as he pulled him, unresisting, to the edge of the dais. Then, looking up at the shadow demon, the emperor slashed his own guardsman's throat.

The man didn't even jerk or shudder. His enthrallment was too strong. He leaned forward obligingly as his lifeblood gushed and spurted into the brazier. The flames hissed but did not ebb; in fact, they rose higher, as if they were greedily consuming Gemelzar's blood.

It didn't take long.

The emperor let the body slide limply to the floor in front of the brazier. "Salakzor!"

This time, the guardsman saw the shadow demon and the lifeless form of his companion and stopped dead in the doorway, not even kneeling down. "What…"

The emperor spoke that word again, and my stomach twisted, a shock of nausea and weakness running through my nonexistent body. Salakzor froze, and the gruesome scene was repeated.

While the only feature in the shadow demon that could be seen was its eyes, I could somehow *feel* it gloat. *Well done, my servant. Now, the things I shall show you…*

The vision faded.

* * *

I wasn't back in the pavilion, though. Instead I stood next to the emperor, his face narrower, more gaunt, perhaps paler, with a faint red gleam in his eyes, as he looked down at the excavation beneath him.

Ruins stretched from horizon to horizon. I didn't recognize the place. It wasn't Barmanak, Myrgarak, or Gremman. In fact, the architecture matched none of those places. There was something almost Roman about this place, with many columns and arches, though there were other structures around the outside that looked blockier, more industrial, if that makes sense. They weren't the sort of high-rises I'd grown up with back in the World, but there was a brutal starkness to their lines, even as they crumbled, that reminded me of some of the worst of modern architecture.

Though it also reminded me of something else. Something far more ancient and horrible. I just couldn't put my currently nonexistent finger on it.

Dozens of men labored to dig into the earth before the crumbled remains of what looked an awful lot like the Greek Parthenon, except different, somehow. Twisted. It took me a second to realize what was different.

The columns were covered in bones. Human bones.

A shout went up from below, and the emperor, who had been staring vacantly into space, turned his gaze toward the pit. Several workmen were brushing the dirt away from what looked very much like a black stone sarcophagus.

One wrapped in silver chains, with a great silver seal holding them all together. I couldn't read the runes, but I didn't need to.

I knew, in a flash of insight, as clear as day, what lay in that coffin.

And I knew what was coming next.

The emperor spoke an incantation. His voice cracked a little halfway through, but he continued. It was different from what he'd used on his guardsmen back in that cave. Longer, more involved. I was sure if I'd still been in my body, I would probably have retched, because the effects were even stronger, even though the spell wasn't aimed at me.

The men down there in the pit stopped moving. They weren't completely frozen; I could see them breathing. Then, slowly, they turned their eyes on one another.

With a sudden scream, they threw themselves at each other. With picks, mattocks, shovels, and bare hands, they proceeded to murder each other gruesomely. Blood, meat, and bits of bone flew and sprayed across the pit and the sarcophagus, until finally the last man, his throat bitten out by the man whose guts he had ripped open, collapsed on the sarcophagus, a cascade of red splashing over the black stone and the silver seal.

The sarcophagus shook then, as if struck a heavy blow from inside. Then again. The seal cracked. The silver chains slid away. Then the sarcophagus itself opened, the lid splitting in half and falling away to either side.

At first, there was nothing but darkness inside. Then a pale flicker of green fire gleamed, until a headless form clad in full plate armor sat up, took its leering head from between its legs, and placed it within the column of emerald flame. Its eyes opened and it looked up at the emperor standing on the platform above the pit, and the evil, sharp-toothed grin on the Dullahan's face grew wider.

The vision faded again.

* * *

This time, the emperor stood in a temple in the city of Ar-Annator. Built atop the rubble of a far older structure, it was dark, utterly windowless, lit only by that same weird, purple fire that had burned in the brazier in the cavern. He was alone this time, except for the dismembered corpse lying on the altar before the brazier, the heart and the severed head burning in the noiseless flames.

The shadow demon slowly coalesced out of the darkness. I wondered, with a bodiless shudder, how long it had been lurking there, watching.

You have done well. The Thirty walk the waking world once again. No man has had the strength to summon them all in many lifetimes of men. Truly you are Chosen. That voice still seemed to come from every surface in the temple, even through the sizzling visage of the sacrifice's severed head.

"Is it enough?" The emperor's skin had become almost scaly, and there was a decided red tint in his eyes.

It may be. The demon was being sly. It wasn't even trying to hide it, though the emperor took the bait.

"What else is there? If there is a greater power that will assure my ascendancy, my *ascension*, then tell me!"

The shadow demon loomed over him, darkening the flames in the brazier. *There is one. A power that dwarfs even the Thirty. The Great Wyrm. The Bane of Commagan. The Eldest of Elder Gods.*

Thoggudan Karataros.

CHAPTER 35

THAT name went through my mind like a lightning bolt, even as the vision disappeared and I found myself in the emperor's pavilion again, the emperor himself still transfixed on the point of the Sword of Iudicael.

He was trying to talk, even as the blood welled around the blade and ran down his front. His lips formed the name, though he couldn't get the air to actually pronounce that dread title.

Thoggudan Karataros.

The gurgle that was his attempt to speak had not even died away when the dragon's voice rumbled through the pavilion. Like the shadow demon's voice in the vision, it seemed to surround us, coming from everywhere at once. "*Thy pleas avail nothing. Thou hast sold thy soul and theirs to me. I shall rule now, without thee. Die, and come to me, where I might torment thee for an eternity.*"

The sepulchral laugh that vibrated through the very ground was one of the most evil, gloating sounds I thought I'd ever heard.

I pulled the Sword free, and the emperor fell to his knees, his own sword falling from slack fingers to hit the floor of the tent with a *thud*. Blood sprayed from his severed carotid, though it was already beginning to slow.

Who knew what price his body had paid for the deals he'd made with the devil?

His end came quickly, the red fading from his eyes as he stared at me, sheer, abject terror in their depths. His flesh withered rapidly as his blood ran out and he slumped to the ground.

I had been transfixed, unable to tear my eyes away from his death, but now the roar of the fight outside returned in full force, and I spun around and plunged out through the entryway.

Diarmodh, Gunny, Gurke, Bailey, and Farrar stood just outside, in a tight semicircle facing four Dullahans. They were keeping their distance, for now, mainly because Diarmodh was chanting at the top of his voice, contending with the guttural murmuring of the Dullahans as they tried to work their sorcery. Bailey, standing out in front with the Sword of Categyrn gleaming in his fist, was the other factor. I'd barely stepped out of the tent when he lunged at a Dullahan wearing a muscled cuirass under a fur-lined mantle with a strangely shaped shield hanging from a strap against its arm.

The Dullahan, its head peering out from beneath that shield, its eyes glowing a sickly green, swayed back, away from the Sword. It lashed out with that whip but yanked it back again as Bailey countered with the Sword's blade, almost managing to lop the chain of human vertebrae in half.

That one Dullahan in plate, its head still floating on that column of green fire, snapped out a single word that made the other flinch, even as it lashed the retreating headless abomination with its own whip.

A strangely detached, dispassionate part of my brain noted the way that the first Dullahan keened under the blow, and smoke rose from the mark that whip left. It seemed that the whips hurt the Dullahans worse than they hurt us. That was interesting.

Yet it was a detail that wasn't going to help us right then and there. We had to break out and get out of there. The job was done. The emperor was dead. Mission accomplished. Yet it hadn't had the effect we'd hoped for. The dragon had simply taken over, and the Dullahans, even if they were no longer bound to the Empire of Ar-Annator—which was questionable—wanted the Two Swords.

Nothing seemed to be going right. For a brief moment, as I looked at what we were up against, I almost despaired.

Yet I had killed the emperor. We had whittled the Thirty down to the Twenty-Seven. This wasn't over yet.

So, I attacked. What else was I going to do?

I might have needed to coordinate with Gunny or Bailey, since their backs were to me, but I didn't even have to say a word. They just parted like the Red Sea, and I went through with the Sword of Iudicael held high, point forward, charging the line of headless horrors with a recklessness born of a certain knowledge that I was going to die.

That Dullahan in the muscled cuirass must not have wanted to incur the plate-armored monstrosity's wrath again. It lunged to meet me, and our blades clashed. This one bore a bone sword not unlike that of the one I'd fought in Cor Legear, if slightly wider at the hilt. It tried to keep itself bladed off to present the shield on its shoulder, and for a moment I could have sworn that its sword got longer to make up for the loss of reach.

Despite the extra strength and endurance that Iudicael's help seemed to lend me when I needed it—and asked for it—that creature was *strong*. It got its blade inside my thrust and battered the Sword aside, riposting so fast that I took a hit square to the shoulder before I could get my buckler underneath it. The force of the blow knocked me off-balance as an icy cold spread down my arm and across my side, and I staggered. It would have taken my head off if Bailey hadn't taken a swing at it, in the split second he had before another Dullahan, this one in a coat of plates beneath a double-layered black cloak, was right on him.

For a moment, the Two Swords brought us up to nearly the level of our adversaries, and we fenced with them in a dizzying series of cuts, parries, thrusts, and ripostes. I say *nearly* the level of our adversaries because they were still unnatural monstrosities with the power of the Outer Dark in them. My opponent actually stopped my swings dead twice, both times jarring my arm so hard that I almost lost my grip on the Sword of Iudicael. The second time, it was noticeable enough that it reached out from beneath the shield, the whip having disappeared I don't know where, and tried to grab the weapon out of my hand.

I withdrew the Sword just in time, dropped the point, and tried to stab it in the face, sliding the edge along the inside of its arm. It twisted its body then, though, and my thrust glanced off the face of the shield.

That almost put me out of position, but I think Iudicael must have pulled me back to centerline, because there's no other way I could have reset that fast, not after the duel with the emperor.

We crossed blades one more time, and then the Dullahan with the green fire coming out of his gorget apparently decided that enough was enough.

He barked an order, in a harsh, screeching voice that sounded worse than fingernails on a blackboard, and suddenly the encircling Dullahans closed in on us.

Gunny was right at my elbow, swinging that axe like there was no tomorrow. Judging by his words up there on the battlements, some time before, he might have been convinced that there *was* going to be no tomorrow. That this was his last stand, and so he was going to make the best of it.

That might have saved his life. That preparedness to die must have made it harder for the Dullahans to touch him.

A moment later, though, that theory was put to the test.

Off to Bailey's right, Gurke threw himself at a Dullahan with its head held in a satchel at its side, its garb the most flamboyant of any I'd seen so far, wearing a brigandine beneath a mail mantle and with slashed puffed sleeves. Its bone sword was more like a longsword, held in two hands, and had close to twice the reach of Gurke's own weapon.

Gurke still put it on its back foot. He drove it back, raining blows against its guard. He was hardly the most subtle of swordsmen. He'd never gotten the best feel for it, but he was making up for his lack of skill and finesse with sheer ferocity and a complete disregard for his own life. He wasn't frenzied, though. In the brief glimpse I got, he was utterly calm, utterly focused.

Right up until the moment that the Dullahan got inside his guard, smashing his forearm hard enough that even while I was engaged with my own opponents, I could hear the bone crack. Gurke's sword went flying, and then that bone-bladed longsword swept up and back, and Ross Gurke's head fell to the ground, his body following with a spray of blood.

There was no time to mourn him, or even to look at where he'd fallen. I ducked under a lashing whip and tried to shoulder charge the one I'd been fighting, though it danced quickly out of the way, allowing another, dressed in what looked like little more than a silk tunic, breeches, and a fur-lined cape, to come at my flank. Gunny smashed his axe into that one's side, doing little damage but throwing it off and giving me a chance to regain my equilibrium.

It was only a matter of time, though.

Then the world itself seemed to split asunder.

The blinding flash and booming thunder drove Marine, Tuacha, and Dullahan alike to our knees, and a blast of wind from the dragon's wings battered us as it swept overhead.

"*I warned thee.*" The demon's voice reverberated through the very stones. It roared overhead like a freight train, banking hard as it crossed the line of the wall and headed out over the plain. In seconds it had come back around and was arrowing toward us.

The Dullahans knew what was coming. Whatever the falling out between them and the dragon had been, it hadn't been healed over the last few minutes by the fact they were fighting us. The one in the plate armor barked another word of command, and the leonine horror it had been riding rose out of the ground beneath it, spreading its wings seemingly out of its ribs—if it had any such thing—and blasted away from the imperial encampment like a rocket. The others weren't far behind, scattering like quail before the dragon's wrath.

We might have hesitated then, with the pressure of the Dullahans suddenly removed. If we had, we'd have died in an instant. Fortunately, Diarmodh was on the ball, and before we could even catch our breath from the Dullahan's abrupt exit, he had grabbed me and Gunny and was propelling us toward the plains below. "Move!"

We ran. Our legs feeling like lead, the air—dry and stifling and stinking of blood, death, and hellfire—burning in our lungs, our hearts pounding fit to burst, we ran.

The camp had been largely emptied to assault the fourth wall, though there were still support troops, camp followers, and some reserves left. They had fallen back when the Dullahans had closed in after we'd killed our way through the imperial guard. None of them wanted to contend with those monsters. Fortunately, the dragon's imminent attack meant that they hadn't exactly come out of the woodwork as soon as the Dullahans had departed. That left us a reasonably clear route to escape.

Presuming the dragon wanted the Dullahans instead of us.

It went overhead again, dipping low as if to strike, though when I glanced up, it seemed to be focused on one of the flying Dullahans, not us. We pushed on, praying that it wouldn't decide, in a fit of caprice, to simply snap one of us in half.

A bolt of pure blackness stabbed at it out of the murk above and behind us, and it responded with another earthshaking thunderbolt. It was occupied, at least for the moment, and the edge of the imperial camp was right in front of us.

Just before we reached the trampled plains beyond, a shout went up and a dozen men, half-armored and bearing arms hastily snatched up in the dark, charged out to intercept us. Without breaking stride or dropping his axe, Gunny drew his .45 and fired, dropping the first man in his tracks.

The rest scattered. We ran into the night.

CHAPTER 36

WE must have run almost a mile into the plains, losing ourselves in the dark—at least to any human pursuers—before Gunny called a halt. We collapsed, exhausted and panting for breath, in a slight fold in the ground that might be a streambed during the rainy season, but right then was dry and provided us a little cover and concealment.

"Fifty percent security." Gunny's own voice was a hoarse rasp. We'd had to slow down considerably to keep him with us, but no one was going to get separated that night. Or day, or whatever it was. "We can't go much farther without some rest. We'll stay here a couple hours, then move out, unless they come for us before then."

Looking out at the horizon, I couldn't see an end to those pitch-black clouds, though the lightning flickered through them at much greater distances from the citadel than I'd thought.

It was eerily quiet out there. The whispers we'd gotten used to out on the plains, on the way back from Gremman, were silent. That trip seemed an awfully long time ago, even though we'd only returned to Cor Legear mere weeks earlier.

"We can't stay here." Farrar sounded every bit as hoarse as Gunny, and he coughed a little as he spoke.

He also sounded beaten down and scared stiff. Not that I could blame him.

The mission had failed. We'd done what we'd stayed behind to do, and it had availed our friends up on the wall exactly nothing.

"No, we can't," Gunny agreed. "And we won't. Just long enough to catch our breath so that we can fight."

Details were impossible to see from that far, but we could make out the glow of the fires, and the flickers of other, less wholesome lights. The battle for the fourth wall continued... unless it had fallen, and they were assaulting the fifth by then.

"I'll take first watch." Bailey was at my elbow. "One of the Sword Bearers should always be up, I think."

I was too tired, too defeated, to argue. I slumped down on the grass and was unconscious in moments.

* * *

I found myself in a glade, surrounded by aspens just starting to turn yellow. The light was golden, and the air was quiet and warm. The grass underfoot was still green, and the purest snow-covered mountain I'd ever seen loomed above, like a spear thrusting into a clear blue sky.

Looking around me, I could hear the whisper of the wind in the aspens, but I saw nothing else moving. Still, there was something about that sound. It almost formed words.

I strained my ears to try to understand, but whenever I really listened hard, the words faded into wind. Yet I couldn't shake the feeling that someone or something was trying to tell me something.

I had spoken face-to-face with Iudicael, but even then, he'd been less direct than the Tuacha—which was saying something. It sometimes felt like the forces of good didn't want to make things too easy. Or maybe they feared to tread on our free will. I didn't know, but sometimes I kinda wished that they'd just go ahead and let us use Easy Mode a little.

Once more, I looked around the idyllic meadow, trying to figure out what I was supposed to understand.

I still hadn't quite figured it out when Bailey shook me awake. I just knew that there was something I'd missed.

* * *

Nothing much had changed, I saw as I took up security, letting Bailey lie back and close his eyes. The clouds were still there, the fires still blazed around the fourth wall, and lightning still flickered overhead. The dragon hadn't pursued us. It was still circling above Cor Chatha. Something told me that it knew exactly where we were, though.

If the vision I'd had was to be believed, and it was the same Thoggudan that had destroyed the Commagan Empire from within and without and had cast the curse on Lost Colcand, then I had no doubt that it could sense us, even at this distance.

So, what was it waiting for?

The more I thought about it, the worse it got. If it *was* Thoggudan, then it was a creature every bit as dangerous as Vaelor, except Vaelor had been imprisoned, and this thing was flying around, completely free. So far, there hadn't been any great outbreaks of madness, like had been described in the fall of the Commagan Empire, but that *might* just be because the Galel hadn't been worshiping this thing for generations.

That wasn't a great deal of comfort. Vaelor had essentially required divine intervention to cram him back into his prison. What possible hope did we have against Thoggudan?

Despair threatened. Try as we might, fight as hard as we had, the enemy had either been a step ahead of us or simply overpowered us every time. And it just seemed to get worse. We'd killed three of the Dullahans, but now we were up against the dragon, and that monstrosity seemed to be so far beyond the Dullahans that it hardly bore mentioning.

A part of me just wanted to lie down and die at that point. I was so tired. Despite the calm and beautiful vision of the meadow that I'd dreamed of during my short nap, I didn't feel like I'd slept in ages. My eyes felt gritty. Every limb felt like it weighed a ton. Add in the crushing sense of loss and despair, and I only wanted to close my eyes and never wake up.

I wasn't going to. I might not feel like fighting on, but I knew that I had to.

It was a funny thing. I didn't *want* to get back up and fight. There was none of that surge of feeling of brotherhood that you're supposed to feel in those sorts of situations, the feeling that you have to sacrifice for the men around you. Feelings really didn't enter into it at all. I knew what I had to do. I would do it, no matter how much I didn't want to. It was as simple as that.

When Gunny woke up, we got up to move. No one complained. No one balked. No one tried to stay down in our hole. None of us wanted to face what now seemed inevitable but face it we would.

Remember, gents, this is what it's all about. When you're cold, tired, hungry, wet, and miserable, and you keep going anyway.

* * *

Things *had* shifted, we saw as we got closer.

The assault on the fourth wall continued, barely visible through the murk and the smoke from the plain below, but it had slowed. Almost faltered. Meanwhile, some consolidation had happened down in the imperial encampment. I couldn't see any sign of the Dullahans, but the dragon circled overhead, and it looked like one of the Peruni generals, in gold-chased armor, had taken command. He stood, surrounded by a considerable bodyguard, on top of the second wall, a banner over his head to mark him for friendly forces.

Our guys must have been either out of ammunition or hoarding it for the dragon. We heard no gunfire. That was worrisome, but as long as the fighting was still going on, I hoped that there were still Marines, Menninkai, and Tuacha up on that wall.

The general who had taken over in the emperor's absence must have known that we'd broken out. Even as we crept through the grass toward the flanks, I heard the thunder of hooves and looked up to see a patrol of Avur horsemen riding toward us.

We dropped flat in the grass in a heartbeat, going perfectly still. It was dark enough that they probably hadn't seen us, unless they had a shaman with sorcerous eyes in the sky overhead.

Or the dragon could walk them onto us if it wanted.

They swept past, however, and I got a closer look through my NVGs. They weren't Avurs, though their equipment was similar enough to account for the mistake. There were a plethora of tribes who formed Ar-Annator's auxiliaries, and this was some other steppe tribe that had been pressed into service.

They passed us without looking down at us, but only after they'd faded into the dark to the south did we start to relax, just a little.

We got up and kept moving.

Gunny had an idea of where we were going and what we were going to do, but I still wasn't that clear on it. Maybe I was just too tired. We were circling around to the south, but I didn't see how we were going to make it back up to the beleaguered defenders without getting caught.

I should have trusted him more, though I was still confused when we kept going around the south shoulder of the mountain, without even trying to get back to the walls. I only figured it out after we'd covered a few more miles.

We're going to try to link up with Olgudach.

I had no idea how we were going to pull it off without a pre-arranged signal plan. If I were those boys, I'd be mighty suspicious of anyone coming out of the dark with all *that* going on above the mountain.

Lightning split the night again, a dancing light show of destruction that flickered around the peak above the uppermost tower for several moments. The dragon was turning up the heat.

It took some serious discipline to follow Gunny as he kept us moving away from that. After the amount of time that had passed, I would have expected the fight to have died down a little. Usually, either the wall had fallen, in which case the enemy would be consolidating their gains, or it would have held, in which case they'd have retreated to consolidate and lick their wounds. The fact that it didn't look like either had happened, but the Peruni and their allies were still throwing men into the meat grinder beneath and on the fourth wall, said something about the dragon's assumption of leadership.

It was an eldritch abomination from the Outer Dark. It didn't care about the lives of the Peruni soldiers who were dying in job lots. It probably got its jollies from *all* the bloodshed, on both sides.

In some ways, that made our maneuver around and away from it all the harder, knowing what was going on up there. Again, it wasn't a matter of *wanting* to go into that meat grinder. It was a matter of thinking that we *should*, even though we weren't in a position to do much more than get killed in short order. The Dullahans would have killed us all, sooner or later, if they hadn't been fighting the dragon, presumably over who got the first crack at the Two Swords.

For hours, we hiked, ran, and crawled through the grasslands, avoiding the mounted patrols that were still out on the plain. They were few and far between, fortunately, but discovery by any of them could be disastrous. We were all low on ammo, exhausted, low on water, and hadn't eaten in I didn't care to think how many hours.

We would put the hurt on our attackers, but we'd probably get dogpiled shortly thereafter. So, whenever they
rode past, we went to ground and hid.

Finally, we were past the shoulder of the mountain,
and while the storm still raged with increasing fury overhead, and the sounds of battle still drifted over the hills
to reach us over a mile away, we found ourselves essentially alone on the plains. Tired as we were—Farrar was
almost stumbling with fatigue, and Gunny was definitely
slowing down—we picked up the pace.

That lasted about an hour and a half or so, before
Bailey threw up a fist and dropped behind a fold in the
ground, a slight rise that had started as a finger coming
off the side of the mountain that loomed to our north.

I didn't need him to pass the word. I'd seen the horsemen galloping toward us, lashing their horses furiously
to make better speed. It was too dark, even through my
PVS-15s, to see much detail, but the profile of their arms
and armor were Avur.

Something about the way they rode told me all I
needed to know. We needed to ambush this bunch, and
make sure they never made it back to the imperial camp.

We had come far enough that every man there, even
Farrar, needed no prompting. We got down on line, rifles up, and as soon as the riders came within a hundred
yards, we opened fire.

The crash of suppressed rifle fire was still achingly
loud on that otherwise quiet plain. It would have been
drowned out by thunder by the time the sound reached
the fighting above and to the north of us, but where we
crouched, it was almost thunderous enough on its own
to make me flinch. Suppressors reduce the muzzle blast,

but they can't disguise the *crack* of a bullet traveling faster than the speed of sound, and those *crack*s echoed across the plain.

Yet our aim had been dead on enough that we needn't have worried overmuch about compromise. All four horsemen tumbled limply from their saddles, smashed off their mounts by dead-on center mass shots.

We got up and advanced, rifles leveled, on the bodies, even as the horses—most of them; one had gone down with a scream, stumbling as it lost its rider, and had broken a leg—scattered across the plain in sheer, mindless panic. Two of the Avurs were still moving, one shuddering where he lay on the ground, his lifeblood leaking out into the dirt and the grass, the other writhing as he tried to crawl after his mount. An up-close look confirmed that neither had long for this world. The other two lay motionless, even when Gunny crouched to flick their open eyes in the time-honored dead check.

No one would reach the imperial lines to tell what came behind them.

I could just make out the faint glow of torches off to the northwest. They were still several miles away, but they were coming.

We resumed our march, heading for the rendezvous with Olgudach's long-awaited relief force.

I just hoped and prayed that they came in sufficient numbers to turn the tide. And that they perhaps brought some hope to challenge the dragon, before Thoggudan swept across the land in a tidal wave of madness, hatred, and destruction once again.

CHAPTER 37

BY the time we could see the vanguard, we were just about spent. Gunny made the call to circle up on a slight rise, not far from the road where the oncoming army would pass by. We huddled up, set security, and waited.

I wanted nothing more than to sleep, despite it all. Despite the thunder and the lightning overhead, despite the distant figure of the dragon still occasionally visible in the clouds overhead, circling the fortress. It had to know that the army was coming, but it hadn't attacked yet. That was disturbing. From what I could see, Olgudach had brought a *lot*, probably over two hundred thousand men and horses. Whether it would be enough to turn the tide after the slaughter of the last few days or weeks—it was hard to tell just how long it had been at that point—I didn't know, but it was definitely going to alter the battlefield as soon as it arrived.

Fighting the heaviness in my eyelids and every other part of my body, I bit the inside of my cheek and held watch, waiting for the vanguard.

They hove into sight some time after we'd set in, coming around the bend and out of the small stand of trees that ran down from a gully in the mountainside above. Two dozen horsemen, every other man bearing a torch atop a staff, rode in a tight formation, fully armed and armored, their eyes up and scanning the shadows around the road.

Not only Galel rode in that group. A good twelve of them were definitely men of Cor Legear and its holds, but there were others as well. The three Tuacha were immediately identifiable as such, though I didn't recognize them specifically.

The sight of those tall, powerful beings riding along with Olgudach's relief force hit me with such a sense of hope and relief that I sagged where I was. We had sent no word across the sea about what was happening. There hadn't been time. Yet apparently King Caedmon had known, nevertheless, and sent warriors to our aid.

I didn't recognize the other riders or their equipment. They tended to be darker men than the Galel, from what I could see in the torchlight, and their armor was different. They wore a mix of mail, coats of overlapping scales, and solid breastplates, and their helmets varied between round iron caps, glorified kettle helms, and a few flaring, ridged helmets that looked almost like a conquistador's morion. Their shields were smaller and rounder than the Galel's and had a much more pronounced dome to their shape. Each man also wore a half-cape fastened at one shoulder and draped across his breastplate or mail on his shield side.

Gunny stood as they came within a hundred yards and called out in the *Tenga Tuacha*. "Lords of Cor Legear! Friendlies here!" Without a set protocol for deconfliction, he had to make up the hail as he went along, and the *Tenga* doesn't work quite the same way as English, anyway.

The lead riders reined in. I almost expected a react to ambush drill, but while the men in the unfamiliar armor looked like they were about ready to charge, the Galel and the Tuacha put up their hands to call a halt. They recognized the words, if not the voice.

"Who goes there?" The Galel knight who bellowed out the words seemed familiar, tall, broad-shouldered, and wearing a tunic of green and orange, the horsehair crest atop his helm dyed a deep red.

"Four Recon Marines and a Tuacha warrior." Gunny stood in the open, unflinching, as the knight rode closer, flanked by two more Galel, a Tuacha who looked nearly as tall as Mathghaman, armored in glittering mail and a white cloak, and one of the darker men, his cape a red so dark, it looked black in my NVGs.

"Tigharn is truly merciful." The Tuacha swung down from the saddle and gripped Diarmodh's forearms. "We feared we might be too late, given the storm."

"Conchar." Diarmodh returned the tall man's grasp. Conchar's hair was a blond nearly as light as King Caedmon's white. "How many have you brought?"

"Come and see." Conchar didn't smile, though there was an air of reassurance about him. "Yet we must ask. Does Cor Chatha still stand? Or are you the only survivors?"

"The fortress still stands." Diarmodh looked over his shoulder. "For how much longer, I cannot say."

"We have little time, then." The Galel knight still sat his horse, his spear in his fist, as he looked over his shoulder at the advancing army along the road. "We will call a halt until you can tell Lord Olgudach and the kings all."

* * *

I hadn't expected any size Tuacha force, let alone the army that marched and rode not far from the front of the column. There must have been ten thousand of them, in tall helms and shimmering mail, spears glittering more brightly than the torchlight could account for. While Mathghaman and his companions had adopted rifles in order to fight our way when they'd accompanied us into battle, the rest of Tuacha da Riamog seemed to be entirely happy sticking to the old ways.

They were quite formidable enough to make that stick without worrying about ever being outclassed.

What was even more surprising than the fact that an entire Tuacha army had crossed the sea to join in the defense of Cor Chatha was the sight of King Caedmon himself riding at their head.

I shouldn't have been surprised. He'd led the way against the hundred-handed Deep One that had attempted to assail the Isle of Riamog to take the Sword of Iudicael from me. Like Mathghaman, or King Uven, he was not the sort to sit back and rest on his throne while there was serious fighting to be done.

He locked eyes with me, then turned his gaze to Bailey. With a nod to Gunny, he swung down off his horse and moved to greet us.

"Conor. Sean. Ronald." He gripped each of our hands, and something about the power in that grip seemed to help us shake off the weariness and the pain. He even greeted Farrar in the same way. "Michael. Come. Rest a moment." He looked up as Olgudach rode up to join us, hardly waiting for his horse to come to a complete halt. He rushed over and wrapped me up in a bear hug. I hadn't realized we'd formed that tight a bond, but I suddenly felt a flush of warmth that this man, whom we had once, not so long ago, suspected of treason, had moved heaven and earth and, from his look of complete exhaustion, had hardly slept for weeks as he'd worked himself to the bone to gather this force and march on Cor Chatha.

"The king?" he asked, searching my face for any thread of hope to hold on to.

"He was still alive when we saw him last." My own voice was a harsh rasp, almost worse than Gunny's. "That was at least a couple days ago, but if they're still fighting, I doubt he's gone down."

Olgudach nodded. It was probably the best he could have hoped for. King Caedmon had patiently waited out the interruption, then ushered us toward a stand of trees just off the road, leading his horse. Most of the other warriors were spreading out to either side of the track, setting security and preparing to wait a little while. The king wanted an intel dump, and Olgudach appeared to be following his lead.

Yet another man joined us then, with a red and black cape over a gilded breastplate, one of the pseudo-morion helmets under his arm, its crest a golden eagle. His features were hawkish, his hair worn longer than most of the Galel's, with a short, pointed beard on his chin and flaring mustaches above.

"Conor, Bearer of the Sword of Iudicael, and Sean, Bearer of the Sword of Categyrn, I present King Monderic, of the Kingdom of Silabor." Olgudach held out a hand toward the richly armored man. "He would also hear what you have to say."

The king of Silabor bowed to both of us. I'd heard of Silabor; in fact, one of this king's ancestors had been one of the first Sword Bearers. I didn't know what he thought about foreigners from beyond the mists carrying them now, but if he had an opinion on that, he kept it to himself. He was older than Uven, and considerably more aloof. This wasn't the sort of man, I thought, that we, as ordinary warriors, could've developed a bond of true brotherhood with, not like we had with Uven. He knew his place, and by extension, everyone else's place as well. He showed some respect to King Caedmon, but there was neither deference nor outward friendliness there.

Maybe that was just the reality of being a battle king among foreigners. He had to maintain a reserve, a certain stature and image. I didn't know, and right then, I didn't especially care. I already disliked him on principle for that cold stare of his. We'd been through hell, fought Dullahans and wyverns and other things almost as bad, watched friends die horribly, and here he was, acting all superior.

I told myself to keep my mouth shut. I could easily get pissed off and torpedo the alliance here if I wasn't careful.

"Now, tell us all that has transpired." King Caedmon, for all the warmth of his greeting, got right down to business. "Leave nothing out."

That took a while. There was a lot, and there were some things that I hadn't seen. Diarmodh seemed to have been everywhere, or else his Tuacha perceptions and gifts extended to a certain telepathy that allowed him to see through more than just his own eyes. He did most of the talking, while the rest of us filled in the details.

Finally, once the broad strokes of the battle had been laid out, King Caedmon looked around at the lot of us. "Does Mathghaman still live?"

"So far as we know." I glanced at Diarmodh. "Bearrac's dead, though."

The words seemed to hang in the air like the pronouncement of doom, and I felt it then, worse than any time since he'd fallen. The near despair at the realization that Bearrac, larger-than-life, the biggest and most boisterous of Mathghaman's companions, a man who had more often than any other volunteered to accompany my team on our missions, was just *gone*.

I'd lost men before. Stanley, Smith, Rodeffer, others who had gone down in combat, training, accidents, or by their own hand over the years before we'd come through the mists. Something about losing Bearrac, though, seemed worse. We'd known, deep down, that the Tuacha could be killed. Cairbre's sacrifice had shown us that. Bearrac had always seemed less like a man and more like a force of nature, though. Nothing could bring him down, least of all something so mundane as a spear.

And yet it had. That bluff, brotherly giant was dead and would never get up again.

I managed to choke back the grief, though King Caedmon bowed his head and placed a great hand on my shoulder. I might have seen a tear glitter in his eye as he nodded grimly. "You say that the dragon has claimed suzerainty over the empire? What sort of beast could this be?"

The echoes of that vision reverberated through my mind. "It's Thoggudan."

All eyes turned to me. Some were uncomprehending, not recognizing the name. Others were filled with horror, as if confronted by a nightmare out of the deepest pits of hell. King Caedmon's hand tightened on my shoulder.

"It would not be wise to utter that name carelessly, Conor." He studied me with a faint frown, the only other sign that he was in any way perturbed. "You are sure of this? How?"

I didn't answer immediately, just because what the king had said had just slid the last piece of the puzzle into place with a mental *click*.

"I saw a vision, when I killed the emperor, of his fall into darkness. Saw him dig up the Thirty. Heard the shadow demon tell him the name." I looked up at the sky. "I know why I saw that, now."

Gunny, Farrar, Olgudach, and King Monderic all looked somewhat confused, but King Caedmon, Diarmodh, and, surprisingly, Bailey, were nodding. They understood what had just dawned on me.

"Did you hear its full name?" King Caedmon asked.

I nodded. I wasn't going to say it, not after the caution he'd given me. "Yeah. I heard it."

The king nodded gravely and looked to Olgudach. "We should halt here awhile. There are preparations to make." Looking first me, then Bailey, in the eye, stretching out his other hand to grip Bailey's shoulder, he kept his voice low. "You know what you must do?"

I looked over at Bailey, who nodded. He'd never been that interested in much outside the job and sports, but now that we were in it, and now that he was a Sword

Bearer, he was beginning to understand the mystical side of this war more. In some ways, given the way he'd simply react to a situation while I was still analyzing it, I thought he had come to instinctively understand it better than I did, and I'd been a Sword Bearer longer than he had.

"We know."

Gunny, as was his wont, didn't ask questions, though he probably still wasn't entirely sure what had just happened. He might be, though. He'd always surprised us at just what he'd picked up on, especially when it was something that the younger guys were trying to slip past him. He was cunning like that. He just started setting a fire, since we were going to be there for a little bit.

King Caedmon knelt next to it, accompanied by Diarmodh and a couple more of his warriors, and we joined him.

We had a lot of preparation ahead of us, and not a lot of time for it. I closed my eyes as the king began to chant.

CHAPTER 38

I still didn't know how we'd managed to hide an entire army in the open, just by staying behind the mountain, especially when the dragon was flying through the stormy skies overhead. I had to offer some thanks to Iudicael, Categyrn, and their master, Tigharn. They must have shielded us from the dragon's baleful glare while we had held vigil, trying to prepare ourselves for the battle ahead.

Our part of it, anyway. Things were about to get very, *very* interesting.

Olgudach's reinforcements had deployed quietly while we were meditating under the trees, circling wide around to the south, with several maniples of Galel and Silaboran knights roving even farther afield to intercept any Peruni reinforcements or their auxiliaries.

Now they were ready, in a great crescent poised to slam the door shut on the imperial rear area. There were infantry in the rear, but the front ten ranks were all mounted men, knights, heavy men-at-arms, and Tuacha warriors. The Tuacha were in the center, behind the front rank, ready to spring out and strike with a fury that the enemy wasn't ready for.

We sat fresh horses in the middle of that formation. Our place wasn't in the vanguard, as much as we might have started to worry about the rest of the platoon, started to feel guilty. We might have found ourselves a reasonably safe haven, away from the fighting, for a few hours, but we had a much harder task than even those guys up on the wall right then, fighting for their lives while lightning hammered the sides of the mountain above them.

I knew what I had to do. I knew why I'd been shown the vision of the emperor's fall into darkness. It had all been to reveal to me the dragon's name.

Names have power. To know a person's name is to give a certain degree of authority. If you just yell, "Hey, you!" they can ignore you.

In an exorcism—this wasn't something I'd been familiar with, but it turned out Farrar had gone on a research kick after watching *The Exorcist* and hearing that it was somewhat based on real people—the exorcist at some point has to find out the demon's name, at which point he can command it more strongly, advancing on the way to kicking it out of the possessed. This is usually done through invoking authority from on high, but I'd been shown the dragon's name without having to play word games with it.

Our hope was that with that name, I could compel it to land, giving us a crack at it. If anything was going to kill it—or banish it; I wasn't sure if you *could* kill an Outsider—it would be one or both of the Two Swords.

I wasn't especially looking forward to the confrontation. While we rode forward, I prayed almost constantly that we wouldn't just get fried on the ground as soon as we tried it. This felt like throwing a rock at a B-52.

We wouldn't be alone. Gunny, Diarmodh, and Farrar were determined to come with us. So was King Caedmon, which should have been a comfort.

Facing that thing, though, knowing what it was…

There wasn't much comfort to be had.

Of course, it was going to take more than just riding out and yelling the dragon's name at it. We'd gone back and forth a little about whether we wanted to try to draw it out onto the plains or find a way to pull it into a fight in the more restricted terrain of the fortress. We'd finally decided on the latter. Once we had brought it down—if that was even possible—then we didn't want to give it room to maneuver. Shackled by the supernatural command I was hoping to issue, it would be bound to the physical constraints its assumed form forced on it.

At least, that was the hope. I wondered how realistic that hope was. This was an Outsider, an ancient and powerful demon of the Outer Dark. What was it *really* capable of?

We were ants going after a lion. And we knew it.

The only one who looked perfectly relaxed was King Caedmon. He was mortal—we knew that just because we'd seen that the Tuacha themselves could be killed—but he was still on a level beyond us. If there was any one man who had the least reason to be afraid of the dragon, it was the king.

Of course, most of the rest of his warriors reflected the same ease. They weren't loose and sloppy, but they were far from wound tight with worry and fear. To them, this was simply one more fight in a life of warfare with dark and eerie forces. Perhaps a greater fight than any since they'd fought the Deep One outside the harbor, but still not that much different.

The Galel and the Silaborans were perhaps a little more nervous, and their mounts were picking up on it.

Even as we began to trot forward, some of the horses were shifting and crow-hopping a little. They smelled what was coming, and they didn't want to go into it.

Of course, the near constant flicker of lightning and roll of thunder was already bad enough, without the winged shapes of wyverns flocking around the dragon as it circled above the citadel. The carnage beneath the walls was pretty awful, too, but these were warhorses. They were used to that. It was the sorcery and the monsters that had them scared.

Still, they were disciplined beasts, and while they shuffled and balked a little, they advanced as their riders—some of whom were every bit as nervous—kicked them into motion. With a rumbling thunder of hoofbeats that rivaled the thunderclaps in the sky above, the army came around the shoulder of the mountain and up over the rise, into full view of the fortress and the imperial camp.

Fires still burned on the fourth wall, glittering in the dark and putting a pall of smoke over the whole of the fortress, only occasionally lit by another lightning flash. The fighting was still going on, but while I felt a sudden surge of hope that the rampart had held, it was dashed as we continued to advance and another bolt of purple-tinged lightning revealed a massive gap blasted in the wall, halfway between the gate and the mountainside. The lower part was obscured by the ruins of the walls beneath, but from the looks of it, an entire angle had been blown out, opening the way to the imperial forces.

We could only hope that most of the defenders had made it back to the fifth wall without being cut off and killed. Or worse, taken from the sky and eaten or thrown to their deaths on the rocks below.

I still couldn't hear gunfire or explosions. I wondered if that meant everyone had gone black on ammo, or if the worst had happened. I hoped and prayed it was the former.

The bulk of the enemy forces still appeared to be pressing the fight inside the walls. Some were still in the encampment, apparently regrouping, but horns brayed as we came into view, and men began to scramble into defensive formations. There were more in the camp than we might have hoped, but still far from the bulk of the army.

Of course, when you considered that even with the reinforcements from Cor Legear, Silabor, and the Isle of Riamog, we were still hugely outnumbered, more than we hoped was still a lot.

A silver trumpet sounded, and a forest of Galel and Silaboran spears descended to level at the enemy, flickering brightly as another thunderbolt split the sky. With a yell, the front ranks kicked their horses into a gallop.

We followed along. That defensive formation was rushing to meet us near the end of the first wall, and we had to break through them to get a chance to move higher up into the breached fortifications.

The Peruni were mostly on foot, and for all the desperation with which it had been thrown together, the imperial leaders clearly knew what they were doing. I had to hand it to them for tactical acumen. They'd looked up, identified the threat, and put together a ten-man-deep shieldwall, bristling with long spears that might have been the cataphracts' two-handed lances, all within minutes. And they'd used the terrain to put the wall on one flank and enough of the camp—with a partially completed stockade around it no less—to present a serious obstacle to the other. The only way to get to the inside of the fortress and the rest of the army was to go through them.

If we were in that much of a hurry. I knew enough of Olgudach's and King Monderic's plan that I didn't think wasting men and horses trying to break through a prepared formation like that was in the cards.

And it wasn't.

At the last moment, within about ten strides of the bristling spearpoints, the trumpet sounded again, and with a dazzling display of horsemanship, the lead ranks veered off. A few riders and their mounts came almost close enough to take cuts from the enemy spears, but the crashing impact didn't happen.

Instead, the men-at-arms, all with their spears thrust into sockets behind their saddles, drew bows as they charged, and loosed a whistling cloud of arrows over the knights' heads.

The gap between those front ranks and the horse archers had steadily grown wider as the charge had crossed the gently sloping ground toward the base of the first wall. That gave them some room to maneuver and to shoot just over the galloping knights.

Many of the arrows either skipped off or embedded themselves in the shields. Some of the less-disciplined Peruni soldiers, however, must have looked up over their shield rims to try to figure out what was happening. Clothyard shafts, tipped with hardened iron, hammered into and under helmets. Some, again, skipped off. Others went beneath the rims or through the eye openings, crunching through skin, cartilage, and bone, dropping the men where they stood. Their formation was tight enough that when one man fell, he dragged down men to either side as well as in front and behind him.

A few arrows even punched right through the relatively thin iron of the Peruni helmets, dropping their targets anyway.

That volley hurt the enemy, but it didn't punch a hole we could get through. That was going to take some doing.

More horn calls blared, and the dragon roared overhead, banking onto a wingtip and diving toward the advancing army.

Here it comes.

This wasn't the place we wanted to fight that thing, but unless the next few minutes went remarkably according to plan, it was where the battle was going to happen whether we liked it or not. We'd tried to plan for that contingency. Time would tell if we'd planned well enough.

We had shifted to the right flank with the Tuacha as the charge had continued, and now we were driving hard out around the imperial camp, looking for the gap where we'd escaped when we'd broken out while the dragon had been distracted with the Dullahans. I was keeping an eye out for those nightmares, but so far, they seemed to have cleared out.

Maybe killing the emperor had had some effect, after all. If the Thirty were no longer bound to him...

No. I couldn't count on that. The one with the green fire in place of a neck wanted the Two Swords. They'd stick around, even if they were trying to steer clear of the dragon now. They'd probably come out of the dark at the most inopportune time, too.

King Caedmon was now at the head of the great wedge of riders, his spear glittering in his hand, seemingly almost on its own. Bailey and I had to ride hard to keep up. We were riding Tuacha horses, which were fast as the wind, but we weren't the sort of riders the Tuacha were.

The king lifted his spear and pointed, and the entire wedge wheeled toward the camp. The riders shifted, and it was a much narrower spearhead that drove between the pavilions, swords licking out to cut lines and collapse the tents as we rode through.

More horn calls sounded the alarm, and spearmen poured through the smashed, open gate in the first wall to stop us. More were trying to turn from the flank formation, since we'd ridden faster than they'd expected, but just then the Galel left wing hit them hard.

I could just barely hear the crash as the knights hammered into the shieldwall, leading with their long lances. They'd waited until the shift had begun and hit it at just the right time. Galel knights were dying, but they were giving better than they got. Horses trampled men underfoot, as lances punched into bodies. Some of the shafts snapped, and the knights let go of the shattered hafts and drew their swords and axes, urging their horses on through the press, weapons rising and falling as they hacked their way through.

Some were knocked off their horses by the impact. Some didn't couch their shields well and were run through with spears. Still others were dragged down as their horses lost momentum in the press and were hacked or stabbed to death on the ground, but even some of them managed to take a few of their killers with them.

We couldn't spare the attention or the maneuvering room to help them. We had our own task. Outnumbered as we were, each element had to drive the attack as hard as possible.

Since we'd entered through such a narrow opening in their perimeter, we had an equally narrow lane of attack, which meant the full weight of the Tuacha's charge was concentrated on a small point on the advancing Peruni line. The smashed gate was the bottleneck. If they could hold that gate, we were stuck.

Mostly stuck. Some of us had a contingency plan for that.

Always expect things to go wrong. It's the only way you're ever going to succeed.

The spearmen in the lead got into the wreckage of the gate and formed a hasty shield wall just before the lead Tuacha warriors crashed into them. Several of the massive supermen had driven their horses hard to get out in front of King Caedmon, and he had let them, simply because he was sticking close to us. He had a part to play in what was to come, as well, and while I was sure that on some level, leaving the front line fighting to others chafed on him almost as much as it would on King Uven, but he'd been around long enough that he had the wisdom to hold himself back when he needed to.

Weapons rose and fell, and men died in that wreckage-choked gateway. The Tuacha were like angels of death, hammering their way through the loose shieldwall and cutting their way through the men before them like a scythe through wheat.

Yet the sheer weight of the enemy numbers began to tell, even then. The flanking element that we had first engaged was falling back, fighting ferociously even as they were pinned between the Galel and the Tuacha, and more were coming down from the inner walls to back up the force at the gateway. The advance slowed, and it began to look, before we even reached it, as if the Peruni might just hold the gate. Not forever, but long enough to delay us.

King Caedmon looked the situation over, even as the Silaborans drove inward to crush the outer forces against the wall, their formation tight and their spears bristling. Another breach in the wall loomed just off our right flank, where we had not yet closed the ring... but neither had the enemy.

He pointed his spear, and we followed him, a close column of riders joining us as we peeled off from the main attack, plunging through the squares and circles of tents toward the gap, riding hard, the thunder of our horses' hooves sounding even over the clash of weapons and cries of men in battle in my ears.

We were almost there when the wyverns came diving out of the clouds as the dragon descended to alight on the second wall with an earth-shaking crash.

CHAPTER 39

THE wyverns had taken a beating during the battle so far, but that wasn't a deterrent. They came at us with every bit the same ferocity that they had displayed from the first moment one had attacked us out on the plains. They dove on King Caedmon, jaws agape, their talons extended to grasp and tear. That same steam-boiler hiss rattled down out of the sky, just audible over the noise of the clash of weapons and the grunts and cries of men fighting and dying.

The king didn't have a rifle. After seeing him fight the Deep One off the coast of the Isle of Riamog, however, I knew he probably didn't really need one.

He reared back in his saddle, a spear in his hand, and cast it skyward with a force that I knew I'd never be able to match if I lifted and did 'roids for years. The weapon sailed into the air and slammed into a wyvern's throat a good fifty yards from the king. The creature's dive couldn't be arrested, but it bucked and thrashed, screaming out its agony, and veered off to smash into the wall not far from our flank, wiping out a dozen tents as it went down.

I had my rifle up, gripping my horse with my knees, and got a snap shot off at another one. Single shots weren't going to do much, but I'd been riding along *behind* the attack for long enough. I had to do *something*. I was pretty sure I missed, since the wyvern was unfazed, and I hadn't exactly trained to shoot a rifle from horseback at a dead run, either.

One of the monsters, a good thirty feet long, snatched at a Tuacha warrior on my left, and managed to get him out of the saddle, its talons digging into his shoulder. It flapped into the sky with him, but while the pain had to be excruciating, he didn't cry or falter. He drew his sword and hacked at the monster, grabbing its limb and climbing higher as he hewed through its taloned foot so that it let go of him. The last I saw of him, he was still swinging as the wyvern screamed and soared into the night, out over the plain.

Then more of them were swirling around us, and the king bellowed for us to close in and fight. The drive for the gap slowed and stopped. To ignore the monsters would mean to lose too many.

The Tuacha's horses were different from any others we'd seen in this world. The Galel's mounts tended to be a bit thinner, more delicate, and flighty than the stocky Menninkai animals we'd ridden in the north, but even the Menninkai's mountain horses were downright panicky compared to the Tuacha's beasts. Those chargers were every bit as courageous as their riders, and they wouldn't stampede for anything. It would have seemed unnatural, were they not raised by people as generally otherworldly as the Tuacha.

So, the horses didn't bolt, didn't panic. They began to circle, trampling down tents and the various other camp detritus, as their riders lashed out with spear and sword at the swooping, screeching wyverns.

There was only so much we could do. Bailey and I had the Two Swords, but the monsters were veering aside from them, so we could only ride with the rest and try to get a shot in when they got close enough and tried to grab one of us.

It was frustrating as hell. The Tuacha were getting some. I saw another spear transfix another wyvern through the jaws, and it sailed limply overhead, crashing to the ground with a *boom*, wiping out two riders and several tents in the process. Still, all we could do was ride.

In moments, everything dissolved into pandemonium as the wyverns swooped and snapped at us, the enemy raced to close up the gap in the wall with men, shields, and spears, and the dragon loomed over it all.

I was too busy in the whirl of the fight with the wyverns to get a good look at that ancient, eldritch monstrosity, but I heard its voice reverberate through sky and stone. Its words were unintelligible, but they carried such a weight of malice and hatred that it almost made me sick.

Those words weren't aimed at us. They were a command, a demand, aimed at the dragon's servants, which, whether they liked it or not, included every man under the banner of Ar-Annator. That thing wanted to throw every man available at us, and it wanted it to happen yesterday.

If ever there had been proof of just what kind of bloodshed that thing desired, it was right there. I might not have been able to understand the words in the strictest sense, but even as a smaller wyvern stooped on me, pulling its talons back just as it snapped at my head like a striking snake, taking a slash across the throat for its troubles, I could *feel* what it was saying. There was no subtlety, no tactics involved. It wanted every man who wasn't then engaged with our forces on the wall to throw himself at us. My guess was that it wanted the Two Swords.

And King Caedmon.

The wyvern had been wounded, but it wasn't dead. It battered me with its wings and sprayed me with caustic black blood as it climbed away with another hiss, only to bank sharply and come back around, enraged to the point of insanity by the hurt I'd given it. I ducked its talons and cut it deeply along the underbelly as it went over once more.

King Caedmon would make a hell of a target. The Tuacha were all somewhat otherworldly, but the king stood another head and shoulders above them all. I'd seen what he was capable of. I'd seen him call on Tigharn and then, in the next moment, hurl a spear sheathed in lightning to strike down a Deep One with one shot. *Of course* the dragon wanted him dead.

That second cut did the trick. With a twisting wrench as it tried to get away from the pain, the wyvern thrashed in midair, its involuntary movement driving its head into the ground and forcing it into a forward flip. It landed on its back, crushing several tents and a few Avur auxiliaries who had moved around to try to get on our flank. It kept thrashing around there, spreading the destruction, as blackened ichor flowed from the wound, turning to smoke as it hit the air.

Then King Caedmon got pissed.

It happened quickly. So quickly that I almost missed it. Yet he brought his horse up on its hind legs, then *jumped* it twenty feet in the air.

That brilliant white horse seemed to glow with its own light as it went over the other warriors' heads, intercepting one of the wyverns in midflight. King Caedmon's sword flashed, and the wyvern's head flew free, sailing over the whirling circle of hard-riding Tuacha to smash into the ground between us and the edge of the camp. Something about the way he'd hit it deflected the body so that while it landed close enough to shake the ground under us, it still missed us except with the membrane of one wing, which almost swept Naoghas off his horse.

The king and his horse alighted just outside our circle, and he stood tall in the stirrups, spread his arms, sword in one hand and shield in the other, lifted his face to the sky, and shouted.

No, it was more than that. He chanted, his voice booming louder than the battle, in that ancient, sacred language. The surviving wyverns scattered.

The dragon roared back, but King Caedmon's voice only soared higher. For a moment, I could have sworn that the glow around the king intensified.

Then it really did.

The swirling black clouds overhead seemed to shrink, and the wind picked up. Thunder rumbled, but it faded into a distant mutter, almost as if the storm had tried to lash the fortress with another volley of lightning bolts but had been somehow prevented.

Some of the twilight we'd been fighting under for days lightened, and a gleam of light appeared in the eastern sky as the wind got stronger. The storm was being driven away.

The dragon roared again, but the wyverns were in full panic and fleeing. Solas, who seemed to have stepped into Mathghaman's shoes in the King's Champion's absence, roared a command, and the wheeling horsemen turned almost as one and thundered toward the gap in the wall.

We raced to keep up, though our Tuacha horses seemed to flow right along with the rest, which made it easier.

The wyverns had delayed us just enough, though.

A massive formation of spearmen and cataphracts stood in the gap. Even though they shifted nervously at the signs of the fading of the dragon's power, they held their ground, and they were going to slow us down, if they didn't stop us dead by sheer weight of numbers first.

The cataphracts sat their horses at the front, backed up by two angled phalanxes of spearmen. They had been ordered to hold that gap in the wall, and so they would. They held their long, two-handed lances ready, as the Tuacha warriors, singing the same battle hymn I had heard from Bearrac's lips, thundered toward them, spears held high, swords gleaming in the glimmer of sunlight now coming through that gap in the clouds to the east.

I was close enough to see that clash, since Gunny, Bailey, Farrar, Diarmodh, and I were in the charge, about four ranks back from the apex of the wedge. I saw the first Tuacha hurtle into the front rank of Peruni cataphracts, hitting with a crash that echoed from the mountain above.

The cataphracts were armored from head to toe, draped in overlapping plates of iron that covered every bit of them, even their faces. Their horses were similarly armored, which meant they were heavy enough that they were the unstoppable force in a charge, the immovable object when holding their ground. Their spears were long enough that they could reach nearly the length of a horse past their mounts' muzzles.

The Tuacha hit them like an avalanche.

Lances splintered under that onslaught, and I didn't see any of the Tuacha go down. They must have used their shields to good effect. Some probably just reached out and battered the enemy's weapons away with swords, axes, and spears. Then they were in among the front rank of the cataphracts, their horses lashing out with iron-shod hooves, the Tuacha warriors striking out with a speed and fury that the Peruni couldn't hope to match.

They didn't break. They fought. But the line sagged back under the force of the onslaught, and the spearmen faded back as well, seeing the light in the Tuacha's eyes and the force with which those glittering weapons clove through iron, leather, and linen.

They weren't actually cutting through that armor, not most of the time. They had a way of finding the weak points, though. Getting through the gaps between plates, the seams between pieces of armor. The strength of the Tuacha could take over from there.

One man fell, his helmet cleaved by Colla's axe. The lean, wiry Tuacha wrenched the weapon clear in a sweeping semicircle that brought it crashing down on another man's neck, while the soft sunlight sparkled off his mail and his coppery hair blew in the wind.

Solas lopped the head off another, sending his gold-chased, blackened helm flying through the air. That was very nearly the straw that broke the camel's back.

The line of cataphracts began to bend. The spearmen behind them started to shift backward. Fear was beginning to take hold. A few of the Tuacha went down, when enough of the Peruni's finest warriors ganged up on them, but too few to stem the tide.

The line bent farther. The first of the Peruni began to break and run. The knowledge of certain death was too much, even after all they'd seen and endured in the siege so far. Six Tuacha had been bad enough. An army of them was simply too much.

Then the dragon intervened.

An echoing shout blasted across the fortress, and for a brief moment, everything seemed to just *stop*.

Then the dragon opened its great maw and spewed out an oily black mist that settled on the Peruni below like tar.

I felt my guts twist. I knew what was happening. We'd seen it before. A glance at Gunny and Bailey told me they knew just as well.

It had taken days of human sacrifices to draw that power from Vaelor where he lurked in his stony prison far to the north, under the Teeth of Winter. The dragon being at least as powerful, and free, it took seconds and a simple act of will.

That oily mist settled on the Peruni and their allies, and a moment later, all hesitation, all fear, all sense of self-preservation was lost. In their place was only hatred and bloodlust.

That unreasoning ferocity stopped the charge dead. Solas was mobbed and dragged down, a cataphract throwing himself bodily off his horse at the Tuacha warrior while others charged, even though their horses could barely move in the press. Weapons were forgotten, and men rushed at the Tuacha, foaming at the mouth, grasping with hands turned to claws and snapping with their teeth.

Bailey and I started forward. I tried desperately to hide the dread that had just settled in my chest. The last time we'd faced this sorcerous nightmare, Vaelor had been far away, the numbers had been far fewer, and we'd still almost all been killed. We'd had to slaughter every single surviving Lasknut and Dovo besieging Vahava Paykhah. They hadn't quit. Had just kept coming until they joined the mountain of corpses in front of the gate or along the walls.

We couldn't fight even a quarter million such lunatics, and I wasn't that optimistic that their losses had been that heavy.

My fears, however, were greater than they needed to be. We hadn't had King Caedmon with us last time.

I was only just beginning to understand just why he was the king, and why Mathghaman, who I thought was the noblest man I'd ever known, revered him so much.

King Caedmon didn't panic, didn't even seem perturbed. He simply stood straight up in his saddle, once again with his face turned to the sky, his arms spread wide.

His chant was different this time, but it still echoed the prayer that had begun to clear the skies. The effect was even more immediate.

With a faint, distant howl, the black mist rushed out of the Peruni and plunged into the ground to disappear. In a moment, the battle had shifted again. With the dragon's influence banished, the terror that had gripped the imperials redoubled, even as the Tuacha, their battle hymn getting even louder, pressed the attack, slaying men with every stroke.

The dragon's howl shook the very ground. It spread its wings and heaved itself into the air. It glared down at the first wall with fiery eyes as it climbed, its jaws agape, its fangs flickering with purple corposant.

Its roar was not a threat like it had made before. It was a blast of sheer hate that hit so hard, I almost blacked out. I think if I hadn't been holding onto the Sword of Iudicael, I would have. When my vision cleared, I looked over and saw Farrar sagging in the saddle. I was just close enough to catch him and shake him back to awareness before he fell.

Gunny being Gunny, he'd gritted his teeth and endured it. He was riding alongside us, his jaw set and his eyes hard.

The dragon spread its wings and dove toward us. King Caedmon was suddenly at my side.

"Prepare yourselves, my lads. The plan has changed. The dragon comes to us." Beckoning to us, he wheeled his white horse and kicked it into a gallop toward the plain. Toward open ground, where we could fight the dragon away from the rest of our comrades.

We rode after him, as that ancient being of hatred and malevolence swooped toward us.

CHAPTER 40

WE rode hard toward the gap in the clouds on the horizon, into the rising sun—it had been so long since I'd seen the sun that I hadn't realized it was dawn until that moment—dodging wrecked tents, wagons, baggage, and the occasional imperial straggler, some of whom tried to fight and others who just tried desperately to get out of the way. Behind us, I could hear the beat of the dragon's wings, though it had ceased to roar as it closed in on us.

King Caedmon in the lead, we broke out of the encampment and galloped onto the plain. The grassland had been trampled down before the rain and hail of the storm had battered it down even further. The sun was blazing on the horizon now, as he wheeled to face the oncoming monster. "Come, Conor! Come, Sean! Now is the time!"

The two of us brought our horses around sharply to flank him, turning to face the dragon as it glided toward us, its wings spread wide, its entire body seemingly shrouded in shadow despite the rising sun at our backs. Only its eyes, crackling with purple lightning, shone through that cloud of utter darkness.

I hadn't thought too much, during our preparation, about what I would say at this moment. I knew the dragon's name, and I knew that it gave me some power over it, but I had no formula in my head until that moment.

Lifting the Sword of Iudicael in a gesture of defiance, I faced the dragon. The sun gleamed on the blade, turning the golden runes and accents to blazing fire. Bailey lifted the Sword of Categyrn in the same way, and it shone just as brightly.

"Thoggudan Karataros!" I brought the full volume of a Marine NCO's voice to bear, but my bellow still roared louder than I would ever be capable of on my own. "I name thee, and in the Name of He Who Stands on High, I bid thee come down and face me!"

The words had simply come to me. I suspected that Iudicael had effectively whispered them in my ear. Iudicael, or someone higher than he.

The dragon had flared as we had lifted the Two Swords, rearing up and spreading its wings to arrest its forward rush, but now, as my voice echoed off the mountain behind with the force and volume of a thunderclap, it dropped toward us suddenly, almost as if it had been grabbed by the throat and yanked down toward the ground.

It struck the ground with an earthshaking *boom*, catching itself with its taloned feet and the knuckles of its wings. Yet that catch was only momentary, as it slammed onto its belly on the ground, its enormous skull crashing to the dirt only a few yards away.

It groaned then, its eyes squinted, and rolled its head weakly from side to side. Its wings flapped, and it tried to bring one up off the ground, but it quavered in the air for only a few seconds before falling again with another heavy impact.

I felt a surge of triumph. All we had needed was that name. The great and awful so-called "elder god" that had destroyed the Commagan Empire, left Lost Colcand a haunted, cursed nightmare of twisted beasts and terrible darkness, and the ruins of the northern marches of the Empire of Ar-Annator and equally haunted place of shadows and fear, had been brought down by a single command.

So powerful was that feeling of triumph that I wanted to charge it right then and there, put my foot on its head, and shout our victory to the sky. What couldn't a man who hadn't just killed a dragon, but commanded it down out of the sky be capable of?

Iudicael was looking out for me, though. Even as I thought it, that first bit of doubt started to work through the surge of emotion. It had taken Galan's death, concentrated .50 caliber fire, the Sword of Iudicael, and Galan's spear, effectively sanctified by his self-sacrifice, to kill the red dragon of Gremman. Could it really be this easy?

No. I knew it then, as sure as the sun was shining through the clouds behind me. This was a trap.

Maybe naming it and calling it down in Tigharn's name really had been effective, but the fight wasn't over yet.

The spell it was working was a powerful one, though. It went beyond the outward show of weakness. That thing didn't need to speak to assert its influence. Only Iudicael's help—Tigharn's help, really, at Iudicael's request—was giving me the ability to see through it, if only a little.

Bailey had started to move forward, though I thought I saw what might have been a luminous figure reaching out to forestall him. He halted, reining in after only a few lengths of his horse, a frown crossing his features, even as King Caedmon reached out a hand toward him in warning.

Of course King Caedmon hadn't even started to fall for the dragon's trick. He was on a whole different level, making even us Sword Bearers look like amateurs.

With a flash of what might have been shame, I realized that we really *were* amateurs, men groping through a role we hadn't chosen and hadn't truly learned. Of *course* King Caedmon was greater than we were. He always had been, and always would be.

Not everyone with us had the same degree of mystical protection, though.

Farrar, with a shout of glee, kicked his horse into motion, racing toward the dragon. I saw its slitted eyes flick to him, and in an instant, I knew what was about to happen.

Kicking my own horse into motion, I darted forward to head him off. He might be an idiot at that moment, but he was *my* idiot, and I'd be damned if I sat back and let him get his head bitten off because he was riding the emotional high of watching the dragon fall to think straight.

I caught him just before the dragon struck. I was just a bit too slow to save the horse, but I grabbed Farrar by the chest rig and hauled him out of the saddle by main strength, almost dislocating my shoulder in the process, and wheeled my horse around just as that massive, viper head darted down and snapped Farrar's mount in half with an awful *crunch*.

I was out of position to try to hit it with the Sword of Iudicael, and off balance from holding onto Farrar, so I kicked my horse away from the dragon, even as King Caedmon, Gunny, and Bailey closed in.

"*Foolish.*" The dragon had heaved itself up off the ground, its head now looming above us, its neck curved like a snake coiled to strike. "*Thou couldst have had unlimited power. Could have used the scrap of power thou wast given to command me. Instead, thou hast only sealed thy doom.*"

It struck at Bailey, then, as I got out of reach and let Farrar slide to the ground. He was pale faced and shaking, but he got his weapon up and went into a fighting crouch next to Diarmodh as I turned back to the dragon.

Bailey had dodged at the last moment, aiming a cut at the dragon as its jaws closed where his head had been a split second before. The combination of the dragon's hasty retraction and Bailey's Tuacha horse quickly carrying him out of harm's way prevented him from doing any more damage than a scratch to the scales along the dragon's jaw, but even that stroke left a brilliant, burning scar along the monster's mandible.

It lunged then, pivoting back toward where I sat my mount over Diarmodh and Farrar. It didn't seem to be able to take off again, but it was still dangerous on the ground. As dangerous as a rattlesnake the size of a train. One that could influence minds and twist and warp the very forces of nature by an act of sheer will.

Under any other circumstances, I should have been dead right then and there. It opened its maw and blasted a bolt of lightning at my head. If some premonition—doubtless thanks to Iudicael—hadn't made me duck, it would have blown my head off and ended the fight in a split second. As it was, every hair stood on end, and I felt a flush of heat as the skin on the side of my face was scorched by the close passage of that electric inferno. Then my horse was thundering around the dragon's flank, opposite the direction Bailey had gone.

That horse was almost picking its movements on its own. It *was* a Tuacha horse, but I also suspect that Iudicael had something to do with it.

The dragon snapped its head back around toward where Bailey was charging it now, but it hesitated a moment as King Caedmon came at it from the front.

It snapped a wing up, I thought at first to try to strike the king down, but it turned out it was shielding itself. King Caedmon still delivered a terrific cut to the membrane, splitting part of it as flames leapt from the wound.

With its wing shielding it just enough from Caedmon, the ancient abomination swung on Bailey, sending out another searing blast of lightning. Except this time, even as he barely avoided getting fried, it struck at him like a cobra. I couldn't tell what was happening from the other side, but only the fact that he had the Sword of Categyrn up in a defensive position kept him from being bitten in half. The dragon didn't want to touch that blade, and it recoiled as soon as it came near it.

Commanding it in Tigharn's name had pinned it to the ground, but actually killing it was going to be another matter.

King Caedmon got another cut in, but the dragon twisted again, lashing out with that wing. It missed him altogether, but crushed his horse, sending the animal tumbling with an awful finality, its limbs loose in a way that spoke of many broken bones, even as the king leaped free.

Then it reared up and came for me as I closed in on its flank, uncovered by that wing.

It was so big and so long that it didn't even need to turn around, but just twisted its neck to bring its head to bear against me. Those massive fangs, each one longer than my arm, glittered through the darkness that still clung to it as it struck.

I got a good cut on it that time, keeping the Sword of Iudicael low until the last possible moment. The blade split its jaw nearly as deep as my forearm before it recoiled away again, rearing up to loom over us all.

"*Thou didst challenge a god. Thy tricks, thy groveling alliance with that meddler on high, have given thee some slight advantage in the beginning, yet now, as is His wont, He has left thee to thy own devices. And I shalt devour thee.*"

King Caedmon was on his feet, flanked by Diarmodh, Farrar, Gunny, and a couple other Tuacha warriors who'd come with us. But despite how formidable the king was, right then, I knew that this was going to come down to the Two Swords.

If we could even get close enough to really hurt that thing, and that was looking like more and more of an impossible task.

I knew that the dragon itself was fueling that sense of despair, pouring its malice into a subtle weight upon our minds. That didn't make the task in front of us any less daunting.

It was Gunny who broke the impasse.

He crossed himself—I'd never seen him do that before—and rushed the dragon.

For a moment, it almost seemed as if the dragon didn't see him. It was so focused on those it thought were a real threat—Bailey, Caedmon, and me—that it was practically ignoring everyone else. It hadn't ignored Farrar, but then, Farrar had been falling for its tricks. Gunny, as desperate as his maneuver might be, wasn't.

He hit the wing that Caedmon had already cut, hacking deeper into the wound in the membrane, cutting it with his axe clear to the bone. Then he worked his way up and started swinging at the joint, whaling on it like a lumberjack. His axe bit deep, and the dragon roared, even as the joint parted, the wing collapsing and dropping it onto its shoulder.

It was still big enough that it was entirely too formidable to be considered disabled, even though it was wounded. But it was apparently in shock, at least for a moment.

It wasn't so in shock that it couldn't counterattack. It twisted its head around, arched its neck, and struck with blinding speed.

Gunny just disappeared into its maw.

It happened so fast, and I was so deeply enmeshed in the fight, that I didn't have time to mourn, or even feel the shock of his death. I simply took it in, a detail logged dispassionately as complete calm settled over me.

The dragon's head was still lowered, though it was beginning to rise again. King Caedmon was out of position, but he didn't let that stop him. He reared back, his sword held in two hands, and flung it, as hard as he could, at the dragon's diamond-shaped skull. Just like his spear during the fight with the hundred-handed Deep One had gathered all the lightning from the clouds above around itself, so his sword seemed to absorb and intensify the light of the rising sun as it whirled through the air to embed itself to the hilt in the dragon's eye.

It roared again, dipping its head and turning toward Caedmon, but then I was right on it, and I threw myself out of the saddle and onto its back.

Bailey had made a similar move, though he was still on the ground, and the Two Swords bit into the dragon's neck at almost the same moment.

The blade sank deep, passing through the scales with only the slightest tug. The dragon's unnatural flesh began to burn even as the Sword if Iudicael came up against its iron-hard spine, and then I hauled the Sword free and struck again, deeper this time, as its massive body bucked and twisted under me, lightning shooting wildly from its maw as it roared and screamed.

"Go back to the pit from where you came!" Bailey's voice boomed as loud as mine had when I had issued my challenge, even as he hewed deeper into the side of the dragon's neck.

We hacked and slashed at it as it kept thrashing around, but it was held to the ground, and while it fought to the very end, it was already dying as soon as we'd gotten our first couple of strokes in.

Its head finally came free of the massive, serpentine body and settled to the earth with a tooth-rattling *thud*. I threw myself clear, rolling as I hit the ground, or at least trying to. The impact knocked the wind out of me, and I almost cut myself on the Sword as I tumbled to a stop. The body continued to thrash and writhe on the ground, digging a great crater in the earth before its throes were over.

Before it had even stopped moving, the carcass had begun to melt into smoking black ichor. The shroud of darkness that had clung to it was gone, burned away by the sun, which grew brighter as the dark clouds overhead continued to clear.

Only then, as a panicked horn call went up from the imperial formations, and all those Peruni, Avurs, and other imperial forces that found themselves with an escape route started to flee, did I sink to my knees, struck down by the reality that Gunnery Sergeant Ron Taylor, the man I'd looked up to since I'd first come to the platoon, a man who had kept us all alive across the Land of Ice and Monsters and through countless fights since, was gone.

King Caedmon's hand came to rest on my shoulder, as I stayed on my hands and knees, gasping for breath against both the impact and the staggering loss that had just clamped its reality around my chest. I looked up at him, as regal and imposing as ever, through a mist of tears that I hadn't realized had blurred my vision.

"He will be remembered for his sacrifice, Conor." He extended his hand to Bailey, who had joined us, openly and unashamedly weeping. "In this life and the next."

EPILOGUE

KING Uven, flanked by Mathghaman and Santos, limped as he came down from the fifth wall to where King Caedmon and King Monderic awaited him with Olgudach and the remainder of the strike team that had stayed behind, days before, in wait for the emperor.

He was covered in blood, and from the slack way his left arm hung and the way he favored his side, some of it was his. Yet he walked as tall as he could, only stopping when he came to stand before us. His eyes went from Caedmon, to Monderic, and finally to us.

Stiffly, obviously in pain, he knelt. "King Caedmon. I could hardly have hoped for your aid. All that I have is yours." He shifted slightly to face Monderic. "Kinsman. Your coming shall be sung of in all the halls of the Galel for generations to come."

Monderic, for his part, despite the coldness he'd displayed when we'd first met him, stepped forward to raise Uven to his feet. "Honor demanded it, my brother. The glory you have wrapped yourself in for holding this fortress, against such odds, for so long, will outlive any honor you might do me."

Uven clasped the Silaboran king to him in a bear hug, then, and from some of the looks of Galel and Silaboran alike, I gathered this was not a normal display of camaraderie between the two nations. A fight like we'd just been through, though, makes brothers of men who might otherwise not even want to pass within arm's reach of each other.

Then he turned to us.

"My friends." He was choking up, and he dropped to his knees again. This time, though, everyone but the Tuacha and our surviving Marines followed suit. "You have done what no man might have dared. You have brought the Two Swords out of darkness, and with them, delivered us from the greatest evil we have seen in living memory. Perhaps the greatest since the Summoner himself walked the earth." He turned his head—with some obvious pain—and lifted his voice. "Glory to the Bearers of the Two Swords!"

"*Glory to the Bearers of the Two Swords!*" The shout thundered off the mountainside and rose to the rapidly clearing blue sky overhead. "*Glory!*"

"We couldn't..." I had to swallow the lump in my throat. "We couldn't have done it alone."

"Get up, Uven. Please." Bailey was as choked up as I was. "We're just men. If not for Iudicael and Categyrn... Without Gunny's..."

Mathghaman came to join us then, clasping each of us by the shoulder. "There is no victory without sacrifice. He will be remembered."

"He will indeed." Uven rose stiffly then, and slowly, almost reluctantly, the rest followed suit. "By his sacrifice, like Galan's before him, in the battle with the red dragon of Gremman, he enabled us to be free." He pointed out toward the eastern plains. "Even now, the Empire of Ar-Annator teeters on the edge of the abyss. Their army shattered, tens of thousands taken, tens of thousands more dead, the emperor fallen without an heir... Ar-Annator will be wracked by civil war within a fortnight."

"There will be a new threat therein," King Monderic said. "Yet now is a time for celebration, despite the mourning we must make for the dead."

King Uven nodded, the gesture returned by King Caedmon. "Come, my friends. Sorrow may temper our joy, but for today, at least, we have won. Tigharn be praised."

* * *

We stayed in the Kingdom of Cor Legear through the winter. There was a lot of rebuilding to do, and it was a watchful, wary winter, even once the bodies were buried, the prisoners secured, and the snows shut down the passes. Word began to filter to the frontiers that the predicted civil war in Ar-Annator was indeed in full swing, and it was worse than we'd expected. The Empire had been so corrupted by its alliance with the Outer Dark that the only worse downfall we'd heard of was that of the Commagan Empire, centuries before. Ar-Annator was too far away for substantive news to reach the frontier, but we knew for a fact that Ar-Karum the Great, Ar-Basamun, and Ar-Kasaron were all in flames. It hadn't gotten better with the coming of spring.

The greatest worry, however, had been the remaining Dullahans of the Thirty.

None of them had been seen after they'd fought the dragon. They had simply disappeared. More than one Galel and Silaboran loremaster had muttered about the possibility that they would step into the power vacuum in the Empire, and the resulting nightmare would be worse than the first. Yet there was no sign of them, no word that they had been spotted anywhere that men dared to go.

So, two weeks into spring, I found myself at the rail of the *Radala Farragah*, once more taking to the waves to return to our new home on the Isle of Riamog, after almost a year of war and loss away.

Gunny's death was still a dull ache in the back of everyone's mind. There weren't many of us left. Chambers had gone down on the fourth wall. There were now only six men surviving, of the twenty-nine who had come through the mists, all that lifetime of two and a half years before. Of the Menninkai who had joined us in the north, only Lintu, Ohto, and Kärsä were left.

I glanced over as Bailey joined me. We weren't alone aboard the ship. There were nearly a hundred Galel warriors aboard, coming with us across the sea to learn the ways of Marine Reconnaissance. King Caedmon had promised the use of the *Coira Ansec* to equip them so that we could teach them our way of war.

It wasn't really *our* way of war anymore, though. We'd adapted, learned from the Tuacha, the Menninkai, and the Galel, and combined their ways into ours. It was the only way to approach warfare. You learn, you adapt, or you die.

They weren't just there to learn to be Recon Marines, though. They were there because of the two of us standing at the rail. They were there to be close to the Sword Bearers.

Of course, the warriors weren't the only Galel who had come with us. There were new families building, and easily a dozen Galel women had come along, several already heavy with our brothers' children.

I looked up at the sky. We hadn't discussed it, but since Mathghaman still didn't want to be our commander, and I'd picked up the Sword of Iudicael long before Bailey had come into possession of the Sword of Categyrn, I had been forced to step into Gunny's boots.

I'd never fill them. That much I was sure of. I just had to give it my level best.

Everything had changed. I had a feeling, as the years went by, that the burden of the Sword at my hip would ensure that it would continue to change.

I was still a Recon Marine. But now I was a Sword Bearer, as well.

Time would tell which one took precedence.

Never shall I forget the principles I accepted to become a Recon Marine. Honor, Perseverance, Spirit, and Heart. A Recon Marine can speak without saying a word and achieve what others can only imagine.

Peter Nealen is a former United States Marine who now writes full time for a living.

https://www.americanpraetorians.com/

Other WarGate Titles Available now:

Forgotten Ruin
Tier 1000

For Updates, New Releases, and Other Titles, visit
www.WarGateBooks.com